ADAM'S SONG

8 MILLION HEARTS: BOOK 1

SPENCER SPEARS

INTRODUCTION

Free Bonus Epilogue

Join my mailing list and instantly get access to *All I Need*, a free, explicit epilogue for *Adam's Song*. You can't get *All I Need* anywhere else! You'll also be notified of my new releases and when I have more free stuff, you'll be the first to know.

Sign up at: http://eepurl.com/deH7Z1

Thanks for downloading this book. I appreciate your support. Visit my website or my Author Central page on Amazon to see the rest of my catalog and keep up with my new releases.

www.spencerspears.com

For Pickle

The soul is like a wild animal—tough, resilient, savvy, self-sufficient, and yet, exceedingly shy. If we want to see a wild animal, the last thing we should do is go crashing through the woods, shouting for the creature to come out. But if we are willing to walk quietly into the woods and sit silently for an hour or two at the base of a tree, the creature we are waiting for may well emerge, and out of the corner of an eye we will catch a glimpse of the precious wildness we seek.

— Parker Palmer

1

ADAM

The first thing you need to know is that it *wasn't* a suicide attempt.

Don't get me wrong. It was embarrassing as hell. And misguided. And definitely not something I'd recommend as a way of dealing with your problems.

But no, four shots of tequila, a hand-full of prescription painkillers swiped off the back table in the green room, and a chugged-down, room-temperature Miller High Life was not *actually* a suicide attempt.

It was just the best way I could think of to deal with the fact that I'd just found out my boyfriend was cheating on me, that he'd outed me in front of the members of my band, a gaggle of sound technicians, and about a dozen concert-goers looking for the bathroom, and, oh—that he was breaking up with me.

Clearly, I would have broken up with him if the asshole hadn't technically dumped me first.

And I suppose you also have to add in the crippling case of stage fright (which you'd really think someone my age who plays music for a living would have gotten over by now) for my decision to make any sense. 25 years old and every show still felt like the first, when I'd had a panic attack at an open mic night in college. So yeah, at least two of those tequila shots happened before Ellis—the asshole ex—walked in and ruined, well, everything.

Look, I never said it was smart. It was just the only way I could come up with to get through the hour long set that lay in front of me at The Grasshopper. After, I'd go back to my falling-apart group house, crawl into my falling-apart bed, and close the blinds and sleep for, oh, approximately 12 years, or however long it took for my falling-apart life to stop sucking.

That had to happen sometime, right?

Only things didn't quite work out as planned. My vision was blurry by the time I walked onto the stage—and okay, if we're being honest, it wasn't a walk, it was a stumble. I was supposed to do the first 5 songs solo and I was cursing my past self for coming up with that brilliant plan.

Put the solo songs first, Adam. Get the hard stuff out of the way early, Adam. Play those, and then it'll be smooth sailing with the rest of the band.

Well, fuck past-Adam and fuck his logic, because now I was supposed to open with *Cardiology*, the world's most emo love song that I'd written the night I'd met Ellis three months ago, drunk on blowjobs and bourbon and possibility. Justin, my friend and occasional drummer, helped me record it and then put it up online without telling me.

For some unknown reason, it had set the hearts of thousands of teenage girls a flutter and I'd gotten more attention as a singer and songwriter in the past three months than I had in the three years since college. And Ellis, a manager and booker in the business, kept getting me and the band show after show, playing bigger and bigger venues each time.

The Grasshopper was an indie rock institution. They hadn't even said yes the first time Ellis tried to book us there. But when the woman who was supposed to play their midnight slot came down with food poisoning, they'd called me last minute to ask if we could fill in.

It was so rushed, I hadn't even had time to tell Ellis about it before the show. It was a shame he'd miss it, but otherwise, I was psyched. Playing there that night was supposed to be our big break. And I figured I'd just tell him about it after the show. Instead, I literally ran into him in the hallway before our set. I was on my way to the bathroom. Ellis was on his way to giving another guy a tonsillectomy with his tongue.

It was clear that he was just as surprised to see me as I was to see him. But what did he say when he realized it was me who'd slammed into him?

"Oh baby, don't look so shocked. You knew we weren't exclusive, right?"

I'd stared, mute, as Ellis put his arm around the guy whose mouth he'd been hoovering and laughed. He'd fucking laughed.

"Who—how—what the fuck?" I'd spit out.

"Adam, be reasonable. You can't expect someone to wait around for you for months while you work up your courage to finally try something most people have been doing since they were 18."

I'd wanted to vomit. In fact, I was pretty sure I was going to. I could feel bile rising in my throat and I'd turned around and walked back into the green room. But Ellis followed me.

"But hey, if you ever put on your big boy pants, Troy and I would be more than happy to show you what you're missing. You're a born bottom, kid, and someone's gotta break you in."

"Get. Out." I'd turned and spit the words in Ellis's face. "Get the fuck out of here."

"Suit yourself," Ellis had said. "But if you ever change your mind... Well, you've got my number. Good luck with your set."

And the asshole had sauntered off like he hadn't just ruined my life.

I couldn't look at anyone when I walked back into the room. My face was hot, my heart pounding, and I kept feeling like I couldn't get enough oxygen into my lungs, no matter how hard I breathed. Fuck, I was pretty sure I was about to have another panic attack.

No no no no no. This was not good. This was very not good. I looked around the room wildly and realized that Justin had started loudly arguing with Clive, our bassist, about whether he was rushing the bridge of our song *Peonies*. If I'd had the spare brain space, I would have thanked him, silently at least. But I was reeling, wishing I could sink into the floor and disappear, and the floor stubbornly refused to turn to quicksand beneath me.

So I did the next best thing—I took two long swigs from the bottle of Jameson on the coffee table, then stalked to the back of the room and grabbed a handful of pills scattered on a shelf, swallowing them down with another drink. I hadn't done something quite that reckless since high school but dammit, if I had to go on stage, I certainly didn't plan on remembering anything that came next. If I was lucky, some of those pills might even be anxiolytics.

And now, only 5 minutes later, wasted, I was supposed to play this excruciatingly earnest, heartfelt, claw-your-eyes-out sappy love song about the first guy who'd made me feel desirable. The guy who'd told me to take all the time I needed, that he was fine with waiting to have sex. The guy who was fine with 'waiting' because he'd been *fucking someone else this whole time.*

So there I was, grabbing onto the mic stand for support, staring down at my guitar like I'd never seen it before and didn't know if you plucked the strings with your fingers or your teeth, wishing the room would stop spinning, when I saw the rum and coke Justin had been drinking earlier, balanced on an amp in the corner.

I lurched over to it, drank it like I was dying of thirst, and somehow made it back to the wooden stool at the front of the stage. I couldn't see the faces of the crowd in front of me, and not because of the lights. I couldn't even see my hands at that point.

Muscle memory and sheer blind luck got me through the

first verse of the song. Then I got to the chorus, and I remember thinking, *fuck, I might actually cry.*

I'm high out of my goddamn mind and my boyfriend just publicly outed, dumped, and cheated on me and I'm pretty sure I'm slurring my words, but the most embarrassing part of all *of this is that I'm about to cry because I have to sing a song about fucking beginnings when I've just been forcibly reminded of how all anything ever does is end.*

Amazingly, I didn't cry.

Instead, I passed out.

And stopped breathing.

Like I said, not the best way of dealing with your problems. Instead of waking up 12 years later, my very public breakup and shame lost to the mists of time, I woke up 12 hours later, in the ER, my sister beside herself with fury and relief as she leaned over my bed, and discovered that my meltdown was on the front page of entertainment blogs and websites across the country. I'd even made it onto the local news.

My big break had turned into my big breakdown. Hell of a coming out party.

∾

"Fuck," I said, starting to put a hand to my head, then stopping when I saw that there were tubes poking out of it. "Where am I? What happened?"

Esther, my sister, smiled down at me, relief washing across her face. "You're in the hospital. New York Presbyterian. Thank God you're okay." She took my hand and gave it a squeeze. "You really scared me there for a minute. How much do you remember?"

"Not much," I said, closing my eyes in an effort to make my headache go away. "We... had a show. At the Grasshopper. I was about to go on—oh, fuck."

My eyes snapped open—headache very much still present, unfortunately—and stared at Esther in horror. Images from the night flashed through my mind, disconnected but with enough detail for me to piece the outline together.

"Oh, God," I said.

"Adam, what happened?" Esther asked, trying her best to use her stern big sister voice and utterly failing to keep out a note of panic. "Why would you do something like that? I know you don't like playing in public, but I thought that was getting better these past few months. You've been doing so many more shows."

"I—it wasn't—" I stopped, unsure of what to say.

"If you were feeling—God, if things were getting this bad, why didn't you tell me? Or someone? We can get you help. I know things can feel really bad sometimes, but you can't— you can't just—hurting yourself isn't the solution."

"I know, Es, I know. I'm sorry. I didn't mean to worry you."

"Adam, I have to ask." Esther bit her lip, which, combined with her too-gentle tone of voice, had me worried. Unsure and mild were not words I'd usually use to describe her. "Did you—did you do this on purpose?"

My eyes widened when I realized what she was saying.

"God, Esther, no. No. Jesus, no, nothing like that. I wasn't—I wasn't trying to like, kill myself or anything."

"Adam, it's okay, you don't have to hide it or anything. It's nothing to be ashamed of. I just—please, let me help you. You don't have to go through this alone."

Oh God, this was excruciating. It was bad enough remembering what had actually happened the night before. But Esther thinking it had been a botched public suicide attempt was somehow even worse.

"Es, please, listen to me," I said fiercely. "That's not what it was. I just had a bad night. Something... happened. I was just trying to get drunk and forget about it. It wasn't smart but it wasn't anything bigger than that either. Just a bad night."

"What happened?" Esther asked, her eyes narrowing in concern.

"It's not important. It was a one-time thing. It won't happen again. Trust me."

'It's not important' wasn't true, exactly. It was important—to me. But if word of what had happened with Ellis hadn't reached Esther yet, if it wasn't written in the sky over New York City, I didn't see the need to enlighten her. I wasn't out to anyone at that point. Well, except for the 20 or so people who'd been within earshot when Ellis had let loose.

But to anyone else? No. I was awkward enough as it was. I'd known I was gay since I was 12 but high school—hell, even elementary school—had been hellish enough when people just thought I was gay and tormented me for it. I didn't need to go confirming their suspicions and making everything worse.

And my family wasn't much better. My mom was chronically checked out, abusing whatever benzo prescription she was taking at the time, my stepfather--well, the less said about him, the better, but my stepbrothers were pieces-of-shit bullies whose favorite activity was beating me up. And my father? The best that could be said about him was that most of the time, he wasn't home.

Esther was the only person I could have come out to. And rationally, I knew she wouldn't care, knew she'd still love me. But old habits die hard and I wasn't ready to spew out the contents of my heart only hours after doing the same from my stomach.

Besides, the rest of what I'd said was absolutely true. It wasn't going to happen again. Because not only was I never going to talk to Ellis again, I probably wasn't going to date anyone else until I was at least, say, 80 years old.

"Adam, this isn't the kind of thing you can brush off," Esther said. Back to the big sister voice. "Even if you didn't mean to do it. Adam, people don't just take half a medicine cabinet's worth of pills with a chaser of bourbon if there's not something seriously wrong."

"There's nothing *wrong* with me," I spit back. Except I knew that wasn't true either. There was a lot wrong with me, but I didn't need anyone else reminding me, thank you very much. "It was just an accident. You're making way too big a deal out of this."

"Too big a deal?" Esther's eyes were on fire. "Adam, you could have *died* last night."

"Don't be so dramatic," I said, wincing internally at the way that echoed Ellis's words. "I'm sure it wasn't—"

"Fuck you, asshole," Esther interrupted. "I'm a fucking doctor and if I tell you you almost died, you have to listen to me. You *stopped breathing*. They had to intubate you. Pump your stomach. You were—" she stopped, tears welling up in her eyes. "It was a lot closer than you realize."

I felt awful. All my life, Esther had just tried to take care of me and all I did was resent her for it—mostly because I didn't want to admit that maybe I needed to be taken care of. It wasn't like our parents had ever filled that role.

"Es, I'm sorry," I said. "I didn't mean to. I didn't mean for, well, any of this to happen."

"Well I didn't go through four years of medical school and three years of residency just to have my shithead little brother question my medical opinion," she said, her face softening. "You're not dying on me, you hear that?"

"Yeah, yeah," I said, smiling faintly. "Got it."

A nurse stuck her head into the room.

"You've got another visitor. Says his name is Justin. Want me to send him in?" she asked with a sunny smile. I wondered if I was one of her patients, if she'd seen my chart and was judging me. And then an even worse thought occurred to me.

"Es, did you call Mom and Dad?"

Esther glared at me. "I called everyone I could think of Adam. I wasn't sure you were going to make it. I called everyone whose name I recognized in your phone."

"Hey, I only gave you my passcode for emergencies!"

"I'll... come back in a minute," the nurse said, ducking back out of the doorway.

"Well what do you call this, dipshit? I don't know what the hell else qualifies as an emergency." Esther snorted. But then she took my hand and gave it a squeeze, carefully avoiding the tubes sticking out of my veins. "Adam, they're not coming. I couldn't even get through to Mom—no surprise there—so I left a message, but I haven't heard back. Dad... Well, Dad—"

"Said something about not wanting to indulge my disgraceful behavior by giving me the attention I'm so clearly seeking?" I finished, rolling my eyes.

It was no secret that my dad had seen me as pretty much useless since I was a kid. Esther didn't get along with him either, but at least they could be civil. With me? Well, the last conversation my dad and I had had was two years ago and you couldn't call it civil.

"I mean, he's in Europe," Esther said. "He said he won't be home until September. I'm sure he'd come if he—"

"Don't bother," I said with a bitter laugh. "We both know he wouldn't." I shook my head. "Anyway, it doesn't matter. I'm actually kind of relieved they're not coming. So who else did you call?"

"Justin. Ryan. Ben," Esther said, ticking the names off on her fingers. "I mean, Justin is the one who called me, actually. He rode over in the ambulance with you and asked me to keep him updated."

"God." I sighed and sank a little lower in the bed. "No

chance of forgetting about it now."

Esther winced. "Yeah, uh. So you're probably not going to be thrilled to hear this, but Ryan's on his way out here from Maple Springs to visit. And Ben's buying a ticket home, too."

"Oh God, no," I said, feeling my stomach sink. "This is so embarrassing. It was just an accident. Fuck, Ryan's already on his way?"

"Arrives at La Guardia in a few hours," Esther said.

"Christ. What about Ben?"

"I don't think he leaves until later this afternoon."

"Can I use my cell phone in here?" I asked, looking around the room frantically. "Maybe I can call him and convince him not to come."

"They're your friends, Adam," Esther protested. "They want to come."

"Yeah, well, I *don't* want them to. Ben's on a fucking world tour right now. There's no reason for him to mess that up for me—for something that isn't even that big a deal."

"Yeah, you and I are going to have to have a talk about what constitutes a big deal," Esther said, standing up. She walked over to a table in the corner of the room that I hadn't noticed. My clothes from the night before were folded up there and she pulled my phone out from under them and handed it to me. "I'll go keep Justin company for a minute. But I want to talk to you about something important when I get back."

With that ominous sentence, she deposited the phone in my hands.

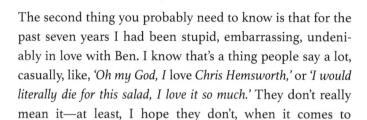

The second thing you probably need to know is that for the past seven years I had been stupid, embarrassing, undeniably in love with Ben. I know that's a thing people say a lot, casually, like, *'Oh my God, I* love *Chris Hemsworth,'* or *'I would literally die for this salad, I love it so much.'* They don't really mean it—at least, I hope they don't, when it comes to the salad.

But the thing was—I did. I meant it hardcore.

Which made the fact that he was straight really awesome. Obviously.

Though I guess if you're a stickler for accuracy, I'd actually only been in love with him for six years and nine months, because for the first three months of college—we were paired as roommates freshman year—I was convinced he was just another close-minded asshole. The body of a lacrosse player and the brains of, well, a lacrosse player.

I barely spoke to him until November. Maybe not *my* most open-minded moment, but in my defense, I'd been sent to—and kicked out of—five boarding schools and preparatory academies between sixth and 12th grade and not once had one of the cool, popular kids turned out to be a decent human being.

So when I met Ben on move-in day, I didn't have high hopes. He had one of those faces where someone's so good-looking you just expect them to be an asshole because they'd never needed to learn how to be nice. And when I'd discovered that he'd only been on campus for three hours and had already befriended most of the bros on our floor? My hopes were downright subterranean.

It wasn't until he came home from a party one night and saw me playing guitar that everything changed. I hadn't even asked him his major at that point, so I was shocked to discover he was studying music as well. And when he called me out for being a dick to him, well, there wasn't much I could say.

So I did what any normal human being would do—stopped hating him and decided to fall for him instead.

In one sense, it didn't even matter. I wasn't out, so it wasn't like Ben had any reason to suspect I had feelings for him. It was pathetic, sure, but it wasn't hurting anyone.

But then, last year, things had begun to change. Ben Kowalski, my best friend, had gotten signed by a label, run through their popstar production machine and extruded out the other side in perfect, cookie-cutter fashion as Ben Thomas. A new album, full of radio-ready hits with earwormy hooks and saccharine lyrics, and a world tour followed. He'd been gone for months. And even though we talked as much as we could, we could both feel the strain that the distance, his crazy schedule, put on our friendship.

About the only good thing to come out of it—or so I'd thought, at the start—was that by the time I met Ellis three months ago, Ben had been gone just long enough that the secret-gay-crush fog had started to clear from my brain. And so I took my first, furtive steps towards being an adult, entering the brave new world of *dating*, leaving behind the dank, comforting garbage bin of illicit-feelings-for-your-best-friend.

And it hardly even counted as dating. Ellis had said he didn't want to look unprofessional, dating one of the musicians he managed, and I definitely wasn't chomping at the bit to come out, so it was more like three months of arriving separately at the same bars, making out in the backseats of cabs, and then blowing each other in his apartment before we passed out or he kicked me out, whichever came first.

And now that I'd seen how that had all turned out, I wished I'd just stayed in my dumpster. Yeah, it was weird and smelly there, but it was also safe. And if I'd just stayed put, I wouldn't have ended up here, in the hospital, somehow still hungover even though I'd had my fucking stomach pumped, terrified of Ben coming home to see me.

Because that would be just the most *Ben* thing ever. My first impression of him couldn't have been more wrong—he was disturbingly well-adjusted, suspiciously kind to everyone, and downright creepily loving and supportive of his friends.

I decided to start with a text.

ADAM>> Hey, Esther told me she talked to you. I'm so sorry for everything but everything's ok here. Please don't come home early - you'd just fuck up your tour and I'm really fine

For all I knew, he could have been on stage at that moment, so I figured a text was a good start. But of course, he called me back immediately.

"Heyyyy..." I said, bracing for impact when I picked up the phone. "How are you?"

"I'm good? Um, how are *you*? Are you okay? Where are you calling me from? Is everything alright?"

I sighed. "I'm fine. I'm in the hospital, but it's not nearly as bad as it sounds. I just accidentally drank too much last night and mixed some pills in with the booze."

"Jesus."

"Yeah." I tried for a nonchalant laugh. "Knew I should have paid more attention in high school health class. Synergistic effects and all that." I paused. "It wasn't... it wasn't on purpose or anything. I don't know what Esther said but, well, it was just... a bad night."

Ben was quiet for a moment. "Adam, are you okay? I know that's like, a shitty thing to ask from across an ocean and I get if you wouldn't want to tell me because I haven't been around for a while. I should have... I should have been a better friend these past few months and I just—fuck, I just, I want you to know that if there's anything you need to talk about..."

Oh God, kill me now.

Sure, yeah, actually, now that you mention it. I guess I should probably tell you I've been in love with you since we were 18 and I think about you naked like, a lot, and even though I try to limit myself to only thinking about you while I jerk off once a week, I still do it. And spend way too much time trying to imagine scenarios where you might fuck me. Desert island. Prison. Old-timey British boarding schools.

Oh, you meant like, do I have psychological problems? Uh, no. Of course not. What could possibly give you that idea? Also, please forget everything I just said.

"Ben, Ben, you're fine. Really." I tried to infuse as much confidence into my voice as I could. "Seriously, you are now and have always been an amazing friend. Dude, you've been traveling the world finally doing the job you worked your ass off to get. Do *not* apologize to me. I'm—I'm okay. It was stupid, but an accident. You do not need to come home."

"I want to."

"Well... don't."

"Real convincing argument."

"Hey dude, I just had my stomach pumped. Cut me some slack."

"And yet you call this *'no big deal.'*"

"I mean, to be fair, I'm not sure I ever explicitly used those words," I argued. "It's like, a modicum of a deal. Not quite a medium deal, but like, more than a little deal, I'll grant you. Still though, don't you have like a contract or something? Are you even allowed to leave?"

"Define *allowed.*"

"Like literally is it permitted in your contract or is you leaving going to put you in legal disputes with Greenleaf Records and have you paying court fees for years?"

"Years? Nah. Definitely not. Months...?"

"Dude. Don't come home. Really truly times a million, I'm fine. I appreciate the offer and you can babysit me all you want when your tour's actually over, but seriously. It's not worth it for you to come all the way back for what, two days? Just to watch me go back to my house and avoid people?"

"I mean, I can think of worse things," Ben snorted. "If you're gonna be hiding out from the attention anyway, might as well have company. It would actually be kind of nice to get away from this craziness and just be myself again for a couple days. Hey, we could finally watch *Twin Peaks*."

"In two days? I don't think—wait, what attention?"

"Uhhh, fuck. Um. Did Esther... maybe... mention... the whole video thing?" Ben asked, his voice growing higher and more hesitant with each word.

"Noooo," I said, starting to feel slightly uneasy. "Should she have? What video thing?"

"Um. Well. So there are maybe, kinda like, a few, uh, videos. Of you. Like, on stage? And then, uh... falling? And then being carried out to an ambulance."

"Jesus Christ." My heart sank. "Are you serious?"

"Yeah." I could hear Ben wincing. "I guess people had their phones at the show, you know. It, um... Well, a bunch of entertainment blogs ran the story. And Esther said something about you being on Channel 9 news?"

"Shit. Did they... did they catch anything from before the show?"

"Before the show? You mean like, before you went on stage?" Ben paused. "No, I don't think so. Why?"

"Just... curious."

"Does whatever happened before the show have anything to do with you suddenly deciding to drink your weight in whiskey and pain-killers?"

"It—it doesn't *not* have to do with it," I hedged. "I, um. I don't really want to talk about it, if that's okay."

Understatement of the year. *What happened? Oh, you know.*

Just found out the first guy I'd ever called my boyfriend was fucking someone else the whole time. But don't worry—he was really polite about it, and extended an invitation for me to join in. Oh, by the way, I like dick, I guess I forgot to tell you for the past seven years.

Ben was quiet, and when he spoke, I got the sense he was picking his words carefully.

"Okay," he said. "I get that. And if you really don't want me to come back, I won't. But I just—I think you should talk to someone. Even if it's not me. I just—I love you man. I don't know what I'd do if something—"

"Eww, gross, stop," I interrupted him. "If we're segueing into the feelings portion of the program, I'd be just as happy to skip that part."

"Figures," Ben snorted. "Okay, fine. You don't actually mean that much to me and I couldn't care less what happens to you. Is that better?"

"Much," I said, heaving a sigh of relief. "You have no idea."

"Just—just promise you'll think about what I said, okay? About talking to someone?"

"I pinky swear," I said, rolling my eyes.

And, as it turned out, I did. Mostly because after I got off the phone with Ben, after Justin came in and then left, Esther cornered me—easy enough, considering I was lying in bed, pantsless, and wasn't about to get up—and asked me how I was feeling.

"Fine," I said for what felt like the fifty-millionth time that day. "Honestly. I just want to go home."

Esther made a face. Her *you're-not-going-to-like-this-but-I'm-saying-it-anyway* face. I narrowed my eyes in suspicion.

"I've been thinking about that," Esther began. "I know you say everything's fine. And that you weren't trying to do anything yesterday. But Adam, I'm worried. What you took, what you drank... that's dangerous. I think maybe you should go somewhere. A clinic or something."

I felt a hot flash of shame in my stomach.

"I don't need to do that," I said, trying to sound calmer than I felt. "Not rehab. Es, I don't even really drink much or anything, except before shows. Just to help with nerves and stuff."

"That's still problematic."

"Okay, so I won't do that anymore. I'm not going to be playing any shows anytime soon anyway."

After the disaster and public embarrassment of last night, I wasn't sure *when* I'd be able to handle that again. I hated the feeling of people looking at me, of being dissected, on display.

"Fine," Esther said. "But clearly something happened. Even if drinking isn't the main thing, it's like, a symptom, right? Of something bigger? I just feel like something's going on that you're not telling me, and that's fine, you don't have to, but you have to talk to *someone*."

"So what," I asked petulantly. "You're going to make me see a shrink or something? I'm not going to spill my troubles out to one of your psychiatrist friends."

Esther gave me a withering glance. "No. That would be ethically gray in the first place, since they know you already, and know me. But Adam, this is serious. I can't like, be around 24/7 but at this point, I'm afraid to leave you alone."

"Jesus, Es, I'm not five, I can handle—"

"There's this place in West Redding, the Peachtree Center."

"What, you're going to have me committed or something?"

"No, it's not like that. It's more like, a retreat. I don't know. Celebrities go there all the time for like, exhaustion and stuff. They have therapists, counselors. And they're really discreet. If you just went for like, a month, no one would know. And I know you're an adult, I know I can't make you do anything but I just... Adam, I'm freaking out. I just want to know you're gonna be okay."

Esther's voice broke on those last words and I looked at her and wished I hadn't. Dammit, her eyes were full of tears and I knew I wasn't going to be able to say no. The thought of having to pour my feelings out to strangers made me cringe. But Esther had always been there for me, even when our parents had been conspicuously absent. She'd taken care of me when I'd needed it, no matter how hard I fought.

I couldn't say no to her.

And on top of that, she was probably right. I was a mess. Anyone could see that. Maybe it was finally time to admit it.

So that's how I ended up spending the next 30 days at the Peachtree Wellness Center, a holistic health retreat where they had horses and yoga and hiking and private rooms with high-thread count sheets—in addition to enough psychiatrists and clinical social workers to fill a Greyhound bus.

I figured it was going to be mostly kumbaya sharing circles and talking about my childhood with a bunch of spoiled rich 20-somethings and there was a lot of that. But they didn't make you talk and mostly I just hiked and wrote and read. I was pretty sure I pissed the hell out of the shrink assigned to my case—excuse me, the psychiatrist assigned to guide me on my personal journey towards wellness—but the month didn't suck entirely, and that was mostly due to Nick.

Nick was a divinity student volunteering at Peachtree three nights a week as one of his pastoral care externships. I hadn't been inside a church since I was eight but when I ran into Nick in the kitchen one night when I couldn't sleep, he was making tea, offered me a cup, and I couldn't think of a good reason to say no.

Turned out, Nick—bi, 26, Mets fan—had almost zero advice to offer me, which ended up making him the one person there I could stand to talk to. And that was how, eight days into my stay at Peachtree, I managed to come out to someone for the first time. He took it with an almost disappointing lack of fanfare and just nodded, asking how I felt now that I'd told him.

And somehow, telling Nick made me think maybe I should tell Esther. And telling Esther made me think that maybe, just maybe, telling other people wouldn't be the worst thing in the world. And the next thing you know, it's 22 days later and I'm waiting for Esther to come pick me up as I check out of Peachtree, trying not to act anywhere near as panicky as I felt.

"I can do this, right?" I asked, glancing over at Nick where he sat in a wicker chair in the atrium. Indoor orange trees rose up around us, stretching to the glassed-in roof. My bag was packed, lying on the terracotta-tiled floor next to the chair I'd been sitting in until I realized I was too nervous to sit.

"You can definitely do this," Nick said. "Unless you can't, in which case, you come back here and we watch more Bob Ross and you avoid talking to any of the people here who are actually qualified to help you out."

"You're qualified," I shot back. Nick arched an eyebrow and I made a face. "Well, kind of."

"I'm flattered you think so highly of me," he said with a smile.

"God. What if like, everyone's seen those videos by now? What if there were even more than I knew about? You know, it's not really fair that they make you give up your phone and internet use here. I have no idea what I'm facing in the real world."

"Well, what *if* everyone's seen those videos. What if there *are* more? How would you feel about that?"

"Terrible."

"And what would you do about that?"

I sighed. "Probably nothing. Ugh, I get it. I know like, I still have to do the whole coming out thing and be honest with myself and all that but why does personal growth have to suck so much?"

Nick smiled. "Beats me. It definitely does, though. You're right."

"What if none of my friends like me anymore? God, that sounds pathetic, doesn't it?"

"It sounds like a question we all ask ourselves like, once a week. That's a normal thing to worry about, even if all you did was talk to someone at a party with food in your teeth."

"What if *Ben* doesn't like me anymore?" I blurted out.

Nick gave me a kind look. "I wondered when that was going to come up."

"He gets back from tour soon," I went on. "I know I have to tell him but I just. Fuck. I don't want to. What if he's mad that I've been lying to him for seven years?"

"What if he says he understands and he still loves you and is your friend no matter what?"

I rolled my eyes. "I don't know. Maybe I should just wait until I'm 80 years old and on my deathbed to tell him I'm gay. Might be safer that way."

"I mean, you could," Nick said, shrugging. "Would you really want to though?"

"Ugh." I ran a hand through my hair. "I might. What if he hates me?"

"He's not going to hate you."

"How do you know? You haven't met him."

"But I've met you. And I'm pretty sure you wouldn't be head over heels for someone who was that much of a dick."

"God, this is so embarrassing," I sighed. "Why can't I just be a normal human person? Like, people come out every day and it's not a big deal. Why does my stupid brain think it is?"

"I don't know," Nick offered. "But your stupid brain is also the same brain that made you the friends you have, that can play any instrument it sees, that got you this far in life. Be a shame to trade it in."

I turned back towards the rest of the building, looking down the hallway to where my room had been. "Part of me just wants to run back there and never leave. Are you sure I can do this?"

Nick stood up and pulled me into a hug.

"You can do this," he said, squeezing my shoulders tight before releasing me and stepping back. "I promise. And you can text me anytime you need to talk."

"Thanks," I said glumly. "God, I wish Esther would just get here so we could get this over with. Even if everyone ends up hating me—"

"Which they won't—"

"—I just want to know."

I turned and glanced over my shoulder absentmindedly, then froze. I was waiting for Esther to pick me up. But the person walking through the front doors wasn't Esther. It was the most gorgeous guy I'd ever seen—6'2", broad shoulders, blond hair, and eyes so blue you could swim in them.

"Ben?" I said, my jaw dropping open. "What are you doing here?"

2

BEN

I was in Tokyo when Esther called to tell me about Adam.

I was at a pop music radio station and had just finished doing some kind of interview that had involved shaving cream, water guns, and an inflatable doll with my face. I hadn't understood half of what was going on, but the translator swore that I was doing fine and apparently the show was huge with my target demographic—teenage girls—so the label was thrilled.

And that was the bottom line, I'd realized—if it made Greenleaf Records happy, I did it. The contract I'd signed made that crystal clear and I'd spent the past year learning just how much Greenleaf now dictated the minutiae of my life.

I'd just stepped out of the studio and Shereen, my manager, had ushered me into a bathroom to change out of my shaving-cream-soaked t-shirt and to wash the glitter off my face, when my phone rang. I didn't recognize the number, but the

917 area code meant it was someone in New York, which made me nervous.

If something had happened to my baby sister, Lacey, my mom should have called me herself. But one time back in college, she'd forgotten her phone and had to call from the hospital to tell me Lacey was in the ER. Now anytime I saw an unknown New York number, I couldn't control the panic that blossomed in my stomach. Besides, not that many people had my cell phone number anyway.

"Hello?"

"Hey. Is this Ben?"

"Uh, yeah. Sorry, who is this?"

"It's Esther Hart. Adam's sister. There's been—there was an accident and Adam—Adam—"

My heart stopped for a second. I broke out in a cold sweat. Adam was my best friend. If something had happened—

"Is he okay?" I asked, my heart clenched tight in my chest. "Is he—"

I couldn't say it.

"He's gonna be okay," Esther said. She sounded on the edge of tears. "He just... he had a show tonight and I guess he took a bunch of stuff—we don't even know what yet—but he passed out on stage and stopped breathing and—he's in the hospital now."

"Holy shit," I breathed. "Do you know—does anyone know what happened?"

"Not really," Esther said. "One of the guys in his band came to the hospital with him, called me. He said he saw Adam take a bunch of pills and drink like, half a bottle of Jameson and I just—Ben, I'm so worried. What if he—what if he did it on purpose? You know what Adam's like. If he did, he'd never admit it and I just... I don't know what to do."

My heart sank into my shoes at the thought. I knew—well, no, correction, I *thought* that Adam had maybe struggled a bit with some mental health issues in the past, but he was so quick to change the subject whenever it rolled around to his family or childhood that I wasn't really sure. It didn't *seem* like something Adam would try to do intentionally, but fuck, what if I was wrong?

"I'll come home," I said. "As soon as I can. I'll get the first flight out."

"Oh shit," Esther breathed. "Oh, fuck, Ben, I didn't realize. I forgot. You're like, on tour or something, aren't you?"

"Yeah but—"

"Oh, I didn't mean to—I thought you were in New York, that's why I called. I thought maybe you could come to the hospital and—"

"I can," I said. "It'll just take me a little bit to get there. But I'm coming."

Esther was quiet for a long moment and when she spoke again, her voice was hesitant.

"Ben, I know—I know this is an awful thing to have to ask, but do you know—can you think of any reason why Adam might have... you know. I mean, you guys are so close. Adam never tells me anything important. But I thought he might —if anyone knows what's going on with him, it's you."

Her words were like a knife to the stomach, stabbed in and then twisted. I *was* supposed to know what was going on with Adam. That was what best friends did. But the past six months had been hard. The tour was exhausting—show after show, new cities every night, and even when I wasn't performing, every minute of my day was controlled.

It had been so much harder to stay in touch with people than I'd thought and most of my friends were now stuck checking my official *Instagram* or *Facebook* pages for updates. With one month left on the tour, the only person I still talked to regularly was my mom, and even that wasn't as often as I knew she'd have liked. Adam and I still texted, FaceTimed when we could. But it wasn't enough. I should have been a better friend.

"I know he's been playing more shows recently," I said, feeling completely useless. "There's some guy, fuck, I forget his name, but he's a manager and he's been booking Adam's band a lot of gigs."

Now that I thought about it, Adam had been a little less communicative in the past few months. But I'd just chalked that up to business, and the awkwardness of trying to talk to someone on the other side of the world. Fuck, maybe it had been more serious. And if I'd made more of an effort, maybe I would have known—maybe I could have stopped this.

I said as much to Esther but she disagreed.

"Ben, it's not your fault," she said, her tone practical. "You couldn't have known."

I sighed. "I mean, he hates playing live shows. Maybe it was just, I don't know, stress or something? From having to do so many?"

"Maybe." Esther paused. "I just hate this. Am I a horrible person if I think Adam should go to like, therapy? Or rehab or something? There's this place outside the city—the Peachtree Center—that's kind of like, a retreat. One of my coworkers told me she recommends it to patients sometimes —they do all kinds of therapy and stuff there. Apparently it's like, full of celebrities and rich people but it's really good."

"You're not a horrible person," I said, trying to sound soothing. "That could be really good. I mean, I can't imagine Adam saying yes to that—"

"Yeah, I know—"

"But if he did, I don't know, he hates talking about feelings and stuff but yeah, maybe it would help."

Esther snorted. "I mean, it's probably a moot point. It's way more expensive than we could afford."

"Hey, if you can get him to go, I'll pay," I said.

"No, Ben, I can't let you—"

"Please, Esther. Let me be useful. Let me help."

"But it's so much."

"What the hell is the point of me making all this money if I can't use it for things that are actually important?" I said vehemently. "Seriously, if he says yes, I'll cover it."

"Are you sure?"

"Absolutely," I said without hesitation. "Just, um... Maybe don't mention I'm paying for it until I get there? I feel like that's the kind of thing I should tell him myself."

"Sure," Esther said. "Absolutely." There was a beeping in the background and I vaguely heard someone else's voice speaking to Esther. "Ah, Ben, I gotta go, they need me to sign some papers."

"No problem. I'll text you my flight info."

"Ben, seriously—thank you so much. You have no idea."

"Esther, he's my best friend. Don't mention it. Just let me know if anything changes, okay?"

We hung up and I pulled up a browser on my phone and began searching for flights. The first one I could get didn't fly out til the next day and cost two thousand dollars but I booked it anyway. I had just texted Esther the information when the door to the bathroom opened and Shereen poked her head in.

"Did you fall in or something?" she asked, staring at me in confusion. "You don't even have your shirt on yet."

I looked down at my bare chest in surprise. I'd completely forgotten what I was doing when Esther called. I pulled on the fresh t-shirt quickly.

"That's what you get for barging into the men's bathroom," I said, rolling my eyes. "Listen, Shereen, I need to talk to you about tonight's show."

Shereen listened, her face a mixture of concern and apprehension, as I explained that I needed to take some time off from the tour. I glossed over the details, just saying that my friend had been in an accident and was in the hospital now. She gave me an apologetic look when I finished.

"Ben, I'm so sorry that your friend was hurt. And it's really sweet that you want to go home and be with him. That says a lot about you as a person. But the thing is, you can't actually leave."

"I already booked my flight," I said, looking at her in surprise. "He's in the hospital, Shereen. I can't just—"

"Ben, unless it's you or a direct family member who's sick, your contract says you're obligated to complete the tour."

"Well fuck my contract," I exploded. "Shereen, Adam *is* family."

"Ben—"

"As good as, anyway," I continued. "He's my best friend, and the thought of something happening to him, of me not being there because of a stupid job—I mean, how would you feel in my situation?"

"Really shitty," Shereen said, giving me a sympathetic look. "I know it sucks. But the label—"

"The label can suck it. They choose the music I sing, the clothes I wear, the same five freaking anecdotes I recycle over and over in all of these ridiculous interviews. I can't buy a latte without getting the decision approved and signed off on by the fucking label. I'm done with this."

"Ben, I know you're upset right now but—"

"Yeah, you're right. I am fucking upset. My best friend could have died while I was on the other side of the world hula-hooping on a Japanese game show. I'm sick of this. I'm sick of this pointless, empty, fake routine that I go through every day. I'm sick of doing music I didn't help write, music I don't even like, just because it's what the label wants. I'm sick of pretending it doesn't bother me. I'm done."

Shereen took a deep breath and gave me a long look.

"Okay. First things first—I get that. No arguments from me. You think I don't know how much of your job is bullshit, is fake? I'm a professional bullshit manager. I get how exhausting it is. And honestly, Ben, I can't stop you from getting on a plane home. No one's going to physically prevent you. And I totally understand wanting to just be done with this. It's been a long fucking tour. You have every right to be sick of it all."

I frowned. "But?"

"But," Shereen said heavily. "I don't know what to tell you to convince you otherwise. I mean, if you leave, you'll be in breach of your contract. They'd have grounds to sue you and trust me, no matter how much money they've paid you in the past year, you don't have enough to win that court battle."

"That would be a really fucking shitty thing to do, Shereen," I said. "Sue me because I went home to help a friend in the hospital?"

"It would be," Shereen agreed. "And they'd do it anyway. Ben, for all that Greenleaf says it cares about its artists, at the end of the day, they're a company. They exist to maximize profits and they're not going to let artists break their contracts without consequences."

I was quiet for a while and Shereen continued.

"I'm not saying it's the same thing, that these things are of equal magnitude, but you could also think about all those people who bought tickets to your show tonight. You might hate this, feel like you're being fake. But they're your fans. They love you, support you."

"Not *me* though. They love the sanitized, sanded-down version of me. The version you've molded, who wears the right jackets, who repeats the sound bites you approve."

Shereen shrugged helplessly. "I don't know what to tell you, Ben. You knew what you were getting into when you signed with Greenleaf."

"Did I?" I shook my head. "I thought I knew. But I don't think I really got it. I don't think I could have."

"Well." Shereen gave me an even look. "Your contract's up in two months. You don't have to re-sign."

"I know." I sighed. "I know. But that doesn't solve the problem of what I'm supposed to do right now."

But as it turned out, Adam solved it for me. By the time he texted me, I'd finished my show that night and was trying to sleep, fitfully, in a hotel suite that was so lavish I didn't feel like I should be allowed to touch anything in it, let alone sleep there. When my phone buzzed, I jolted awake and my breath caught when I saw his message.

Of course I tried to convince him I should come home. I wanted to, regardless of what Shereen said. But Adam had to go and be so Adam-ish and insist that I shouldn't come. That he didn't *want* me to come. And in the end, he won. I could never say no to him and he knew it.

That also meant I wasn't going to be able to tell him I was paying for Peachtree. Not for another month, anyway. But if I were honest, I didn't mind putting off that conversation. I could already see Adam getting really touchy and embarrassed about it and I didn't feel the need to dive into that headfirst anytime soon.

So I stayed on tour. Made my fans happy, made Shereen happy. Made the label happy. And that was my job. Shereen told me the label wanted to re-sign me, that she was doing everything she could to negotiate an even better contract. But as that last leg of the tour ground on, I was more and more convinced that I was just done with it all.

The thought of going independent was scary. For the first two years out of college, I'd been scraping by. Adam and I would write together—hell, he wrote almost all the songs on the demo that got Greenleaf's attention—and I did everything I could to get noticed. Which meant taking every gig I could, even if it cut into my shifts at the two restaurant jobs I worked, even if it meant performing for free and eating ramen for weeks on end just to get my name and face out there.

It was kind of ridiculous that the demo that convinced Greenleaf I had major popstar potential was basically indie rock with blues inflections, songs Adam wrote and we recorded together. Greenleaf had barely wanted me to touch a guitar since signing me. It didn't fit the image they'd chosen for me—sort of a wholesome Justin Bieber crossed with a former boy-band member trying to break out on his own, only I didn't have a former boy-band. But that was the persona that tested well with Greenleaf's target demographic, so that was who I'd become.

If I went independent, I had to hope Adam would still want to write with me. I wasn't sure I was good enough to do this on my own. But still, doing the music I wanted and failing at it, instead of bubblegum pop music chosen for me and then produced and auto-tuned within an inch of its life, would be worth it. I just wanted to be myself again.

If anyone ever tries to tell you that flying from Australia to New York is *fine* and *no big deal* because you'll be in first class and you're just going to sleep the whole time anyway, they're either lying or one of those crazy people who actually *like* flying. I'm neither, so I can honestly report that it's torture.

The last stop of my tour was in Sydney and I didn't sleep more than 3 hours of the 20 hour flight back to JFK, and those 3 hours were filled with restless dreams about the plane falling out of the sky. Because I don't care what people say about *science* and *physics* and *perfectly safe*—there is nothing safe, normal, or natural about hurtling through the atmosphere in a giant metal coffin.

It might help if I'd flown more than three times in my life before this past year, but aside from three trips to perform at Disney World with my high school choir, my experience with flying was limited to watching the pilot episode of *Lost* and deciding never to board a plane again. Of course, that was before signing with Greenleaf. Try asking a record company executive if there's some way you can get to Asia by boat. Really. It'll make their day.

I'd been in a weird fugue state since I got back to my SoHo loft, alternating between deep, dreamless stretches of sleep and weird periods of wakefulness where I watched *Cheers* reruns and ate increasingly bizarre combinations of whatever non-perishable food was left in my apartment after my six months away.

I had just finished a bowl of mac and cheese with sriracha sauce and was peering into my now bare cabinets, wondering if I needed to suck it up and go to the grocery store, when my phone rang. It was Esther.

Shit, what day even was it? I checked the date quickly. Fuck, Adam was coming home today. How long *had* I been asleep?

"Hey Es, what's up?" I tried to keep my voice casual and not betray the pit of worry gnawing inside me. Why was she the one calling me instead of Adam himself?

"Ben, thank God. I wasn't sure you'd pick up, but I didn't know who else to call."

"What's wrong? Is Adam okay? Did something happen?"

No hiding the panic that time.

"He's fine." Esther's voice was soothing. "Sorry, didn't mean to worry you. I just need a favor and I didn't know who else to ask."

"Anything."

"Well, I was supposed to pick Adam up from Peachtree today but I just got called in to cover another shift at the hospital. I know it's a pain in the ass but is there any chance you could—"

"No problem," I said, already glancing around my too clean and too stark apartment for my car keys. "I don't mind at all. What time are you supposed to be there?"

"I told him 2 p.m. Sorry, I know that's really soon."

"Nah, it's no big deal. There's plenty of—" I cut off when I actually registered the time. There was a minimalist clock hanging on the wall, one that looked like one of those molecule models you make with marshmallows on toothpicks. Shit, was it really noon already? My internal clock was so off. "Well, I can get there."

"Ben, you are a lifesaver. Seriously."

"Don't even. It's totally fine. We'll call you when we're back, ok?"

"You're amazing. If I don't pick up it's because I'm in surgery but you can leave a message."

"Got it."

I hung up with Esther and spent the next five minutes hurtling around the apartment like I was trying to win a personal grooming triathlon, trying to brush my teeth, put on deodorant—and clothes, find the keys to the car I hardly ever drove, and I was still buttoning my shirt when there was a knock on my front door.

"Coming," I called, wondering who the hell it was. Right after I'd signed with Greenleaf, they'd moved me here—provided the car, too—because the building had a doorman. But there'd still been a couple times when overzealous fans had made it up to my apartment. Before I could even make it to the door, though, it opened and Shereen stuck her head in.

"Ben? Oh good, you're up." She smiled brightly.

"Jesus, Shereen, what the hell? Why even knock if you're just going to come in anyway?"

"Habit. I thought you might be asleep though and wasn't sure you'd hear me."

"At least give me a second to answer. I could have been naked." I gestured to my half-buttoned shirt. "I practically *am* naked."

"So?"

Well, she kind of had a point. Shereen referred to herself as *'the biggest lesbian on the planet.'* But still...

"What if I'd had somebody else here? Also naked."

Shereen gave me a level look. "Somehow I highly doubt that. Unless you and Mia—"

"God, no." I shook my head. "I still don't know why I let you talk me into that."

"Because you know that I'm the smartest, savviest, most brilliant manager in the whole universe?"

"I seem to recall it was more me being sleep deprived and you refusing to let me nap until I'd said yes."

"Just an illustration of my brilliant managerial tactics."

"Yeah, that and constantly surprising me when I'm shirtless."

Shereen smirked. "If only your fans knew how deeply, truly prim and proper you are, Ben. They'd be so disappointed."

"Yeah, but their moms would be happy. Anyway, is there a reason you're barging into my apartment or is this just an exercise in keeping me on my toes?"

"Technically speaking, it's the label's apartment—"

"Oh don't worry, I hadn't forgotten." I snorted. "If it were mine, I would have changed the locks months ago."

"Anyway," Shereen said, rolling her eyes. "I was on my way home from the office and I wanted to tell you the good news."

"What good news?" I asked warily.

Shereen's idea of good news and mine often differed wildly, since *'good news'* for her usually meant, *'Ben does something that makes him deeply uncomfortable.'*

"Upper management just finished reviewing the tour financials," Shereen said cheerfully. "Ticket sales and merch way exceeded expectations. Revenues through the roof. They're head over heels with you."

"That's... um, great?" I frowned.

"It *is* great," Shereen pressed. "Because it means you're now in a position to renegotiate your contract on *your* terms."

"Shereen, I still don't think—"

"Ben, honey, just think about this for a second. I know right now there's nothing that appeals to you less than the thought of another year with Greenleaf, but you only just got home. The amount of money they're talking about—"

"Is still not enough."

"Really? Even if they were willing to up your fees by fifty percent?"

I paused. I hated myself for pausing, but I paused.

That kind of money... that kind of money would be huge. That was the kind of money that meant my parents wouldn't have to worry about anything for the rest of their lives. All of Lacey's bills—completely taken care of.

Lacey had been a late and unexpected pregnancy—I was 12 when she was born. My parents had always wanted a third kid but had given up trying after I turned eight, accepting that it probably wasn't in the cards. And then Lacey happened, their miracle baby.

The doctors had warned my parents that they'd discovered some abnormalities during the second trimester. But my parents never thought once about not keeping her, even after they found out Lacey would have health problems her whole life. Lacey was born prematurely and had spent almost as much time in the hospital as she did at home for her first two years, her body struggling to develop the organs and systems it needed to keep her alive.

I still remembered peering through the window at her in the NICU when I was a kid, wishing I could hold or even touch my baby sister. She was so tiny, so fragile looking. She still was, to be honest, even at age 13. But she was also smart and funny and the bravest person I knew. You kind of had to be, to go through as many surgeries as she had and come out on the other side.

We all knew there were more surgeries ahead. More bills, more sleepless nights in the hospital. Part of the reason I'd been so eager to sign with Greenleaf in the first place was knowing that I'd be able to help my family out. And as much as I wanted creative freedom—it was hard to turn the kind of offer they were making down.

"Just think about it, okay?" Shereen gave me a stern look. "You don't have to make any decisions until after the benefit at the end of the month. If you re-sign, you get to stay here. Keep the car. Keep everything. If you don't..."

"I'll think about it," I sighed.

And I knew I would. Much as I wished I wouldn't. You didn't grow up poor and then turn your nose up at that kind of money. And for all my mom told me that money didn't buy happiness, it definitely bought at-home-nursing services and top notch medical care.

"Good," Shereen said. She frowned, seeming to notice for the first time that I was getting ready to leave. "Where are you going? You're supposed to be taking this week off."

"I am," I said. "What, I'm not allowed to leave my apartment?"

"What are the car keys for?"

"I'm going to meet a friend," I said with a shrug. "Is that okay, *Mom*?"

"Why are you driving?"

"He's outside the city," I said carefully. "An old friend. His family's in Connecticut."

All technically true. Adam's family *was* from Connecticut, though I was pretty sure he hadn't actually seen them in over a year. And it wasn't like I was going to be driving out to the palatial estate his dad owned anyway. Adam avoided that place like the plague.

But I also wasn't going to tell Shereen I was headed to the Peachtree Center specifically. For one thing, that was Adam's business, not hers. And for another, I didn't want Shereen to start getting any ideas.

She was an amazing manager and tireless worker—and one of the few people I worked with who I genuinely liked, despite the fact that most of her job seemed to be getting me to do things I didn't want to do. But part of what made her so good at her work was that her mind worked a mile a minute coming up with possible disasters and figuring out ways to mitigate them.

If she heard the words *'Peachtree Center'* from my lips, I knew she'd start wondering if my 'friend' was just a ruse and I was really going to check myself in there for exhaustion or whatever else famous people cited because their management wouldn't let them use the words 'mental health reasons.'

"Fine," Shereen said. "But really think about this, okay? I know what that kind of money could mean to your family. And I know that matters to you."

"Oh my God, Shereen," I laughed. "Did you just accidentally admit that you care about me?"

"All appearances to the contrary, I'm not actually a heartless bitch," Shereen said. "I have at least a quarter of a heart."

"Aww, you're so sweet."

"Also, I make more money when you make more money," Shereen said with a laugh. "So there's that."

I walked Shereen out and rode the elevator down with her —she got off in the lobby and I continued down into the parking garage under the building. I still couldn't get used to the fact that I now had a car at my disposal, with private parking, below my 2 bedroom fucking modern loft—all for free. Granted, the car was a red convertible that made me look like a total asshole and that Adam was going to tease me mercilessly about, but still.

I could drive it anywhere I wanted—was expected to, actually, even though I'd be just as happy taking the subway—and just expect someone to park it for me. I could get in anywhere I might want to go, when before I'd just haunted the same dive bars that had three dollar PBR specials. And no matter where I went, people recognized me.

I tried not to be a dick about it. I'd been un-famous for most of my life—it's not like I didn't get the thrill of seeing someone you idolize out in the wild. And New Yorkers were actually pretty blase about it, compared to some cities. But I just had the urge to shake everyone who asked me for a selfie by the shoulders and say, *'I'm not that important. The person you think you love isn't really me. Please go find someone who actually deserves your attention.'*

If I didn't re-sign with Greenleaf, if I let the contract lapse and went independent, all the attention would have to die down. Without carefully calibrated public appearances and social media accounts faithfully tended to by someone on Greenleaf's payroll, I'd fade from the public eye, I was sure. I'd gone from unknown to on-the-verge to fully-fledged pop sensation, my first single with Greenleaf playing on the radio and people stopping me on the street, in the space of about eight weeks.

Surely I could slip back down just as fast?

I'd been away from home for over six months, but the

absence hadn't been long enough to change one of the central tenets of my life: Fuck Connecticut.

Fuck Connecticut because it's too hard to get to, for one thing. Even after you get through the eternal mess that is the FDR Drive, you've still gotta deal with the highways. And I-95 is always full of traffic or construction or accidents, so you have to take the Merritt Parkway, which has a fucking 45 mile-an-hour speed limit in some places and is way too nice looking for a highway besides.

Have you seen its bridges? Like freaking works of art. I grew up in Queens, where our highways are self-respecting, graffiti-covered concrete monstrosities. I don't trust a place that has highways that look like they could be in the Louvre.

But that's Connecticut for you. Too fancy by half. The part close to the city, anyway, and anything north of Bridgeport and you're in Red Sox territory, so let's not even talk about that.

Down in Fairfield County though? Just hedge fund managers and their stay-at-home wives as far as the eye can see, living in these opulent mansions that look like their own private country clubs. It always made me feel a little uncomfortable to be there, like someone was going to ask to see my 'old money' credentials and kick me out of the state when they discovered I was an interloper.

Rich kids, country clubs, and ostentatious highways. Nothing good has ever come out of Connecticut, except for Adam. But he was the exception that proved the rule, and besides, he'd probably agree with me.

Adam didn't talk much about his childhood. But he'd let bits and pieces of it slip over the years, usually when he was drunk, and I'd patched together enough details to know that it hadn't been pleasant.

His parents divorced when he was seven and he and Esther had moved to California with his mom and stepdad for a while. Somehow he'd ended up back on the east coast, despite the fact that his dad seemed disinterested at best, an emotionally abusive alcoholic at worst—though getting Adam to talk about his dad was just about impossible. I'd gathered Adam had been bullied a lot. And then rebelled. He'd get kicked out of one school, then shipped off to another, and the pattern would repeat.

I wasn't sure what was at the root of it, exactly, but there was a wariness about Adam. He reminded me of a wild animal sometimes, ears constantly pricked up, searching for danger. And even when he decided he liked you, there was still this sense that he could decide at any moment to just disappear.

I'd never understood why Adam liked me. Although he was quiet at first, once he let his guard down, he was breathtaking. So much smarter than I was, so much more talented. Hilarious, if more than a little cynical. I didn't understand why he'd picked me to be his friend—he could have had anyone—but I counted myself lucky.

I just hoped he hadn't changed his mind. I felt awful about how busy, how *gone* I'd been while I was on tour. I wouldn't blame him if he was fed up with me. But I hoped... Well, I was going to be a better friend from now on, that was what mattered.

The thought of losing Adam, in any way, was heartbreaking. Something in Adam made me want to protect him. Show him that the world wasn't as terrible a place as he thought.

Show him that even if he'd been dealt a shitty hand, there were people who cared about him.

Of course, he'd tease me mercilessly if I ever said that out loud. That or get mortally offended—and embarrassed. So I'd keep it to myself. Just like I'd avoided pressing him for details about what had happened the night of the accident. If you pressed Adam on anything, he froze or ran away. But if you waited, if you gave it time—sometimes he'd come to you.

There was a weird feeling growing in my stomach as I drove, tense and jittery, and I didn't like it. Just nerves, probably, but I couldn't make it go away. Finally I turned off the Merritt and began driving through woodsy, wild country until the road I was on made a hard turn to the left.

Right at the curve was a pair of old brick gateposts, surrounded by wild rose bushes. There was a little gold plaque that said 1915, the street address, and *Private*. Peachtree took discretion seriously. Esther had called ahead and given them my name and license plate number and as the woman in the gatehouse waved me through I wondered if this was one of the few places I wouldn't have been able to get into with just my face alone.

The pea gravel driveway snaked through an alley of old oak trees, sweeping past what looked like tennis courts and maybe even a lake in the distance. There were stables on the right as I neared the main building. Shit, no wonder Peachtree was so expensive. It looked like somewhere you'd come for vacation.

That live-wire, jumpy feeling in my stomach got stronger as I pulled into a parking space and turned off the car. Trying to ignore it, I got out and started up the flagstone walkway towards this sprawling old mansion that looked like a location from the Great Gatsby. I half expected to see girls in flapper clothes smoking long handled cigarettes as I entered.

But of course, I didn't. What I saw instead was Adam.

When I opened the doors to the building and saw him standing across the room, the sight of Adam hit me with so much force that I stopped walking mid-stride. My breath caught. He looked so much smaller than I remembered.

That had to be my imagination, right? Adam was only two inches shorter than I was but something tugged at my heart when I saw him. Pale skin, dark brown hair falling into his eyes, a tentative smile on his face. He was talking to some guy underneath an orange tree—because apparently the lobby was a fucking greenhouse—and as I watched, that protective urge rose up in my chest again.

Whatever it was that Adam said, it made the other guy lean in and give him a quick hug. My heart twinged. And then Adam turned around and his sharp green eyes, the only part of him he could never quite keep from showing emotion, widened when he saw me.

"Ben? What are you doing here?"

3

ADAM

"Uh, picking you up?" Ben's blue eyes crinkled in amusement. "That is, if you want me to. I mean, if you'd rather stay..."

I laughed. "Actually yeah, sorry. I don't know if you like, know this, but I'm kinda busy and important? Do you mind waiting in the parking lot for like 12 hours? But like, keep the engine running."

God, it was good to see him again, even if it was under slightly embarrassing circumstances.

"Get over here, asshole," Ben said, but rather than wait for me to come to him, he walked over and pulled me into a hug. And suddenly, everything felt better.

This, at least, was normal. Ben teasing me and making me hug him. Me begrudgingly hugging him back but secretly loving it. I was still terrified of the rest of my life crashing back down onto me, and I wasn't sure why Ben was here, but at least this—us—hadn't changed

Don't count your chickens, dumbass. He doesn't know about you yet.

I wanted to squelch that voice in the back of my head, wanted to tell it it was wrong, that Ben wouldn't stop wanting to be my friend. But it was the same voice that was reminding me not to be so obvious about smelling Ben's cologne, warm and spicy, not to hug him quite so tightly, and I couldn't fault it there.

"Seriously, though, what are you doing here?" I asked, making myself pull away from Ben before the hug got weird. Just because he'd come up to see me unexpectedly wasn't an excuse to surgically attach myself to his body. "I mean, not that I'm not happy to see you, but..."

"Esther got called into the hospital," Ben said with a smile. "She promised me her firstborn and free botox in exchange for picking you up."

"You hate Connecticut, though," I said, looking at him suspiciously.

"I know." Ben gave me a serious look. "So start thinking of ways to repay me because you're definitely in my debt now."

"I don't suppose you'd take my firstborn too?"

"Already got one of those, try again."

"I'll think better in a moving vehicle," I said with a grin. "I'm sure I'll come up with something on the road."

"You'd better," Ben said darkly. "Or I'm abandoning you on the Throgs Neck Bridge."

I was already packed up so it only took a minute for me to get ready to go. After introducing Ben to Nick, officially signing myself out, and picking up my cell phone, we were back in Ben's car—a red convertible that I was definitely going to give him shit for—and heading down the driveway. I tried to quiet the fear bubbling in my gut at what was waiting for me outside the Peachtree Grounds.

"Seriously man, thanks for coming up here," I said as we turned onto the road. Talking seemed like a good way to distract myself from the thoughts of my real life waiting for me back in New York. "I know it's a shitty drive."

"Dude, you've *got* to stop thanking me," Ben said, glancing over at me from the driver's seat. For a second his eyes were the exact same color as the summer sky above and my breath caught in my chest. Dammit. Not off to a good start.

It wasn't like I'd really expected to *stop* being in love with Ben just because I'd done the 30 day free trial of '*Self-Esteem—More Fun than You Think.*' But still, a boy could dream. Part of me had been hoping that coming out to Nick and Esther, simply deciding I *would* come out to other people, would magically make my feelings for Ben disappear.

No such luck.

"What can I say, I'm still trying to get used to this whole my-best-friend-is-famous thing," I said, rolling my eyes. "Are you even allowed to be out in the wild without a leash? I'm amazed they let you out of their sight."

"You have no idea," Ben said grumpily. "How would you feel about not going back to the city at all? If we just keep driving south, we could be in Key West by tomorrow morning."

"And what, you sell homemade sea-glass windchimes while I restore antique rattan furniture?"

"Exactly. We just run away together and spend the rest of our lives in rum-soaked obscurity," Ben grinned. "Whaddya say?"

"Tempting."

Way more tempting that he realized. But that was Ben for you—just when you think it's time to start getting over him, he taunts you with phrases like 'run away together' and 'rum-soaked obscurity' and suddenly you're getting a boner in the passenger seat thinking about him bare-backing you in a hammock.

What, just me?

"Seriously though," I went on, giving Ben a long look. "Aren't there supposed to be paparazzi trailing you every-where you go now? I saw the pictures from Paris."

"Oh God, don't remind me." Ben ran a hand through his hair.

"'*Popstar Ben Thomas falls for singer Mia Lee—and off her balcony*'," I quoted. "'*Ben Thomas caught sneaking out of Mia Lee's Four Seasons suite—this new couple is music to our ears.*' Dude, it was in like, every tabloid."

"Since when do you read tabloids?"

"Since I spent the past month in a mental hospital with no phone and limited internet access? It was either read those or finally make a dent in Anna Karenina and even I'm not that crazy."

"Fair," Ben said.

Peachtree put a big emphasis on whole-body healing, whatever the fuck that meant. So you were supposed to spend your free time doing yoga or communing with nature. They did have a music room and for a while, Nick had encouraged me to play, thinking it might help. But every time I got close to their piano, anytime I heard someone strumming a guitar, something inside me felt hot and tight. I'd never gone this long without playing, but right now, it felt like playing music would break something inside me.

"Gotta say though, making a drunken spectacle of yourself and getting caught on camera?" I snorted, trying to pull my thoughts back to the present. "That's *my* MO. Get your own PR crisis and stop trying to steal mine."

"Imitation is the highest form of flattery," Ben said, laughing, as he pulled onto the highway.

"So what's the deal?" I asked, trying to keep my voice casual. "You're dating Mia Lee now?"

I turned and looked out the window as I spoke, not wanting Ben to see my face. I didn't trust myself not to give something away. The forest around the highway shot by in streaks of green and gold as we sped down the road.

Ben was quiet for so long I began to get worried, and when I finally turned to look back, he glanced at me and bit his lip.

"Okay, so. Um. You're definitely going to make fun of me for this. Which, well, I deserve. Because it's pretty ridiculous. But uh, Mia and I aren't actually dating." Ben spoke in a rush. "It's all fake, just for publicity. Mia's got a new album coming out, I was on tour, and the label thought it would be like, good synergy or something. So Shereen—my manager —orchestrated the whole thing. The Paris bullshit was completely staged. Shereen even called the photographers ahead of time to make sure they'd be there."

"Holy shit, Ben. That's—"

"Insane? I know." Ben exhaled. "The whole thing is just— like you think you know what it's going to be like, being famous, being part of this machine, and then you get inside and you realize that even the biggest horror stories you'd heard didn't prepare you. Every aspect of this business is micromanaged. I don't even get to pick my own music, let alone anything else. They care about what I eat, drink, wear, what I do and where I go. Every move is like a fucking mili- tary maneuver, precise and then analyzed to see how much it's building my brand. It's just—fuck, sometimes I feel like I'm drowning. Like I'm losing myself."

"Shit." I blinked. "Ben, I'm sorry. I had no idea."

"Well, you had your own shit you were dealing with," he said. "I know the past month hasn't been great for you either."

"Yeah, but that's nothing new. I've always been a bit of a mess."

"That's not—"

"It is true and we both know it. But dude, you're supposed to be like, the well-adjusted one. If you haven't been happy, I feel like—I dunno, I should have seen it. I should have been there for you."

"Been there for me?" Ben arched an eyebrow. "No offense, but who are you and what have you done with my friend Adam?"

"Hey, asshole, maybe I grew a little as a person in the past month, you ever consider that?" I glared at Ben and he laughed. "I know things have been crazy for you since you got signed. I should have, you know, made more of an effort to like, talk to you about stuff. Feelings and all that bullshit."

"There's the Adam I know and love," Ben snorted. "Feelings and all that bullshit."

I rolled my eyes in an attempt to conceal the grubby little part of me that was turning over the word 'love' in my mind like some precious jewel. *'The Adam I know and love.'* Yeah, I was definitely going to spend the next nine years or so obsessively returning to that phrase, I could already tell.

"Anyway," Ben continued. "Don't worry about it. You know now—my sham of a relationship, my sad man-angst and rich person ennui. All my deepest, darkest secrets." He batted his eyelashes at me. "You still love me, don't you?"

"Eh, you're alright," I said with a shrug. "Hey! Off! Gross!" I ducked and tried to lean away, but couldn't quite evade Ben's hand as he reached out and messed up my hair. "I actually washed it this morning in preparation for my grand return. You're going to mess it all up."

"Aww, you showered? For me?"

"Not for you, jerk. For Esther. If I'd known you were coming, I wouldn't have bothered."

"Well that's a relief," Ben snorted. "What with all your growing as a person, I was worried for a minute. Good to know the fundamentals haven't changed."

He had no idea. Still the same incompetent romantic, wishing for the unavailable. I couldn't help but be satisfied knowing that Ben wasn't really dating Mia Lee. Which was insane. And self-sabotaging in the long run, too, I was sure. I was supposed to be trying to get over my feelings for Ben, not finding ways to prolong them. I should really just drop the whole subject.

"So what happens," I asked, "if either of you actually wants to date someone else for real?"

Good job dropping it, asshat.

"Sesquipedalian," Ben said with a smile.

"What?"

"It means—"

"No, I know what it means. But what does it have to do with anything?"

"It's our eject button." Ben laughed. "Our safeword. If either one of us ever needs to get out of the relationship—insert air-quotes—we can say that and we'll break up and support the other person however we can. No matter what the label wants."

"That's... almost unbearably cute," I said. "God, are you sure you shouldn't actually be dating her?"

"What, and give you a chance to make fun of me for buying into my own hype? Give you more ammunition to rip into me?"

"I'm glad that my reaction is your primary concern when you consider any romantic entanglements."

"Obviously," Ben snorted.

We lapsed into silence then, but I didn't want to break it. It was that comfortable kind of quiet, the kind you can only get when you've known someone for so long that you don't need to talk just to fill space.

Besides, once we started talking again, I was going to have to tell Ben what was going on with me. I could tell he was trying not to pry. And I appreciated it.

But dammit, if I was going to actually give this whole mental health thing a shot, I'd have to start being honest with him. Not confessing my love or anything—I wasn't insane. But telling him what had happened that night at The Grasshopper, for a start.

Except there was no way to explain the accident without explaining about Ellis, without coming out and it was just— it was a lot. I would tell him. I would.

Just... not yet.

I risked a glance over at Ben. It was a risk, because every goddamn time I looked at him, I could feel my heart pressing up against my ribcage. He was still as flat-out gorgeous as he'd been when he walked into our tiny, cinder-blocked dorm room the first day of freshman year. And just as patient, just as easy-going, just as kind. I'd never been able to figure out why he liked me and for the first few years I'd been convinced he'd wake up one day and realize what a weirdo I actually was.

I thought I'd finally gotten over that fear but now that there were things I had to tell him, it was back, like no time had passed.

I knew—or I was supposed to know, anyway—that me being gay wouldn't bother Ben. But it's one thing to know something intellectually and another to actually feel it, to get your stupid, panicking heart to calm the fuck down and believe it. Ben was liberal. Ben was kind. Ben had tons of friends who weren't straight.

But I wasn't tons of friends. I was me. And what if me telling him changed something?

Worse, the scenario I couldn't stop fixating on: What if I told him and suddenly he could somehow see how crazy, blatantly in love with him I was? What if he didn't want to be around me anymore?

If you thought about it, I'd basically been lying to him for seven years. It made me feel kind of gross. Letting him think all I felt for him was friendship. Even grosser? I knew that if I could keep Ben from seeing how hung up on him I was, I'd keep right on being head over heels and do absolutely nothing to change it.

I was pretty sure Nick would tell me that as long as I felt this way for Ben, I'd keep putting myself in the position of getting hurt, of loving someone who could never return those feelings. He was 100% right. And I 100% did not give a shit.

So much for growing as a person.

I'd tell him soon. I'd get it out of the way on this drive. Just rip off the bandaid. I'd do it once we crossed the border from Connecticut into New York.

Except that happened, and I didn't say anything.

Once we crossed the river and were officially back in the city, I decided. After all, I didn't want to say it too early and then leave time for things to get awkward after. But then we were across the river and I didn't say anything then either.

When we got back to Brooklyn, I promised myself. I'd say it then. That should still be plenty of time to stammer it out in extremely awkward and roundabout fashion, right?

But suddenly we were blocks away from Derelict Manor, the crappy old rowhouse I lived in with 8 other people, and I still hadn't said anything.

Crap. Why had I put it off so long? If I started now, I probably wouldn't be able to finish before we got to my house. Which meant Ben would have to idle there awkwardly as I choked it out. Shit shit shit.

Maybe I could just never tell him? That seemed like a viable option. As long as I just never dated anyone for the rest of my life, it'd be fine. And let's be real, there was a decidedly non-zero chance of that happening anyway, considering how fucking gone I was for Ben.

Shit. Okay, maybe I'd grab my bag from the backseat and then be like, *'Thanks for the ride, I'm gay now, byeee!'* That way, if Ben were weird about it, I could just jump out of the car and run away forever. Totally reasonable solution, right?

Just tell him, jet, and go live with the mole people in the subway? The L train was going to be shut down for a while anyway—I could make a whole tunnel apartment down there for myself. It might even be cozy.

Fuck. I took a deep breath and turned to Ben.

"Hey, so I actually wanted to—wait, what are you doing?"

I stared in surprise as Ben flicked his turn indicator on and pulled up to a parking spot on the street, still a few blocks from my apartment.

"Uh, parallel parking?"

"Why?"

"Because I wanted to get some practice in?" Ben laughed. "Why do you think?"

"But you don't have to—"

"Adam, stop being such a weirdo and let me make sure you get home okay?"

"Jesus, Ben, I'm not made of glass. I'm not going to break if I have to walk into my apartment by myself."

"Humor me, asshole," Ben said, throwing the car into park, and there was nothing to do but grumble and let him walk down the sidewalk next to me while I hyperventilated.

I couldn't tell him now. We were out of the car and he might want to hug me to prove we were still friends or something equally as mortifying. Worse, he might have follow-up questions. Supportive, understanding follow-up questions. And if he didn't have his car to worry about, there was no way I could outrun him to the Jefferson Street subway station with my bag.

Oh God, and what if we got to the door and one of my band-mates was there? Someone who'd actually heard what Ellis had said to me that night. What if Just was over and opened up the door like, *'Hey Adam, you gay old so-and-so. So good to have your gay self back home.'*

It didn't matter that no one had ever greeted anyone like that in the history of time, my brain was suddenly convinced that was exactly what was going to happen. Which meant, of course, that I wasn't at all prepared for what did happen instead.

Ben followed me up the stairs on the stoop and watched as I slid the key into the lock, jiggling it back and forth a little to get it to open. I stepped in and stared in confusion.

There was a cardboard box with my laptop, my winter coat, and some old sweatshirts sitting in the front hallway, facing the door.

"Hey, who's home?" my housemate Carson called out. I heard his feet padding across the bare floor from the living room and then he was in the hallway in front of me. "Oh, hey Adam! You here to get your stuff?"

"My stuff?"

"Yeah, I mean, I know we sent most of it to Connecticut but this is the stuff we found in the last couple of weeks." Carson nudged the cardboard box with his foot. "Actually, it's awesome that you're here. Saves me a trip to the hardware store. Yvette needs your key."

"My key? Wait, what?" I stared at Carson in confusion. "Why does she—who's Yvette? Why the hell did you send my stuff to Connecticut?"

"Oh, fuck, did no one tell you, man?" Carson winced. "Sorry bro. We needed someone to cover your rent and Jill said her friend Yvette needed a place to stay."

"So you just kicked me out?"

Carson gave a helpless shrug. "I mean, we couldn't really keep it empty."

"Are you serious? I was gone for like, a month. A month I'd already paid for, by the way. Why didn't you ask—I mean, you didn't even try—you could have—" I spluttered. "And you sent my shit to my dad's place in Connecticut?"

"We didn't know what else to do, man. Your name wasn't on the lease. And we couldn't really pay for storage, plus there's no space for it around here. When we asked Justin, he said he had that address from like, a while back. It was your in case of emergency address on something?"

"Jesus, that address was from when my sister was staying there, for like, two months, a year ago. Fuck, Carson, now I'm homeless. What the hell am I supposed to do now?"

"Adam." I felt Ben's hand on my shoulder and jumped. I'd almost forgotten he was there. I turned and stared at him, dumbfounded. "Adam, why don't you just come stay with me?"

*O*f course, it wasn't that simple. When was getting Adam to admit he needed help ever simple? He just stared at me, so I repeated myself.

"Seriously. Just stay with me."

"With you." Adam still looked confused.

"Yeah."

"In your apartment?"

"No, I was thinking you'd take the car. You have to sleep and eat in the trunk though. I'm really particular about crumbs."

"But—"

"I'm gonna... let you guys sort this out," Carson said. "Good to see you again. Adam, just toss the key wherever, man. Oh, and y'all should totally come back on Friday for the drum circle. Leslie's friends are gonna do capoeira."

He waved and wandered back around the corner. I watched him leave in disbelief. He kicked Adam out and then invited us to come back for a drum circle in the same conversation? What the hell?

I looked back at Adam, whose face was full of misgiving. I didn't like that look—it was too similar to how he'd looked on the drive down here. Like something was bothering him, and all I wanted to do was ask what. How was I supposed to help if I didn't know what was wrong?

But now there were more pressing issues. Knowing Adam, he'd rather be homeless than ask someone for help. So I'd focus on getting him to stay with me first, then worry about the rest.

"I can't move in with you, dude," Adam said, shaking his head like he was clearing it from a fog.

"Why not?"

"Because it's not fair."

"How so?"

"I dunno, because I can't afford your rent? Shit, man, I've seen your place. Greenleaf must be paying you a fuckton of money if you can afford a two bedroom in SoHo."

"Doesn't matter. I can't afford it either, dude. It's free. It came when I signed with them."

Adam's eyes widened for a second but when he got them back under control he sighed.

"Well, then I really can't live with you. I'm sure your label doesn't want some random—"

"You're not random, you're my best friend—"

"Random-to-them dude crashing in their property."

"Then they can take it up with Ben fucking Thomas," I said with a grin. "They're trying to get me to re-sign with them when my contract's up. They'll do whatever I want right now."

"Ben, seriously." Adam looked pained. "I appreciate it, but I can't."

"Why not? Honestly, man, why not?" I reached out and nudged his shoulder gently with my hand. "Are you afraid I came back from the tour as a stuck-up asshole or something? I swear I'm just as cool as I used to be."

"Well that's—" Adam began with an automatic smile

"—Not saying much, I know," I finished for him. "But seriously, dude. It'd be fun to have you around. You don't have to think of it as moving in, if you don't want to. Just, like, hanging out with me while you decide your next move."

"I don't want to be in your way," Adam said. "I mean, you've got work and stuff and I'm sure you're exhausted after the tour. You don't want to have some headcase around, taking up your space just because he can't take care of his own damn life."

"Hey, that's my friend you're talking about," I said, raising my eyebrows. Adam gave a half-hearted laugh. "I'm sorry," I continued, "but you don't get to yell at me from a hospital bed about how completely, totally fine you are last month and then tell me now that you're completely messed up and awful to be around. One or the other, dude, but you can't have both."

"God, I forgot that you actually *listen* when I talk," Adam grumbled. "And like, believe me. Why do you have to do that?"

"Eh, we all have our flaws. Adam, come on. Why not come stay with me, even if it's just for a bit?"

Adam looked down at the floor and I inhaled deeply, forcing myself to let it out slowly. Why the hell was he being so squirrelly? Was it the money thing? Or God, was he mad at me for not being there when he'd needed me? What if he thought I'd gotten famous and decided to drop him?

"Wait, Adam, you don't—I mean, we're still cool, right?" I put my hand back on his shoulder but he flinched, so I dropped it. "Everything between us is okay, isn't it? I know I wasn't always there when I should have been, but I didn't mean to—"

"Oh my God, Ben, no." Adam looked up, his face incredulous. "I promise you, it's nothing—there's nothing wrong. And you definitely didn't *do* anything wrong. I just... I don't know, I wasn't sure you'd want to have me in your space. I'm sure you're busy enough without having me hanging around all the time."

"Are you fucking kidding me? Adam, you're my *best friend*. You've known me since before my life became this insane circus. You'd be doing me a favor if you stayed." I shook my head. "Seriously, if I didn't have you, I'd probably go crazy."

Adam gave me a strange look and I regretted sounding like such a weirdo. But honestly, I probably *would* go crazy if I didn't have Adam in my life and if he thought that I didn't want him to be a part of it, he had another thing coming.

"Ben, I didn't mean—"

"No, listen for a second," I said, catching his eyes with mine and holding them. "You are my oldest and best friend and I will always want you around. God, when Esther called me, when she told me about the accident, I was terrified at the thought of losing you. I didn't know what I was going to do it —I *still* don't know what I would do if—"

"Okay, God, jeez, enough with the feelings already," Adam interrupted me.

"Fuck you."

"Yeah, fuck you too," Adam said, but he smiled. Finally. That crooked smile that made his eyes go crinkly. I'd missed that. "But fine, if you're going to be that pathetic, I *guess* I could do you the *favor* of moving in with you."

"You're too good to me," I said, laughing to cover up my exhale of relief.

Adam's default setting was to interact with the world through 14 layers of irony, like feelings were contagious and he might catch them if someone sneezed. But reluctant, vaguely insulting Adam was the Adam I remembered, the Adam I'd missed.

"I know." Adam glanced down at the box of his things and laughed. "Well, at least you won't have to worry about me filling your place up with my crap."

"Do you wanna go out and get the rest of your stuff from—"

"God, no," Adam shuddered. "No, I'd like to put that off for as long as possible, in fact. Even if my dad's gone for the summer. My mere presence might be enough to summon him from whatever hell dimension he's currently in."

I snorted and bent down to pick up his box of stuff. "Fine then. Let's get this down to the car."

"Jesus," Adam said as I opened the door to my apartment.

He spun around in the space slowly, taking in the sun streaming in from the large, south-facing windows as it illuminated the cement floors and smooth granite surfaces of the loft.

"I forgot how nice your apartment was," he said, completing his rotation. "You have a baby grand piano in here?"

"It feels like I'm living in a spaceship," I grumbled. "A spaceship with a piano, sure, but still a spaceship."

There was an absurdly high amount of chrome and steel, weird angles protruded throughout the apartment, and my couch was a bright, futuristic orange and shaped like a trapezoid. Not the decor I would have picked. The Steinway in the corner looked completely out of place.

My family's house in Queens was a lot more... well, my older sister Jessica called it shabby chic. I called it shabby. But it at least felt lived in and comfortable. This... didn't.

"A fucking expensive spaceship," Adam said. He took a few more steps into the apartment and turned and looked at me. "It's strange. It feels sort of like a museum. I'm afraid I might break something."

"Maybe it wouldn't feel so weird if you came over here a bit more," I needled, "instead of always making me come out to

Brooklyn. You've been here like, twice in the whole year I've lived here."

"Hey, you weren't even hear for six of those months," Adam pointed out. "You think going to Brooklyn's bad? Maybe if you hadn't abandoned me, *in my hour of need*, no less, I would have come here more often."

Well, that was a punch in the gut. But I couldn't argue with it. I bit my lip and looked at Adam, feeling like I needed to apologize. Adam took one look at me and laughed.

"God, Ben, I didn't mean that. You're right, I should have come here more. And you don't need to feel guilty about being on tour. I'm sorry, I was trying to be funny, not serious. Please don't go and be all sulky all night."

I brightened. "Fine. But just for that, I'm gonna put on my 80s power ballads playlist."

"Do it and I'm moving out," Adam threatened.

I grinned. "Don't even try to pretend you don't love it."

Adam walked into the guest room to unpack—not that he had a whole lot of stuff, but I figured I should give him some space—and I briefly considered flopping down on the couch. But it looked so uncomfortable that I'd never tried that before and I decided tonight wasn't the night for new things. I flung myself across my bed instead. God, it felt good to lie down.

I wondered how long I could convince Adam to stay with me. Knowing him, he'd probably try to move out as soon as possible and claim he was doing me a favor. But I wanted him here. I'd been on tour for months and I just wanted to relax, hang out with someone who knew the real me.

And fine, okay, maybe there was a tiny bit of concern in there too. I didn't want to press Adam to talk about what had happened. But I couldn't help but wonder. And him staying with me, at least for a little while, would be give me some peace of mind that he was okay.

I just had the strangest sense that something was still bothering him. He'd been so quiet for the second half of our drive and not in a good way. He'd seemed tense, somehow. And I couldn't figure out why. Maybe it was just nerves about coming home? I turned the idea over in my mind as I started to drift off.

"Did moving my one box exhaust you that much?" Adam asked as he walked into my room. I picked my head up from where it had been smushed into my comforter and saw him standing in the doorway. "I'm not supposed to be the stronger one of us, but even I'm not *that* tired."

"Hey, I'm entitled to be tired. I just got back from freaking Australia and I didn't sleep at all on the plane." I gave him my best puppy dog eyes. "Can't I get a little sympathy?"

"For flying first class across the ocean after finishing a world fucking tour as a real deal famous person?"

"Yes, my life's very tough."

"Sounds like it," Adam laughed. "I was gonna go hunt something up for dinner in your kitchen. You hungry?"

"Don't bother," I said, rolling onto my side so I could face Adam. "I've denuded it. There's no food left."

"Fine, then come to the store with me."

"Adam, I'm *tired*. Not to mention weak from hunger. I don't think I can move." I flailed my arms helplessly around on the mattress and looked at him with a pained face. "See?"

"I remain unimpressed."

"You're cold. I'm weak and all you can do is be cruel."

"Ugh, get *up*, asshole. I'm not going to the store without you."

"Make me," I said with a smile and a crook of my eyebrow.

Adam walked over to the bed, grabbed my wrists, and unceremoniously yanked on them. But I refused to budge and when his tugging subsided, I pulled hard, sideways. Adam yelped and fell onto the bed in surprise, sprawled on top of me in an ungainly heap.

"You're ridiculous," he said, pushing up onto his elbows and scrambling off of me. He stared at me from the far side of the bed. "You realize that, right? I'm supposed to be the crazy one in this friendship."

"Maybe I'd be less crazy if you let me nap, ever think about that?" I smiled slyly. "Come on, you see how comfortable this bed is now. What harm would a little nap do?"

"Ben, I know you. Your naps are multi-hour affairs. You should probably send out save-the-dates for them."

"Ugh, you're no fun." I turned over onto my side again. "You're gonna owe me big time if you make me get out of this bed."

"Add it to my tab," Adam said. "Now come on, I'm starving and I've been eating nothing but fermented quinoa and organic yak's milk yogurt for the past 30 days. I would murder someone for the chance to walk to the store like a normal person and buy a bag of pork rinds and some Skittles."

"Oh, you should text Es," I said, pulling a baseball cap on as we walked out of the elevator and into the lobby of my building. "I told her I'd let her know as soon as we were back in the city."

Adam stopped at the front door and gave me a look. "Es? Since when do you call her Es?"

"I don't know," I said as I patted my jacket pockets for my sunglasses. "That's what you call her, isn't it?"

"Yeah, but I'm related to her. She hates that nickname."

"So you call her that because..."

"I'm her younger brother and it's my duty to annoy the shit out of her?" Adam said like it was the most obvious thing in the world. "I didn't think she'd put up with that from anyone else."

I shrugged, checking my pockets again. "She didn't seem to mind the last time we talked. I mean, she's never told me not to or anything."

"Wait, last time you talked? What are you two, best friends now?" Adam frowned.

"No, we're just—I don't know, we just talked a few times this past month. Since you weren't using your phone at Peachtree, I was just checking in." I shook my head. "Fuck, I left my sunglasses up in the apartment."

"Why do you need sunglasses? We're not gonna be outside that long and it's gonna get dark soon." Adam gave me a quizzical look. "Also, for the record, I can't decide if it's sweet or creepy that you wanted to check up on me."

"Well, decide while we walk," I said, pushing the door open. "It'll probably be fine. It's only a few blocks to the store and—"

"Oh my God, there he is!"

Both Adam and I turned to follow the sound of a shriek across the street. Two teenage girls clutched each other and pointed at us. After they noticed us looking, one of them jumped, then waved. The other pulled out her phone.

"Jesus," Adam said under his breath.

"Just smile and wave," I said, bringing my arm behind him and giving him a nudge on his lower back to start moving. "Smile, wave, and keep walking. Most of the time they're happy with just a picture."

Adam shot me an incredulous look but started walking, matching my brisk pace.

"*That's* why the sunglasses," I said as we made our way down the sidewalk. "There's a middle school around the corner and their sports practices let out around now. I've learned not to leave the apartment around 3:15 or 5:30, but when I have to, the hat and sunglasses help. Sometimes."

"Were they waiting there for you?"

I shrugged. "Who knows. Honestly, that was so low key, it barely even registers. I don't even mind the autographs and selfies. Like, yeah, if I'm in a hurry, it's a pain, but otherwise... there's no need for me to be a dick about it. Well, except for the people who ask to take a picture and then ambush-kiss you once they're close."

"What?" Adam stared at me as we waited at the stoplight at the end of the block. "That *happens*?"

I shivered. "Yeah. It's pretty weird. And I get off easy. You should hear some of Mia's horror stories."

"That's nuts." Adam shook his head. "God, if I ever look like I'm going to get famous, you have my permission to sabotage my career, okay? I don't think I could handle getting recognized by strangers all the time."

"Sabotage Adam's career, got it. Any particular way you'd like me to—hey, what's wrong?"

Adam didn't answer. He just stared across the intersection, frozen. I followed his gaze. There were two guys talking to each other, a woman with a stroller, and a family of four gesticulating wildly at each other. None of them were looking at us.

The light changed and I nudged Adam. "Hey, is everything—"

His eyes widened as the people on the other side of the street began to cross. Before they could take more than two steps, Adam had turned around and began walking back in the direction we came from.

"Adam, what are you—is everything—Adam!" I called as I jogged to catch up with him. He turned right and walked up to the doorway of the first building he came to, tucking himself behind a set of columns.

I put my hand on his shoulder as I reached him, trying to turn him around so I could see his face, but he kept his back resolutely turned away from the street. Confused, I snuck around in front of him, wedging myself into the tight space between his body and the front of the building.

"Adam, what's wrong?"

"Nothing," Adam said.

But that was clearly a lie. His face had gone white and his breath was coming out in short little bursts. I could feel his muscles tensing underneath my hand. I had the strongest urge to pull him in for a hug. Whatever he'd seen had rattled him badly and I found myself wanting to protect him —not that I knew what from.

"Adam, please," I said, trying to make my voice low and soothing. "Can you tell me what's wrong so I can help?"

Adam closed his eyes tightly. "Are they—are they gone? Those two guys?"

I glanced over his shoulder. Our whole conversation had taken about 20 seconds and as I watched, the two guys from the intersection walked down the sidewalk in front of the building where we were standing. They didn't look at us once and I tracked them with my eyes until they were out of sight.

"They're gone," I said. I brought my left hand to Adam's other shoulder and squeezed them both, like I could somehow impart warmth and strength into him. Adam looked so freaked out and whatever it was he'd been worried about earlier, this was orders of magnitude worse. "They never saw us."

Adam nodded slowly, then opened his eyes. They looked so pained that I decided then and there that I didn't need to ask anymore questions. I just wanted that look of fear to go away and I was going to concentrate on that.

"You wanna go back to the apartment?" I offered. "We can just order takeout and be complete wastes of space. You don't—you don't have to talk about it."

"No," Adam said, and I was taken aback by the resolution in his voice. "No, I—I need to tell you." He closed his eyes again for a brief moment and when he opened them, they were full of determination. "That guy—the tall one—that was Ellis."

"Ellis?" I blinked. "The guy who was booking you all those shows a while ago?"

"Yeah," Adam said heavily. "He's also—he's also my ex."

5

ADAM

"*Y*our what?" Ben stared at me.

"Um. Ex?"

"Like boyfriend?"

"Like... boyfriend. Yeah."

"Holy shit."

"Yeah." Of all the ways I'd thought about telling Ben, blurting it out after almost running into Ellis was *not* one that I'd considered. Fuck, my heart was beating a million miles an hour. But I couldn't take it back now. I took a deep breath. "I can, uh, tell you about it. If you want."

"You don't have to," Ben said quickly. He gave me a strange look and took his hands off my shoulders. My stomach sank. Fuck, this was... not going well. I'd freaked him out already.

So much for Ben taking it well. So much for him not caring. When he'd pulled me down onto his bed back in the apartment, I'd jumped away, afraid to linger the way I so badly wanted to. I wished I'd known that was going to be the last time he touched me.

"Okay. I just meant like... nevermind. It's not a big deal." I looked down. "I can just go back and get my things."

"Wait, what?" Ben's hands flew up and suddenly he was pulling me into a hug, squishing me tight to his chest. I froze, completely confused. "Adam, do you think—why would I—Adam, you'd better not be thinking about moving out right after you moved in. This—whatever happened with Ellis—doesn't change anything between us. You know that, right?"

"But you—I mean, you said—" I mumbled into his shoulder.

"Adam, I was trying to give you space." Ben squeezed me tighter. "When you said you could tell me about it, you looked like you wanted to die."

"Oh." I flushed, relief washing into my system, followed quickly by embarrassment. "Oh. I thought you were like, weirded out by it. By me."

"Never." Ben laughed as he released me but the look he gave me was fierce. "Seriously, all I've been trying to do today— for the past month, really—is not push. But trust me, if it will make you feel better, I am *dying* to pry. Tell me every-thing. All the gory details."

I laughed weakly. "*All* the details? You sure about that?"

"Fine, most of the details. You can keep back like... 3% if you want."

"I just—" I shook my head. "I'm sorry, I just envisioned this going a lot worse."

Ben gave me a disbelieving look. "Adam, how much of an asshole do you think I am?"

I snorted. "It's less to do with you and more to do with my pathologically low self-esteem—something I learned lots about at Peachtree." I glanced around. "Do you wanna, like, go somewhere? I—I'd like to tell you about this stuff but not necessarily standing in this doorway the whole time."

"You realize you still look like you're about to get a root canal with no anesthesia when you say that, right?"

"Okay, well, maybe 'want' to tell you is a bit strong. But I... I've been doing some thinking for the past month and I think it's probably *good* to tell you."

"You wanna go back to the apartment?"

I shook my head. "No. That feels too... I don't know, too serious. I kinda wanna just like, sit in the back of a bar somewhere, if that makes any sense. Be around other people, but not have to actually talk to them."

"I know just the place," Ben said with a smile.

Three blocks later, Ben had led me into a bar called Maggie's that looked like a cross between a mechanic's garage and a garden center. It appeared to be a tiny hole in the wall when we walked into the narrow front room. Bench-seats from old minivans clustered around milk crate tables and I couldn't even see a bar.

But Ben walked through a green velvet curtain in the back and suddenly we were in a massive, airy, open space with three walls of exposed brick, and two huge, glassed-in garage doors in place of the fourth wall that had been rolled up to open onto a courtyard. Motorcycle parts dangled from the ceiling and jade plants, golden pothos, and potted citrus trees dotted every flat surface, including the floor. An old guitar was hanging up on the wall behind the bar. I loved the whole place immediately.

"This is amazing," I said, a smile spreading across my face.

"Isn't it?" Ben grinned. "I stumbled across it a while back and it's my favorite place. Never too crowded, always open, and no one's ever asked me for a selfie. The guy who owns it, Gray, lives above the bar and I think it's just open whenever he's awake. Here, come say hi and then we can grab a table.

Ben walked over to a long, wooden bar where a guy with dark brown hair and about 4 days worth of scruff on his jaw was pouring someone a beer. He set it on the counter and turned to Ben with a smile.

"Hey! I haven't seen you in a minute. When'd you get back?"

"Yesterday," Ben grinned. He tilted his head in my direction. "This is my friend Adam. Adam, Gray. Gray, Adam."

"Hey man," Gray said, sticking his hand out with an easy smile. "How's it going?"

"Good," I said, taking his hand. "Nice to meet you."

I could almost feel warmth and an easy-going confidence radiating off of Gray. I also had the strangest sense I'd seen him somewhere before, but I couldn't place where.

"What are you drinking?" Gray asked.

"Just water for me," I said quickly.

I hadn't had anything to drink since the night at The Grasshopper and while I wasn't quite *worried* about having a beer, I wasn't quite sure I *wanted* one either. Ben got coffee and then led the way to a booth in the corner.

"I feel like I'm met him before," I said as I slid down onto the seat.

Ben smiled. "I'd ask if you'd been here before but we both know you never leave Brooklyn, so..."

I squeezed my lemon wedge into my water and then threw it at him.

"Hey," Ben objected. "Rude."

"Well be nicer to me and maybe I won't pelt you with citrus." I shrugged. "Besides, I can't be held responsible for my actions. I'm in a very fragile, delicate place right now."

"Clearly."

And then he was quiet, and then I was quiet, and then I wanted to crawl under the table because I didn't know how to begin. I wished Ben would just ask me something but of course, he was trying to be respectful of my boundaries or some bullshit, which meant I had to actually be a grown-up and start. But waiting longer wasn't going to make it any easier, so finally I took a deep breath and looked Ben in the eye.

"I'm gay."

"Okay." Ben nodded. "Wow. Okay. Awesome."

"Awesome?"

"Uh, yeah." He smiled at me. "Sorry, I didn't mean to be flippant. I know—I'm sure it's not like, easy to say that. If you don't know how someone's going to react. But seriously. I think that's great. Spectacular. Marvelous."

"Okay, you can stop thumbing through your mental thesaurus now," I said, rolling my eyes. "And I appreciate it. I wasn't looking for any specific word, I'm just... I don't know, it just feels a little anticlimactic compared to what I'd built up in my head."

"Oh, I'm sorry," Ben said with a laugh. "Did you want me to be more shocked? Hold on, let me try again." He cleared his throat, brought a hand to his brow, and widened his eyes. "Oh my stars. Adam Hart, *gay*? Why I never. How simply inconceivable. What will papa say? And the family name? Oh lordy, how will we survive?"

I looked for something else to throw at him but came up empty.

"I guess I shouldn't complain," I sighed. "Could be worse."

"Adam, I really do think it's great. Thank you for telling me. For trusting me with that."

I shrugged like it was no big deal. "Sure."

Ben was quiet for a moment and I could almost see the questions swirling behind his eyes.

"So how long have you—I mean, since when do you—"

"I mean, I always knew," I said, jumping in. "I just didn't really want to admit it for a long time."

Ben gave me a funny look. "What I was going to say was *since when do you date*? Like, anyone, full stop."

Since you were gone for six months and I realized how truly pathetic it was to be as in love with you as I was. Am. Probably evermore shall be.

"Oh. Yeah. um, so that's a more recent development."

"I always just kinda figured you were asexual or something," Ben said. "All through college, you never like, brought someone back to our room. I mean, as far as I know."

Oh, well that's easy enough to explain. You see, I was too busy being obsessed with you to even think about anyone else, let alone actually pursue them.

"Yeah, I was still kinda like, overwhelmed by everything back then. In addition to being super awkward." I laughed. "I don't think anyone, of any gender, would have wanted to hook up with me, anyway, so it's not really like I was missing out."

"You're too hard on yourself," Ben said with a frown. Then he cocked his head to the side. "Wait, does that mean that Ellis was like, the first time you—"

"No, no," I said, blushing furiously. God, I was pathetic but it was suddenly paramount that Ben know I wasn't *that* pathetic. "He wasn't like, the first time I'd done anything. But he was the first guy I dated. Like, saw regularly."

And okay fine, maybe I *was* that pathetic, because it's not like Ellis and I had ever actually had sex. Obviously. That had apparently been the whole problem. But it wasn't lying, was it, to just not specify what we'd done and let Ben draw his own conclusions? Coming out as gay was hard enough. I didn't need to add *virgin* to the list, too.

"Oh, okay," Ben said, nodding. "God, I can't believe there's like, this whole part of you I didn't know about til now."

"Are you mad?" I hated how small my voice sounded.

Ben reached out and covered my hand with his own.

"Not at all," he said, giving it a squeeze. "It's your life, you don't owe me or anyone else anything you don't want to share. But I hope you know this doesn't change anything about our friendship."

"You're sure?" I knew I sounded needy, but dammit, this was what I'd been dreading and I had to know. "Because if it's weird or something, I understand."

"It's only weird that you think I *would* care."

"Sometimes people do. Or at least, you know, they get bothered about why you didn't tell them earlier."

"Adam, it's your life. You get to do what you want with it and decide who to tell what to when. I don't have any right to demand you tell me anything. You told me when you wanted to—that's all that matters. Besides," Ben said, "half my friends are something other than straight. So it doesn't bother me at all. Gray's bi. You remember Luke, from college?"

"Yeah." I made a face. "You still talk to him? Didn't he go into finance or something?"

"Now who's being judgey?" Ben said, cocking an eyebrow. "In addition to being pretty awesome, Luke's my accountant now. Anyway, the point is, he's gay. Even Jess dated a girl for a bit."

"Your older sister?"

"Yep." Ben smiled. "It was this whole torrid summer affair years ago, until the girl moved to Oregon to find herself. So I promise, it's not weird at all."

I heaved out a relieved breath. I felt so much better. Sure, there was still the pesky fact that I was completely in love with Ben, but at least he didn't hate me. Though it might have made the whole becoming *un*-completely-in-love-with-him process a little easier if he had. Hmm.

"So, if I'm allowed to be pushy and pry-y," Ben said, "uh, what happened with Ellis? I'm guessing things didn't, um, end well?"

"You could say that." I groaned and ran a hand through my hair. "Ugh, it's such an embarrassing story, but if you want the gory details—"

"Which I obviously do—"

"—then the long and the short of it is that I met him after a show like, five months ago and he was all, *'You guys were so good,'* and I was all, *'Oh my God, this guy's cute, is he really talking to me?'* and he was all, *'Let me buy you a drink,'* and I was all, *'Holy shit, he really is,'* and he was like, *'Come back to my place,'* and I was like, *'I'm just drunk enough for that to sound like a good idea!'* so… I did."

"Damn. Good for you."

"Well, yeah, for like, a minute. I mean, it was fun. And I didn't think I'd ever see him again. But then I ran into him at another show a month later and it turned out he was a manager and he was like, *'Oh, let me help you guys out,'* and I don't know. I was just dumb and lonely, so I let him take me home again and convinced myself that my life wasn't a hot mess and that I had a real boyfriend."

"Well wait, but didn't you?"

"I mean, that's what I thought," I said bitterly. "But then again, it's not like I have a lot of experience in this area. I wasn't ready to come out so when he said he wanted to keep things under wraps, so as not to make himself look 'unprofessional,' I probably didn't think that was as sketchy as I should have."

"So then..." Ben prompted me.

"God, this is excruciating. So then, basically, the band got called in last minute to fill in this slot at The Grasshopper. So I wasn't supposed to be there that night, which must have been why Ellis thought it was perfectly fine for him to be there. With a guy he was sleeping with. Some guy named Troy."

"Shit."

"Yeah. Pretty much."

"How did you—"

"Find out? Literally ran into them in the hallway."

"Fuck."

"Yep. And then Ellis basically made it out like I was the crazy one, claiming he'd told me the whole time what the situation really was. Which—to be clear—he definitely had not. Oh, and he outed me to everyone in a 20 foot radius."

"Jesus Christ, Adam." Ben's face darkened. "I can't believe

that guy. What a dick. Can you give me his address so I can go punch him?"

"And then end up on the news for assault and battery?"

"Might be worth it."

"My knight in a Yankees cap," I said wryly, gesturing to Ben's hat. "I appreciate the sentiment, but I'd really rather just never think about the guy again. I let him fuck up enough of my life, he doesn't need to take up anymore space."

"So after you found out—"

"I realized I had to go on stage five minutes later. And that I was about to have another panic attack. So I did the first thing I could think of that might help, which was swallowing a handful of pills with some Jameson and hoping some of them were Xanax."

"Fuck, Adam." Ben's grip tightened and I realized with a start that he'd never moved his hand off of mine.

God, it was too easy to get used to the warmth of his skin. If I had any self-respect—or any intention of making good on my attempt to get over Ben—I would have moved my own hand out from under his. But I didn't. I just let myself soak in that illicit heat and consigned another part of my eternal soul to the great dumpster fire in the sky.

"Anyway," I said, realizing I'd let the silence between us stretch out a little too long, "I know it was dumb. I hadn't used pills like that since high school, and back then, I usually knew what it was I was taking. So, yeah, stupid. But I think you know the rest of the story after that. Just me being as melodramatic about a breakup as possible."

"Dude, you are allowed to feel things, you know that, right?" Ben gave me an encouraging smile. "What Ellis did was fucked up. You don't have to be a robot about it."

"I think I'd prefer that, frankly," I snorted.

Honestly, if I were a robot, I might have some kind of kill-switch that I could use to stop feeling this awful yearning for my perfect, amazing, clueless, *straight* best friend.

"Well I wouldn't," Ben said. "I like emo Adam. Even if everything you say is filtered through industrial strength ironic remove. I know he's got feelings in there somewhere and I'm kind of attached to him."

"Gross, dude." I laughed. "I mean, fine, live your lifestyle or whatever but don't shove it in my face, you know?"

"Good point." Ben snorted. "Think of the children."

"Exactly."

"So what now?" Ben asked, finally moving his hand and leaning back in his seat. He folded his arms across his chest and gave me a long, assessing stare. "What's next for the new and improved Adam?"

"Old and slightly less closeted is I think what you meant to say," I said. "I don't know. I mean, I think I need to talk to the band about officially going on hiatus. I never even really wanted to play that much and I don't think I can stomach doing shows for a while. And then I guess back to work? I've been living off the royalties for the last batch of songs I sold —I should actually have a couple more checks coming in soon. But eventually I'm going to have to start writing new material or I'll be broke *and* homeless."

"You're not homeless. You have a place to stay."

"Temporarily."

"Permanently," Ben said. "Honestly, as long as you want. I'm happy to have you."

"You really need to stop being so nice, man. You're gonna skew my expectations for the rest of humanity."

Ben laughed. "If I haven't already managed that in the past seven years, I don't see why I should stop now."

"Yeah, but I'm supposed to like, start coming out to people and shit. You're going to trick me into thinking everyone's gonna be this chill about it."

"Maybe everyone *will* be this chill about it," Ben said.

"Maybe," I said darkly. "I don't know, I mean, I guess now I've basically told the important people—"

"Aww, I'm important to you?" Ben gasped. "Adam, you're so sweet."

"Fuck you."

"Such a sunny disposition too." Ben grinned. "But honestly, if you don't wanna do it—come out I mean—well, it's your life..."

"Yeah. I know. But I guess I like, did a lot of thinking this past month. I mean, there wasn't really a lot else to do. And I guess I don't want to be in denial of who I am or whatever. I just wish there were like, a lever I could pull and then everyone would just know and I didn't have to go through the process of actually telling people."

"Fair," Ben nodded. "After all, telling people generally involves talking to them—"

"And talking to them involves them paying attention to me. Looking at me. Asking me shit about my feelings."

"Honestly, how dare they?"

"I know, right?" I sighed. "I just wish I could fast-forward through all of it, you know? Like, I know in theory that I'm supposed to feel better after all of this and Nick claims I won't feel quite so awkward but I honestly don't think the guy truly comprehends the depths to which my awkwardness extends."

"It's true, it is very deep. Fathomless, almost."

"Scientists have yet to reach the bottom," I agreed. "I don't know, it's just like, how the hell am I ever supposed to be able to play in front of people again? Especially now that I'm not supposed to use alcohol as a coping mechanism or whatever. Like, I could barely do shows before this. Now that videos of me passing out on stage have been seen by the entire population of New York City?"

"Maybe not all of New York."

"Brooklyn, then. Still," I shuddered. "No thank you."

"Yeah, but people get over shit quick, Ben said. "Trust me, there's a social media assistant at Greenleaf whose entire job is to make sure I don't fade out of the public's consciousness. I'm pretty sure most people have forgotten about you already."

"Ah, the comforting obscurity of failure."

"Shit, I didn't mean—"

"No, Ben, really," I interrupted him. "You're fine. I chose this, remember. I never wanted to be up on stage like you. I'd much rather be scribbling away in the dark, handing my songs over to people who aren't completely socially inept."

"Well, I know it probably runs counter to your whole self-improvement plan or whatever, but you really can just hide out in my apartment for as long as you want and never tell anyone you're there. Like if you want to merge with the couch and watch people build treehouses on cable for the rest of your life, I fully support you."

"Such an ally."

"I really am, aren't I?" Ben smiled. "I mean, I don't know what *Nick* would say about that, and I guess he's a trained therapist so *maybe* you should listen to him, but—"

"Actually, he's gonna be a minister. And don't worry, I definitely need a devil on my shoulder to balance out his angel."

"Excellent. More than happy to be a bad influence," Ben said with a wicked grin. "Just remember, we can always run away to Key West."

"I'm going to hold you to that. Just watch, you'll be about to start your next tour and I'll be like, *'Nah, dude, time for our road trip,'* and you're going to regret saying that but you're not going to have a choice."

"If I'm lucky, there won't be a next tour."

"What? Why?"

Ben sighed. "I just—okay, this probably sounds really spoiled and awful and you have my permission to punch me in the face if you think I deserve it, but you know how I only signed with Greenleaf for a year? Well, the contract runs up in a month, right after this benefit thing. And I'm kind of... thinking I might not renew my contract with them?"

"Why does that make you spoiled and awful?"

"Because I'm a hypocritical whiner! Because all I've done since college is try to get signed by a major label and as soon as I do, I decide I don't like it and want to quit! A job people would die for. What the fuck is wrong with me?"

"I don't know. If you don't like it..." I didn't like seeing Ben be this upset. And since he always put so much energy into being sunny and smiling and making people happy, something had to be seriously wrong for him to be... not that. "Is there anything you like about it?"

"I mean, it has its good parts? I like performing. I like getting to meet people and connect with fans and stuff. It just—it feels so fake, at the same time. Like everyone's so excited to meet Ben Thomas, popstar, but he's this complete fantasy. Benjamin Thomas Kowalski is an actual person but no one gives a shit about him."

"That's legit. God, I can barely stand to have three people looking at me at the same time. I can totally see how it would be weird being the center of all that attention and not feeling like anyone even knows who you are. Like they're looking through you or something." I paused, looking up from the napkin I'd been shredding. "Sorry, that was kind of dark."

"No, but that's exactly it," Ben said excitedly. "It feels super weird. But then I feel like an asshole for complaining, because people would kill to be in my position and I feel like such a fraud that I can't even enjoy it. What right do I have to complain when I didn't even earn my way here?"

"Okay, well, *that's* bullshit." I said, fixing him with a glare. "You totally earned it, or am I hallucinating the past years of work you put in, doing every show you could, constantly putting out songs, writing, getting yourself out there. Greenleaf never would have signed you if your last demo hadn't kicked ass."

"Okay, but if you wanna get technical about it, *you're* the one who wrote most of those songs. I can sing, yeah, but I kind of suck at songwriting. I don't know. Maybe I just need to suck it up. Tons of people have jobs they're not passionate about."

"Yeah, but those people are all accountants. Don't be an accountant."

"I'm telling Luke you said that."

"Do it," I retorted. "I distinctly remember telling Luke sophomore year that majoring in business was bullshit. He knows how I feel."

Ben laughed, then got a glint in his eyes. "Hey, wait a minute."

"What?"

"I was just thinking. Have you actually seen Luke in a while?"

"No. Why?"

"I don't know. I mean, he's gay... you're gay..."

"So therefore we should fall in love and have all the sex and make lots of babies?" I arched an eyebrow. "Because of this one thing we happen to have in common? Trust me, he's not my type"

"Okay, you have more than *that* one thing in common," Ben said.

"Right, we have our idiot friend Ben."

"Your well-meaning, loving, idiot friend Ben. Who's so pathetic he can't be happy even when his life is objectively really freaking awesome."

"You're not pathetic," I said confidently. "If you were, you couldn't be my friend. Any friendship pair can only have one person who's failing at life at any given time and I'm sorry to tell you but I've got that market cornered."

"Thanks," Ben said. "I think."

"Don't worry, dude. You'll figure out what you want. And if you don't, you'll make a snap decision at the last minute and live with the consequences."

"Great, I'll look forward to that." Ben tilted his head to the side. "Since when are you so zen?"

"I did just spend the past 30 days doing nothing but horse therapy and talking about my feelings. And trust me, it's way easier to be zen about someone else's life than your own."

"Fair enough." Ben paused. "Wait, I'm curious though. Not that I'm trying to set you up with him or anyone. But like, who *is* your type, if not Luke?"

You. You are my type. My type starts with you and ends with... you.

I flushed. "I don't really know that I have one."

"Sure you do," Ben said, narrowing his eyes. "You just don't want to tell me 'cause you think I'm going to tease you for it, don't you?"

"I would never think something so uncharitable of you," I protested.

"Sure you would," Ben said with a laugh. "You'd just lie about it after."

"Whatever, nosy."

Ben snorted, then glanced over at the bar. "You hungry? I can go get some menus from Gray."

"Sounds good. Oh shit, I still need to text Esther."

"Dude, do it. I don't want her getting mad at me."

I laughed. "Glad you guys are best friends now."

"God forbid two people who actually care about you talk sometimes."

"It's awful," I pouted.

"Yeah, it's pretty bad," Ben agreed. "We've actually started weekly dinners where we just sit around and talk about how much we love you. I'm like, *'Thanks for being such a good sister, Es, Adam's so lucky to have you.'* And then she's like, *'No, thank you Ben, for being such a great friend to Adam. Wow, you're letting him stay with you too? God, you're just the best person in the world.'* And I'm like, *'No—we* both *are.'* And then we clink our champagne glasses and trade anecdotes about you all night."

"You'd better be fucking joking. That is my actual worst nightmare."

"Me and Esther talking about how we care about you?"

"I literally cannot think of anything more horrible in the world."

"Dude, that's a serious failure of imagination on your part," Ben said before walking to the bar to pick-up menus. When he came back, he frowned at me. "What's with the sad face?"

"It's not sad," I protested. "It's just. You know if you and Esther actually want to be friends... like I'm not saying you can't be."

"I know," Ben said, handing me a menu. "I get it."

"Get what?"

"Get that you hate being in people's debt and you're afraid that if Esther and I talk more, we'll end up talking about how much we secretly resent you."

"I—fuck. What are you, like, in my brain?" I stared at him, dumbfounded. "That's creepy."

"Dude, I've known you for seven years. I know you've got your whole dark and mysterious vibe but you're not *that* hard to figure out."

"I find that distinctly uncomforting."

"Deal with it," Ben said, looking at his menu. But after a minute, he peered at me over the top of it and smiled. "You do know we don't actually secretly resent you, right? And that you're not actually in either of our debts? People help the people they care about. That's normal."

"Yeah, but that's like, someone gets the stomach flu and you go get them Gatorade on the way home. You dogsit for a weekend. Normal stuff. This is beyond normal. You're letting me invade your apartment for God knows how long. And Esther... Fuck, do you know how much a place like Peachtree must cost for a month? And she won't take money from our dad, so she must be paying for it herself. There's no way I could pay her back."

"Well lucky for you, you don't have to," Ben said with an odd look. "I'm sure she doesn't care."

"She might. And you should, too. You should make me do something for you."

"You can buy me the grilled cheese I'm about to order."

"Thank you," I said with emphasis. "Just seven million more of those and I'll have restored some balance to the universe."

"Good. Now hurry up and pick something to eat," Ben said, "because I'm starving."

I rolled my eyes but smiled as I looked back down at the menu.

Sure, my life was still kind of falling apart. And yeah, Ben had no idea how I actually felt and, if I had my way, never would know. But against all reason or logic, he still liked me, still wanted to be my friend. I was grateful for that and I wasn't going to ask for more.

I wasn't.

Really.

6

BEN

"Hey, dude, do you have a washer and dryer in the apartment or is it in the basement—oh, shit, sorry."

I heard Adam's voice but I was pulling my shirt off over my head and couldn't see him until I got it off. I turned around once I was free and saw him standing, his face flushed, in the doorway to my bedroom.

"Oh, sure, yeah." I turned back around to drop my old shirt in the hamper and walked towards him. "It's out here, lemme show you."

"Sorry, I didn't mean to—" Adam said as he followed me into the kitchen.

"Didn't mean to what?" I asked, confused.

"Uh—interrupt you while..." Adam stammered, his cheeks growing redder still.

Oh. Now it made sense. Well, kinda. Knowing Adam, he probably thought he seemed like some kind of sexual predator just for talking to me while I was changing. Which was ridiculous, but this was Adam we were talking about, so of course he'd found a way to be worried about it.

"It's not like I had my door closed," I said with a smile. "Don't worry about it. Anyway, it's one of those all-in-one washer-dryers and it's just tucked under here."

I showed him the cabinet where it was located, right next to the dishwasher.

"Ooh, fancy," Adam grinned.

I snorted. "Not really. The dryer function kind of sucks, so it's easier if you just dry your clothes on a rack. Here, let me get you that, too."

I walked back into my bedroom and pulled the folded clothes rack out from under my bed.

"You need to borrow anything else?" I asked as I pulled open the drawer to my dresser. "All my clothes are in here or the closet, so just take whatever you want."

"Um, I'm pretty sure I'd look like a child in your clothes," Adam said with a laugh. "Since when did you get so jacked?"

"Since Shereen insisted I get a personal trainer." I rolled my eyes. "Something about needing to keep my stamina up on the tour. Another reason letting my contract with them go sounds tempting—no more protein shakes and muscle confusion workouts."

"That sounds truly awful." Adam made a face. "Can't say I blame you."

"Right?" I pulled a shirt out of the drawer and began pulling it over my head. "But on the other hand, all of my clothes are now like a size too small because they're supposed to show off the muscles, so they'll probably fit you anyway. See? Don't I look dreamy now?"

I popped my head through the neck of the t-shirt and pulled it over my chest. It was form-fitting, just shy of obscenely so, but I had to admit, Shereen had a point—it did look good. I glanced at Adam who seemed to be in a state of perpetual blushing.

"Uh, yeah," he said, clearing his throat. "Well, I've still got some clean clothes but, uh, thanks for the offer."

"I have a couple meetings today," I said, grabbing a pair of sandals from my closet and walking towards the front door, "but I'll be back around four?"

"Cool," Adam said. "I figured I'd call Angela at Indigo Records and see if she had an update on when I'd get paid for those last two songs I sold. And then, after that shocking burst of productivity, I thought I'd lie around on the couch?"

"Sounds perfect," I grinned, grabbing my keys and sunglasses from the table in the entryway. "I can't wait to join you."

"Hey Ben?"

I turned around and saw Adam giving me a worried look.

"What?"

"Just—thanks, you know? For, I don't know, everything, I guess. It really—it means... Well, thanks."

I rolled my eyes. "I know it's hard for you to believe this, but I do actually like spending time with you. But if it makes you feel better: You're welcome."

As I walked to the subway to meet up with Luke, I wondered how long it was going to take before Adam actually believed I still liked him. Him coming out had been a surprise, sure, but it didn't change anything. If anything, it made sense of some stuff that had always tickled the back of my mind, like why I never saw him with anyone, why he never joined in when people were talking about girls.

I'd always just assumed that was Adam being Adam—quiet, a little shy. I hoped he didn't feel like he couldn't tell me about guys he was dating now. At the very least, because I deserved the right to veto anyone who seemed like an asshole. I wanted Adam to be happy, and I didn't want him to end up dating some tool who I'd have to pretend to like just because he had a big dick and was good in bed.

I flushed, realizing suddenly that I was picturing Adam with someone, Adam naked. Adam in someone's arms, head tilted back, eyes closed. Adam underneath someone, Adam letting himself go for once.

Something hot and a little uncomfortable pulsed in my stomach. I didn't even know what Adam liked, I didn't know the first thing about his sex life. I should probably get my mind out of the gutter.

But still—Adam deserved someone as amazing as he was. And I wasn't going to let him settle for less.

~

"So what's up man, how was the tour?" Luke asked as he returned from the counter carrying his giant green smoothie.

When I'd asked if he had time to talk today and he'd suggested a lunch meeting, I'd assumed he meant actual lunch. Instead, the address he'd given me was a juice bar and instead of the burger I'd been counting on, I was drinking some kind of orange-carrot concoction with turmeric, ginger, and so many other powders I'd stopped paying attention.

"It was good, man, it was really good," I said, forcing a smile after I swallowed a sip of my punishment lunch.

"Right. Because that sounds convincing." Luke raised an eyebrow. "Your smile couldn't look any faker."

"Maybe it's because I'm still getting over being forced to drink my lunch today. What even *is* turmeric?"

"It's good for inflammation," Luke said with a smile. "You gotta take care of yourself, man. That juice is gonna give you tons of vitamin C, vitamin A, vitamin K and B6—the ginger's got manganese. Trust me, you'll thank me for it later."

"It's truly appalling how healthy you are, you get that, right?"

Luke grinned. "Tell me that again when I'm 120 years old. Anyway, how was the tour really?"

"It was..." I sighed. "It was *fine*. It was fun at times. And exhausting at others. I don't know, I'm not sure I have another one in me."

"You could just be burned out right now," Luke said, frowning. "But if you want, I've got some friends who are lawyers who could take a look at your contract and see if there's room for negotiation."

"That's actually kinda what I wanted to talk to you about," I said, taking another sip. I couldn't decide if it was tasting better or if I was just getting the juice version of Stockholm syndrome. "I'm thinking... okay, this isn't like, for sure yet, so don't say anything—"

"My lips are sealed."

"—But I'm thinking I might not renew my contract with Greenleaf."

"Whoa." Luke blinked. "That's big."

"Yeah. I don't know, there's a lot to think about. But I just— I'm not even doing music I like, really. But the thing is, I want to make sure this isn't going to completely fuck me over financially. Is there... like do I have enough to, like—"

Luke snorted. "Ben, when was the last time you actually looked at any of your accounts?"

"Uh. It may have been a while." I winced. "Is it that bad?"

"Bad?" Luke looked at me like I was crazy. "Ben, it's the opposite of bad. Greenleaf's contract has been very good for you. Now, granted, I've been diverting a solid chunk of your earnings into your retirement accounts and some other mutual funds with an eye towards long-term profits but if you want, we can redistribute some of that and take a more aggressive investing strategy, if you're looking for income in the short-term. There are a couple of—Ben! Ben, are you even listening?"

"Sorry." I shook myself. "Sorry. Really. I'm trying to listen. But I can't help it if finance stuff just makes my eyes glaze over."

"Dude, you need to understand this stuff. It's important."

"Or I could just keep paying you to understand it for me."

Luke rolled his eyes. "Okay, well long story short, yes, you've got enough money to live comfortably for quite a while. Like years. If you think your income's going to take a hit—if you're not going to renew with Greenleaf, for instance—we should sit down and actually look at everything together and talk strategy. But in general, yeah, you should be okay."

"That's really good to hear." I heaved a sigh of relief.

"Yeah, you're good." Luke glanced at his watch. "Shit, I gotta get back to the office soon. Anything else you wanted to talk about?"

"Nah, I don't think—Oh, wait. Can you move some more money into my parents' account this week?"

Luke frowned. "I can. But didn't you say they got mad at you the last time you did that?"

"Yeah, but if I'm gonna be poor soon—"

"Poor?"

"Okay, earning less, well, I wanna make sure I transfer some more to them while I can."

"Is everything okay there?" Luke's voice was kind. "How's everything going with Lacey?"

"Everything's fine. She's actually been doing really well. But you just kind of never know when something could happen, and if there are bills their insurance can't cover."

"Say no more. I'll transfer the money when I get back to my computer." Luke paused. "Actually, that reminds me—I meant to check in with you about this, there was this kind of massive transaction a couple weeks ago on one of your credit cards for this place called the Peachtree Center and you don't have any records of dealing with them before. Is that something new for Lacey?"

"Oh. Uh, no. Not exactly. It's, uh, kind of complicated. They do a lot of great work down here in the city though with like, low-income communities and medical clinics. Actually, I might ask you to make a donation to them too."

"Whatever you want, bossman," Luke grinned. "God, I can't believe I'm moving money around for someone who used to smuggle extra food out of the dining hall to supplement his meal plan."

"A penny saved, man."

"Yeah, yeah." Luke stood up and dropped his smoothie cup in the recycling bin. "I gotta head back now but we should hang out soon, okay? Now that you're back."

"Definitely. Back and hopefully not going anywhere for a while."

Of course, Shereen had other ideas. Even though it had only been a day since I'd told her I was thinking of going independent, it didn't surprise me at all that she'd called me in for a meeting. Knowing her, she was going to do everything she could to keep me with the label.

I rehearsed my arguments for not renewing as I walked over to the Greenleaf offices in Alphabet City. They'd bought a whole building there back in the 90s when it was shitty and condemned and held onto it. Now it was worth millions but instead of selling, they'd put a recording studio in the basement and added client offices in the upper floors.

Shereen's office overlooked Tompkins Square Park and she was in there on the phone with someone when I stuck my head in.

"Carter, I'm telling you," Shereen said, sounding exasperated. "You can't just make a DUI go away. I can't wave a magic wand and make it go poof. You're going to have to— No, no, we can't do that either. You just need—right, I hear that, but the fact of the matter is, you got arrested and he didn't. Unless you can build me a time-machine, I can't go back and change that."

She glanced up at me, rolled her eyes, and motioned for me to come in. "Listen, Carter, I have another meeting. Just sit tight, don't give any interviews, and I'll call you back in 30, okay? And for God's sake, do not *drive* anywhere, got that?"

I arched an eyebrow as Shereen hung up the phone. "That sounds fun."

"Boy bands," Shereen said as she hung up. It sounded like a curse. "God knows they're popular but working with 18 year olds who think they know everything is going to give me wrinkles even Botox can't fix. Carter fucking McElroy got wasted last night and he and his friends thought it would be a good idea to have a drag race down Sunset Blvd. Thank God he crashed his car into a lamppost before he hit anyone."

"Jesus. Is he okay?"

"He's fine. Stitches for a cut on his forehead." Shereen shook her head. "Maybe if he'd actually gotten hurt, he'd realize how serious it was. As it is, he thinks I can just fairy-godmother his DUI away."

"Yikes. I can come back later, if you need to deal with this."

"No, no. Sit, stay. Honestly, I need a break from that whole mess anyway and this won't take long."

I arched an eyebrow. "That confident, are you?"

"Confident." Shereen blinked. "About what?"

"Getting me to renew with Greenleaf? Or is that not what this meeting is about?"

Shereen laughed. "Oh sweet Ben. No, I've got much more nefarious plans to get you to stay with the label. And don't you worry, they're in motion. They're just not quite finished yet."

"That sounds ominous."

"Good," Shereen said. "It'll keep you on your toes. Anyway, no, that's not why I called you in. What I wanted to talk to you about was—oh, good, Mia, you're here too."

I turned around to see Mia Lee walking into Shereen's office, a cloud of curly hair, scarves, and a wide-brimmed straw hat. She looked like she should be riding a Vespa down a cobblestoned street in Rome. How did she always look so put together? When I wasn't on stage, I basically lived in sweat pants.

I said as much to Mia and she smiled.

"It's easier to do that as a guy," she said. "You in sweatpants equals, *'Stars! They're just like us!'* Me in sweatpants equals,

'Heartbreak for Mia Lee? The secret story behind why she's let herself go.'"

She took off her hat and pulled me in for a hug.

"It's good to see you," I grinned. "How was Paris after I left?"

"Delightful," Mia laughed. "Shereen's little PR stunt basically ensured I couldn't leave the hotel without 20 paparazzi following me everywhere."

"You're welcome for that," Shereen said drily from her seat behind the desk.

"Your new album's coming out soon, right?" I asked as Mia and I sat down across from Shereen.

"Yeah, couple of weeks." Mia grinned nervously. "So you know, it'll either be awesome and inescapably popular or everyone will hate it and I'll question my worth as a human being."

"Sounds about right."

"And that," Shereen broke in, "is why I called you guys in."

"Uh oh." Mia looked from me to Shereen and back. "Why does that sound vaguely threatening."

"To be fair, three quarters of what comes out of Shereen's mouth sounds vaguely threatening," I said.

"I'll take that as a compliment," Shereen said with a snort. "Anyway, here's the deal. Upper management wants to leak a couple of tracks from your new album, Mia."

"Like, on purpose?" Mia frowned. "I mean, can't we just release a few early? That's pretty standard, right?"

"Precisely. Which is why we're going to do something a little different." Shereen smiled wickedly. "This Saturday, we're going to hold a pre-release party. Invite some journalists, PR folks, other artists—you guys can invite your friends, of course. And Mia, you're gonna do a couple of songs off the new album."

"And you're just gonna hope that someone records them and leaks them?" Mia asked.

"Oh, you sweet, innocent chickadee," Shereen said with a smile. "No. We're gonna pay someone to record them and leak them. People always want what they're not supposed to have. Best way to make them want your album? Make it clear they're not supposed to have it. Well, not yet, anyway."

"That's..." Mia laughed. "I was going to say that's surprisingly devious, but knowing you, I really shouldn't be surprised by anything anymore."

"If it makes you feel any better," Shereen said, "this was kind of a surprise to me, too. But I'm not going to bite the hand that keeps me in my Louboutin's, so if they want a massive but top-secret party in a week, they'll get one. If I can find a space that hasn't been booked yet."

Shereen's eyes swung over to me and she frowned. "Ben, you're making your thinking face, so before you even say it, let me gently remind you that your presence is required. This is, after all, your girlfriend we're talking about. The woman you love most in the whole wide world—aside from me, of course. It's bad optics if you're not there to support her."

"Hey, I'm not a total asshole," I protested. "I'll be there. I was just thinking—I might know a good place, if you're looking for a venue. My friend Gray own's this bar, Maggie's. I don't know if it's quite the vibe you're looking for, but I can text him and ask if he could maybe slot us in?"

"Just give me the address," Shereen said. "I'll pop over after I'm done dealing with this Carter nonsense."

"Sounds good."

"Alright, then you lovelies are free to go," Shereen said with a smile. "Oh, but if you don't want your picture taken, make sure you leave by the back exit. Lucy Grace is coming in to record later and I've got photographers posted out front."

"Thanks for the tip." I waved bye to Shereen and then turned to Mia as we walked out of the office. "Wanna take the back exit with me?"

"Hell no," Mia laughed. "I look cute today. I'm not wasting that. You'd better look cute on Saturday though."

"Oh, don't worry," I called as I headed towards the back stairs. "I'll wear my most expensive sweatpants."

My phone rang as I walked back to my apartment and I smiled when I saw that it was my mom calling. It must have been hard for her, to know I was back in the country for a whole two days and resist calling. I'd texted her when I landed at JFK just to say I was back, exhausted, and planned on sleeping for a week. Frankly, I was pretty impressed she'd held out this long.

"Hey Ma," I said, ducking into the park as I picked up. "How's it going?"

"Oh Ben, sweetie, it's so good to hear your voice! I was worried about you."

"Worried? Why?"

"You said you were tired when you got back…"

"Ma, I'd just gotten off a 20 hour flight and I hadn't slept. That'd make anyone tired."

"Well I just want to make sure you're taking care of yourself," she clucked. "I can't imagine you're eating enough vegetables when you're living out of airplanes and tour busses and everything."

"Then you'll be relieved to hear that I ate an orange and carrot juice for lunch. With turmeric."

"Oh, that's supposed to be good for inflammation. I just saw something about that on Oprah."

Was I the only person in the world who hadn't heard about the miraculous healing powers of turmeric?

"Well I'm feeling very non-inflamed, so it must be working," I snorted. "And for the record, I'm fine. Got some sleep, back on a normal schedule now. Oh, Adam's going to be staying with me for a little while."

"Adam? Oh, that's wonderful. How's he doing?"

"He's good. Taking a break from playing shows for a while. Working on some new songs and stuff, I think."

"Well you tell him I say hi and send my love, okay? And bring him over for dinner soon. He's always so skinny, and you can't survive on juice alone."

"Will do," I said with a laugh.

Freshman year of college, I'd come back from Thanksgiving break a little early to try to get some more time in one of the studios they let undergrads use and discovered that Adam hadn't gone home for the holiday at all. And when I'd mentioned it in passing to my mom, she'd insisted on inviting him to spend Christmas with us. And that was the beginning of my mother's long, ardent, unquenchable love for all things Adam Hart.

From then on, Adam was invited home for every holiday, included in every care package. Hell, when we graduated, neither of Adam's parents came, but my mom pulled Adam and Esther into every picture and basically adopted them. Adam grumbled about it—but he never asked her to stop.

I wandered around the park as my mom caught me up on everything going on with the family. My dad had taken on a couple new clients—he was a plumber—and business was good. Jess, my older sister, was sick of her commute and was thinking of moving out of the city and over to New Jersey where she taught.

"Oh, of course, there's Lacey's birthday in two weeks," my mom added towards the end of the conversation. "Do you think you'll be able to make it?"

"Wouldn't miss it for the world," I said, smiling. "Where else am I going to get my funnel cake fix?"

When Lacey was five, we'd gone to Coney Island for her birthday and she'd fallen in love. So we'd done it every year since. I loved the tradition—spend the day on the beach, then come home sunburned and exhausted for pizza and cake. Especially after how draining things had been, I couldn't think of anything I'd rather do.

"Do you think you'll want to stay overnight?" my mom asked.

"Yeah, for sure." Even though I'd be sleeping on the fold-out couch, I'd probably sleep better there than in my apartment. Something about being home just made me feel whole.

"Good, I'll make sure there are clean sheets then."

I caught my mom up on how the tour had gone and after promising yet again to pass on her love to Adam, she let me off the phone. I had a new message waiting for me, a text from Gray.

GRAY>> Apparently I'm hosting a party for you on Saturday?

Damn, Shereen worked fast.

BEN>> Yeah, I'm gonna be a real diva about it though. I want 50 million individually peeled cocktail shrimp and someone needs to walk around and put them in my mouth all night

GRAY>> Your label's paying me enough, I could probably make that happen

BEN>> Sweet. See you Saturday

"Honey, I'm home," I called out as I twisted the key in the lock and stepped into my apartment.

"Cool." Adam's voice floated up from somewhere in the living room. "If you think I've spent all day making you dinner though, you're sadly mistaken."

I smiled. It had only been a day, but it did already feel more like home with Adam in the apartment. I wondered how long I could convince him to stay. I walked into the living room and saw Adam lying on the couch, reading.

"Don't worry," I said. "I'm not sure I'd want to eat anything you cooked anyway."

"Hey, I make a mean cup of noodles, I'll have you know," Adam said, looking up from his book. "Besides. I was very busy. I texted Angela and then when she called back, I actually picked up. And talked to her. Like a real adult."

"Holy shit, dude."

"I know. Impressive, right?"

"Very." I nudged Adam's legs with my knee. "Now move over. I had a hard day adulting too."

Adam sighed and made a big show of laboriously sitting up and scooting over to one end of the couch. I grinned, dropped my keys on the coffee table, and then stretched out in the space Adam had just vacated, laying my head in his lap.

"Hey! Wait, what?" Adam squawked. "Since when is that fair?"

"I never said it was fair. But it's on you for not asking clarifying questions before you moved. Anyway, I'm exhausted and might have an attack of the vapors if I can't rest on my fainting couch."

"You have a perfectly good bed like, 15 feet away," Adam grumbled. "Besides, who says I want your big head in my lap?"

"Yeah but then I'd have to yell at you through the door. This makes it easier. Just be happy I'm not putting my feet on your lap. I've been walking around Manhattan in sandals all day and they're are disgusting. Anyway, I'm too tired to get up now and move."

"You poor thing," Adam said drily. "You have my deepest sympathies."

"Your support means the world to me."

"So?" Adam said after a moment's silence.

"So what?"

"So what was hard about your day? I mean, I doubt it's going to compare to the suffering I went through lying here on this couch, avoiding all human contact and most responsibilities, but you can try."

I snorted. "I found out I have to go to a party on Saturday. For Mia's new album. How's that for anguish?"

"Ok, you win. That sounds truly awful."

"Good." I smiled up at him. "You're coming with me."

"Excuse me what now?"

"Yeah." I wiggled my eyebrows at him. "Consider it rent for staying here. You have to come and hang out with me at this party so I don't feel like an asshole with no friends."

"It's a party for your girlfriend."

"Fake girlfriend."

"Still, you're going to know like, everyone there."

"But they're all work people. And Mia's going to invite people and I can't look like the loser who doesn't actually know anyone outside of the industry."

"Ben, I hate parties."

"But you love me, right?"

"Not that much," Adam said, giving me an odd look. "Anyway, isn't it going to be weird if I'm there? Just hanging on like some kind of third wheel?"

"Trust me, no. Mia's going to be busy and I'll probably talk to her for like, 15 minutes all night. Pleeeease?"

"I don't know..."

"You know, it is even conceivable you could have a good time," I said, giving him a stern look. "It's going to be at Maggie's so Gray will be there and you know him."

"Barely. And he'll be working, won't he?"

"Fine, then you should invite someone too. A fourth wheel. That way if I even have to leave your side for like, five seconds, you'll still have someone to talk to and you won't die of acute social embarrassment."

"I'd pretend to be insulted by that," Adam laughed, "if it weren't entirely true."

"Why not invite Nick?"

I was very proud of myself for mentioning Nick's name in what I thought was a normal voice. I couldn't explain the weird antipathy I had towards the guy—he seemed perfectly nice, from everything Adam had said about him and the 30 seconds I'd spent in his presence. Maybe I was just feeling possessive of my friend after being gone for so long, but still, not the most attractive quality.

"Seriously, he seems like a great guy," I continued. There. I was being open minded. Good for me.

"Hmm." Adam frowned and looked at his phone. "I guess I could do that. I'm not sure he'd be able to come though. Or even want to. But I could ask."

"Do it," I said with more confidence than I felt. "It'll be great."

It would be. Even if Nick came and turned out to be a total asshole. If it would make Adam happy, that was what counted.

And maybe I'd get lucky and Nick would be busy.

7

ADAM

*G*etting over Ben would have been a lot simpler if he'd stop putting his mouth within inches of my dick.

I guess I was grateful that me coming out hadn't changed that particular habit of his, but it almost would have made my life easier if it had.

Because when he flung himself onto the couch that afternoon and threw his head in my fucking lap, it was only sheer terror that kept me from getting hard. Terror that he'd be able to tell, that I was giving off *I'm in love with you* pheromones or something. I desperately wanted him to move before something went wrong.

And just as desperately, I wanted that moment to last forever.

Ben was just so... drapey. He always had been. Maybe that was just what happened when you grew up with parents who actually, you know, cared about you? And demonstrated that fact?

Ben wasn't afraid of showing affection and he'd confused more than one girl—and guy—in college because of that. The way he'd casually throw an arm around your shoulders when he came up next to you, the way he'd hug you *so* enthusiastically to say hello or goodbye. With anyone else, you'd be forgiven for thinking that meant something, that those long hugs were a subtle signal to you. With anyone else, you'd probably be right.

But Ben didn't think like that. Didn't calculate or play coy. He was always himself—and comfortable enough in who he was that he didn't modulate it for anyone. Rachel, the girl he dated senior year of college, had even asked him to tone it down around other girls. And Ben had no idea what she was talking about. I still remembered the night it happened.

The two of them had gone out to see some movie but Ben came back to our apartment early because Rachel had a test the next day. We were living off campus that year in a tiny apartment we shared with Luke and an engineering student named Craig. I'd been sitting on our IKEA futon watching *Leprechaun 4: In Space* and Ben had sprawled out on top of me—again.

"Am I too touchy with people?" he asked out of nowhere during one of the commercial breaks.

"What?" I was confused by the non-sequitur—we'd been talking about ordering pizza only 10 seconds before.

"Rachel says I'm too touchy with other people," Ben repeated.

"Like, in that it makes her uncomfortable, or other people uncomfortable?" I asked.

"Oh shit." Ben blinked and stared at me. "I think she meant her. But I didn't even think about the other thing. God, *do* I make people uncomfortable?"

I couldn't help it. I burst out laughing. Because despite the horror on his face, Ben was also pinning me to the couch with his legs.

I glanced down at them significantly, where they lay across my lap and then smiled back up at Ben. "I mean..."

"Fuck." Ben's eyes followed mine and he flinched, starting to sit upright and move his legs. I stopped him, resting my hand on his shins.

"Dude, you're fine." I fixed him with a serious look. "I was just kidding. You don't make people uncomfortable."

"How do you know?" Ben shot back. "You're not all people. Maybe everyone on campus dreads running into me. Maybe every time I come into a room, people try to leave and I don't even notice. I could be that weird guy people avoid at parties."

"You're not that weird guy." I snorted. "If anything, people die from happiness when you walk by them at parties. You're not that bad at reading people—it's not like you force yourself on anyone. You're just not afraid of showing people affection."

"You're sure it's not weird?" Ben's eyes narrowed. "You never touch anyone."

"That's just because I was raised by frigid, unfeeling robots. You should *not* be using me as a standard for comparison."

Ben didn't seem convinced.

"Seriously dude, you're fine. I'm sure Rachel's just feeling a little possessive, that's all. That's probably a good thing, right? Means she likes you. You're just overthinking this."

Ben made a face. "Damn. If Adam Hart thinks I'm over-thinking, you know that's bad."

"Asshole." I threw a pillow at Ben, which he caught and shoved behind his head.

"Why are we even watching this?" he asked, gesturing to the TV. "*Leprechaun 4* is the worst of the whole franchise."

But we spent the next two hours sitting there and watching it anyway, arguing over which toppings to get on our pizza. We talked for so long that the pizza place closed and we never ordered.

It was a night in which absolutely nothing of substance happened. And it was one of my favorite memories.

Ben and Rachel didn't last. And Ben never changed how he acted around people. I had no idea if the two facts were related, but I didn't mind either outcome.

The truth was, I wasn't super touchy, and people who were kind of weirded me out. Except for Ben. Sure, for the obvious reasons. My insanely hot best friend who I was head over heels for wanted to put his head in my lap. Boo fucking hoo.

But it was also just... nice. What an insipid word to use. But it was. It felt warm, comfortable. When Ben had his arm around me or was otherwise invading my personal space, I felt oddly safe.

The only problem was that all the tolerance I'd built up to

Ben's touch over the years seemed to have dissipated when he was on tour. And now that we were sharing the same apartment, I felt like I was constantly yelling at my body to chill the fuck out. Every touch from him gave me goosebumps, every casual hand on my arm might as well have been a hand on my cock for the way it turned me on.

But I was *not* going to repay Ben's kindness, his friendship, by jerking off while thinking about him. No matter how much I was tempted.

Before the accident, before the month at Peachtree, I'd always done a weird mental calculus. It was okay to think about Ben sometimes, I'd decided, okay to get off on fantasies of sucking his dick, of feeling him inside me, of his breath on my neck as we tangled together in bed, because it didn't mean anything. I wasn't ever going to date Ben, but I also wasn't planning on telling him I was gay. So what was the harm in a few sordid fantasies?

But now that I was supposed to be doing this whole out-and-proud thing, owning my truth or some bullshit like that, I wasn't supposed to be ashamed or embarrassed of myself anymore. So it probably wasn't a great idea to keep indulging in my definitely shameful, definitely embarrassing lurid daydreams about my best friend.

My feelings for Ben, I decided, were some weird, fucked up coping mechanism. But new and improved Adam didn't need maladaptive behaviors. New and improved Adam wasn't going to hang onto the feelings I'd nursed for Ben for years, clutching them to my chest like some kind of security blanket.

The only problem was that new and improved Adam's dick

didn't seem to have gotten the message. Infact, new and improved Adam's dick seemed suspiciously similar to old and worse Adam's dick, and frankly, I didn't think that was very fair. How the hell were you supposed to go about growing as a person when your cock had no interest in playing along?

And until someone developed a mindfulness manual for my cock, I was stuck with the disobedient one I had. The one that throbbed insistently when Ben finally rolled his head off my lap that afternoon and said he was going to go for a run.

I forced myself to take a cold shower after he left, which settled things for the moment. But it was clear that new and improved Adam had his work cut out for him, at least as long as he was living under the same roof as old and still-stupidly-hot Ben.

"So you're inviting me to a party you don't want to go to?" Nick asked when I called him later that week. "Tell me again why I should say yes?"

"Because you've missed me desperately since I left Peachtree?"

Nick snorted. "It has been a little more boring since you left. But Adam, I don't really know if it's appropriate for us to like, hang out, after—

"After I bared my soul to you and told you all my disgusting secrets?"

"Well—"

"Dude, you're not, like my counselor anymore. You never even were, not really. Just come as a friend. And if it feels unbalanced, you can just dredge up some shameful secrets of your own to share."

"Again, you're not really selling this night as a tempting experience," Nick said with a laugh.

"Dude, come on. Ben's probably going to be busy the whole time and I need someone to hang out with."

"Correction: you need someone to be your backup friend, who you can drop the minute the cool kids—aka Ben—start talking to you."

"God, who scarred you in middle school?" I asked. "Nick, come on. If I have to watch Ben be all cute with his girl-friend by myself the whole night, I'll probably drink myself into a stupor. And then you'd feel really bad. So when you think about it, really, it's kind of your professional responsi-bility to come and keep an eye on me."

"I thought I wasn't your counselor anymore."

"But you're training to be a shepherd to lost souls or some-thing, right? Come tend to your flock. By which I mean me."

"You know I'm not actually Christian…"

"Great, neither am I. Come on, Nick. You're my only hope. We can make fun of famous people together. There'll prob-ably be an open bar. And froofy little trays of appetizers." I sighed. "Look, I know I'm an asshole a lot of the time, but it would actually like, mean a lot. If you came. Please?"

Nick sighed. "I have a feeling I'm going to regret this."

"Which means you're saying yes!" I grinned. "Awesome."

"I'm only saying yes because I'm pretty sure that's the first time I've heard you say please. And actually talk about your feelings without being prodded. How'd it feel?"

"Terrible," I retorted. "But I suppose it's possible—just possible—that you might be right, that talking about them is good."

Nick laughed. "First you say please, then you acknowledge I might, occasionally, know what I'm talking about? Will wonders never cease?"

"If you keep that tone up, they definitely will."

"So. Aside from having to attend fancy parties, how're things going? How're you feeling now that you're back?" Nick asked, his voice gentle.

I was silent for a minute before speaking.

"Honestly? I'm a mess. Because it's pretty fucking clear that I'm not going to get over Ben as long as I'm living with him, maybe even friends with him. Like, every day, I wake up and I'm like, *'This is it! This is the day I open Craigslist and start looking for a new place to live.'* And every day, I don't. And since I'm not gonna stop being friends with him... I think I'm just screwed."

"You don't need to stop being friends with him, Adam," Nick said, his voice soft. "But you do need to take care of yourself. You have to be honest about what you want and what you need."

"I am being honest," I protested. "Fuck, Nick, I even told him."

"You did? Holy shit, how did that go?"

"Uh, wait, to clarify, I did *not* tell him that I want to like hug him and kiss him and have all his gay babies. I'm not that brave. Or dumb. But I did, uh, come out. And tell him about the whole Ellis thing."

"How did that feel?" Nick asked.

"Terrifying? Nauseating? I mean, it didn't help that we'd almost run into Ellis on the street right before that and I panicked and lost my shit. There wasn't really any avoiding telling Ben, after that. But yeah, aside from the whole wanting to sink into a tar pit while I told him thing, I guess it wasn't that bad."

"And how do you feel now?"

"Jesus, okay, if you're coming on Saturday, you're not allowed to ask these questions. You have to act like a normal person. None of this touchy-feely shit."

"Right. Because normal people don't have feelings."

"They don't. Or if they do, they have the decency to hide them under rocks and not talk about them in polite company."

"Fine," Nick said. "I'll be *normal* on Saturday if you'll be honest with me now. How are you feeling about everything?"

"How am I feeling about everything?" I paused to take a breath, which turned into a high-pitched giggle. "Nick, I feel like I'm about to pass out every time I'm in the same room with him. I'm so horny I can barely move without poking my dick into things, I jump every time he says my name, and I know I'm just hurting myself in the long run because I need to move out and get my life back on track but all I actually want to do is just stay in his guestroom forever and press pause. Like, I'd actually make that trade. I'd accept never getting to be with him if it also meant we could just do this—me living with him and avoiding my life—for the rest of forever. How do I feel? I feel completely and totally fucked."

"That sounds really hard," Nick said. "Have you been playing at all?"

"No. Not that that shocks you, I'm sure." I sighed. "My housemates packed up all my shit and sent it to my dad's, which means I don't even have my guitar. And Ben's got this piano in his apartment, because of course he does, but mostly it just sits in the living room and taunts me."

"That sucks." Nick's voice was gentle. "I'm sorry it's been hard. But thanks for the honest answer. For being honest with yourself. That's important."

"That's it?" I blinked. "I don't get some lecture from you about how I need to grow up and pour myself back into music because that's what'll heal me? And that I deserve to have fulfilling romantic relationships in my life, that I need to move on and give myself a real shot at happiness, and I'll never get that if I keep clinging to this adolescent crush?"

"Do you... want that lecture from me?"

"I don't know. All I know is that I'm supposed to be doing better now, I'm supposed to be like, fixing my life and shit. But I don't have any idea how I'm supposed to do that, how I'm supposed to move on from him, when he's still the best, kindest, most genuine person on the planet who I in no way deserve as a friend but who, for some bizarre reason, seems to like having me around."

Nick laughed softly. "Oh Adam. I don't think you need any lectures from me or anyone else right now. I think you just need to be kind to yourself."

"Eww. Gross."

"I mean it."

"Well it's easier said than done," I grumbled.

"It is," Nick agreed. "That's one of the challenges of being human, really. Kindness to others or kindness to ourselves. Most of us are struggling with one or the other of those most of the time."

"Well that's something to look forward to," I snorted. "I thought not living in denial anymore was supposed to make things better."

"It does," Nick says brightly. "But it doesn't make the hard shit go away. It just means that when it comes, you can kind of wave at it cheerfully, instead of closing your eyes and pretending it's not there."

"You don't have to sound so chipper about it."

"I'll make a note for Saturday. *Be normal, act marginally depressed.*"

"Perfect," I said. "You'll fit right in."

"Holy shit. Ben, look what's on TV," I called as I heard him say goodnight to the delivery guy and close the apartment door.

"Please tell me it's a *Lifetime* movie with a murderous nanny. Or a philandering husband. Or both."

"Okay, well now I *wish* it were that, but sadly, no. It's *Leprechaun 3*."

"Oh my God, even better." Ben walked over to the couch with our box of pizza and looked down at me. "Move."

"Hell no." I shook my head. "I learned my lesson last time."

As though Ben putting his head in my lap again weren't exactly what I wanted. But no, I was supposed to be being responsible and not finding ways to get him to touch me.

"I don't suppose suggesting that you're my guest and you owe me would work."

"What, *now* you decide that me being here is an imposition?" I rolled my eyes. "Nice try."

"What if I write a song about how amazing you are for making room for me?" Ben asked. *"Adam, oh Adam, I do love your face. But Adam, oh Adam, you're taking up space. I need this sofa, is it that hard to see? Oh Adam, please, Adam, please make room for me."*

I snorted. "How long have you been carrying that one around in your pocket?"

"Couple weeks," Ben grinned. "Tune popped into my head when I was listening to some TV jingle in Seoul. It was just waiting inside me, bursting to get out the whole time."

"Definitely has hit single potential," I deadpanned. "But I'm still not moving."

"You're the worst," Ben said, but he smiled and sat down on

the floor, leaning back against the couch. He opened the pizza box and handed me a slice.

"Oh my God, this is heaven," I sighed. "Cheese on bread, how I've missed you."

"Was it really that bad?" Ben asked, tilting his head up and taking a bite of his slice. "Peachtree, I mean?"

"The food or the experience?" I asked, suddenly nervous.

Ben hadn't asked me anything about what my time at Peachtree had been like. It wasn't that I minded telling *him*, exactly. If I were going to talk about it with anyone, it would be Ben. But talking about it at all...

You know how sometimes you pick a scab off before the skin underneath is completely healed? I wasn't sure that I wouldn't start bleeding again if I had to talk about it now.

"The food," Ben said quickly. "Definitely the food."

"Offensively healthy," I said with a laugh. "Every meal was at least 80% chia seeds. And if I never see a sprouted almond again, it'll be too soon."

"Eww, chia seeds are those little, like, gelatinous things, right?"

"The ones that look like frogs eggs? Yeah. They taste about as good, too."

Ben nodded and leaned back against the couch and I had to shift slightly to make sure I didn't get crumbs in his hair. This close, I could smell the subtle citrus scent of his shampoo and I found myself wondering if there were a way to get him up on the couch with me after all. So much for being responsible. I should have just moved when he'd asked me the first time. Maybe if I got up to get water, he'd lie down on it and I could wiggle my way in there somehow?

Except dammit, that was exactly what I *wasn't* supposed to be thinking. New Adam wasn't supposed to waste his time on a pointless crush. New Adam wasn't supposed to be letting his gaze linger on the muscles in Ben's arms, or the place on his neck where his hair turned into peach fuzz, just behind his ears.

New Adam definitely wasn't supposed to be flashing back to this morning when I'd walked into the bathroom to find Ben brushing his teeth in just his boxer briefs, the tight black fabric leaving very little to the imagination.

"Hey, Adam?" Ben said after a few minutes.

"Yeah?"

"Do you *want* to talk about Peachtree? Like, other than the food, I mean?"

He asked it casually and the words sort of hung there between us like a string of lights in the dark. I couldn't decide whether or not to step into the glow they cast.

"Nevermind," Ben said after a moment. "I was just—you don't have to. I just—if you *wanted* to talk about it, I'd be happy to listen."

"Thanks," I said slowly. It was all I could think of to say.

I turned over onto my back and stared up at the ceiling, completely giving up any pretense of still watching the movie. Fucking Ben. I didn't want to talk about it. The thought made my stomach sort of curl up on itself, like a dog that's trying to wrap itself up into a ball for protection. And yet.

"I did a pretty shitty job of being there," I said after a moment. It wasn't what I'd expected to say—I hadn't even expected to start talking. But now that I'd opened the door, the words were just sneaking their way out.

"I mostly just feel like a dick because I know Esther spent all this money and for the first two weeks I didn't even talk to anyone except Nick," I continued. "They had all these counselors, and like, psychiatrists if you needed something stronger, or some kind of prescription. But I don't know, I don't think what's wrong with me can be fixed with a pill."

"What's wrong with you?"

Ben's voice was soft, curious, but he kept his eyes locked on the TV. I wondered if he was doing that on purpose, if he knew it made it easier to talk that way.

"I don't know. Everything?" I barked a laugh. "It's so dumb, because it's not like anything that horrible happened to me. I don't really have an excuse to be as messed up as I am."

"I don't think you need an excuse," Ben said.

"Yeah but some people—some people have like, trauma, you know? Straight up *bad shit* happened to them and you're like, holy shit, you're actually really functional, all things considered. But unless I've got deeply repressed memories or something like that," I snorted, "I'm basically just every other sad, rich, white boy. Boo hoo, my parents got divorced when I was little. Whose didn't? Yeah, high school was hard —but that's nothing new. High school's supposed to suck. But you're supposed to go through your whole 'my dad doesn't love me enough' phase and paint your nails black with a sharpie and put safety pins through your ears and then *grow out of it*. I'm just the asshole who never did."

"Holy shit, your ears are pierced?" Ben asked in surprise.

I laughed. "Figuratively speaking. I guess I couldn't even do the emo rebellion thing right."

"You never really talk about high school," Ben said after a moment. "I guess—I always figured it wasn't great, but, I don't know. I didn't know how bad it was."

"What's to talk about," I said, unable to hide the bitterness in my voice and burning with embarrassment because of that fact. "Fourteen year old boys are assholes. Especially at boarding school. There's an order, you know, a hierarchy. And once they've decided you're at the bottom of it, there's not much you can do. And if they're just gonna call you gay, if they're just gonna beat you up any time you try to stand up for yourself. I don't know, it just becomes easier not to. No one wants to be your friend. So you just... learn how to not have them, I guess."

"Shit. Adam that's—"

"I mean, they weren't wrong, when you think about it. I was gay. Not that it would have made any difference to them if I weren't. That was just the thing you ripped into people for. It just happened that in my case, it was accurate."

"But they still shouldn't have—I mean, that's awful."

"I know. I know." I had the strangest sense I was the one trying to calm Ben down now, not the other way around. I laughed. "God, I remember the spring of my freshman year. Tommy Somers and Steven Bozeman stole my clothes and room key when I was showering—oh, and my towel. I had to walk down to the house master's office naked to ask him to let me back into my room. Tommy lied and said he'd thought he'd grabbed his own clothes and key. They didn't even get a slap on the wrist."

"Jesus, that's—"

"That was the night I broke into the teachers' lounge." I smiled, remembering. "I grabbed two bottles of vodka and the football coach's spare key for the locker rooms. I doused Tommy and Steven's uniforms in Grey Goose—only the highest quality for America's future leaders, of course—and set them on fire."

"What the—"

"In my defense, I made sure they were on a concrete floor. I wasn't trying to burn down the school or anything. I just didn't think through the whole smoke alarm issue." I shook my head. "By the time the fire alarm went off, I was up on the roof, drunk off my ass. It took them hours to find me. And minutes to expel me, once they did. But still—worth it."

"Adam, that's—" Ben finally turned around and looked at me. "I don't even know what to say to that."

"Yeah. Sorry. It's probably not great finding out that your friend's a vandal. I probably should have told you all of this before. I just—well, honestly, I wasn't sure you'd like me anymore if I did. Anyway, I promise, I haven't lit more than a cigarette since then."

"Okay, well I definitely still like you." Ben shook his head vehemently. "My only complaint, honestly, is that you should have burned their regular clothes too. Hell, I'd have been right there with you, adding lighter fluid."

"Let's just be glad you weren't. Your poor parents would have had a heart attack. My mom was too stoned out of her mind on Valium to understand what the problem was when the school called her. And my dad—well, my dad had always told me I was an embarrassment to the family name. Dramatic, weak, *sensitive*. Code for disgusting, in his mind. The music thing never went over well with him—far too effeminate for his tastes. And now he got the pleasure of being proven right. Hell, I wouldn't be surprised to find out he'd given Tommy and Steven the idea. Probably hired those assholes right out of business school eight years later."

"That's awful." Ben stared at me, his blue eyes full of pain. I had to look away. If I stared at them too long, I was afraid I was going to start crying. "God, Adam, I'm so sorry."

"Eh, it's okay," I said, lying back down on my back and staring at the ceiling until I felt that shaky, breathless feeling in my chest subside. "That's basically all high school was. People being shitty to me, my parents being shitty to me, and me realizing that no matter how much school guidance counselors clucked about wanting to help me fit in, no one actually gave a shit. It was easier to just not try."

"Fuck."

"I mean, don't get me wrong. It sucked. I'm pretty sure I spent half that time drunk or high. And it's not like I'm encouraging drug-use-as-escape for 16 year olds in general. But it's over now. And it made me into the unique, remarkable, one-of-a-kind human being I am today," I finished in a sickening, lilting voice. "I really have so much to be grateful for."

"Adam, you—" Ben started, then stopped.

I waited for him to keep going, to tell me things about myself I'd never be able to believe. I could see him out of the corner of my eye, still facing me, his arms folded on the couch as he sat there on the floor below. But he didn't say anything. He just put his hand on my arm.

I froze. Ben's skin was so warm, his fingertips almost hot against me, and I felt so cold in comparison. I wanted to wrap myself up in him like a blanket. And then, as I stared at the ceiling willing my emotions to calm the fuck down, he leaned in and pressed a kiss to my arm, his lips warm and dry on my skin, for an instant before pulling away.

And instead of doing anything normal in response— instead of turning and asking him what the hell he thought he was doing, or just lying there and saying nothing or even, fuck it, confessing everything right then and there—instead of doing *anything* normal, I started to cry.

Tears spilled out from the corners of my eyes before I could stop them. I reached up with my free hand—the one attached to the arm Ben wasn't holding—and wiped them away, feeling my breath catch and hating how I was coming undone.

"I'm just sick of feeling broken, you know?" I said.

My voice was high, shaky. Super attractive. Totally the way you want to sound when your best friend kisses you (On the arm! Who the fuck kisses someone on the arm?). Your straight best friend who your gay ass is desperately in love with.

God, this was not good. This was very not good. Crying? Losing my shit over stuff that happened over 10 years ago? I needed to get out of there.

I sat up abruptly, swinging my legs down off the couch and pulling my arm out of Ben's grasp.

"I... need to go," I said, standing up. I felt shaky, not entirely sure that my limbs would hold me. "Sorry. Thanks, uh... just, thanks."

I couldn't even look at him. I walked away from the couch quickly, crossing to the door of my bedroom like I was walking on hot coals. I was pretty sure I'd left my cell phone lying on the coffee table, but I didn't care. I couldn't let Ben see me like this.

"Adam, wait," Ben called out. And I stopped. Of course I fucking stopped.

I squeezed my eyes shut tight and took a deep breath before forcing them open, making myself turn around. "Yeah?"

Ben was standing now, next to the couch, looking at me like he'd never seen me before. Oh, God, I'd probably disgusted him.

"For the record. I don't think there's anything wrong with you." He gave me a small smile. "Okay?"

"Okay."

I turned back around and walked into the bedroom, closing the door behind me before I could get any ideas about staying, about lingering, about asking him what the fuck that kiss had been about. Because yeah, it had been on the arm, but still.

I threw myself down onto the bed, trying to stay afloat in the swirl of emotions churning inside me. Crying in front of your best friend. About shit that didn't even matter anymore. And maybe I could have carried it off, acted like it didn't still bother me. But then Ben had to go and kiss me.

What was that about? That was out of nowhere—even for Ben. He must have just been trying to comfort me—and God, it made me cringe to realize how pathetic I must have looked for him to want to do that. It couldn't mean anything else. The arm's not exactly an erogenous zone.

I tried to slow my breathing, tried to calm my heartbeat down. It wasn't fair. Because I was weak when it came to Ben. And no matter how much my mind yelled at my body that that kiss was nothing more than a fluke, something *Ben* sure as hell wasn't lying awake thinking about, my body refused to relax.

The longer I lay there, the more my mind kept returning to that moment. Ben's hand on my arm, his touch firm but gentle. The feel of his lips against my skin, soft and silken. What if I hadn't started crying at that moment? What if I'd had the courage to turn and look him in the eye? What would have happened?

Fuck, I could feel myself getting hard. This was a bad idea, this game of what ifs. It couldn't lead anywhere good. I should stop, stand up, go throw myself under the cold, harsh pulse of the shower. But I didn't do any of that.

Instead, I let my hand drop to my cock. Fuck that felt good, even just the light stroke against my shaft over the fabric of my flannel pajama pants. Jesus, this was exactly what I promised myself I wouldn't do. But I couldn't stop. I hadn't jerked off in over a week, and when I had, I'd forced myself to think about anyone *but* Ben.

What if I'd looked at Ben? And what if I'd seen the look I'd so often dreamed of seeing in his eyes—nerves, excitement, hope? And if I'd turned, rolled over onto my side, brought my face within inches of his?

My hand dove underneath my pants in a flash and I bit my lip to stifle a moan as it came in contact with my skin. Fuck, I was aching, so hard at just the thought of Ben leaning in and kissing me, his lips smooth and sweet against mine. We wouldn't need to say anything—he'd know, without needing to hear it, that I'd do whatever he wanted.

I stroked myself hard and fast as I pictured Ben reaching up to grab a fistful of my shirt, pulling me towards him and then down onto the floor. I'd land on top of him and I'd be able to feel how hard he was and I'd know, for the first time, that he wanted me as badly as I wanted him.

God, I could see myself grinding down onto him, rolling my hips and thrusting my cock down against his thigh. I could feel his fingers slide under my shirt, around my back, dipping under my pants to tease my ass. Feel his grip tighten, pulling me down onto him.

And if I slid a hand in between our bodies, felt the warm girth of his cock pressing up into my grasp, would he do the same? Would he tell me how long he'd wanted this, how long he'd waited, as his hand slid down to stroke me, telling me how he wanted to make me come?

It was too much. I stroked myself faster, one, two more

times, and bit down on my lip again. But it didn't work, and as I came, shooting hot and hard into my own hand, a whine escaped from my lips like a secret I could no longer keep.

It was a long time before I even trusted myself to move, to roll over and grab a tissue from the nightstand. My eyes were wide in the dark. And it wasn't just the worry that Ben might have heard me. It was the sinking realization that no matter how much I knew I should let go, no matter how much I knew he wasn't even mine to hold, there was no part of me that was ready to give Ben up.

8

BEN

I wanted to hate Nick from the minute I saw him walk into the party at Adam's side. I didn't care if it was petty, or territorial, or inexplicable. My antipathy to the guy was rock solid. I'd given up trying to figure it out and just accepted the fact that I'd probably never like him. But then the asshole didn't even have the decency to act like a dick and actually let me hate him, which only annoyed me more.

When Adam and Nick finally showed up to Mia's party on Saturday night, when I caught sight of them on the far side of the room, across a sea of people who I kept pretending to know because they all seemed to know me, my first thoughts were, in quick succession: relief that Adam had actually showed up and annoyance that Nick had the gall to accept the invitation I'd encouraged Adam to make. How dare he?

It was absurd. Just because Adam was my best friend didn't mean he wasn't allowed to have other friends too. Hell, I couldn't blame him if he wanted to hang out with someone other than me, since I'd pretty much forced him to spend every waking minute with me for the past week. God, especially after that... whatever the hell that had been the night we'd watched Leprechaun 3.

I still didn't know what to make of that kiss. It had seemed so natural that I hadn't even thought about it, just did it without stopping to consider. Adam was upset and I'd wanted him not to be. But then he'd gotten up and basically run away right after and I'd realized how inappropriate I'd been.

My best friend had just come out to me as gay and here I was randomly molesting his arm like some kind of overeager teenager. No wonder he'd gotten out of there. Knowing that I'd made Adam uncomfortable made me sick to my stomach and even though he'd acted normal the next day, I'd felt guilty ever since.

It took me a while to make my way over to Adam and Nick at the party. I had to extricate myself from a conversation with Molly Ides, one of the Greenleaf execs, and some journalist whose name I couldn't remember who seemed to be angling for some kind of job. And even once I'd started walking, people kept snagging my wrist and stopping me as I crossed the floor of Gray's bar.

The space worked surprisingly well for this kind of party. There was enough room for people to mingle, but lots of little booths and corners for quieter conversations. An excited, tipsy kind of hum permeated the air as people greeted each other, gossipped, and vied for position.

And I had to be the perfect Ben Thomas all night. It was everything I hated about my job, but I had to admit, it was probably going to be a success as an evening. At least Shereen would be happy.

The closer I got to Adam, the more my progress slowed. All I wanted to say was, *'Sorry, but I really need to talk to my friend,'* but even something as innocuous as that could be taken the wrong way, spun into, *'Ben Thomas, rude and entitled,'* or, *'Who does Ben Thomas think he is?'*

I could hear Shereen's voice in the back of my head: approachable yet unattainable. That was the mantra I was supposed to live by. Always friendly, always on, and never really myself with anyone I talked to. So as I made my way over, I had to keep stopping and smiling at anyone who wanted to talk to me, making at least two minutes of conversation before I was allowed to leave—always, of course, with a promise to find them later.

"Someone's popular," Adam said with a laugh when I finally made it to the corner of the room where he and Nick were standing. Nick was holding a beer and Adam had a glass of something limey and fizzy in his hand. He caught my glance and arched an eyebrow. "Don't worry, it's just seltzer."

"Dammit. If it were something stronger, I'd be stealing it from you right now."

"Having a good night, then?" Adam grinned. "Should I order us some tequila shots?"

"I could use a gallon of tequila right now," I sighed. "Shereen never lets us drink at these things and I swear I'm going to scream the next time someone tells me they love my music but really just wants to pump me for gossip. It's bullshit. *I* don't even like my music—not the last album anyway—and everyone's just jockeying for position and talking to me as some kind of elaborate social ploy."

"Damn." Adam said with a laugh. "Tell us how you really feel."

"Sorry." I grimaced. "It's just been a long night and it's not even half over yet. I always get grumpy at these things."

"Key West is looking pretty good right now, huh?" Adam laughed.

"Don't even say those words," I begged. "It hurts too much thinking of what I can't have."

Nick's eyes had been bouncing back and forth between me and Adam as we talked and I saw his confusion when Adam said 'Key West.' I tried and failed to stifle a flash of smug triumph that Adam and I had something he didn't share.

What the hell was wrong with me? Of course Adam and I had inside jokes. That was nothing to be proud of. And I was being a jerk by coming over and then not even including Nick in the conversation.

"Sorry," I said, looking at Nick. "I'm being incredibly rude, aren't I? You're at a party and should be having fun and I'm over here raining on your parade." I gave him a warm smile, forced myself to hold it and mean it. "I'm really glad you could make it. It's good to see you again."

Even if I didn't like Nick, Adam did. I should at least try to make an effort, right?

"Don't worry about it," Nick said with an easy laugh. "To be honest, Adam made this sound about as enjoyable as back surgery. If you'd come over here beaming and overjoyed, I'd almost be disappointed."

Dammit. He wasn't supposed to be nice and easy-going.

"Besides," Adam put in, "we got dinner first to gird our loins. We're still riding out the tail end of our food-coma, so we're looking at everything through an MSG-flavored haze right now. Can you believe Nick's never been to Peking Palace before?"

"Unconscionable," I said in a serious voice, trying to ignore my irrational annoyance that they'd gone out for dinner together. "I'm glad you remedied that."

I turned to Nick. "Did he make you order the spicy pork?"

Nick made a pained expression. "He did."

"Bad?"

"Ben, I thought I might actually die, and I was okay with that, because it meant the burning would stop. Seriously, I saw my life flash before my eyes."

Ugh. Easy-going and funny. Why couldn't Nick suck more?

"It's awful," I agreed. "But you should have at least 30 more minutes of an endorphin high from the peppers before you come down." I jerked my finger at Adam. "I honestly don't think this one has taste buds anymore. That's got to be the only way he can eat as much of it as he does."

"Hey, just because you mere mortals don't understand the beauty that is Michelle Yang's spicy pork doesn't mean you need to slander me for it," Adam complained. "Keep that up and I'll stop bringing you guys with me when I go. Which, for the record, would be fine. More pork for me."

"Do you live in the city?" I asked Nick, searching for something to ask that wasn't, *'What's your deal and what are your intentions with my best friend?'*

"Yeah," Nick nodded. "Lower East Side. You?"

Well, shit. I'd been hoping he'd say something like Williamsburg so I could feel smug and superior.

"SoHo." I paused. "Adam and I used to live in the Lower East Side, actually. This shitty old apartment on the corner of Hester and—" I looked at Adam "—it was Orchard, right?"

"Yeah, Orchard."

"Right." I turned back to Nick. "The first two years after college, there were 8 of us crammed into this 3 bedroom place and I kid you not, we had honest-to-goodness bunkbeds. Complete fire hazard, but the landlord couldn't report us because I'm pretty sure the whole place should have been condemned."

"That sounds... way too familiar," Nick laughed. "Until last year, I was actually sleeping in someone's closet, and paying $1100 a month for the privilege of doing so."

"How long have you been in the city?"

"Just a few years," Nick said. "I moved in for work, then stayed for div school. I grew up close by, in East Rutherford —Jersey," he added at my look of confusion"—but I'm not dumb enough to claim I'm from New York."

I laughed. "Good. I'm from Queens so I'd be contractually obligated to rag on you if you did."

"Ben takes these things *very* seriously," Adam said with a snort.

"Hey, I'm open-minded, at least," I protested. "I'm friends with you, after all, and you're from fucking Westport."

"Wait, you're from Connecticut?" Nick looked at Adam, aghast. "How did that never come up?"

"Um, maybe because I didn't want to face everyone's anti-Connecticut bigotry and prejudice?" Adam said. "You guys don't know what I suffer."

"You really *are* open-minded," Nick said to me. "Connecticut's awful."

"I know, right?" I said, and when I grinned, I actually meant it. Ugh, I'd wanted to hate him so badly. Why wouldn't he let me do that? "You said you moved in for work?"

"Yeah," Nick nodded. "I work at a nonprofit that provides housing and support services for domestic violence survivors and families. We have housing all over the city, but the offices are at Houston and Avenue B, so—"

"Holy shit. Do you work for the Family Futures Project?" I stared at Nick.

"Uh, yeah?" He looked back at me in surprise. "You... know about them?"

"Yeah." I blinked. "Yeah, I uh, I used to do volunteer work with them when I was in high school. One of your buildings was pretty close to my parents' place. We'd go and do reading and homework help with the little kids after school.

Actually, I'm going to be performing at this benefit thing they're doing at the end of the month."

Nick smiled in surprise. "That's awesome, man. I've always been out of town when they do the benefit, this is the first year I'll actually be able to go. That's really cool that you used to tutor for them, too."

"I wasn't like, saving the world or anything—" I began, blushing, before Nick cut me off.

"Seriously, Ben, volunteering like that makes a huge difference. The kids in our programs *love* having an older kid hang out with them, even if it is to do homework. You'd be amazed what an impact a positive older role model can make."

"I mean, it was only two days a week, though. You're doing that on a daily basis." I shrugged, suddenly uncomfortable as I looked around the scene in Gray's bar. "It kind of puts what I do, nights like this, in perspective. I *really* shouldn't complain about my job."

"Well, I actually spend half my time doing grant-writing," Nick said with a laugh, "and the other half, I'm working with adults, not kids. So don't make me out to be too much of a saint."

"Still, it's definitely—" I trailed off as I saw someone—Gray himself, actually—approaching us from the side.

"Hey," Gray said, his broad smile taking in all three of us as he approached. "I hate to interrupt, but Ben, someone named Shereen appears to be holding a very tense meeting in my supply closet? She caught me as I was walking past and asked me to come find you."

I sighed. "That's my manager. I should probably go see what the crisis is."

"Thank you." Gray gave me a relieved look. "I got the distinct impression that if you didn't come, she'd find a way to murder both you *and* me and I don't have time to get murdered tonight. Micah, one of my bartenders, is out sick and someone forgot to change two kegs that kicked last night."

"Don't worry." I squeezed his shoulder with a smile. "I'll be right there, and I'll make sure to tell Shereen to put you on the '*do not murder*' list."

"Thanks, man, I owe you one."

Gray walked off before I could protest that if anyone was owed something, it was him, for letting us fill his bar up with a bunch of rude, self-absorbed entertainment industry types who were probably bad tippers besides.

"I swear, that guy looks so familiar," Adam said, shaking his head as Gray walked away. "I really don't think I've met him before, but something about him..."

"Wait, are you serious?"

Adam and I both turned to look at Nick, who was glancing between us and Gray's retreating figure.

"Uh, yeah?" Adam said, looking confused. "Why?"

Nick tilted his head to the side. "Wow, ok, now I feel like an asshole. Maybe I'm not supposed to say this? I don't know what the etiquette is here. Probably it's *not* talking about somebody when they're not here and part of the conversation, but—"

"Oh come on," Adam said, his eyes lighting up. "You can't say something like that and then not actually tell us what the hell you're talking about."

"Yeah, come on," I grinned. "What's the deal? Is Gray hiding some kind of huge secret?"

It was hard to imagine anything less likely. I'd never met someone as uniquely confident in himself and relaxed as Gray. The guy just gave off an air of perpetually not giving a fuck. Tonight was actually the most fucks I'd ever seen him give, come to think of it.

"Um. Shit." Nick started to blush. "Okay, well, he's not hiding it, but I still feel like I have to say that obviously, a person should be able to do whatever they want with their lives and their bodies as long as it's not harming other people and they shouldn't be stigmatized or judged for it and society has a long way to go in understanding and improving the way we react and treat people and probably even me talking about this like it's a *thing* is part of the problem—"

"God, Nick, we get it, you're a good person and you don't advocate assholery," Adam said. "Spit it out."

"Ok, well, um," Nick looked between the two of us, "I guess it kind of makes sense that Adam might recognize him. And Ben wouldn't. You, uh," he nodded at Adam, "probably have seen him before. Maybe not in, uh, person? But, uh. *Hiding* things... is not what I'd say... you'd, uh, think of... him for?"

As I tried to wrap my mind around the syntax of that sentence, Adam's eyes narrowed, then widened suddenly in a rush of comprehension.

"Ohhh."

"What?" I looked back and forth between them. "What am I missing here?"

"Gray does porn," Adam said bluntly. "Or, well, did, I think. I haven't uh, seen him in anything in a while."

Nick nodded. "Yeah, he's actually retired now."

"Wait, what? What, do you like, *follow* him?" Adam asked.

"No! He was on NPR!" Nick said, flushing bright red. "Seriously, he's super open about it actually. That's why I didn't think it was too big a deal to say. He's given tons of interviews about like, the adult entertainment industry and fighting the stigmatization of sex work in general."

"Shit. That's really cool." Adam paused for a second, then looked at Nick and laughed. "Honestly, dude, I didn't know ministers were allowed to watch porn."

"Okay, well, number one, I'm not a minister yet, I'm still in school, and number two, yes they are. Unitarian ones anyway. And number three, who are you to judge me?"

"Um, a self-loathing head-case who's watched, albeit furtively, a metric fuckton of porn. In the name of research, of course."

"What better way to figure out your sexuality than by watching a bunch of dicks touching?"

"Exactly," Adam laughed. "The first 500 hours of gay sex pretty much sorted it out for me, but I figured I should watch at least 500 more just to be sure."

"For science," Nick said sagely.

"Of course."

"I... I feel weirdly left out," I said with a laugh when they turned to look at me. I meant it as a joke, but honestly, I did, kind of. It was stupid, but I couldn't help being bothered that Adam and Nick shared this thing that I'd never have a part in. "And like I have a lot of NPR to catch up on. And maybe also gay porn? God, what have I been doing with my life?"

"Making bad choices, evidently," Adam said with a grin.

Nick laughed. "Don't worry though, we're your guys if you need advice. Well, Adam is, anyway, since he lives with you. I'm sure he'd be more than happy to give you some pointers."

"Thanks, asshole," Adam grumbled. "But I don't listen to NPR."

Nick smiled at him innocently. "I know."

"I'll, uh, keep that in mind." I said with a laugh. I put my hand on Adam's arm. "I should probably go find Shereen, though, before she actually does murder someone. I'll see you later though?"

Adam nodded. "Sounds good."

I began threading my way back across the room, trying to keep my face pleasantly neutral despite the avalanche of thoughts tumbling around in my mind. It was absurd that I felt *left out* by the fact that I hadn't seen whatever videos Gray had been in, but I did. Like I was in fucking middle school and hadn't been invited to sit at the cool table in the cafeteria.

It wasn't the Gray part of it that bothered me. Good for him. But it was one more thing that Nick and Adam shared, which somehow only made it more annoying that Nick was actually pretty awesome and I couldn't hate him. Dammit, why couldn't he be an asshole? More importantly, why the hell did I care so much?

By the time I made it to the supply closet, Mia was crying on a box of cleaning supplies and Shereen was crouching down on the floor in her stilettos, holding Mia's hands and telling her how beautiful and perfect she was.

"Uh, hi?" I said, slipping inside and shutting the door quickly behind me. "Gray said you were looking for me?"

"Ben, thank God." Shereen looked over her shoulder at me in relief. "Will you please tell Mia what a gorgeous, talented badass she is?"

"Um." I took a step further into the room and looked at Mia. "I mean, you are, Mia. All of those things. Also smart and funny and you probably could kick my ass because I know you do Krav Maga."

"Exactly," Shereen said, nodding her head like I'd just settled an argument.

"Mia, what happened?" I asked, kneeling down on the floor next to Shereen.

"Tate!" Mia wailed, looking up at me. Her mascara was running and I hoped she had some tissues in her clutch. "He—he—he just—"

As she lapsed back into sobs, Shereen filled me in on what I'd missed. Tate Bryan was an actor—moderately talented, in my opinion, but more than moderately good looking— who Mia had dated until this past April.

The official story was that their schedules had made it too difficult to stay together but Mia had told me she was pretty sure Tate was cheating on her with Emma Hayden, another actor on his TV show. He'd denied it when she asked him but then claimed that he couldn't keep dating someone who didn't trust him.

Mia had been more than happy to agree to Shereen's fake relationship proposal back in May. She'd claimed to be over Tate but I was beginning to think that was very much not the case. Because apparently Tate and Emma really *were* dating and, well...

"It's all over Instagram!" Mia cried. "They got matching tattoos!"

"Aww, Mia, I'm sorry," I said. I pulled her into a hug. "That really sucks."

"It's not even fair," Mia mumbled. "I'm the one who supposedly moved on first. I'm not allowed to be upset."

"Yeah, but you still can be." I smoothed her hair. "He's a dick."

"Thanks," Mia said, pulling away and wiping at her eyes. "God, I must look terrible."

"You look perfect," I said.

"Not helping," Mia said, rolling her eyes.

Shereen laughed as she stood up and walked towards the

door. "I'll go see if I can find someone with some concealer and mascara. I'll be right back."

"A compact mirror too," Mia called as Shereen slipped out the door. She frowned at me. "How much did I just fuck up the schedule tonight with my pity party?"

I settled down onto the floor next to Mia and pulled my phone out. "Eh, not too bad. Besides, you're like, a diva, right? You're supposed to be dramatically late."

Mia snorted. "I've got a couple decades to go before I get to claim that crown. And by then Tate and Emma will probably be married and have 10 children, five biological and five adopted from war-torn nations for which they'll be helping organize relief efforts as Goodwill Ambassadors for the Red Cross or something. So that'll be great."

"Yeah, but they'll still be those idiots who got matching tramp-stamps. And when they break up seven years later, they're going to have to get them removed."

"I guess there is that," Mia sighed.

"Besides," I said, nudging Mia with my shoulder. "You're way prettier than she is."

Mia laughed. "I know I'm not supposed to care or like, *want* you to say that. But... thanks."

"Any time."

"You're a pretty decent fake boyfriend, you know?" Mia said with a laugh. "You're gonna make someone a pretty good real one someday too."

Shereen popped back in and handed Mia a makeup case. She looked at the two of us and gave us a thumbs up sign.

"You two good to go?"

I looked at Mia. "Whaddya think? Ready to go knock 'em dead?"

Mia pulled a tube of mascara out of the little bag Shereen had given her and smiled. "Give me five minutes. I might be heartbroken but I'll be damned if I'm going out there looking anything less than hot as fuck."

"Damn straight," Shereen grinned.

True to her word, Mia was ready and waiting in the hallway less than five minutes later and when we walked out together, she was beaming. And she was fantastic. The songs were great and Mia flirted, bantered, glowed in between each one.

At one point, she thanked me for being her rock and pulled me up on stage and I hammed it up for the photographers there, planting a giant kiss on her cheek and gazing at her as adoringly as I could. If Tate Bryan was going to see these pictures tomorrow—and I was willing to bet he'd still be checking up on Mia, new girlfriend be damned—I was going to do everything I could to make him feel like shit about his life choices.

I could see Adam smirking at me as I got up on stage and I had to fight the urge to roll my eyes right back at him. I knew he'd make fun of me for how fake this all was and honestly, I kind of wanted him to.

Nights when I was surrounded by people from the label, by journalists and industry people, I craved having Adam there to puncture everyone's self-importance with his sarcasm. All I could do was grin back at him and hope he'd move up front so I could talk to him once I got off-stage. But I was pretty much pinned to Mia for the next hour and by the time we were done giving out sound bites and playing the disgustingly-in-love couple, Adam was nowhere to be found. Neither was Nick.

I pulled my cell phone out to see if I'd gotten any texts from Adam and sure enough, there was one waiting.

ADAM>> Went home early, a little tired. Party was great, have fun!!

I snorted. The nicer Adam was about something, the more likely it was that he was lying.

BEN>> Liar. Since when do you use double exclamation points??

And then, because I couldn't stop myself,

BEN>> Is Nick still here? I can go find him and make sure he has someone to talk to

ADAM>> Nah I think he went home. Said he was tired too

A wave of relief washed through me. Once I'd seen them both missing, my mind couldn't help but jump to certain conclusions. It felt strangely good to be proven wrong.

BEN>> Cool. Well thank you both for coming and putting up with me

BEN>> I'll be home as soon as I can but Shereen's bossing me around, so that might be a while

ADAM>> Don't worry about it. I'm probably just gonna pass out. Have fun with your gf

ADAM>> !!!!!!!!!

BEN>> Cute

"Ben, my love, I need you," Shereen called out.

I slid my phone back into my pocket and looked up, making sure my smile was firmly in place. It was going to be a long rest of the night.

9

ADAM

"*H*appy to give him some *pointers*?" I asked Nick incredulously after Ben was out of earshot. I watched Ben's back as he wove through the crowd, wishing I didn't feel so much like I was losing something as he walked away. "What the hell, man?"

"I mean, you are, aren't you?" Nick asked, barely concealing his mirth.

"Fuck you." I rolled my eyes. "Just because it's my deepest fantasy for Ben to ask me for advice on gay porn consumption does *not* mean I need you telling him that. I'm living in his guest room, now really isn't the optimal time for him to discover how fucking creepy I am."

"I'm pretty sure you could tell him you have a freezer full of severed heads in a storage locker on the Upper East Side and he still wouldn't think you were creepy." Nick laughed. "Frankly, I'm just glad I passed the test."

"What test?"

"The one where he was deciding if I was allowed to be your friend."

"Wait, what?" I stared at Nick. "What the hell are you talking about?"

"Dude, were you not a part of the conversation we just had? The one where he spent the entire time subtly reminding me of how close you two were and grilling me to see if I was acceptable?"

"That's—what?"

Nick smiled and mimicked Ben's tone. *"Did Adam make you try the spicy pork? He loves it so much, I know that because I hang out with him all the time because we're best friends. Where do you live? Oh, that's close to where me and my best friend Adam used to live, back when we lived together, because we're best friends. How long have you lived in the city? Is it as long as my best friend Adam and I have been here? Probably not, which is a shame, because it means you'll never be cool enough to be his best friend like I am."*

"That's... not what he was doing, I think?"

"Adam, that's one hundred percent what he was doing. Honestly, I don't know what you were so worried about with Ben. He might be dating Mia, but dude's completely in love with you."

"What?" My voice was a yelp, and I glanced around, panicked that someone had heard. "Jesus Christ, Nick. A, could you try not to talk through a megaphone when you say shit like that? And B, also, you're just—it's not—no. Just no."

"No what?"

"No, Ben doesn't—" I paused, looking over my shoulder again before answering. "He doesn't like me."

"Are you sure about that?"

"Yes I'm fucking sure," I whispered furiously. "You don't think I'd know if my best friend, the guy I've been in love with for years, had ever showed any amount of interest in me? You don't think I've wanted that to happen for, oh, let's see, *forever*, and driven myself crazy over-analyzing things in the hopes that maybe the fact that he said '*Hi, Adam*' to me that one time senior year instead of '*Hey, Adam*' meant he was secretly pining for me too?"

I was breathing hard by the time I was finished and Nick gave me a sympathetic look.

"Sorry. I didn't mean to upset you," he said, and for once his tone was as soft as I could have asked for. "I'm not trying to make things feel worse or tease you. Maybe Ben wasn't aware of what he was doing, but he obviously cares a lot about you. And frankly, it's sweet. He's definitely protective of you. That whole hand-on-the-arm thing?"

"That's just how he is, Nick. Ben's just... I don't know, he's like that with everybody. It doesn't mean anything." I sighed. "If he likes you, he lets you know, doesn't leave you trying to interpret vague signs. And he's never once mentioned being into guys."

"Just because someone's never talked about being interested in men doesn't make them straight," Nick said, raising his eyebrows. "Case in point: you, up until a month ago."

"Yeah, but that's because I'm '*damaged*' and have '*issues*,'" I said, bitterness twisting my words. "Ben's about as undamaged as they come. If he liked dudes, he'd just say something."

"Well maybe he just hasn't realized it yet," Nick offered.

"Right."

Nick laughed lightly. "I'm doing a terrible job of being a normal friend, aren't I?"

"What, encouraging wishful thinking and an unhealthy attachment to someone who will never be available or interested?" I snorted. "That's exactly what a normal friend's supposed to do. I'm just a bottomless pit of need who's determined to wallow in the hopelessness of my romantic prospects."

"Got it."

"Is that Adam Hart?"

I jumped at the sound of a voice just over my shoulder and when I turned and saw a statuesque woman with long black hair standing behind me, I froze. I was pretty sure I'd seen her talking to Ben earlier that night. How much of our conversation had she just overheard?

"Uh, yeah," I said, trying to smile. I felt a little sick to my stomach. "Hi."

"Molly Ides," the woman said, pulling me in for what turned out to be a quarter of a hug and some air kisses. Jesus, when did people stop shaking hands? "Greenleaf's chief talent scout. Darling, it's so good to see you. I've been keeping an eye on you."

Darling? Had I missed the part where we'd become best friends?

"Uh, this is Nick," I said, gesturing towards him.

"Not a musician," Nick said, grinning cheerfully. "Just a plus one."

"Oh, you're a cheeky one," Molly said, her eyes flashing. "Well let me know if that ever changes. You've got a sort of rugged boy-next-door look we could work with. But in the meantime—" she turned to me, "you and I need to talk."

"Uh. We do?" I wasn't entirely sure where this conversation was going but I didn't like her tone. It sounded... hungry.

"We do indeed." Molly flashed a predatory smile. "I've been watching you. Have you ever considered professional management, Adam. Greenleaf could do a lot for you if you were so inclined."

"I uh—I mean, no, not really," I stammered. "I appreciate the offer but uh, I'm more of a songwriter than a performer."

"That's ridiculous. With Greenleaf behind you, we could have you up on stage in no time. This whole angsty vibe you're working would be catnip for the 18-35 crowd."

"No, that's not what I—I mean, I have performed. I do. I just... it's not... I don't really like to—I don't think you'd actually want me."

I was starting to sweat. The longer Molly talked to me, the louder she was getting. People around us were starting to turn and watch our conversation.

"Oh, sweetie. Are you talking about that little incident at The Grasshopper?" Molly asked, her voice like a foghorn in the crowded room. "That's nothing. That can work *for* your image. Dark and troubled loner musician, tragically misunderstood. We can definitely work with that."

"I can't—I mean, I don't—"

"Honestly, darling, who hasn't overdosed at this point?"

It wasn't just that I didn't know what to say—I couldn't have gotten the words out if I had. Everyone in a ten foot radius was staring at me and given how crowded the room was, that was a lot of people.

"Thanks," I finally choked out. "But I don't think—"

I was saved from having to figure out how to end that sentence when a younger guy with bright red hair came hustling over to Molly and whispered something in her ear.

"No rest for the wicked," Molly said with a smile as she turned back to us. "I'm needed elsewhere, but Adam, think about what I said, okay? Your career could vault into the stratosphere with Greenleaf behind you."

I turned and looked back at Nick in distress as Molly walked off and the people around us started to drift back to their own conversations.

"I don't *want* my career to vault into the stratosphere," I said, pained. "I'm a songwriter. The band, me playing, that was never meant to be—"

But a cheer from across the room cut me off. We turned to see Ben and Mia walking out of somewhere in the back of the restaurant, arm in arm. Mia did a little twirl when she reached a raised area on the far wall--usually it was full of velvet couches and low-lying wicker tables but Gray had cleared it off and made it the stage for the night.

Ben stepped back as Mia walked towards the microphone, playing the supportive, adoring boyfriend. He did it well. The two of them made a disturbingly cute couple and the whole time Mia sang, Ben beamed up at her. If I hadn't known it was fake, I'd have no trouble believing they were deeply in love. Hell, even knowing it *was* fake, I still kind of believed they were.

I knew Ben said there was nothing between them, but I wouldn't have blamed him for falling for Mia for real. She was pretty and her voice, light and ethereal, sent shivers down my spine. She had a presence. Sweet and vulnerable, but a little bit playful. It was hard not to be captivated by her.

So no, I wouldn't blame Ben if he fell for Mia.

I just wished someday he'd look at me the way he was looking at her. Adoring. Delighted. Wrecked.

Before her last song, Mia called Ben up on stage and gave a little speech about how much his support meant to her. Ben's eyes swept over the crowd and I feigned swooning when he made eye-contact. He grinned right back at me and made a little motion with his hand for me to come forward. But I could see Molly standing up front and I wasn't in the mood to dive back into that conversation.

Besides, the longer I watched Mia and Ben together, the worse I felt. Even if it was fake, even if it was just the most convincing act of all time, it's not actually all that fun to watch the guy you're in love with pretend to be in love with someone else.

"I think I'm gonna head out," I said to Nick, finally. "Do you mind?"

Ben and Mia looked like they were giving an interview and I could see other people swarming around, waiting for their chance to talk to them. The likelihood of getting to talk to Ben for the rest of the night was looking pretty slim.

"Nah, not at all," Nick said. "I should probably go home too."

"You can totally stay if you want. I just... I don't know, I'm not really feeling it."

"You don't have to justify anything to me, Adam." Nick smiled. "Besides, I've been up since 5 a.m. I've been more or less asleep on my feet since we got here. Passing out back at home sounds nice."

Passing out did sound nice. I texted Ben to let him know I'd left early but even after I lay back on my bed, I couldn't fall asleep. I was too wound up, the events of the night buzzing around inside me like fireflies in a glass jar. Ben looking at Mia like she'd hung the moon. Nick teasing me, saying Ben might be interested. It didn't matter that he'd meant it honestly. It wasn't true—I knew it wasn't—and so it still stung.

And then there was Molly Ides, her loud, confident voice reminding everyone of just how messed up I was. I knew she meant well. At least, it was a lot nicer to assume she did than to imagine that she'd wanted me to feel like I needed to sink through the floor. I could still feel everyone's eyes on me as she spoke, still feel their curiosity poking and prying at me like invisible fingers. Maybe sometime I'd get to the point where everyone staring at me didn't make me want to hurl, but tonight was not that night.

Eventually, I flicked off the lamp and just lay in the darkness. I wasn't tired, but I thought maybe I could incept myself into sleep if I just closed my eyes long enough. Eventually I heard the door unlock, Ben walking back into the apartment. He must have thought I was asleep, because he didn't say anything.

I listened to him set his keys on the table by the entryway, walk into the kitchen, pour a glass of water. I thought he'd go to bed after that, but he didn't. Instead, I heard his footsteps pad through the living room and moments later, I heard the soft plink of piano keys. Oh God, he was playing the 'Adam get off the couch' song.

'Dude's completely in love with you.' Nick's words pricked at the back of my mind. How the hell was I supposed to forget them? And after that bizarre arm-kiss—which Ben and I still hadn't talked about and I was beginning to think I'd imagined? What was I supposed to do?

It didn't matter how wrong he was—Nick had given me the thinnest thread of hope and I was grasping onto it like a dying man clutching a tuft of grass as he dangles over the edge of a cliff. I needed to let go already. The fall would suck. The landing would suck more. But it was the right thing to do.

Which was why, of course, I had no intention of doing it. And finally, my better judgment screaming at me, I got up and walked out into the living room.

"Hey! I didn't know you were still up," Ben said, looking at me in surprise.

"Yeah," I shrugged. "Couldn't sleep."

"Oh shit." Ben looked stricken. "I didn't wake you up, did I?" He gestured to the piano.

"No, no, definitely not."

I didn't want Ben to feel like he had to change anything about his routine just because I was around. I felt bad enough taking up space as it was, no matter how much he said it was okay. Besides, he really hadn't woken me up.

"I could hear the piano," I continued. "But trust me, that wasn't what was keeping me awake." *Don't worry, it was my deplorable crush on you instead.* "It was actually kind of nice. Weirdly repetitive."

"If that's your way of telling me to stop fucking around with this song," Ben laughed, "I can take the hint."

"Same one as before?" I asked, coming to stand next to the piano bench.

I tried not to let my gaze linger for too long on his arms, extended and relaxed as his fingers rested lightly on the keys. How could something as innocuous as a forearm make my breath speed up?

Looking at Ben's smooth skin, the blond hair on it downy soft, I was struck by a sudden urge to reach down and run my fingertips along his arm from wrist to elbow. I wanted to feel the warmth, the steadiness of Ben's body. God, what would it feel like to have his arms around me?

"Yeah. I don't know, I keep feeling like there might be something here but I can't make it come out right." Ben made a face. "I don't know why I bother, I've never been good at this.

I probably should just stay with Greenleaf. I might hate the music they make me do, but at least I get to complain about it. If I go solo, I'll have only myself to blame when everything I write sucks."

It was strange to see Ben, sunny, optimistic Ben, looking so lost and confused. It did something funny to my stomach— made *me* want to wrap my arms around *him*, which was weird, because I was supposed to be the broken one and all I ever did these days was think about how badly I wanted Ben.

But suddenly, that all took a backseat to my desire to wrap Ben up, to hold him, to somehow show him how amazing he was. How talented, how passionate, how inspiring— everything that he'd somehow forgotten. The desire to comfort him, to give instead of take, was disconcerting and it made something flutter in my stomach. But it wasn't entirely unpleasant.

So of course, I felt all that, but just stood stock still, my arms dangling awkwardly at my sides like I'd forgotten how they worked.

"Okay, first of all, you don't suck. At any of this. And second of all, even if you did, you still shouldn't let that scare you into continuing to do something that doesn't make you happy."

"God, I must sound so pathetic. What a fucking nightmare, people want to give me an insane amount of money to keep doing something that I don't suck at and all I want to do is complain about it."

"Hey, no one's got a monopoly on suffering," I said. "That's something Nick says a lot, anyway. Like just because there's a famine right now in some other country doesn't mean your pain doesn't count."

Ben blinked at me and then barked a laugh. "Jesus, Adam, that's supposed to make me feel better? Now all I can think about is people starving to death and I *really* feel like an asshole."

I winced. "Somehow it sounds better when Nick says it."

"He's gonna make a hell of a minister one day," Ben said darkly.

"Seriously though. I know I'm not like, the poster child for perfect mental health right now but I don't know. You're allowed to feel bad about your shit, is what I'm trying to say. If nothing else, you've earned it. You're being so nice to me, letting me stay here and basically mooch off of you for free. You've built up some complaining points."

"I hope that's *not* how this works. Because if it is, I haven't earned shit." Ben looked at me sharply. "Having you here really isn't some kind of burden, Adam. I *like* having you here. It's nice getting to spend time with you again."

Spend time with you. A weird phrase. It was the kind of thing you said after having lunch with your grandmother, how much you'd enjoyed getting to *spend time* with her. It felt so formal. But still... nice? Like, better than *'hang out with you,'* right? Maybe not quite as good as *'be with you,'* but I should probably just take what I could get and be happy with it.

"This is where you say, *you too*, asshole," Ben said and I realized I still hadn't responded.

I blushed. "You too, asshole."

Ben rolled his eyes and I felt flushed with warmth. This was good. This was how things should be. I should be happy with this. If this was all I got from Ben, it was enough, wasn't it? How could I convince myself that this was enough?

But then I realized I was doing it again, the falling silent and not talking for too long thing. So I blurted out the first thing that came to mind.

"What's the problem with the song?"

Ben laughed bitterly. "You mean aside from the fact that I'm a talentless hack? You think anyone would complain if I just did covers of 80s power ballads for the rest of my life?

"Well I would," I said. "Because those are cheesy as hell. And also, dude, complaining allotment reached. You're not a talentless hack and if you say anything else like that I'm just going to think you're fishing for compliments."

"But will you still give them to me anyway?" Ben batted his eyes innocently and he obviously meant it to be absurd, not adorable, but somehow it was adorable anyway, because it was *Ben* and he could be standing in a dumpster covered in banana peels and still make my heart skip a beat.

"Play me the song again and we'll see," I said, doing my best to sound severe and not like I wanted to pull myself onto Ben's lap, let him pick me up and push me back against the keys and fuck me into the piano.

No, definitely wouldn't want him to know you're thinking about that.

"It's just not... coming together, I guess," Ben said. He ran through the melody once with his right hand. "It's too simplistic. Like, so straightforward it almost sounds childish. But every time I try to add anything it just sounds need-lessly baroque, like I'm trying to merge Tchaikovsky and Row, Row, Row Your Boat and basically I suck at writing songs and want to die."

He blanched as soon as the words were out of his mouth and looked up at me in remorse. "Oh God, I didn't mean—"

"Dude, it's fine," I said, waving his apology away. "You didn't mean it. Besides, it's not like I meant it either. It was an accident. I promise."

Ben squinted at me and I wondered if he believed me. God, I was ridiculous. Wondering if maybe it were possible for Ben to feel something for me when here he was, convinced I was some kind of fragile glass ornament.

"Seriously, dude," I went on. "Please don't censor yourself around me. If you do, I'm just going to feel weird and like I have to censor myself too, and I'm like, supposed to be trying this whole *comfortable in my own skin* self-esteem bullshit, which I'm pretty sure is the opposite of censoring myself so—"

"Okay, okay," Ben raised his hands in surrender. "You win."

"Good." I glared at him. "I'm not going to break, you know?"

"Oh don't worry," Ben said, reaching out and shoving me. "I know you're too much of an asshole for that."

"Thank you." I grinned, then frowned down at the piano. "Have you tried transposing it down a fifth?"

"Have I tried transposing it down a fifth?" Ben repeated. "No, why would I do something as simple as that? Why would I do something so elementary, so basic that I'd be an idiot *not* to try it?"

I blinked. "Oh. Okay. Sorry, I didn't mean—I didn't realize you'd already—nevermind, it's fine." I started to turn away.

"Adam, jeez, stop," Ben said, and I felt a hand on my arm.

When I looked back, Ben was holding my wrist. His grip was loose, light. More a supplication than a demand. I wanted to drink in that warmth, like I could osmose some of that light up through my skin and save it for later, when I was lying in the dark with nothing else to hold onto.

"I was joking," Ben continued as I stared down at him, still dumbstruck by the feeling of his skin on mine. "It literally never *did* occur to me to try that. Because I'm a dumbass. Please, I'm sorry, I didn't mean to snap. I was talking to *myself* like I was an idiot, not you. God, I'm in a terrible mood but that's not an excuse to take it out on you."

I smiled, relief flooding through me. "It's okay. I mean, I just told you not to walk on eggshells around me. Here, move over."

I shoved Ben aside on the piano bench and sat down. Telling myself not to pay attention to the warmth of Ben's body next to mine—because flannel pajama pants are no kind of boner camouflage—I put my fingers on the keys. They were cool, pearly, as I ran my hands up and down their backs before setting my fingers into place. I ran through the snippet of the song Ben had been playing earlier, calling it up from memory, my fingers flashing across the keys.

"That's what you're starting with, right?" I said, glancing at Ben who was looking at me in awe.

"I can't believe you can just—after only hearing it once?"

"Only seeing it once," I corrected him. "I've heard it about 400 times in the past half hour."

"Cute," Ben said, rolling his eyes.

"So," I said, bringing my fingers back into place. "What is that, G major? Yeah, a little goofy. But if you bring it down just a bit and then maybe wait a beat on the four before you launch into the next measure, you can—"

I stopped talking and started playing, running through Ben's melody again and making changes as I went. I played it a few times, tweaking each round until I finally found a key I was satisfied with, then brought my left hand up to join my right, adding in chords in counterpoint to the melody.

It just felt good, to be sitting at a piano again. Any instrument, really. Feeling the music course through me. It was almost like my body was part of the instrument, that it was being played as well, swelling and filling with the notes my fingers drew from the air. For once, I felt like I belonged.

I wasn't sure how long I played before I finally wound down, letting my fingers drift to a stop on the keys.

"So yeah," I said into the silence, not quite ready to look up. "Just imagine that with like, lead guitar taking the melody, a strong bassline. Throw in some drums and you've got a song. Well, maybe change the words though. I don't think anyone's gonna buy a hit single about you trying to get me to move off your couch."

"Holy shit," Ben said when I looked up at him. "Holy shit."

"Sorry." I flushed. "I didn't mean to like, take over. You don't have to use any of that, I was just—"

"You have nothing to apologize for," Ben said. "Fuck, I just—I can't believe I forgot how you can just... do that."

"Do what?"

"*That*," Ben said, waving his hands in a gesture that took in me, the piano, and maybe the whole right side of the room. "You hear just a snatch of a melody and you can build a whole song around it. In 15 minutes."

"I was playing for 15 minutes?" I flushed. "Jesus, I'm sorry."

"Oh my God, will you please stop apologizing? If anything, I'm the one who should be saying sorry, making you work on my stupid song when you've probably got tons of your own pieces you're working on."

"Actually, no," I laughed, embarrassed. "Um, actually, that's the first time I've played anything since the accident."

"What?" Ben looked at me in confusion. "But I thought—I mean, you said you were going to work on more songs to send to Angela."

"Uh, yeah. I said that. That's what I've been meaning to do. But in terms of actually *doing* it? Not, uh, not so much, yet."

"Why? How? You're always working on something or other."

I shrugged. "I don't know. It's... hard to explain. It was just like—like there was something stopping me. Something sort of in my way, barring my path from even thinking about music. And at first I thought it was this external thing, like having something put a hand on your chest, all 'thou shalt not pass,' but I don't know, now I'm kinda thinking maybe it was just like, my brain trying to protect me? Or something? Does that sound crazy?"

"Not at all." Ben shook his head emphatically. "It makes a lot of sense, thinking about what happened. It sounds really hard though."

"I mean, it wasn't great. It was... lonely, I think, is maybe the best way to describe it. But it just felt safer that way?"

"Shit, and I just made you—"

"No, no, you didn't make me do anything." I ran my right hand along the keys again. "It was kinda nice, actually. I didn't get that weird, *'I'm gonna puke,'* feeling this time. So that's progress, I guess. Sorry, that probably sounds really weird."

"We really need to stop apologizing to each other. Let's just agree that we're both awesome, talented, handsome, humble geniuses and let it rest."

"Well. Maybe one of us is," I snorted.

"Hey!" Ben shoved me lightly, his shoulder pressing into my body and I had to stop myself from leaning into him. "First you won't let me fish for compliments, now you insult me?"

"I meant you, asshole," I said, shoving him back. "You're the awesome, talented, humble genius."

"You forgot handsome," Ben grinned.

"No fishing, remember. It's not polite."

"Well it's not polite to not tell your very handsome friends how handsome they are either."

"If you know you're so handsome, then you don't need me to tell you."

"Sure I do, " Ben laughed. "My ego yearns for it."

"Well it can keep yearning." I could feel my cheeks starting to heat up. God, Ben truly did not have a clue what he did to me.

"Ugh, you're no fun," Ben grumbled. He looked back at the piano and then over at me. "If I promise to back off, will you show me that song again tomorrow though, when it's not the middle of the night, so that I can write it down? I mean, I still kinda think I should just do 80s power ballads for the rest of my life but I *guess* I could try your amazing song instead."

"Sure," I said, rolling my eyes. "Whatever you want."

And I meant it.

10

BEN

*T*he morning of Lacey's birthday, I woke up exhausted. Shereen had had me doing press with Mia all week in the lead up to her album launch. Then there'd been prep for the Family Futures Project benefit at the end of the month—agreeing on the setlist, fittings with the stylist, letting my publicist take endless photos of me for a week's worth of social media posts.

I'd come home drained every day but Adam had started playing and writing again in the last week and we ended up staying up too late working on songs and just goofing around. Adam still didn't seem to understand how talented he was, no matter how many times I told him. But it was just fun to be working together again. I'd missed it.

So when I woke up that morning, I stumbled into the kitchen to make a pot of coffee, only to discover that we were out. I already had a headache and the lack of coffee seemed particularly cruel.

"Hey, we're out of coffee," I called, walking over to Adam's room. I poked my head in the door. "Do you wanna just—"

I stopped. Adam wasn't there. That was odd—I usually got up before him. It wasn't like he had to tell me where he was going or anything. I was just a little surprised—he hadn't even texted. So where'd he go?

Disgruntled, I wandered back into the kitchen and stared at the empty coffee maker on the counter. Dammit, I was going to have to go out if I wanted coffee, wasn't I? I sighed and walked into the bathroom to brush my teeth—and stopped short again. There was a note from Adam taped to the mirror.

We're out of coffee :(At Maggie's with Nick for breakfast. Didn't want to text in case it woke you up. Come!

It figured it would be Nick. He was probably one of those natural early risers who just woke up feeling cheerful and ready to take on the world. I bet he didn't even get morning breath. And now he and Adam were going to hang out all day while I was out at Coney Island.

What a childish thing to be jealous about. But I wasn't going to let that stop me.

But it wasn't like I had anything else to do and I *did* want coffee, so 10 minutes later, I found myself walking in the door to Maggie's. Adam and Nick were sitting in the courtyard and I waved and gestured to the bar—I'd join them once I'd gotten breakfast.

Gray came out from the back carrying two large boxes.

"Hey man, how's it going?" he said with a smile.

"Good. You need any help with those?" I asked.

Gray set the boxes down on the counter behind the bar and shook his head.

"Nah, I'm good, but thanks." He pulled two bottles of Jameson out of the first box. "Still recovering from your party last week."

"Not my party," I said.

Gray laughed. "Close enough. You're the reason we hosted it here. Not that I'm complaining. Business is up, which is great, but we're still restocking and catching up on inventory."

"That's awesome."

"It is," Gray said as he shelved the bottles in his hands and continued unpacking the box. "Timing could be better, though. I usually shut down the bar for a week in July and take the staff out to my place in Montauk."

"Shit dude, you have a house in the Hamptons?" I stared at him. "That's fancy."

"Eh, it was my aunt's," Gray said with a shrug. "Same as this place, actually. I didn't really need it, but it seemed like a shame to get rid of a place she was so attached to. Anyway, we're going out there this week—I'm shutting down at noon today—so it kind of sucks to lose our momentum. But what are you gonna do?"

"You are the most relaxed small business owner I've ever seen," I said, shaking my head. "I can't believe you just—oh, hold on a sec."

My phone started ringing and when I pulled it out of my pocket, I saw that it was my mom calling.

"Sorry, do you mind if I—" I said to Gray.

He shook his head. "Take it. I'll get your order in. Cafe con leche and a blueberry scone, right?"

"What am I gonna do without you for a whole week?" I said, giving him puppy dog eyes before I turned and answered my mom's call.

"Hey, Ma. Couldn't wait the two hours til you saw me, had to talk to me now?" I said with a grin.

"Sweetie, I just wanted to know what time you think you'll get there. You know traffic can be a nightmare on a day like today."

"I know," I said rolling my eyes. "But I'll be leaving in just a few minutes. I'm grabbing breakfast and I need to check in with Adam but I should be on the road right after."

"Oh, is Adam with you?" My mom's voice perked up. "How is he? Can I talk to him? It's been ages."

"Uh, yeah," I laughed. "Let me go get him."

I walked over to the table where Adam and Nick were sitting and, it appeared, having a very intense conversation about orange juice. Adam looked up at me with a grin as I approached.

"Back me up here Ben. Pulp or no-pulp?"

"Oh, pulp, definitely."

"Told you so." Adam shot a triumphant look at Nick, then quirked an eyebrow at me as I held out the phone. "What?"

"My mom wants to talk to you," I explained.

"Uh-oh. Why?"

"Because in her mind, she adopted you seven years ago? I don't know, she's just being mom-ish."

"Your mom has way too high an opinion of me," Adam said with a pained look. "One of these days she's going to realize she adopted a trash son and understand what a mistake she made."

"Oh please. You could tell her you'd murdered someone and she wouldn't care. Just take the phone."

Adam reached out and took the phone, his fingers cool on my hand. I smiled at Nick and tried to think of something to say so I wasn't just standing there awkwardly. But I failed.

"You want more coffee?" I asked, spying his mostly empty cup.

"Oh." Nick looked surprised. "Sure, yeah. Thanks."

"I'll be right back."

Gray pushed a plate with a scone on it towards me as I walked back over to the bar, feeling incompetent. I was going to learn how to like Nick. I *was*.

"Thanks," I said, taking a grateful bite. "Can I also get a refill of whatever he was drinking?"

I pointed over my shoulder at Nick and Gray looked up and nodded.

"Sure, that's easy. It's just the house coffee. I'll get you guys a carafe." Gray smiled as he bustled behind the bar. "You were talking to that guy at the party, right? He a friend of yours?"

"Yeah. Well, Adam's friend more, I guess."

"You don't like him?"

My head snapped up. "I didn't say that."

"You didn't need to," Gray said with a laugh.

"He's not—it's not that—I mean, he's... fine. Really. I like him. He seems like a cool guy. I don't know him that well but Adam seems to like him and I'm happy to get to know him better. In fact, I think that—wait, why are you laughing?"

"The Ben doth protest too much," Gray snorted.

"I *do* like him. I do."

Gray just gave me a long look and set the carafe of coffee on the bar.

"Okay, fine, I hate him and I don't know why and it's completely ridiculous because he actually seems really cool." I glared at Gray. "Is that better?"

"No idea?" Gray said, cocking his head to the side. "Really?"

"Yes." I looked over my shoulder at Adam and Nick. Adam was leaning back in his chair, running his fingers through his hair and laughing at something on the phone. Nick was sitting eating a bagel, completely inoffensive—and I felt a wave of antipathy. "All the times I've talked to him—which, granted, is a grand total of three, but still—all the times I've talked to him, he's been totally chill. So what the fuck is wrong with me?"

Gray quirked an eyebrow. "You want my actual opinion or was that a rhetorical question?"

"Your actual opinion, if you have one. Please. Enlighten me, because I sure as shit can't figure it out and I don't like feeling like such an asshole."

"Well. He's Adam's friend, right?"

"Yeah."

Gray gave me a level look. "Isn't it possible you're jealous?"

"Well yeah but isn't that a little, like, grade school? Like coming home from vacation and finding out your best friend made a new friend over the summer? I should be more mature than that," I fumed.

"That's not... exactly what I meant," Gray said, his voice picking over his words carefully, like someone walking on a rocky path. "Ben, I never asked you this before because it's not my business. I always just kind of assumed. But... are you sure you're, well, straight?"

"What does--" My eyes widened. "Oh."

I whipped my head around to look back at Adam, then tried to turn back to Gray—but I couldn't. I couldn't take my eyes off of Adam. Something was tightening in my chest all of a sudden, like the last few cranks of the lever on a jack-in-the-box, and I couldn't look away.

Adam. Gray thought I liked Adam. *Like* liked him. My Adam.

But that didn't make any sense. I mean, sure I could see how that would maybe make me—but no. Not with Adam. That was too—

Wouldn't I have felt something? Thought something? Before this? I'd known him for seven years, wouldn't I have looked at him and felt... fuck. Felt a fraction of what I was feeling right now, as I watched him, something blossoming inside my chest.

Jesus Christ. Was that where that bizarre arm kiss had come from? Did I like Adam?

When I thought of Adam—whether he was right in front of me or I had to close my eyes and summon up his image —I felt this warmth, this incredible warmth like something was bursting from my heart. And as I watched him... Fuck.

My eyes ran down the taut, lean muscles of his arms as he reached behind his head and stretched. They dipped hungrily down onto his collarbone, just peeking out from the neckline of Adam's shirt, and then swooped down further still, to where the hem of his shirt was just starting to pull up and—

Fuck. I had to rip my eyes away, force myself to stare at a spot above Adam's head on the far side of the courtyard. I focused on the leaves of a potted orange tree, shiny green against the cinderblock wall, as I waited for my heart to calm down.

What the hell was I doing? I couldn't be thinking this. Couldn't be feeling this, this feeling where every cell in my body was on alert, for my friend. Not for Adam. There was no way I could—but then, why couldn't I—

I slowly turned back to look at Gray, my eyes wide. "Fuck."

Gray gave me an amused smile. "I mean, it's just a thought, but—"

"Fuck." I blinked. "Fuck fuck fuck fuck fuck."

"That's... a lot of fucks," Gray said, looking for all the world like he was suppressing a laugh.

"It's not funny, asshole," I said, glaring at him. "I can't—I mean, I'm not—"

"Ben, being attracted to men—whether it's a million or just this one guy—doesn't actually have to be a big deal. It's not a bad thing. You're aware of that, right?"

"No, I mean, yeah, that's not—I mean, it's not that," I stammered. "It's just, I'm not sure I can—Gray, this is Adam we're talking about. I know you don't know him that well but I just —he's not the kind of person you can just explore something casual with. Well, not with me, anyway. It would have to be... He's—we're—fuck."

"Hey, you don't have to know anything man, and you definitely don't have to do anything. Give yourself some time to figure it out." Gray smiled ruefully. "God, I remember when I was first figuring out my sexuality. It was confusing as hell. You don't need to rush it."

"How did you know?" I asked, staring at him like he could throw me some kind of rope. Because all of a sudden, I felt like I was drowning.

Adam. My best friend. Who'd just come out to me, who was working hard on taking care of himself. The last thing he needed was some asshole like me saying, *'Hey, I got an erection when I watched you talking to my mom this morning. Wanna maybe blow each other and see what happens?'* Jesus Christ, I was fucked.

Gray shrugged. "I don't know man, I just kinda did? It's hard to argue with what gets your dick hard, you know. Even if it's not what you're used to, or what you'd expect. Don't beat yourself up over it. Though I guess if you realize you're not into women at all, you probably need to have a talk with your girlfriend. But otherwise, no need to do anything drastic, unless you want to."

"My girlfriend," I repeated softly.

God, that was a wrinkle I hadn't considered. Not that Mia would give a shit. But would Adam be willing to—Jesus, what was I even thinking? Putting my cock before my horse much? But still. There was a lot invested in my public persona. Even if I went independent... God, it was just layers more complicated, each time I thought about it.

All I really wanted to do was just freeze time for about, maybe three months, just to think about this and figure shit out without having deadlines and decisions breathing down my neck. To explore this without consequences. But every choice, every option felt so loaded.

I couldn't tell Adam that I *maybe* felt something for him and not expect that to blow our friendship up. Even if we hadn't been friends, Adam wasn't the kind of guy you did that to. He deserved better than someone who wasn't sure of himself. He deserved someone who could see how amazing he was.

But could I really dive in there on just a hunch? Tell Adam I wanted something more when I'd never so much as kissed a guy before? What if I was wrong? What if this feeling in my gut was just me being protective, possessive? Was it really possible that I could be interested in Adam—could want Adam—and I was only just realizing it now?

Then again, Adam had only just come out. So maybe I'd just

never considered it before. Maybe it was like one of those genetic things—you have a predisposition to something, but you need the right conditions for that gene to be expressed.

I snorted. That would go over well. *'Hey Adam, I think I'm into you. Yeah, I know it's sudden, but it's kinda like obesity or bipolar depression. Guess I'm just lucky you decided to come out!'* Right.

How was I supposed to know what I really felt? On the one hand, I *did* feel protective of Adam. And I didn't want to confuse that with something else. But I didn't think that was what this was. This feeling in the bottom of my stomach, all rumbly and jumpy, was nothing like what I'd felt when I'd picked him up at Peachtree two weeks ago.

It didn't bother me, the idea that I could be attracted to a guy. To guys, really. You liked who you liked was the way I saw it, and it wasn't anyone's business but your own. Except that this wasn't just a question of whether I was into guys, or even just *a* guy. It was Adam. That was huge. And I had no fucking clue what to do.

The only thing I knew for sure was that I was still holding that carafe of coffee and I'd been standing over at the bar long enough that it was starting to get weird.

Adam was just hanging up when I got back to their table and he handed me my phone with a smile. Same smile as always, a little crooked, the left corner of his mouth curling up a bit higher than the right, his green eyes crinkling, but this time it felt like a punch in the gut. I had to force myself to keep moving, to grasp the phone he was holding out and sit down, because I felt like I was frozen in place.

How had I not noticed that his smile, always warm, always self-deprecating, was utterly gorgeous?

"How's my mom?" I asked, hoping my voice sounded normal.

"Disgustingly affectionate as always," Adam said, laughing. "Uh, but, um, she invited me to Lacey's birthday this afternoon."

"Oh my God, I should have warned you," I said apologetically, even though my stomach appeared to be doing jumping jacks on a trampoline at the thought of spending the day with Adam. "I mean, if you don't want to come, you totally don't have to, I'll just tell her something came up."

"No, it's okay," Adam said. "I mean, unless you don't want me—"

"No, I totally want you! To come, I mean," I added, annoyed with myself. *Get a fucking grip, Ben.* "And Lacey will be thrilled. She hasn't seen you in ages."

Adam laughed. "I know. She told me. Your mom put her on the phone."

"Well then it's settled. Get ready for a day of sunburns, sand in your hotdog, and really long lines for the bathrooms, followed by my mom trying to get you to sign formal adoption papers."

"That's all I've ever wanted, Ben. All I've ever wanted."

～

"Boys, do you need to reapply sunscreen?" my mom asked,

peering over the edges of her paperback romance novel at me and Adam where we lay sprawled out on beach towels.

We'd flopped down there thirty minutes ago after spending hours on rides, consuming worrying amounts of funnel cake, and staining our tongues blue and red with Italian ice. We probably did need more sunscreen but the thought of moving at that minute was too much. I had no idea how my dad, Lacey, Jess were upright, splashing around in the water right now.

"Later," I said, flailing my arms uselessly. "I'm too tired now."

"Later, you'll be burned to a crisp," my mom retorted. "Don't you have an image to maintain?"

She scooped a bottle of sunblock out of her tote bag and tossed it at me. I let it fall into the sand at the edge of my towel and contemplated it with a frown. Picking it up just seemed like it so much work.

"Yeah, Ben," Adam grinned, looking over at me from the notebook where he was writing out notes for some kind of song. "Do you really think your adoring Instagram followers want to see you in your natural summer look—lobster red, skin peeling off your face?"

"Okay, that happened *one* time," I grumbled, "and it was five years ago. Give me some credit. Besides, if I remember correctly, you got almost as burned."

"Yeah, but no one gives a shit what I look like," Adam said with a laugh.

"I'll give a shit. I'm the one who has to look at you."

"Fine," Adam sighed. "Hand me the sunscreen. You might want to look like a tomato but some of us have standards."

I tossed him the bottle and tried not to watch as he squeezed the lotion into his hands and began to rub it in. Just like I'd been trying not to watch him all day. It wasn't *my* fault that the day Gray pointed out that I might have a bit of a crush on my friend was the same day we were going to spend the afternoon in bathing suits.

Every time I'd looked at Adam, I'd gotten--God, the only word I could think of was butterflies, which felt so adolescent, so... silly. But that was it. That goofy, beginning of a crush, intoxicated by possibility feeling that beat inside my chest? Butterflies.

And now, as I watched Adam tilt his head to the side, rubbing sunscreen into his shoulder? I needed that to be my hand on his shoulder, my skin on his. I'd been staring all day and suddenly I needed to touch. To know for sure.

"Here, let me get your back," I said, holding my hand out. Adam looked at me in surprise but then dropped the bottle in my hand and turned around.

And suddenly everything felt... different. Slow, almost, like the world around the two of us had faded away. I opened the bottle slowly, felt the creamy lotion drizzle into my palm. Fuck—my hand started to shake. I brought it to Adam's skin swiftly, hoping the quick movement would cover up the jitters.

What I was *not* prepared for was the way the feel of his skin underneath my fingers would make my breath hitch, the way that running my hand along his back, over the vertebrae of his spine, would start to make me hard. I wanted to press pause, to run away, to either wait for my body to calm down or to jerk off frantically. I wanted the moment to last forever.

I took a shaky breath, forced my hand to move, mechanically rubbing the last of the sunblock into Adam's skin. *Don't feel how soft he is. Don't feel the way the sun has warmed his skin. And for fuck's sake, do not feel the way his body moves when he breathes and wonder what it would feel like if you could put your head on his chest.*

"There," I said, clearing my throat a little more forcefully than strictly necessary. "You're good to go."

"Thanks, man," Adam said, giving me a strange look. "Do you want me to—"

He didn't finish, just gestured to the bottle of sunblock.

"Oh, uh, yeah. Thanks."

Because it would have been weirder if I'd said no, right? Thankfully, Adam's hands were efficient, running over my back in quick, firm strokes, not even giving my cock enough time to realize it wanted to go from half-hard to completely fucking noticeably erect, for which I was grateful. I took the bottle from him when he was done and coated my arms and legs with the stuff, forcing myself to think about homeless kittens and global warming—anything sufficiently depressing to be a boner-killer.

I lay back down on my stomach—still not totally trusting my dick to behave—and picked up my phone, idly flipping through some promo images my publicist had sent me for approval. It was hard to keep my mind on the task, though, with Adam so close to me. And it was frustrating as hell.

Because it was unmooring, right? To realize that someone you'd only ever seen one way, you suddenly saw in a totally different light? But the person I'd normally talk about that with, the person I'd make listen to me be confused and excited and scared about it, was the one person I couldn't tell.

If I were sorting through feelings about guys in general, I wouldn't hesitate to tell Adam. But how the hell was I supposed to have that conversation now?

Hey Adam, um, listen bro. How did you know you liked guys?

Well, I was attracted to them, so that was kind of a major clue. Why?

No reason. I just... think I might want to kiss you. Like maybe a lot. And also just like, feel your skin on mine? And maybe also see you naked. No big deal.

I'd been scanning my memory all day, trying to come up with instances when I'd ever felt this way about a guy before. I'd never had trouble identifying guys who I thought were attractive. But there was a difference between them being attractive and me being attracted *to* them, wasn't there? Except, maybe there wasn't. Maybe it had just taken a push to get me to realize that.

Adam had gone back to writing in his notebook. I glanced over at him out of the corner of my eye and had to bite my lip to keep myself from reaching out and touching him. The curve of his back as he propped himself up on his elbows, the muscles in his shoulders and arms? I wanted to stroke my fingertips along them. Run my tongue down his spine. Kiss that space on his neck right behind his ear.

Jesus. So much for wondering *if* I was attracted to him. But the bigger question still remained—what the fuck was I supposed to do about it?

"What are you staring at, weirdo?" Adam asked, not looking up from his notebook, and I jumped, realizing I'd been watching him unabashedly for a few minutes now.

"Oh. Um, just zoned out, I guess." I glanced down at his notebook. "What are you working on?"

Adam held it up for me to see. "Remember the song you showed me last week, after Mia's party?"

"You mean the random bit of melody that *you* turned into a song?"

"Yeah, well," Adam said, shaking his head. "I can't stop playing around with it, so I thought maybe if I wrote it down, I could get it to behave."

"That's—"

"Oh my god, are you Ben Thomas?"

A shadow fell across the sand over me and Adam and we both looked up to see three girls, high-school aged, from what I could tell, standing between us and the water.

"Hey," I said, snapping into fan mode and smiling broadly. "Yeah, I am."

"Oh my God, I *told* you," said the girl in the middle.

"Hi there," I said, rolling over and then standing up. "I'm Ben. It's nice to meet you guys."

Adam, I noticed, was content to watch with a smirk from his position on his towel. It turned out that Courtney, Ashlyn, and Isla, rising seniors at Bronx Science, were my *biggest fans*—well, according to Courtney anyway. They asked what I was doing at the beach and I explained that it was my sister's birthday, which Ashlyn declared to be the *Cutest. Thing. Ever.*

I introduced them to my mom—I'd get major brownie points from Shereen there, she loved it when I played up the family angle—and then to Adam, who finally deigned to roll over and at least sit up and look in our direction.

"Oh my God," Isla said when Adam finally sat up. "Are you Adam Hart? I *love* you."

Adam blushed. "Uh. Thanks?"

"Our Adam's very shy," I said, smirking at him, "so you'll have to forgive his manners. What he meant to say was, *'Thank you so much, that's very sweet of you. He's so happy you like his music, and he wonders what your favorite song is.'*"

"Oh my God, *Cardiology*, obviously," Isla said. Courtney and Ashlyn nodded fervently.

"Thanks," Adam said, looking marginally less like he wanted to die. "I really like that one too."

My mom offered to take pictures of the five of us and after at least 30 seconds of pure squealing, the three of them handed over their phones for the photoshoot. Finally, the girls left and Adam gave me an incredulous look.

"Jesus, I know you're supposed to be nice to fans but you're like, serial killer nice. I thought you were going to invite them to stay for dinner."

I shrugged. "I don't know, it's not that bad, is it? Like, 99% of people who come up to you are just super nervous and sweet."

"You think it's sweet when total strangers tell you they love you?"

"It's..." I paused. "I mean, it's weird if you stop to think about it. Because they don't. Even if they meant the word *love*, it's not me they love, it's the perfect version of me Greenleaf presents to everyone. But it's not *their* fault, you know? The fans, I mean. Even if the person they think they know isn't really me, that person... he means something to them. Ben Thomas made an impact on their lives. It'd be shitty to ruin that for them by being a jerk."

"You're a way better person than I am," Adam said, shaking his head. "You go on being philosophical about modern day stardom. I'm gonna crawl back under my troll bridge and get back to yelling at people who walk across it."

"I mean, it's not entirely selfless. It's free publicity too. Shereen squirts a little every time a *'17 Reasons Why Ben Thomas Is the World's Nicest Celebrity'* article gets written."

"You probably *should* have invited them back for dinner then," Adam said with a laugh.

"Speaking of dinner, Adam sweetie," my mom interrupted. "Why don't you come back for dinner with us tonight? We'd love to have you."

"Oh, I don't know if—" Adam paused and looked at me. "I mean, it's fine if you want—"

"Stay," I said, "it'll be fun."

And it'll give me more time to sort out what it is you're doing to my stomach every time you look at me.

"I'm not sure if—I mean, are there even trains back to Manhattan from your place?" Adam asked, skeptical.

"The E and the F, for your information," I said. "And you're one to talk. At least I don't have to take—"

"Oh sweetheart, just spend the night with us," my mom cut in before I had time to get in my sick burn about Connecticut. "Ben's going to be on the pullout couch anyway, there's room for two there."

"Are you sure—" Adam looked at me in hesitation.

"I don't mind if you don't," I said, priding myself on how nonchalant I sounded.

"And Lacey will be thrilled," my mom said with a smile.

Lacey was more than thrilled, it turned out.

"You're staying?" she asked excitedly when she and my dad and Jess came back up from the water, shivering and dripping salt droplets everywhere. Adam nodded and Lacey darted in for a damp hug. Even though she only came up to his chest, Adam pretended to stagger under the force of her blow.

"Jeez, Lace, you been working out?" he asked when she let him go.

"Yeah. Wanna arm wrestle?" she laughed, pretending to show off her muscles.

"No," Adam said, his voice very serious. "What I want is a Go Fish rematch. Don't think I've forgotten the dirty tricks you pulled last summer. We're throwing down tonight, and I am definitely winning this time."

"Are not," Lacey shot back, sticking her tongue out at him.

Well this wasn't helping. Now my mind couldn't stop going all sorts of insane places. Adam and Lacey got along so well. How easy would it be, how great would it be, if Adam and I were dating? My family already loved him. It would just be... perfect.

Except that it was crazy to be thinking all of that before I even knew if Adam might return my feelings. Whatever they were. There was no reason to think he would.

"Yeah, yeah, you talk a big game," Adam said to Lacey, "Bring that attitude with you tonight, Kowalski. You're gonna need it."

"I'm gonna wipe the floor with you," Lacey grinned.

"We'll just see about that."

In the end, they played three rounds and roped me in to playing with them. I lost soundly each time. But it was fucking hard to remember who's got any sevens when I kept getting distracted by the way Adam's fingers curled around the cards in his hand, or the way he worried his bottom lip whenever he was thinking. I found myself staring at the pale skin on Adam's throat, wondering what it would taste like, what kinds of sounds Adam would make if I traced my tongue across it.

So yeah, not the best games of Go Fish I'd ever played.

We watched *Moana*—excellent—and *Airplane*—excellenter —all crammed into my parents' tiny living room. And there in the dim light of the tv, Adam squished in next to me on the couch, me trying to pretend I didn't notice the warmth of his skin where it grazed mine, I felt like I was home for the first time in a long while. The most important people in the world to me were all right there. Wherever they were *was* home and I felt something unknot inside me, releasing a tension I hadn't even realized was there.

Later that night, after everyone had gone to bed, Adam helped me fold out and make up the bed from the sofa in the living room. It was the strangest feeling—we'd done this exact same task on this exact same bed more times than I could remember—but it felt like the first time. Everything inside me felt buzzy and breathless and I kept fumbling with the sheets as I tried not to stare at Adam's arms.

Be normal, I scolded myself. But it didn't work. The best I could do was try to tamp down my nerves as we climbed into bed and yell at myself not to do anything stupid. Adam and I had shared a bed—this bed specifically—plenty of times when he'd stayed with us for the holidays. Nothing about tonight was different—except me.

As I lay on my back that night, trying to force myself to think about anything other than the fact that Adam was only inches away from me, I realized I'd made a decision.

"I think I really am going to go independent," I said softly.

Adam, who'd been reading by the low, golden light of the table lamp, closed his book and looked over at me.

"Yeah?"

"Yeah."

I rolled over onto my side, looking at Adam, and felt a flash of warmth in my core when Adam did the same thing. His face was shadowed, the light behind him setting the edges of his hair on fire with gold, but I could still make out his delicate features—the soft curve of his lips, the long line of his nose. I found myself wanting to kiss his brow, smooth out the almost perpetual furrow between his eyes.

"It might be a huge mistake," I said. "But I just—I think it's the right thing. For me."

"I mean, if it's what you want," Adam said slowly. "You should do what makes you happy. Fuck everything else."

I smiled, nervous. "I just want to go back to being *me*, you know? I want to play the music *I* want, the kind of thing that made me want to perform in the first place. You gotta be true to yourself, right?"

"God, you're so wholesome, I'm gonna puke," Adam said with a smile.

"Shut up, you love it," I said, reaching out and shoving him on the shoulder.

Adam put his hands out, trying to fend me off, and somehow I found myself taking hold of one of his wrists. It was small, thin, in my hand, but I knew there was strength behind its apparent fragility.

"No, I don't," Adam protested. "You can't make me say it. I have an image to maintain."

"Deep down, you are just a big, mushy sap." I slid closer to him in bed, my body moving of its own accord. I poked his chest with my free hand. "You can't fool me."

"I deny it. I deny your charges. Baseless accusations."

"You're the one who just told me I had to do what made me happy."

"Ugh." Adam grimaced, squeezing his eyes shut for a second. "It was a moment of weakness. You and your stupid family being all loving and actually wanting to spend time together. You tricked me into lowering my guard."

"You have feelings, Adam Hart, and you can't lie to me."

"Maybe." Adam raised his eyebrows. "But accuse me in public and I will definitely lie to everyone else."

I snorted, and moved my fingers from his wrist up to his hand, my heart racing. "Hey, thanks for coming today."

I squeezed his hand in mine and it was like time stopped. Adam looked down at my hand on his, then looked back up at me. Our eyes met and all I could do was look, just look, into that deep green gaze and wonder what he was going to say next. For a second, it felt like we were standing on the edge of something.

And then Adam shook his head and laughed. "Are you kidding? Your family is like, the only place I feel normal. Besides, my Go Fish battle with Lacey is epic. There's no way I was turning down a chance to win back some honor on that front."

"You know, for someone who claims to be an asshole, you're really good with her."

I let go of his hand, drew my arm back to my chest. What

the hell had I been thinking, touching him like that? Even if I did want something more with Adam—and the more we lay here in this dim glow, snuggled under blankets with a cruel foot of separation between us on this thin, coiled mattress, the more I knew it wasn't really an *if*—but even if I did, there was no guarantee that Adam would feel something in return.

"Disgusting," Adam said, making a face. "If you're just going to be nice to me, I'm turning off the light and going to sleep."

"You know my mom gets up at like, 6 a.m., right? We should go to bed anyway. But fine—you're an asshole and I hate you. Feel better?"

"Yes. Thank you—order's been restored."

"Good night, Adam. My dearest, favoritest human in the entire world," I couldn't resist adding.

"Gross. This is harassment."

"Love of my life, light of my world, beat of my heart, sun in my—"

"God, shut up," Adam said, and he flicked off the light, plunging the room into darkness and rolling over onto his side. I was pretty sure I could feel every inch of distance between us, like a cord was pulled taut between his body and mine.

"Night, Adam," I said after a moment.

"Night, loser."

It was the middle of the night when I woke up again. For a second, I wasn't sure where I was or what had woken me up. But then my eyes focused on Adam in bed next to me. Adam who was sliding closer. Adam, who put his arms around me and lay his head on my chest.

I thought I might stop breathing.

"You awake?" he whispered.

I could feel his heart beating against my chest and I pulled him in tighter. "I am now."

"I'm cold," Adam said, tilting his face up to me in the dark.

And I did the only thing that made sense—I tipped my head down and kissed him, catching his lips with my own. Adam hummed his approval, his lips parting, begging me to deepen the kiss, and I did, my tongue sliding into his mouth, tangling with his. I kissed him hungrily, desperate to taste the lips I'd been watching all day, finally feeling their soft heat.

Adam pressed his body to mine and I could feel his cock, warm and hard, pushing against my stomach. I inhaled sharply. It was one thing to daydream about Adam, to wonder if the butterflies I felt were real. It was entirely different to feel Adam's arousal, to know he wanted me.

It was better. And I could feel my cock getting hard in return.

I rolled Adam over onto his back, pushed his legs apart and slid my leg between them. I needed friction, needed heat. Adam moaned as I rubbed my cock down along his, the fabric of our pajama pants bunching and sliding as I ground my hips down into him. And as his hands slid up my back, underneath my t-shirt, I did what I'd been wanting to do all day--I kissed my way down onto his neck and licked a long stripe up his Adam's apple.

Adam whined underneath me, hipping up to meet me as I rolled my hips onto him. His hands gripped my waist as I sucked the sensitive skin on his neck, worrying it with my teeth. I liked the idea of leaving a mark, of showing the world that Adam was mine.

I thrust down harder, rutting against Adam. One hand of his slid up, tangled in my hair, as he spread his legs, inviting me to move between them. Adam—my Adam—wanted me. And I was going to take care of him, give him exactly what he needed. I slid a hand down, found his cock and stroked him through the flannel between us. Adam moaned in pleasure, opening his legs wider, his breath hot and fast in my ear.

"God, Ben," Adam whispered. "You have no idea how long I've wanted this. Please, I need you to fuck me."

His words were like a match, striking a spark down into my core, setting my body on fire. My orgasm blazed out from deep within me, my muscles spasming as I released, Adam's hands holding me tight to him as he breathed my name in the dark.

I woke with a start, my heart pounding. Disoriented, confused, I looked around in the dark wildly. Where was I? Had I dreamed that? It felt so real, so true. I could still feel Adam's heat beneath me.

But as I looked over in bed, Adam was curled up on the far side, just a shape underneath the blankets. Feet of space between us. He slumbered on, unaware of what my brain had just made him do—made us do, together.

I shifted, started to turn over to my side, disgusted with myself, when I felt it—something sticky and wet in my boxer briefs. My eyes widened in shock. When was the last time that had happened? Not since I was in high school. Dammit, I had it bad if just a dream about Adam could do that to me.

God, I felt disgusting. More specifically, disgusted with myself. It had nothing to do with what I wanted, but rather, who. It wasn't that I'd had a sex dream about a guy. It was that I'd dragged Adam into it without his consent.

It was bad enough that I'd spent the entire day lusting after him in secret. But to dream something like that? My stomach clenched in self-loathing. How would Adam feel if he knew what I'd imagined him doing, what my subconscious had made him do? Would he be able to stand being around me, if he knew how badly I wanted him? Jesus, what was wrong with me?

I felt sick, and as I slipped out of bed and headed towards the bathroom to clean up, shame bubbled in my stomach like a pool of tar. It was going to be a long rest of the night.

11

ADAM

I couldn't move when I woke up in the morning. As light filtered in through the unfamiliar windows, it took me a second to remember where I was. I almost thought I was back at Peachtree. And something was pressing against my chest.

But then I looked down and saw an arm—an arm that wasn't mine—flung across me and it came back to me. I was at Ben's parents' house. In a sofa bed. And Ben, in his sleep, had turned over onto his stomach and apparently decided to take up the entire bed, starfishing his limbs out and trapping me against the mattress.

His arm was a comforting weight across my chest, his body rising and falling slowly with his breath, his lips parted in sleep, looking incredibly kissable. Fuck. Even when Ben was sleeping, he found a way to drive me crazy.

He'd been so weird the day before and I couldn't figure out why. It was hard to put a finger directly on how Ben had been different. But I'd kept catching glimpses of him staring at me and naturally, I'd started to spin worst case scenarios. I was getting on Ben's nerves. Ben was sick of me. Ben was trying to find a polite way to tell me to get out of his place, his life, already.

I wondered if I should get up, or, at the very least, move Ben's arm. But, creep that I was, I was enjoying his touch way too much to push him away. I could hear Ben's mom moving around in the kitchen and it was just *nice* to lie there, all peaceful and puddled in that pool of blankets and sunlight, pretending like this was my real life, that Ben and I shared a bed every night, that every morning began with his touch.

Ben's phone rang, breaking the silence. But he didn't seem to hear it.

"Hey, your phone's ringing." I poke Ben in the side.

He didn't move.

"Wake up, asshole," I said louder this time, shoving him hard in the side.

"Voicemail," Ben mumbled, turning his head but otherwise refusing to move.

I sighed, wondering if I should just give up, but then his phone rang again.

"Ben, I swear to God, if you don't pick up your phone, I'm going to answer it for you and spread slanderous lies about you. Ben. Ben. Ben. Bennnnnn." I picked up his arm from my chest, bent it, and made him hit his head with his own hand. "Wake up, wake up, wake up."

"Ugh, fine," Ben said, his voice a sleepy grumble.

He shifted, moving his arm off of me, and leaned over the edge of his side of the bed to get his phone. I tried not to mourn the loss of contact.

"Hello?" Ben said, his voice thick with sleep still. "Shereen, it's so early, why are you—wait, what?"

His voice snapped awake and even his posture changed.

"Holy shit, is she—Uh huh... Uh huh... Has anyone— Jesus... Okay... Okay, yeah, I can do that."

Whatever Shereen was telling him, it wasn't good. Ben's voice sounded tense now, tight with worry.

"No, I'm at my parents'," he said after a moment. "Yeah. Yeah, I'll call—Right. Yeah, I'll let you know. Can you—let me know if anything... Yeah. Thanks."

He hung up and looked back at me, his brow furrowed.

"What happened?" I asked.

"Mia..." Ben shook his head in disbelief. "Mia and her ex got married?"

"What?" I sat up in bed and stared at him. "When?"

"Last night, apparently? In Vegas?" Ben's eyes were wide. "Apparently two nights ago, she ran into him at *Rose Red*, some club in the Meatpacking District, and they got in a screaming match... and then last night they showed up in Vegas, drunk and very definitely married."

"Holy shit."

"Yeah." Ben shook his head again. "I need to call her. I can't —she was just talking about getting over him. And he—I thought he had a girlfriend? This is such a mess."

"Anything I can do?" I asked, not sure what the hell I could do. But it couldn't hurt to offer.

"Yeah, actually," Ben said, sighing heavily. "The other thing is, Shereen wants me to lay low for a while. Apparently paparazzi are hounding Mia and Tate out in Vegas and she doesn't want to add more fuel to the fire by anyone asking me what I think about all this."

"Makes sense."

"So I guess I'm supposed to get a hotel room? Shereen said she's already sent someone by my place and there are photographers waiting outside."

"Shit." I grimaced. "Do you want me to—"

"Would you mind making the reservation? It's usually easier if I don't do it under my name. I'll pay for it and everything, it just kinda helps keep things on the DL if my name isn't on the books."

"No problem." I pulled my phone out, then stopped and stared at a text from Esther. "Ugh."

ESTHER>> I'm headed up to the Hell Mouth today. Need anything from there?

The Hell Mouth was what we not-so-affectionately called my dad's place up in Westport.

"What?" Ben asked and I realized I'd spoken aloud.

"Esther's going up to my dad's place today," I said, making a face. "She asked if I needed anything."

"Don't you?" Ben frowned. "You still haven't gone and picked up your stuff."

"Yeah, but I can't ask her to carry that all back for me. I should probably go get it myself."

"Wait, Adam." Ben's face lit up. "Isn't your dad in Japan all summer or something?"

"London, but yeah. Why?"

"What if we just hung out in Connecticut until this all blows over?" Ben asked. "Literally no one would expect me to be there, you have to go there anyway, and if your dad's not gonna be around, why not? If you want, we can set some of his clothes on fire before we leave."

"Jesus, I tell you one story..." I snorted. "I don't know, I mean, I guess we could. You don't think you'd be bored? It's just country clubs and yachts up there, mostly."

"We'll make it fun then. Play house. Drink brandy out of crystal snifters and eat caviar. I assume your dad stocks caviar in his kitchen, right?"

I laughed. "I don't know. There's definitely brandy though. Given that my dad's drunk half the time, that's pretty much a guarantee. But yeah, we could ask Lydia to get some caviar the next time she does the shopping, I guess."

"Lydia?" Ben looked at me in confusion.

"My dad's housekeeper. She's awesome, actually. She was pretty much the only person who was nice to me once I moved back there." I smiled. "Actually, you know what? Let's do it. I haven't seen her in ages. It'll be fun."

"You sure?" Ben gave me a long look. "Don't let me peer pressure you."

"Please. You couldn't peer pressure me if you tried."

"That sounds like a challenge," Ben said, wiggling his eyebrows. "But fine then, it's settled. Just let me call Mia and then we can go live a life of dissolute luxury for a week."

"Sounds like a plan."

The closer we got to Westport, though, the more nervous I got. Ben kept up a steady stream of non-sequiturs and once we got off the Merritt, started pontificating on how many ghosts lived in each of the houses we passed. I appreciated his attempt to lighten the mood, but I couldn't stop feeling unsettled.

I'd told Esther our plans, told her we'd see her there. I tried to concentrate on that fact—seeing Esther would be nice. Focus on the good things.

But even so, going home—and technically, I realized, that's what this trip was, since I was otherwise homeless right now —felt awful. There was this sinking, twisting feeling in my gut that only grew as we drove down familiar streets that I hadn't seen in two years. I felt so melodramatic, seeing portents of doom as we drove along those sun-dappled lanes, passing by ivy-covered mansions with old stonework walls that I remembered from when I was a kid, dragged to garden luncheons and Christmas parties before my parents had split up.

The memories came in flashes. The clink of glasses, the flash of someone's red scarf, the cool water of a fountain where Esther and I decided to go swimming as we waited for my mom to finish her tennis match. My dad had been furious when he'd come to pick us all up, refusing to let us into the car because we'd get his leather seats wet.

And always, always—a feeling of tension in the air, like thunderheads on the horizon, a storm cell about to break. All my early memories were thick with it, a sense of foreboding that hung like Spanish moss around those pictures in my mind.

I didn't remember much before my parents' divorce when I was seven. Though to be honest, I didn't remember much about the four years Esther and I spent in LA with my mom after that either. She'd gotten remarried to Eamon, my stepdad, who had two kids of his own. Caleb and Andrew—the kids who taught me what the word bully meant.

I don't know what it was about me that they decided they didn't like. It didn't seem to matter. Any moment the adults were out of the room was fair game for them to torment me, saying whatever they could to get a rise out of me, and once they got older, beating me up whenever they got the chance.

Andrew was only one year older than me and I got the impression that if it hadn't been for Caleb, he might have left me alone. But Caleb, three years older, took after his father and had a mean streak as wide and deep as the San Andreas fault. He was the instigator and when he was around, Andrew was just as cruel.

Things were bearable as long as Esther was around, but after she'd left for college, they'd made my life hell. So I made my mom's life hell in turn, refusing to do my homework, throwing tantrums, running away—anything to get in trouble, until she finally decided she couldn't take it anymore and sent me back to live with my dad. I'd been so relieved when I first got back to Connecticut.

I'd had no idea just how much he'd despised me coming back.

And now here we were, turning onto Damson Lane, driving down that gently undulating road until we came to the end, house number 24. I'd had to give Ben directions for the last few turns—he'd only been here a couple times—and he gave me a concerned look as we pulled up to the gate at the end of the driveway.

"You still wanna do this?" he asked, his voice quiet.

"Yeah." I nodded firmly. "Yeah. It's just a house. And he's in Europe. It's gonna be fine."

"Definitely," Ben said with an encouraging smile.

He pulled up to the gatehouse and punched the button on the intercom. A low tone pulsed, then a woman's voice answered, slightly obscured by static.

"Delivery?" she said. "If it's flowers or catering, you can just pull around to the back when you come through."

Catering? That was weird.

"Uh, no," I said, raising my voice and leaning over Ben to get closer to the intercom. "Lydia, it's Adam. We were just—"

"Oh, Adam, honey, I didn't know you were coming! Come on in." Lydia's voice was cheerful as she buzzed us through, the gates opening slowly, as if by magic.

"I will never get used to that," Ben said, shaking his head. "Who the fuck lives in a gated compound?"

"To be fair, you're the one who has people stalking your every move right now," I said. "Maybe you should look into gates."

Ben snorted as he put the car in drive and pulled forward. "It's not like these actually do much good, though, right? I mean, we could just drive around them on the grass, couldn't we? There's no fence."

"You can't, actually. There are spikes."

"What?" Ben threw me an incredulous look. "Spikes? What is this, the Middle Ages?"

I shrugged. "A while back my dad got really paranoid about people trying to steal company secrets from him, so he had them installed. They're pressure sensitive, so you don't see them until they've punctured your tire. Or your stomach, if you're my pet dog who died when I was 12."

"Jesus."

Ben continued up the drive as it wound its way across the sweeping lawns and curved towards the house. Eventually it forked, and a discreet wooden sign indicated that the formal entrance was to the left, service entrance to the right.

"Right," I said when Ben looked at me, hesitating. "The fucking formal entrance is such bullshit."

It wasn't until we'd pulled around to the far side of the house that we saw all the trucks, with people in uniform carting out tables and chairs, others bringing out large boxes from a truck with a dinner wear logo. A large tent was being set up back by the pool house.

"Uh... Adam?" Ben stared at me in confusion. "Is there... something happening here today?"

I stared back at him, at a loss. Obviously *something* was happening. But I had no idea *what*. Or why.

Before I could get any further, the door to the kitchen opened and Lydia flew outside, beaming at me. She came over to the car and I had no choice but to get out and let her hug me.

"Oh, Adam love, it's so good to see you," she said as her stout arms pulled me in and squeezed me. She squinted up at me as she released me. "It's been far too long. Next time, let me know ahead of time that you're coming and I'll make sure we've got that LaCroix that you like. Though I suppose if you're just here for the party, you won't care. But are you staying with us tonight, honey?"

"I—what—Lydia, what party?" Well that was a stupid question, it was obvious what party she was talking about. "What's all of this for?"

Lydia frowned at me. "It's the annual board member dinner tonight, sweetheart, remember? Didn't your father tell you?"

"Wait—what? Is my dad—I thought he—" God, I felt like such an idiot, standing there stammering, my face heating up. "Is he home?"

"Of course, sweetheart." Lydia looked at me in confusion. "They couldn't very well have it without the CEO. But sweetie, if that's not why you're here—"

"Lydia, this is simply unacceptable. If you're not able to keep
—" my dad's voice, pitched at a yell, as always, started
suddenly as he came striding out of the house through the
kitchens and stopped just as suddenly when he saw the
group of us clustered in the driveway.

"What are you doing here?" he asked, stalking over, his
voice cold.

I wanted to disappear.

"I'm—I'm just—I just came to—"

"Disgrace me in front of the board?" my dad finished for me,
his lip curling in disgust. "Make a spectacle of yourself in
front of them just to embarrass me? Or were your plans
more private this time, just to remind me of what a failure
you are as my son?"

As he spoke, his hulking figure grew more imposing,
looming over the three of us. Lydia stepped back, clearly not
interested in catching my dad's ire. I couldn't blame her—
she needed to keep her job. All I could do was stare up at
him, sandy hair framing his cruel, sneering face, and try to
remember to breathe.

"No," I choked out. "No, that's not—I didn't know
you were—"

"You'd better not be here to ask for money," my dad said,
taking a step forward. I could smell the liquor on his breath.
"It won't work. I don't care what sob story you've got this
time. I haven't wasted a penny on your choices since that
farce of a degree I paid for and I'm not about to start now."

He took another step forward and I couldn't help it, I backed
up—right into Ben, who put a hand on my shoulder. I'd

almost forgotten he was there. It was so hard to think straight in my dad's presence. It was like he could warp the air around him, make it as cold and dark as his feelings for me. Ben's hand was like an anchor, a rock in the storm raging inside me.

"I wasn't asking for money," I stammered. "I was just—I wanted—nevermind. We'll just go."

"Adam, we don't have to go," Ben said quietly, fiercely, next to my ear. "We can still get your things, you don't have to—"

"Good," my dad interrupted. "Go, before you find a way to ruin everything I've been working on this summer. Do you have any idea how long it's taken to put this merger together? Endless negotiations, countless rounds of golf at the club. I'm putting it to the board tonight and I will not let you distract from the proceedings with whatever ridiculous cry for attention you've dreamed up."

"I'm not here to do some cry for—" I stopped, my dad's words sinking in. "All summer?"

"Yes, Adam," my dad said with a withering glance. "Some of us actually work. I know that might come as a shock to you but—"

"Esther said you were in Europe. That you were going to be there til September."

My dad didn't say anything, just pressed his lips together in a hard line.

"Were you even gone at all? Or did you just not want to come see me—were you that ashamed of me?"

"And what would me visiting you have done? I won't

condone your behavior by giving you the attention you're so clearly desperate for."

"Dad, I was in the hospital, how could you—"

"Dad?" Esther's voice rang out behind us. I turned to see her stepping out of her gray Camry. "Dad, what are you doing here? I thought you were in London."

"Apparently your dad's a sociopath," Ben said, his voice heated, "who's been lying to you for months."

"I don't need to defend my—" my dad began, but Esther stalked up to him and cut him off.

"Dad, Adam could have died. Died. And you lied to me? To him? What the fuck is wrong with you?"

"I was busy, Esther. I didn't have time to take away from work at that moment and anyway, he's obviously fine. Returned to form, ready to make himself a nuisance again."

"God, I knew you were an asshole," Esther began angrily, "but I never thought..."

I tuned her out. I couldn't take it anymore, couldn't *be* there anymore. I could feel my breath getting short, choppy, and sweat broke out across my body. I had to get out.

"Can we go," I asked Ben, turning around and giving him a pleading look.

"We can," Ben began. "But Adam, don't you want to—"

"No." I shook my head. "No, I just need to—we need to leave. Now."

I started walking back to the car. I didn't care what my dad was saying to Esther right then, didn't even care about saying goodbye to poor Lydia, still standing at the edge of the driveway, trying to make herself invisible. I just needed to be somewhere, anywhere else.

Ben caught up to me when I reached the car. "Are you sure you don't want to at least get your stuff?" he asked, his voice threaded with concern.

"Please," I begged him. "Please, just get in the car and drive."

12

BEN

I glanced at Adam out of the corner of my eye as I drove back towards the Merritt. He was slumped over in the seat, his body as curled up as he could get it in the car. He was staring straight ahead but I didn't think he was seeing anything. Not anything we were driving past, anyway.

All I wanted to do was pull him into my arms—and not even in the way you're probably thinking. Not mostly, anyway. I'd never seen someone look so defeated and I wished there were something I could do. But the way he'd begged me to get in the car and drive, I figured the best thing I could do was to get him away from there.

I knew Adam and his dad didn't get along and had always gotten the impression the guy was a douche, but I'd never actually talked to him until today. And actually, I'm not even sure today qualified. Talked *at* might be the better way of putting it.

God, no wonder Adam avoided going home. I couldn't

blame him and I completely regretted proposing we make the trip. It was just hard to fathom how someone as caring, as sensitive as Adam, had grown up with a man like that for a father.

Eventually, we had to stop for gas. Adam looked up in confusion as I pulled the car to a stop, seeming to surface from whatever well of memories he'd fallen into.

"Where are we?" he asked, looking around. "Sorry, I, uh, kind of zoned out."

"New Canaan service station," I said.

"Right," Adam nodded. God, he looked so lost.

"I have to fill up the tank, but I'd love you forever if you bought me some of that disgusting, off-brand popcorn," I said with a grin, pulling my credit card out of my wallet and then tossing it to him. "And maybe some gummy candy?"

Adam turned my wallet over in his hands like he'd never seen such a contraption before. Finally he looked up and did something with his mouth—I think it was supposed to be a smile, but it was just a rictus baring of teeth, like he'd forgotten how his face worked.

"Any particular kind of gummy candy? If you don't give me specifics, I might just buy out the whole store."

"Go nuts," I said with a grin.

After I got the gas started, I pulled my phone out and texted Gray.

BEN>> How do you feel about surprise houseguests?

GRAY>> Awesome, if they're you? Are they you?

BEN>> Yeah. And Adam, if that's ok?

GRAY>> Definitely. Any particular reason?

BEN>> I'll explain when we get there. Too complicated for a text

GRAY>> Sure

GRAY>> But does it have anything to do with what we talked about yesterday though?

BEN>> Nosy

GRAY>> My house, I get to be nosy

BEN>> That's also complicated

GRAY>> Fine. But I expect full details soon

BEN>> Yeah yeah. Thanks for letting us crash

GRAY>> Any time. I'll text you the address

Adam came back outside with popcorn, candy, and two bottles of store-brand seltzer water. He seemed marginally more recovered and looked at me in curiosity as I shut the pump off and got back in the car.

"So where are we going that requires so many snacks? I'm gonna be really disappointed if it's just back to Manhattan."

"I would never tease you like that. Roadtrip snacks are for roadtrips, obviously."

"So where then? Key West?"

I laughed. "Almost. How do you feel about the Hamptons?"

"Full of rich people and snobs, why?"

"Gray has a house in Montauk and he and some friends are

spending the week there. He said we could join. I thought it might be a good place to get away for a while."

"Oh." Adam paused. "Okay, yeah. Sure."

"I mean, we don't have to go, if you don't—"

"No, let's do it." Adam smiled—a real one this time—and nodded. "I think being around people will actually be good."

"Cool. I'll see if we can rustle up some rich people to make fun of, too."

"You *are* rich, Ben," Adam snorted. "I can just make fun of you."

We settled back into silence as we got back on the road, but it no longer felt so empty, so stark. Adam turned on the radio after a while and refused to change the station whenever one of my songs came on. When we got onto the Long Island Expressway and headed west, he leaned back in his seat and sighed.

"I wish I'd told him to go fuck himself. I should have."

"We can turn around if you want," I said.

Adam grinned and there was a mischievous glint in his eye. "Serve him right if I did come back in the middle of his dinner, told him what a shit father he was in front of the board. God, what an asshole."

"Yeah." I nodded. "Gotta say, you were not exaggerating about him at all."

"Pretty much."

"I'm sorry I dragged you back there," I said after a moment.

"I should have—well, I don't know. I shouldn't have suggested it."

"You didn't know," Adam said with a shrug. "No one did. Don't feel bad."

"But if I hadn't—"

"I still would have had to go up sometime this summer," Adam said. "I would have found out he was here one way or another. I mean, Esther was going up today anyway. She would have told me. Because unlike my father, she's not a lying piece of shit."

"I'm so sorry, Adam."

"It's okay."

"No, it's really not. He should have been there for you. He should have visited you in the hospital. I can't believe he'd treat you like that, say those things."

"I can," Adam said darkly. He barked a laugh. "You know the thing that hurts the most? The fact that I'm not even surprised by any of this. Hearing what he thinks about me? Not a surprise—it's not like he hasn't told me that before. Finding out he was lying to me, avoiding me? Not a surprise —the guy was barely home from the time I turned 14. Knowing that he wishes I weren't his son? Not a surprise at all. Just a reminder to never expect anything different."

"I wish there were something I could do," I said, feeling helpless.

"There is. You bought me gummy candy."

"You know what I mean."

"I do. Gummy candy's a sacred thing, man. We've got an unbreakable bond now."

"Because we didn't before?"

"Eh, you know how these things go. Can't hurt to reinforce it," Adam laughed. "Wasn't it Thomas Jefferson who said that the tree of friendship must be refreshed from time to time with the blood of gummy worms and octopi?"

"I'm not sure you've got that one *quite* right," I said. "But who am I to argue with the keeper of the gummy worms? I'll take a green and yellow one, please."

∼

"So I was promised a story," Gray said as he settled into the outdoor armchair on his deck. Adam and I sat across from him on a couch that faced out towards the water. The house was a rambling, two-story building with weathered gray shingles, a wrap-around deck, and rooms and wings that stuck out in odd directions. "What inspired the change of plans?"

Adam shot me a quick, panicked look but I shook my head and smiled. "Work stuff," I said with a grin. "Well, kinda."

"Oh shit, is this about your—uh, I mean, does it have anything to do with—" Micah, one of Gray's friends looked around for support from his perch on the other end of the couch. "Seriously guys, am I the only one who reads celebrity gossip?"

"No," said Chris, another one of Gray's friends. "But you're the only one gauche enough to say something about it in front of him."

Chris glanced at me and I laughed. "Don't worry about it," I said, shaking my head. "I used to read that shit all the time too. And I'm still not used to thinking of myself that way."

"So are you and Mia like, you know—" Micah went on.

"We're... I don't know what we are, right now," I said.

Which was the honest truth. Mia hadn't picked up when I'd called this morning, or just 10 minutes ago when we'd gotten to Gray's. Hadn't responded to any of my texts either, including *Sesquipedalian?*, which I'd sent right after Shereen had called.

But on top of that, while I didn't *think* any of Gray's friends were going to randomly contact a tabloid to report what I'd said, I could pretty much feel Shereen sitting on my shoulder telling me to shut the hell up and jamming the heel of her shoe into my neck to hammer her point home.

"I just want her to be happy," I said after a moment's pause. "I hope she is."

"That's like, creepily well-adjusted, dude," Micah said, frowning. "Are you sure you're human?"

"Ben is basically a saint," Adam said with a snort. "This is honestly pretty typical for him."

"Hey," I said, giving him a shove. "I can be mean."

"You couldn't be mean if you tried," Adam said, shoving me back.

"Maybe he's just not an asshole like you, Micah, ever think about that?" Gray put in.

"I don't have to listen to this slander," Micah said with a

smirk. "Or if I do, I'm at least going to do it from the hot tub. Who's with me? Ben? Adam?"

"Uh, we didn't really bring anything," I said after a minute. "This was kind of an unexpected trip."

"Trust me, I've got tons of stuff here that will fit you guys," Gray said. "You can borrow whatever you need."

"What, you keep all the clothes from the guys you've fucked over the years?" Micah asked sweetly.

Gray shot him a haughty look. "Don't be jealous just because I actually get some and you don't."

"Hey, I get some."

"Yeah," Chris said, leaning in from the far side of the deck, "but no one would pay to watch you have sex, Micah. That's the difference."

Gray looked over at me apologetically. "Oh, I should probably mention—"

"Don't worry, he knows," Adam said with a laugh.

"Really?" Gray tilted his head as he looked at me. "How'd you find out? Or do you watch more gay porn than I realized?"

"Nah, I told him," Adam said, and the asshole reached over to ruffle my hair. I could feel my face turning red. "I offered to give him a tour of your greatest hits but the poor baby just blushed and stammered no thanks."

"Not true!" I protested. "You never offered. And besides, you don't know what kind of porn I watch."

Adam arched an eyebrow. "Please, I lived with you for four

years in college, I think I would know if you watched gay porn."

"Well by that logic, I should have known what you were watching, too. And I didn't. So maybe I'm just a treasure trove of secrets of my own."

"Trust me, I think I'd know if you swung that way," Adam said with a smirk.

Would you? Because I sure as hell didn't. God, part of me wanted to just say it, right then and there. Tell him everything that had been running around in my head for the past two days.

But I didn't. Of course not.

"Adorable as this all is," Micah said, "I don't see anyone getting in the hot tub."

"Show me where I can get a swimsuit," Adam said, standing up, "and I'll join you."

"I'll catch up in a second," I said, pulling my phone out. "Just need to—" but no one was listening.

Which was fine. I didn't actually need to do anything with my phone at that point. It was just camouflage. What I needed was a second to process that conversation.

Adam thought he'd know if I were interested in guys. So he obviously thought I wasn't. Which meant he probably hadn't ever thought of being interested in me. And that stung—even though I knew I was being completely unreasonable to demand that Adam return my feelings.

Fuck, my feelings were so new, I still wasn't quite sure of their shape. I liked him. That much was clear. I couldn't look in his direction without feeling my chest tighten. But what I wanted to do with that information was still an open question.

"So that was an interesting conversation."

I looked up and saw Gray walking over to join me on the couch.

"Yeah," I said, shoving my phone back in my pocket. "Tell me about it."

"So I'm too old to be cute about this shit. Have you thought any more about how you feel about him?"

"Thought any more about it? Gray, I haven't been able to stop thinking about it. You were completely right. And now that I've realized that, I'm a fucking mess."

"Why? Because of the Mia thing?"

"Oh God, no. Listen," I lowered my voice, "please don't go spreading this around, but the Mia thing... we were never anything more than friends. I really do hope she's okay but I don't have any like, private angst over that."

"Okay." Gray nodded slowly. "Well then in that case, why the—"

"Because I don't think it's ever occurred to Adam that I *could* be interested in him. I don't think he sees me as anything other than a friend. And I can't go fucking up our friendship on a hunch."

"You sound pretty convinced for a guy who only just realized he might be into his friend two days ago. Maybe Adam does feel the same but just never thought it was a possibility. No way of knowing unless you ask him."

"What are you, some kind of mature and pragmatic adult? Get out of here."

Gray looked at me, exasperated. "Man, if you're freaking out about not knowing something and there's an obvious solution..."

"I can't." I shrugged my shoulders helplessly. "I can't. It'd be too awkward. And even if I wanted to, I can't do it *now*. Adam's... Adam's dealing with some shit. Telling him now would just make things worse for him."

"Or, it could make it better. Couldn't it? If he feels the same?"

"But how do I know before I say something?"

"Ben, man. You don't. That's the risk, buddy. But the other option seems to be walking around never saying anything and hoping his dick falls into your mouth by accident, so pick your poison."

I looked over at Adam as he climbed into the hot tub with the other guys. He was smiling and laughing but there was a tightness to his grin, a sharp edge to his laughter. He was trying to forget about earlier today, I could tell. And I was sitting here whining about whether or not he liked me. Whatever I did or didn't do about my feelings for Adam, being his friend came first.

As if he could feel my eyes on him, Adam turned around and smiled at Gray and me.

"Hey Gray, just so you know," he called, "you're my new best friend."

"I thought I was your best friend," I shot back.

Adam grinned. "Get a hot tub and maybe we can renegotiate. Now come on, get in here. I don't want to have to keep yelling at you."

"Fine," I said, standing up. "If it'll stop you whining."

Maybe it was the beer we'd been drinking. Maybe it was Gray's words in the back of my head. But I walked over to the hot tub instead of ducking inside first to grab a suit and when I made it to the edge of the water, I pulled my shirt off.

"Seriously?" Adam said as I stripped down to my boxer briefs.

"Just trying to make you happy, schnookums," I said, and Adam splashed me.

"If you meant that, you'd buy me a hot tub."

"Cute." I stuck my tongue out at him. "Now move over, it's cold out here."

There wasn't a lot of room left in the water at that point, but Adam slid to the side and I slipped in next to him, letting the heat envelop me. I tilted my head back and closed my eyes, sighing. Even if nothing else made sense, this moment, at least, was good.

"How you doing?" Adam said after a minute, ducking out of an argument Micah and Chris were having about whose beer was whose.

"Good," I said, opening my eyes and looking at Adam. "Actually really good. You?"

Adam sighed and settled back against the wall of the tub, his leg grazing mine in the water below. "I've been better," he said quietly. "But honestly? I'm sick of letting him make me feel bad, you know?"

"You're allowed to, though," I said. "You know that, right? You don't have to apologize for how you feel."

"I know." Adam nodded, not looking at me. "I know."

It was the middle of the night when I woke up.

It was pitch black, my eyes unadjusted, and I blinked, not sure what had woken me. I was crunched up in a twin bed with Adam—Gray's place had four bedrooms but our arrival had meant some people had to double-up. It hadn't seemed fair to make anyone else share a bed, so Adam and I had volunteered while I pointedly ignored Gray's suggestive eyebrows.

I started to make out shapes in the dark, the starlight spinning down from the night sky through the open window, and I realized it was a sound that had woken me up. The sound of crying. Furtive, quiet crying—the sound of someone trying to hide it. But crying, nonetheless.

It was coming from Adam.

I froze, hot and cold all at once. Adam was crying. In bed with me. Every muscle in my body wanted to wrap him up in my arms but I couldn't move. Adam could barely admit he had emotions—acknowledging that he was crying, that I'd heard him? I wasn't sure what he'd do if I moved. He might get mad at me, for all I knew. And he was clearly trying to be quiet. But I couldn't just do nothing.

For a second I wondered if this was another dream, like the one I'd had last night. But no. The hushed noises coming from Adam, the faint roar of the waves outside, the crisp folds of the sheets crumpled around us in the dark. It was too detailed, too real.

Adam, my Adam, was hurting. And he was lying curled up in bed, just inches away from me. I couldn't just do nothing.

Holding my breath, I reached out and put a hand on Adam's shoulder in the dark. The noise stopped immediately. Adam didn't move and I was frozen for a second time, not sure what to do next. But I'd already started—might as well see it through now.

I pushed myself up onto my elbow and inched closer to Adam in bed, leaning over to try to see his face. I could see his eyes, at least, and the whites around his green irises were bright in the shadowy room, tears glistening in the corners.

"Are you okay?" I mouthed it more than whispered it. The snores from the other bed told me that Chris, our roommate, was still sleeping, but I didn't want to push it.

Adam looked scared but finally he nodded. "Yeah." I could barely hear him.

I wanted to say something else, but I didn't know what it was. I felt like I was standing on the edge of some massive cliff, about to jump off, with no idea whether I'd fly or plummet—and no way of knowing til I took that leap.

"Your dad?" I said after a minute.

Adam grimaced and nodded, then squeezed his eyes shut as a swallowed sob shook his body. He kept his eyes shut for a long moment and when he opened them again, he gave me a watery smile.

"Sorry. I'm fine. Go back to sleep."

And then he turned further onto his side, sliding closer to the edge of the bed. I collapsed back down, feeling sick. I should have said something, should have done something more. To comfort him, at least. Let him know he wasn't alone.

And then I heard it again—another quiet gasp, a stifled sob ripped from Adam's chest. And before I knew what I was doing, I wrapped my arms around him and pulled him close.

I half-expected Adam to freeze, to push me away as I drew him in, his back to my chest, but he didn't. He just let himself be pulled and when I slid my arm over his shoulder and pressed it to Adam's chest, he clutched my hand. His body began to shake, racked with silent sobs, and I just held him, pressing my face into the back of his neck, trying to offer whatever comfort I could.

Adam's body was warm for once, but it felt so small, so fragile against mine. I wished I could hug strength into him somehow. I still couldn't quite believe he was even letting me hold him like this, knowing how he hated to feel weak.

Adam was just a little shorter than I was and I couldn't help noticing how perfectly our bodies fit together, like puzzle pieces that had found their mates. I breathed in the scent of his skin, deep and cool, like forest streams and moonlight.

Finally, Adam stopped moving and I could feel the breath in his chest slow.

"Sorry," he whispered after a minute. "I didn't mean to—"

"Shh," I quieted him. "You're fine."

"I can—I can sleep on the floor tonight," Adam said, starting to pull away. "You don't have to—"

"No." It came out more forcefully than I'd expected. "No. Stay." I squeezed my arms tighter around him and felt Adam freeze, and then, so slowly, relax against my chest.

"Stay," I repeated, a murmur this time.

My nose was behind Adam's ear, the hair at the back of his neck tickling my cheek. And maybe it was because it was the middle of the night. Maybe it was being in a strange house after a long day. Maybe it was because I was just tired of holding myself back.

But quietly, slowly, so slowly I was barely aware of what I was doing, I pressed a kiss to the side of Adam's neck.

Adam froze immediately. I pulled back an inch, leaving my arms wrapped around him, my lips hovering above his skin. I could still feel the heat of his body on my lips and I waited for Adam to move, to pull away, to say something, anything.

But he didn't. Instead, almost imperceptibly, he tilted his head down towards the pillow, opening just a bit more of his neck towards me. My eyes widened, not sure I was really seeing this, half convinced I was dreaming. But I gathered my courage and leaned in, touching my lips to Adam's skin again. They felt cool on the smooth surface of his neck.

This time, it was more obvious. Adam shifted again, exposing more of his neck, and that was an invitation if I'd ever seen one. I bent down and kissed him again, letting my lips linger longer this time, flicking my tongue forward to taste Adam's skin. God, was it really only two days ago that I'd realized what I felt for him? It seemed like I'd wanted to know what he tasted like for years.

I didn't pull back this time, just slid my lips further down Adam's neck to where it met his shoulder and disappeared into the stretched out collar of the t-shirt he was borrowing from Gray. A noise escaped Adam's lips, more than an exhale, not quite a moan. A sound of pure need, and it stirred something deep inside me.

I pushed myself up a bit, and over, and as I started to move my body on top of Adam's, Adam shifted and rolled onto his back, leaving me hovering over him, the two of us chest to chest. My heart beat so hard I was amazed it didn't wake up the whole house.

Adam stared up at me. His eyes were full of fear and confusion and hope and I wondered if they mirrored my own. I smiled, almost not daring to believe this was real, this was happening, and Adam's smile answered mine, just as tremulous.

I thought of saying something, but what was there to say? *I like you? I want you? Everything I feel for you has changed in the past 48 hours, except maybe it hasn't changed at all. Maybe I've felt this way the whole time, and I'm just now opening my eyes.*

Anything I could say was too much or not enough and I didn't want to ruin this, didn't want to stop to question things or let either of us get trapped in our heads. So I leaned down and brought my lips to his. And it turned out that silence was all we needed to say.

Adam's lips parted for me, warm and firm, and I ran my tongue along them, tasting their sweetness, wondering how I'd known Adam for so many years and was only just kissing him now. It felt right, it felt exactly the way it should. It felt like something I should have done seven years ago.

And then Adam bit down on my lower lip and I lost all capacity for rational thought, pushing my tongue into his mouth and tangling it with his. I could taste all of him, feel his breath in short, hot puffs, mingling with my own. I couldn't hold back any longer. I lowered myself down, pressing my body against his.

Adam's hands moved, one to my chest, clutching the fabric of my shirt, and one to my waist and fuck, the soft skin of his fingertips gripping my waist, pressing into my lower back, was enough to make me completely hard. Adam wanted me —really wanted me, wasn't just putting up with this or kissing me out of some weird sense of obligation or guilt. He wanted me at least a fraction of the amount I wanted him.

I ground my hips down onto Adam and shifted further until my cock found his, both of us hard. I needed to feel him and I rolled my hips forward, thrusting and sliding our cocks together through the thin fabric of his pajama pants and my boxer briefs. Adam pushed up against me, his hand on my chest pushing me back and I froze. Had I gone too far?

But Adam wasn't just pushing me back, he was pushing me over, rolling me onto my back and then moving on top, shifting until he was straddling me, his legs on either side. Fuck, he made my cock throb, looking down at me, his eyes hungry.

I pulled at his shirt, used it to guide Adam's body down into contact with my own. Our mouths crushed together and my breath, my heartbeat, seemed to mix with Adam's, our bodies crashing together like the waves of the ocean outside. Adam ground down onto my waist, and my breath caught as I felt his warm, hard cock press against mine.

The reality of what we were doing hit me then. This was Adam. My best friend. My male best friend and I was hipping up into him, desperate to feel his cock slide against mine. If I'd had any doubts about what my feelings meant, they vanished at that moment. I wanted this. I wanted Adam.

I pressed upwards, driving my cock into Adam's hip, and Adam gasped and writhed, biting at my neck. I slid my hands down slowly, one going to Adam's lower back, then ass, to squeeze it—and fuck did that feel good—and the other sliding between our bodies so I could feel his cock.

Finding it, my fingers stroked along its outline through the fabric covering him and I felt it twitch. Adam moaned and I tilted my head, catching his mouth with mine. I stroked him again and Adam pushed harder into my hand as I slid my thumb under the waistband of his pants, desperate to feel his bare skin. Adam moaned into my mouth a second time and—

A loud grunt came from the other bed. Both of us froze as we listened to Chris turn over in bed noisily. We waited, silent, to see if we'd woken him up and as I gazed up at Adam, I could feel a nervous laugh bubbling up from my chest. I tried to stifle it but it came out anyway and Adam clapped a hand over my mouth, looking down at me in horror.

By the time the laugh subsided, the coast was clear. We hadn't disturbed Chris's beauty rest. But Adam slid off of me and fell down onto his back anyway. We lay there next to each other, only our arms touching, our chests rising and falling in time.

My mind was racing, thoughts and questions and desire spinning through it and I wondered if Adam felt as terrified, as exhilarated as I did. Finally, Adam turned over onto his side, facing the far wall. I stared at him from the corner of my eye for a moment.

Was that a sign? Did he want me to leave him alone? I knew we couldn't do anything else tonight—one close call was more than enough. But that didn't mean he had to sleep as far away from me as he could get, did it?

I thought of Gray and his advice. *Just ask him.* I couldn't really make things weirder now, I supposed.

Turning onto my side, I moved over to Adam and wrapped an arm around him. I brought my mouth close to his ear.

"Is this okay?" I whispered.

The seconds it took for Adam to answer were torture, but finally, he nodded. "Yeah." He glanced up at me, a secret smile darting across his face. "Yeah, it's okay."

I pulled him tighter as I lay back down. I had no idea where we went from here. No fucking clue what happened tomorrow. But for tonight, Adam was in my arms. And everything was okay.

13

ADAM

*N*o. Fucking. Way.

There was no way that just fucking happened. Impossible. You could have told me the earth was *actually* flat and I'd be more willing to believe you than if you told me that Ben kissed me last night.

It had to be some kind of fever dream, right? Maybe I'd gotten some kind of fast-acting disease from the hot tub, except instead of crabs or athlete's foot, it was some kind of prehistoric parasite that could only reproduce in a human body flooded with serotonin so it burrowed into your brain and made you hallucinate the crazy things you desperately wanted to come true but knew, in your right mind, never would.

Honestly, that would have made more sense than the thought that Ben really *had* pulled me into his arms last night. The hot press of his lips on my neck, like rose petals falling onto my night-cool skin. His weight on top of me, pushing me down on the mattress like a trap I never wanted to spring free of. The taste of his tongue, the grip of his hands on my waist and then, fuck, the way he'd stroked my cock. And he'd been just as hard as I was?

No way that was real.

Ben was straight. And even if he weren't, he wouldn't be into me. He was perfect—this blond-haired, blue-eyed teenage girl's wet dream and I was just... me. Awkward, gangly, nothing-to-write-home-about me. Brown hair, swampy green eyes, no one you'd do a double-take for on the street.

There was just no way.

Which was why, in the end, it didn't surprise me to wake up alone. Completely alone, in fact. The other bed in the room was empty too and it was just me and the sunlight streaming in from outside. I lay there for a second, trying to pull myself together. I could still hear the waves out the window.

It was a dream. That was all it had been. No matter how real it had seemed, no matter how much I swore I still felt the ghost of Ben's body cradling mine. No matter how much I missed that warmth.

I couldn't miss it—because you couldn't miss something that wasn't real. So I just had to let it go. For now, anyway. Didn't mean I wasn't going to store it up and come back to it night after night when it was just me and my hand. But better to stop thinking about that now before I got hard again. The idea was to get *out* of bed, not spend the next 30 minutes lying around in it.

I threw back the covers and stretched as I got up. A glance out the window was enough to tell me it was another perfect day. And I was going to enjoy it, dammit. Yesterday, that shit with my dad—well, I wasn't going to let him ruin a second day in a row. Though I did send Esther a quick text to let her know I was okay. She'd only texted me 13 times, so, you know, it seemed like maybe I should finally answer.

I could smell coffee wafting towards me from down the hall and I followed the scent down the hardwood floors of Gray's place until I turned right and entered the huge open kitchen at the far end of the house. It was all light marble and stainless steel appliances, stone floors, walls painted a light blue, the color of the morning sky.

Most of the guys were already in there, including Micah and Gray, over by the bagels, and then Ben, of course, peering into the refrigerator.

"Hey, not to be an ass or anything, but do you have any skim milk?" Ben asked, looking over his shoulder back at Gray. He started when he saw me. "Hey, look who's up. Morning sleepyhead."

"Hey," I said, trying not to seem like the sound of his voice made me want to break out in a song-and-dance routine. That was *not* an appropriate reaction to have to your friend, even if you were in love with him, even if you had just had the world's most realistic sex dream about him. Though, come to think of it, it hadn't technically been a sex dream. Even my subconscious must have known how crazy that idea was, and stopped short of the real thing. "Sorry, didn't mean to sleep in."

"No worries, man," Gray said with a smile. "There's no rush, it's not like the beach is going to pick up and run away if you don't get there fast enough."

"Do I smell coffee?" I asked, wrinkling my nose hopefully.

"Yeah." Gray jerked his thumb over to a small breakfast bar on the far side of the room. "Mugs are in the cabinet above the machine."

"Awesome, thanks."

I nodded at Micah as I passed and gave Ben a brief smile as I walked by the fridge where he was still examining Gray's dairy options. And then, just after I'd turned my head away, I felt his hand on my lower back. It was gone in a moment, just the briefest contact, but that warm, soft touch almost made me stop in my tracks. I kept going towards the coffee by sheer force of will but my mind was completely blank by the time I got there.

I turned around and looked back at Ben, who'd evidently found something acceptable in the fridge and was now raising his coffee mug to his lips. He gave me a satisfied smile over the brim of the mug and I stared in shock. Holy shit.

Holy shit.

What?

Had I... not... dreamt all of that, after all?

That had been Ben's hand. It had to be, it's not like anyone else had been standing by the refrigerator next to him. And the glint in his eyes now as he watched me watch him was decidedly... amused. Which meant he'd not only put his hand on my back on purpose, he was enjoying my reaction.

Holy shit.

What was happening?

My head was spinning. I forced myself to turn around and

pour my coffee before everyone else in the kitchen realized what a weirdo I was being, or caught sight of the wordless conversation volleying back and forth across the room between Ben and me.

"Milk?" Ben asked sweetly when I turned back around. He was standing right behind me. When the hell had he crossed the room?

"Uh, I'll—black's fine," I stammered, and I slipped by him and headed towards the table.

None of that made sense. I *did* take milk in my coffee and I desperately wanted to stand close to Ben. But I had a sudden, overwhelming urge to talk to him about, well, everything I'd assumed was a figment of my overactive and undersexed imagination. But that wasn't a conversation we could have in public and I wasn't sure I trusted myself to act in any way that even resembled 'normal' if I was around him.

So I took my gross black coffee to the large wooden kitchen table in the corner, the worn wooden surface warmed by the morning sun outside the windows. I sat at the edge of one of the long bench seats and listened with half a brain to the conversation Micah was having with some of the other guys about the merits of skinny jeans. I was in too much of a state of shock to contribute anything useful.

"Garlic salt, right?" Ben's voice cut through the chatter around me and I looked up to see him walking towards me from the island in the center of the kitchen.

I blinked in confusion. "What?"

Ben smiled. "Garlic salt bagel, toasted with cream cheese? That still your order?"

"That's—yeah. Yeah, it is." I shook my head, my eyes widening even further when Ben reached the table and set a plate down in front of me. A garlic salt bagel, toasted to perfection, with just the right amount of cream cheese. "How did you—"

"Remember your bizarrely stringent rules about the proper cream cheese to bagel ratio after four years of living with you where that was basically all you ate? Adam, it's tattooed on my brain. I'd forget my own birthday before I forgot how you liked your bagels."

And with that, he put his own bagel—everything with cream cheese and lox, which, for the record, I remembered too—and coffee down on the table, sat down across from me, and immediately stretched his foot out and found mine.

I tried not to choke as I felt his toes begin to push up the inside of the pajama pants I was wearing. And I was suddenly very, very grateful that I was at least wearing those. If I were dressed the way Ben was—wandering around in dark green boxer briefs and an old Operation Ivy t-shirt and looking incredibly sexy, of course—I would have had a much harder time concealing the boner I was now in danger of sporting if Ben's foot kept exploring me so intently under the table.

"So you guys still wanna head down to the beach today?" Gray asked as he sat down at the far end of the table. "Looks like perfect weather for it."

"Sounds great!" Ben said cheerfully. He grinned at me. "You in, Adam?"

"Uh, yeah," I said weakly, still having trouble focusing. "Totally."

In case you've never tried it, I don't recommend trying to eat breakfast while someone casually works his foot up and down your calves and even your thighs under the table—a breakfast table you're sharing with five other relative strangers. It's not conducive to remembering how to eat— you know, chewing, swallowing. Little details.

Finally everyone started to stand and clear up.

"Just leave everything in the sink," Gray said when Micah tried to start loading the dishwasher. "This is supposed to be vacation, right? We'll deal with it later."

"Actually, I was going to volunteer to clean up," Ben said to the group. "You guys have been so awesome letting us crash your week off. Let us help out a little."

"You really don't have to do that," Gray said, but Ben waved his objection away.

"Nah, let us. Adam will help," Ben said with a smile.

"Oh, right." I nodded, coming out of the trance I'd gotten sucked into, watching the way the muscles in Ben's arms rippled as he carried plates to the sink. I'd been busy remembering how they'd felt around me last night. Which apparently, I hadn't dreamt. "Yeah, no worries."

"We'll catch up to you guys," Ben added.

Gray shrugged. "Suit yourself."

I carried forks and coffee mugs over to the sink while everyone else filed out and had just started to walk towards the island to grab the big platter the bagels had been on when I felt those arms wrap around me again from behind. Ben pulled me back against his chest, his arms settling around my waist.

"Hey," he said softly into my hair. I heard him inhale deeply and when he breathed out, his breath was warm on my skin. His nose tickled the back of my ear as he kissed me and it was so reminiscent of last night that I just about died right there. "Good morning."

"Good morning," I said, closing my eyes for a second and enjoying the moment.

I wasn't sure what was going to happen next and in case everything went wrong—which, knowing me, seemed very likely—I wanted to savor this, wanted to make sure I could call back the golden morning light, the smell of coffee, the weight of Ben's body behind mine whenever I returned to the memory in months to come.

"Sorry to draft you into dish duty," Ben said, his lips still pressed up against my neck. "I just thought maybe we should talk."

"Right, yeah. Talk. Of course." I forced myself to pull away, to turn around and face him. Time to talk. Fuck. Things were maybe, possibly, probably, about to get very bad. "I mean, we don't have to, though, if you just wanna—"

"I *want* to talk," Ben said insistently.

Uh-oh. Was that a good sign? Didn't sound like it. Who *wants* to talk? "Okay, yeah, Um, let's talk about it then."

Ben tilted his head to the side and looked at me. "Wait, why are you being so weird? I thought... I thought last night was... good?"

"Oh." I blinked.

"Was it... not... good for you?" Ben asked, looking confused. He ran a hand through his hair. "Fuck, Adam, I didn't mean to—fuck, I wasn't trying to like, take advantage or anything or like—shit, why didn't you say something if you wanted to stop?"

"Stop?" I stared at him. "Why would you—God, no, Ben, it was good. Fuck, it was *very* good. You have no idea how long —" I cut myself off there before I could say anything truly embarrassing and tried a different tack. "I just—I didn't know if you were like, into it. Or wanted to talk about it. I mean, we've never—like, I wouldn't be mad if you wanted to just pretend it didn't happen."

"Are you insane? God, come here," Ben said, extending a hand impatiently. When I took it, he pulled me to him and circled his arms around me. I let him press me close, my face resting right below his chin. "Did you really think I was going to say I wanted to pretend it didn't happen? That I pulled you over here just to tell you I wanted to forget about it?"

"I mean, I don't know," I mumbled into his chest. My protests sounded sillier, my fears absurd now that I was in Ben's arms again. "My whole world is just kind of turned upside down right now. I don't know what to think."

Ben tipped his face down and kissed my forehead. It was exactly the kind of sweet gesture that usually put my back up, that I made fun of people doing whenever I saw it. But now that it was *Ben*, kissing *my* brow? Well, maybe I was starting to see the appeal.

"I like you," Ben said quietly. "I know that probably sounds insane, I know this probably seems crazy sudden. But I just... I do. I like you. So that's the first thing I wanted to say."

"Well I like you too, dummy. I'm pretty sure we established that years ago."

Ben snorted. "Not like that. I mean I *like* you. I just... I wasn't sure you felt the same way and I didn't want to press, didn't want to make you feel like you had to—I dunno, like just because we're friends I didn't want you to feel obligated to— fuck, I don't even know what I'm saying."

"No, it's fine. Trust me. Obligated is, uh, not the way I feel when I think of you."

I buried my face in Ben's neck and breathed deeply. There were so many other questions I had, so many things I wanted to know... And the rational part of me knew that Ben was my friend and he wouldn't get mad if I asked them. Why me? Why now? What had changed? And how real were his feelings, really—or were they maybe not even feelings at all, just the product of a late night and being horny and me being way too willing?

But the irrational part of me, the part that still couldn't wrap its mind around what had happened, was urging me to shut my damn mouth and just clutch onto this for as long as I could. That part of my brain knew me too well, knew I was all too likely to fuck this up. And it was telling me to just shut up and enjoy whatever Ben wanted to give me.

"God," I murmured. "If you'd told me a year ago. A week ago, hell a day ago—"

"That we'd be kissing in a twin bed in Montauk—"

"And then practically waking up the other person in the room?" I finished. "Yeah, definitely would not have believed you. This is still just so crazy."

"I mean, we can still take it slow," Ben said. "There's no pressure to like, decide anything too soon or whatever."

"Right. Right, yeah, totally," I said, turning my face down to Ben's chest. That made sense, that he wouldn't want to put a label on this... whatever it was. I couldn't blame him for that. But I also didn't need him to see the disappointment in my eyes.

Which was completely ridiculous, anyway. What right did I have to be disappointed that Ben wasn't getting down on one knee and proposing to me when he'd just kissed a guy for the first time, a guy who happened to be his friend and a total weirdo? No right at all.

I was probably still just feeling needy because of what had happened with Ellis. Of course Ben didn't want to blow up his whole life over something that probably wasn't going to mean anything to him, something that probably wasn't going to last past this week.

"Let's just enjoy this," I said, making myself smile. It wasn't that hard to do. Even if I was being a ridiculous sap, I still knew better than to squander whatever chance I got with Ben, no matter how brief. "For whatever it is."

I looked up at Ben then and caught him smiling down at me and there was a look in his eyes I couldn't interpret, but then he was kissing me and it didn't matter anymore—I had more important things on my mind.

Ben's lips were soft and smooth as they pressed against mine but I wasn't in the mood for softness. I slid my tongue against his bottom lip and he opened up, letting me inside. Fuck, I still couldn't believe this was Ben I was kissing, Ben who I'd dreamed of kissing oh, maybe only a million times.

And here he was, the heat of his body merging with mine, bending down to claim my mouth greedily. His tongue was velvet, sweet as it explored my mouth and someone—okay, me—made a noise that might have been a whimper—okay, it was—but I couldn't even bring myself to care.

My hands went to his face, his back, his neck. I needed to feel his skin under my fingertips, needed to reassure myself that this was truly happening. And then Ben's arms squeezed me tighter, pressing my body firmly against him and any doubts were banished because fuck, I could feel his cock, hard and hot, up against my hip. I rolled my body forward, seeking friction and was rewarded with a moan from Ben when my cock slid against his.

"Fuck," Ben groaned when he finally pulled away. "Fuck, I'm... kind of tempted to say we should just go back to bed while everyone's out of the house, but we did say we'd do the dishes and then they might start wondering where we are."

"Yeah, I'm not sure we need to go two for two with getting interrupted by Gray's friends," I laughed.

"Good point." Ben smiled at me. "Besides, there's no rush, right? We've got all the time in the world."

I smiled. No matter what happened, no matter what came next, I was going to enjoy that. And I wasn't going to complain, or ask for more.

"All the time in the world sounds excellent."

"What's up?" Ben asked me later that day as he walked back towards me from the cooler. He glanced significantly at my phone as he handed me one of the two beers he was carrying and flopped down onto the blanket we'd spread out in the sand.

"Just heard back from Angela," I said. "She wants me to send her the new stuff I've been working on."

"That's awesome." Ben smiled. "Congrats."

"It *is* awesome." I grinned. "Not going broke is pretty exciting. Besides, if I manage to sell most of the new stuff, I think I really will be able to start paying Esther back for Peachtree too."

Ben sighed and looked out at the campfire Gray and Chris were building. "Didn't she say not to worry about that?"

"Yeah. But still. I don't want to be a burden."

"That's not how family works," Ben said, sounding a little exasperated.

"Maybe not yours," I shot back. "But mine... Rationally, I know Esther doesn't resent me for it. But it just... it feels like as long as I owe her, I'm never going to be like, me again. Better. Fixed or whatever."

Ben shot me an intense look. "Nothing about you needs to be fixed. And I promise you, Esther doesn't care. When people love you, they don't calculate things like that."

"Eww, get out of here with that *'love is patient, love is kind'* bullshit."

"There's a reason people quote that, you know."

"That doesn't make it any less gross."

"Seriously, Micah?" Gray's voice cut across the evening air and we all looked up to see Micah coming down from the house with a guitar in hand.

"What, man?" Micah said, feigning hurt. "How am I ever supposed to get better if I don't practice."

"How come your practicing only ever happens when my ears are around to be tortured?"

"Shut up, I'm awesome," Micah said, making a face. He sat down on a long piece of driftwood and brought the guitar into his lap.

"Awesome's one word for it. Like a donkey stepping on a banjo is another word."

"That's like, six words. Besides, all great artists were disparaged in their time, only to be appreciated years later."

As Micah started to play, Ben slid closer to me on the blanket and put his hand on my leg. I looked over at him in confusion.

"Dude. Everyone's here."

"Eh, I don't think these guys are gonna care."

"You wanna call Shereen and tell her that?"

Ben rolled his eyes and then took my hand, twining our fingers together. "You're taking all the fun out of this, you know. Unless—" he looked at me, frowning, "unless it bothers you?"

"No. No. It's..." I laughed softly. "It was just unexpected. It's nice."

"Don't sound so surprised. It's *supposed* to feel nice."

"Well, first time for everything, I guess."

Ben squinted at me. "First time you've liked letting someone hold your hand or first time someone's tried to do it?"

"I plead the fifth."

Ben just looked at me and his eyes were so bright and so earnest and so blue that I had to look down.

"Hey Adam?"

I risked a glance up. Ben's eyes were still shining and he was biting back a smile.

"What?"

"I'm just... I'm really happy right now."

I looked around at the setting sun, the bonfire, the waves lapping at the shore down on the beach and realized that I was happy too. Happier than I could remember being in a long time. Maybe almost ever. And that terrified me.

I squeezed Ben's hand tighter.

"What the hell is Micah even playing?" Ben asked a little later as Micah finished one song and launched into another.

I'd stopped paying attention a while ago, just letting my mind merge with the sound of the waves, and I pulled it back and listened with some effort.

"Oh God, I think that's *Good Riddance.*" I frowned. "Well, it might be. If it is, he's flubbing every other note so it's kind of hard to be sure."

Ben cocked an eyebrow. "*Good Riddance?*"

I sighed. "*Time of Your Life.*"

"Ohh, right." Ben laughed. "I think I knew that." He looked over at me and batted his eyelashes. "Do you not like me anymore because of my ignorance of Green Day's 1990s catalog?"

"You're on probation, maybe."

"Hmm." Ben wiggled his eyebrows. "I wonder what I could do to get off of that."

My stomach turned a somersault.

"Five bucks says he plays *Everlong* next," I said, mostly just to distract myself from the way my body wanted to launch itself at Ben right then.

"Oh yeah?"

"Every guy with a guitar learns how to play that and they all think you've never heard it acoustic before and that it'll change your life."

"I mean, it is a pretty song," Ben said.

"It's overdone. And maudlin. Too sentimental by half."

"Right, I forgot." Ben snorted. "Displays of feeling are capital offenses in Adamland."

"Exactly. See, you're learning."

"God, how do you tolerate me?"

"With great difficulty," I said, giving him my most put-upon look.

"Next thing you know I'm going to be trying to take you out on a date or something."

"Gag me. You can ask, but good luck getting me to say yes."

Ben laughed. "Challenge accepted."

I rolled my eyes but squeezed Ben's hand again. Going on a date with him was not something I'd ever let myself picture. Somehow, that would have felt even more forbidden than imagining Ben's cock up my ass—and that was saying something.

God, I was truly depraved. Going on a date and holding hands. My most shameful kinks.

"Adam." Gray's voice pulled me out of my reverie. "Adam, don't you play guitar?"

I expected Ben to drop my hand but he didn't. Gray's eyes flickered over our hands but he didn't say anything.

"Uh, yeah. Yeah, I mean, a little. So does Ben."

"He's being modest because he thinks it's cute," Ben said. "He actually plays incredibly well."

"Then will you please take the guitar from Micah's meat paws and save us from his artistic stylings?"

"Oh, I don't know." I felt myself flushing. It shouldn't have been a big deal. It's not like we were a big group, and I knew the guys pretty well after spending the day with them. But still, I could feel my pulse quickening.

"Come on, consider it rent for the week," Gray said with a

smile. "Do us all a favor. I don't think I can stand to listen to another butchered Oasis song."

"You don't have to," Ben said, so quietly that no one else could have heard. I turned and stared at him. "Not unless you want to."

Something warm and gooey washed all over me at those words. God, what was happening to me? It was like heart jizz or something. Was I really that pathetic?

But somehow, I did feel better. And fuck it—maybe it would be good to try. Ben would be there anyway. That made it feel easier.

"Fine," I said, standing up and brushing the sand off my pants. "But you guys have to tell me what you want to hear."

I walked over and joined Micah on the driftwood log, taking the guitar as he offered it to me. It took a second to get my bearings, feeling the light body of the guitar in my hands. Instruments always felt alive to me and each one had its own personality.

I ran my hands along the wood, getting a feel for this particular guitar. It had a really nice sound, when Micah hadn't been strangling it. I removed the capo he'd been using and then tuned the E string, which had been sounding a little flat.

"Uh, what do you want me to play?" I asked, looking up at the group.

"*Everlong*," Ben called out. "It's my favorite."

I rolled my eyes. "Anything *other* than *Everlong*."

"*Total Eclipse of the Heart*," Ben shouted out again.

"Okay, anyone other than *Ben* wanna make a request?"

"Can you play *Layla*?" Gray asked.

I nodded. "Sure."

Everyone wants to learn that song when they pick up a guitar, usually with no idea how different it sounds when you're playing by yourself instead of with a full band. But still, it was nice to play something so familiar, so... obvious. When my fingers slid along the strings and started plucking, I still felt a bit disconnected from what I was doing, so at least it was a song I knew well.

I stared down at the instrument, willing myself not to fuck it up. But after my fingers almost slipped, I realized I was concentrating too hard. I snapped my head up, meaning to look out at the ocean beyond us. But my eyes were drawn to Ben instead.

He was smiling at me with the goofiest look on his face and it was so pure, so fucking joyful it should have made me want to throw up—or at least make fun of him. But somehow, when his eyes met mine, it was just what I needed. He stared at me and smiled until I smiled back and suddenly, I was there again. Back in the song, connected to the instrument in my hands. It felt good. Right. By the time I got to the end of what was usually a piano coda, I was actually enjoying myself.

I played for ages after that, or at least it felt that way. The guys kept shouting out songs and if I didn't know them, I made them sing a little bit until I could pick out the chords underneath. It was nice, doing it that way—I was less on the spot and they seemed to like performing. And despite his atrocious guitar skills, Micah did actually have a nice voice.

Eventually, though, I made Ben come up and join me so that I could stop singing entirely. I can carry a tune just fine, but my voice isn't anything special. Ben's voice, though. Ben's voice is like liquid sunshine. It's like butter melting into fresh baked bread. It's like church and sex at the same time. It gave me chills, the first time I heard him sing in college. It still did.

Finally, Gray suggested we go inside. It was almost too dark to see and while I didn't need the light to keep playing, it was getting a little chilly. I started to stand and join the others, but Ben tugged on my hand, pulled me back down onto the log.

"What?" I asked, giving him a bemused look.

He stared back at me, his eyes wide. "You were amazing tonight."

"Eh, I was okay."

Ben snickered. "Well, that's basically your version of saying, *'Yeah, you're right,'* so I'll take it. How did it feel?"

"Actually? Not that bad. I don't know. This is going to sound so dorky—"

"Oh my God, say it, I can't wait—"

"But I think maybe it's easier to play when you're here. I don't get so—so panicky, I guess?"

"Hmm." Ben smiled. "Sounds like you'd better keep me around then, huh?"

"Yeah, maybe."

Don't read too much into that. He's just being Ben. Being sweet is

the same as breathing for him. He wants to take it slow.
Remember that.

But still—keep him around? I'd keep him forever if I could.

I started to stand again but as I did, my hand strummed across the strings and the sound plucked at something in the back of my mind. That song of Ben's. What if I added a G chord to...

I sat back down, smiling in response to Ben's questioning look, and ran through the melody again, then shifted into what I'd begun to think of as the chorus. But this time, I shifted the chord structure slightly so that—yes, that was it. There was that rich, warm sound, the notes dancing like red and orange flames, the chords burning like embers. Fuck, that was it—that was perfect.

Ben was staring at me when I finished.

"That was amazing," he said, his voice hushed.

"Now you just have to think of lyrics for it."

"Why do I have to do all the work?" Ben pouted. "It's your song."

"It's *our* song," I corrected him. Ben's eyes went wide and I heard what I'd said. "Eww, God, no, *not* like that, *not* what I meant."

"Nuh-uh, you can't take that back now," Ben said, clearly delighted. "You said it, not me. We have a song. *Our Song.* Oh, Adam, you really *do* like me." He clasped his hands to his chest.

"Okay, you have to stop or I will stop talking to you entirely."

"Doesn't matter," Ben grinned. "You'll never be able to unsay it. This is an unalterable fact in the history of time—we have a song. A song that you wrote—for me."

"I hate you so much right now."

"Are you two coming in?" Gray asked. I looked up and realized everyone else had packed up and Gray had just finished dousing the fire.

"Yeah, we'll be in in a second," Ben said. He took the guitar from me and held it out to Gray. "You mind taking this in for us?"

I expected Gray to say something, make some kind of comment, but he didn't. He just smiled, said, "Sure," and took the guitar. I watched him walk away, amazed at his unflappability. He had to know, didn't he? But he apparently really didn't care.

I looked back at Ben. "Why did you wanna—"

Ben leaned in and kissed me, almost knocking me off the log with the sudden movement. My hands flew to his shoulders to steady myself and his arms slid around my waist. When we broke apart, I was breathless.

"What if someone—any of them could have seen."

"Fuck it," Ben said, his smile wicked. "I've been wanting to do that all day. Do you have any idea how gorgeous you are?"

"What?" I practically yelped it, followed by a high-pitched laugh. "No."

"No you don't know or no you're not?"

"Either. Both." I squirmed. "Stop being weird."

"I'm not being weird. I'm just trying to tell my best friend that he's hot."

"Right, 'cause that's normal. Just hitting on your friend. Like bros do."

"Just guys being dudes." Ben fixed me with a stare. "You are, though."

I could feel my face heating up. This was the part where I was supposed to learn to believe Ben, to see myself the way he saw me, but the idea that I was hot somehow just seemed ludicrous. I wasn't hideous, but I'd never felt attractive either.

If I were honest, I'd always felt vaguely uncomfortable in my own body. Too skinny, too gangly. I got the feeling that if I thought about it too hard, I'd forget how to make my limbs work. One of the reasons I liked music so much was that it got me *out* of my own body.

It was like I could live in the instrument in my hands, in the song itself. The part of me that was *me* merged with the notes and I left that awkward, bony exoskeleton that was 'Adam Hart' behind. It was when I felt most at peace.

Ben laughed softly. "I can see those gears turning in your head, trying to find a way to deny it."

"Shut up."

"Great comeback there."

I pushed him on the shoulder.

"Oh good, we're regressing even further. Next you're going to pull my hair and then run away from me during recess."

"Hey, I never claimed to be any good at this..." I trailed off, because I still didn't know what to even call *this*, this thing we were maybe doing.

"You're perfect." Ben's voice was quiet but assured.

He stood up and held out his hands for me to follow. I looked at him questioningly but let him pull me up and walk me over to the blanket we'd been sitting on before. He must have grabbed another one when I was playing because once we were lying down, facing each other, he smiled and pulled the second blanket over us.

"I wanted to make sure we had some time to be alone tonight," Ben said, grinning. "Before we go back to our twin bed and our bunkmate."

My stomach somersaulted again and my heart began beating even faster. Everything seemed to have gone very still all of a sudden. The night felt clear, crystalline, like any sharp movement could shatter it.

"Where'd you go?" Ben whispered.

"What?"

"Your eyes," Ben said. "You just... you do this thing, sometimes. Where you're looking at something but you're not really seeing it. It's like you go somewhere else."

"Oh." I flushed. "Sorry."

"No," Ben said. He took my hand in his own. "It's nothing to be sorry for. I just wanted to know. So I could go with you."

"I'm just..." I didn't know how to put it into words, this feeling like this might just be the best night of my life, the exquisite terror of finally getting the thing you've dreamed of for so long. The panic that something is going to go wrong. The certainty that you don't deserve this. "Just nervous, I guess."

"We don't have to—I mean, if you're having second thoughts—"

"It's not that," I said quickly. "It's just... It's just, you're my best friend, you know? What happens if this goes... wrong, somehow? And we're not friends anymore?"

"I promise that won't happen."

"I know you believe that, but you can't actually promise that, you know? Like, I want to believe that too, but there's no way to know and that's a little terrifying, don't you think?"

"Okay." Ben nodded slowly. "Okay, so maybe you can't believe that. But can you believe me? Believe that I believe that this is good? And worth taking a chance on?"

What are we taking a chance on though? What is it that you want?

And why am I not brave enough to ask?

"How can you know, though? If you've never..."

Ben smiled. "I just do. I know you. I want you."

He brought his hand up to my face, rubbed his thumb along my cheek. I leaned into his touch, embarrassed but unable to stop myself. God, I'd wanted this for so long and now that this crazy, unbelievable fantasy was coming true, I was trying to find ways to push it away? What was wrong with me?

And so I opened my eyes. "Okay." I bit my lip, nodded. "I believe you."

"Good."

Ben's hand moved to the back of my head and he pulled me in for a kiss. His lips tasted salty, slightly chapped from the sun and the wind, and I ran my tongue along his lower lip, pulling it out and sucking it into my mouth. Ben moaned and my eyes flew open. His eyes were closed but he looked, improbable as it seemed, like he was enjoying himself.

And fuck it. Tonight, at least, I was going to stop second guessing.

I pushed forward, rolling Ben over onto his back and straddling him. Ben's hands went to my waist and I liked the way they fit there, liked the comfort of being in Ben's grasp, safe under the blankets, the sand underneath still warm from the day's sun.

I propped myself up on my elbows and rolled my hips forward, pressing up against Ben. I could feel Ben's cock hardening beneath me, feel my own cock stiffening in response to the friction, and I smiled. The thin fabric of our bathing suits left little to the imagination and I was grateful for it.

"Fuck," Ben groaned as I rolled my hips again again, and his eyes flew open. The blue of his irises was a pale gray in the dark but they were still beautiful. "Fuck, Adam."

He pulled my face closer to his, taking a hungry kiss. I was needy, responsive, my cock twitching as Ben's strong, warm hand rubbed the back of my neck. I couldn't stop a moan from escaping me as his other hand slid from my waist down to my ass.

Fuck, he was really going for it.

For the amount of times that I'd fantasized about this, I was suddenly scared shitless. What if Ben didn't like whatever we did? What if it grossed him out—what if I grossed him out? I couldn't handle that. But I also couldn't handle stopping right now.

Ben's hand cupped my ass, then squeezed it. I whimpered and Ben thrust his hips up, his cock pushing against mine. He was kneading my ass with both hands now as he thrust upwards and I rolled my hips in response, meeting his movements with answering friction, our bodies working together like they'd been designed for this.

"Oh, fuck, Ben," I breathed, mortified at how needy, how pleading my voice sounded and unable to do anything to stop it.

Because I did need Ben, and he seemed to get that, gripping me tighter now. My hips moved faster in response. I'd been thinking about blowing him but fuck, I was so close now and I didn't want to stop.

It should have been ridiculous, the two of us rutting against each other like teenagers in the backseat of a car, but with the cool air above and the heavy scratch of the wool blankets and the warm, firm anchor of Ben's body under me, it was just... perfect.

I ground down onto Ben harder. His breath was coming out in pants now, the two of us moving together like we shared a body. I was so close, and when Ben pulled me down and kissed my neck, running his tongue along the same spot where he'd kissed me last night, I knew I was going to lose it.

Ben's tongue moved to my ear, swirling around the inside once before licking the lobe, then sucking it in between his teeth. A shudder of pleasure ran through me.

"Fuck, Ben, I'm gonna—" I tried to pull away, tried to warn him, but I couldn't get the words out. It felt too good and Ben kept hipping his body hard against my cock.

"Come with me," Ben whispered, biting down on my earlobe, and his words unlocked something inside me.

My body took over, grinding down onto Ben, letting out a wordless moan of pleasure as I came. My orgasm unfurled across me in waves, nearly knocking me senseless in its intensity. Years of desire, years of pent up longing, finally coming out.

I thought I might have been saying Ben's name, confessing all sorts of embarrassing things, but I couldn't tell because I was seeing fucking fireworks and not really in my body anymore. Ben's movements grew faster, more frantic, and then his hands tightened on my ass as he stuttered beneath me.

"Adam, oh God, Adam," Ben whispered as he came. From his lips, my name was a perfect note, ringing out beneath the stars. Our bodies and the night sky--bound together in the dark.

This, I thought. This is it.

This is our song.

14

BEN

"So," Gray said, coming to stand next to me on the deck later that week.

Adam was watching Micah play the guitar down on the beach and correcting his technique. And I was standing there, leaning against the railing, just watching Adam. Like you do.

"So," I said, glancing back at Gray.

"You and Adam seem... different."

I snorted. "That's a diplomatic way of putting it."

"You took my advice then?"

"Well, it's more that I just kinda kissed him in my sleep. But it seems to have had the desired effect."

"That's one way of doing it," Gray laughed. "But good for you. You seem happy."

"I am." I grinned at him. "I really, really am. It's been a good week."

"When you two get married, I'm telling that story at your wedding though. *'I just kinda kissed him in my sleep.'* So romantic. Also, btw, I'm taking all of the credit for this."

"Gray, I'd be disappointed if you didn't."

My phone buzzed in my pocket and I pulled it out to see that my mom was calling me.

"You mind if I?"

"Take it," Gray smiled. "I'll be in the kitchen, putting the calligraphy on your wedding invitations, if you need me."

I rolled my eyes as he walked away, then answered the phone.

"Hey Ma. What's up?"

"Oh, just checking in," my mom said. Her voice had that too-casual sound that meant she was most definitely *not* just checking in. "How're you doing, sweetie?"

"Um... good?"

"Have you talked to Mia recently?"

"Ma, I've told you, she and I are just—"

"Well I *know* that," my mom said fussily. "But I couldn't help but see all these things about Mia in the news this week. And you know, sometimes your feelings for a friend can turn into something more when you least expect it. I just wanted to make sure you were doing okay."

She had no idea how right she was.

"I really am. I promise." I sighed. "I wish she'd return my

phone calls because I still have no clue what's going on with her. But honestly, I'm fine. I'm at the beach, actually."

"Oh, well that's exciting." My mom perked up. "Whereabouts?"

"Montauk, if you can believe that." I shook my head. "One of my friends has a house out here, it turns out. Shereen wanted me to keep a low profile until all this Mia stuff calms down so we decided to just head out here for a while."

"We? Is Adam still with you?"

"Yeah." I smiled. "Yeah, he is."

"Good," my mom said firmly. "I worry about him sometimes, you know?"

"I'll be sure to pass that along. Anyway, now that we've established that I'm not dying of a broken heart—and that you spend too much time reading gossip blogs—anything else new?"

"Oh, not much. Work's always slow in the summer. Though actually, that's been good because we had to take Lacey to the doctor a couple days ago and I was able to take off. It's so different when school's in session."

"Wait, what? Lacey had to go to the doctor?"

"She just needed to get some tests, honey, everything's fine."

"Ma, you're supposed to tell me these things."

"I didn't want to worry you, sweetheart, not until we knew what we were dealing with. And it turned out to be nothing so there was no reason to bother you about it."

"Running tests doesn't sound like nothing," I said, frowning. "What happened?"

"She just hasn't been feeling herself lately," my mom said. "And you know that her heart problems may get worse with age, so we wanted to check. But the results looked normal, so the doctor thinks she probably just had the flu. She seems perkier already, so please don't worry, honey."

"Do you want me to come home? What do you mean *'not feeling like herself?'*"

"No, sweetie, you don't need to come home. Why don't you come out for dinner again soon, though? That could be fun."

"I will," I said seriously. Lacey had seemed fine just five days ago when Adam and I were there. I felt like an asshole, spending the past week on the beach while she was sick. "But seriously Ma, can you tell me about these things when they happen from now on? How can I take care of her if I don't even know what's wrong?"

"Honey, you don't have to take care of everything. You know that, right?"

"I know but—"

"Oh, there goes the timer," my mom said, over the sudden sound of beeping in the background. "The broccoli's done. Sweetie, I have to go but we'll talk soon, okay?"

"Okay. But—"

"And yes, I'll tell you if anything else happens. Give my love to Adam!"

"Bye, Ma."

BEN>> Sesquipedalian?

That was the text I'd sent to Mia the morning Shereen called me at my parents' house. And after she hadn't responded, or answered my calls, I'd sent a series of increasingly more frantic ones. As the week went on, reports only got stranger. Mia and Tate had had another huge fight at a casino. Then she'd disappeared and popped up again in LA after cutting off all her hair—not shaving her head, just doing a hatchet job like a kindergartner with safety scissors. And now, apparently, they were getting the marriage annulled.

Shereen had told me she'd finally caught up with Mia in LA and to sit tight, so I was surprised when my phone buzzed on our sixth day at Gray's house.

MIA>> Hey, um, sorry I'm the worst

I texted her back immediately.

BEN>> You're not the worst at all.

BEN>> Are you ok?

MIA>> Yeah. Kind of. Mostly

BEN>> Fair enough

MIA>> Shereen'll probably update you on everything but I just wanted to tell you how sorry I am for fucking everything up. It's not just my career I'm ruining, I know this affects you too. I'm gonna be taking a step back for a while and sorting some things out

BEN>> Do whatever you need, take care of you

BEN>> You did NOT fuck everything up. I promise

MIA>> I mean, I kinda did. I married my cheating ex boyfriend and then let him dump me all over again. And my hair looks like someone ran a lawnmower over it

BEN>> Pssh it's the new pixie cut. You're a trendsetter

MIA>> Maybe.

MIA>> Have you heard of a place called Peachtree?

BEN>> Uh yeah. Why?

MIA>> Shereen wants me to go there and like, find myself or whatever. So I'm gonna take some time off. A few weeks maybe. And I probably won't have my phone with me. But just... know that I'm sorry and thanks for being such an amazing friend

BEN>> Nothing to be sorry for

BEN>> Hugs

MIA>> :)

Before I could even put my phone back in my pocket, it buzzed again, this time with a message—a novel, really— from Shereen.

SHEREEN>> Mia said she talked to u, she's going to Peachtree Ctr tmrw. Announcing that she's taking some time to focus on herself. Need u to be supportive bf still. Prob do some press. We can salvage this for Mia - ur sales will prob go thru the roof too, ppl love this shit. Come by Mon to talk, k?

BEN>> Ok. See you Monday

I sighed and put my phone away. I wanted to do what I could for Mia and if playing the loving boyfriend role would help, I would do it. But I wasn't thrilled about it. Not when things with Adam were going so well.

Granted, it had only been a week but still—I'd been looking forward to getting free of Greenleaf and getting to be myself again. But even if I did go independent now, how long was I going to have to keep up the charade with Mia?

I glanced over at Adam where he sat on the far side of the deck, alternately strumming something on the guitar and scribbling in his notebook. God, how the hell had I gotten so lucky? He was a fucking genius. How was it possible he felt the same way about me as I did about him?

I didn't have any answers. But I didn't want to waste the day feeling disgruntled when I could be spending it with him instead, so I wandered over and sat down across from him at the deck table.

"How's the work coming?" I asked.

Adam jumped, noticing me for the first time, and I grinned. When he got really focused on music, he zoned out completely. You could sing the Star Spangled Banner naked while juggling frogs and he wouldn't notice.

"Sorry," he said with a sheepish grin. "I didn't—uh, what did you say?"

"I said how's the work going?"

"Good, actually?" He laughed, sounding surprised. "I'm feeling weirdly inspired."

"I'm glad to know I inspire you," I said, arching an eyebrow.

"I never said it was *you*," he retorted. "Maybe it's Gray who inspires me."

"Dammit, I really have some porn to catch up on, don't I?" I peered over at his notebook. "Songs for Angela?"

"Some," Adam nodded. "There are some I'm kind of attached to, though. I don't really want to sell them, but I don't know what else to do with them."

"Play them?"

Adam made a face. "I'm not sure I'm gonna be doing that for a while. Or maybe ever."

"Really?" I blinked. That was new.

"I don't know." Adam shrugged. "Ever since the night at The Grasshopper, the thought of playing in public just kind of makes me nauseous. And I never really liked performing anyway."

"We used to play together all the time," I said. "I always thought you liked that."

"But that's different. That was just us fucking around. It was fun. And playing with you isn't stressful in the same way. But the band... the band was never supposed to last anyway. It was just supposed to be a way to record some of the bigger songs for demos so I could sell them. And then it just took on this life of its own and I didn't feel like I could tell them I didn't want to do it anymore—didn't want it to be my fault the band fell apart."

"A really wise person once told me you have to do what makes you happy," I said with a grin. "So I'm gonna quote them right back at you. Even if it does make me a little sad you might never play a show again."

"Yeah?"

"Yeah. I was going to stand in the front row and flash my tits at you."

"You would," Adam said, rolling his eyes.

"Anyway, are you at a good stopping point?" I asked, gesturing to the guitar.

"I could be. Why?"

"I feel cooped up. Wanna walk into town and get ice cream or something?"

Adam looked at me suspiciously. "Aren't you supposed to be staying out of sight?"

"I just got the all clear from Shereen. She wants me back in the city by Monday. Apparently Mia's going to be taking some time off—at Peachtree, of all places—so we need to hold a strategy meeting or something like that. And if my life is about to become ridiculous again, I want to enjoy the rest of this week while I can."

Adam gave me a strange look but then nodded. "Sure, then. Why not."

The day was gorgeous—hot, dry, and almost windless, which was impressive for a strip of land as far out into the ocean as Montauk is. The sky was a blue bowl overhead and gulls screeched as they circled above us, looking for food. I reached for Adam's hand as we walked along the sandy path to town and Adam looked at me suspiciously.

"What?" I said, grinning. "You admitted the other day it wasn't the *worst* thing in the world. And it sounds like you've got years of practice to make up for."

"Remedial hand-holding, huh?" Adam asked.

"Yep. Next comes Cuddling 101 and then Advanced Pet Names."

"Pardon me while I vomit out my insides," Adam said drily. But he didn't drop my hand until we got to town

"Civilization, remember?" he said when I frowned. "You're kind of famous, in case you've forgotten. You probably shouldn't be seen holding hands with a guy."

Even though Adam had a point, I didn't like it. I knew I was probably freaking out over nothing but there was a part of me that couldn't help but worry about Adam's reaction to, well, all of this. He did like me, right? It wasn't like I was surprised by his aversion to everything romantic. But it would have been nice if I didn't feel like I had to pry every bit of affection out of him with a crowbar.

But of course, Adam was completely right. Because as soon as we got in line for ice cream, a girl standing in front of us with her mom turned around.

"Are you Ben Thomas?" she asked, her voice so breathy and nervous that it was almost inaudible.

"Yeah." I gave her a big smile, hoping it would put her at ease a bit. "Yeah, I am."

"Holy shit," she squeaked.

"Language, Samantha," her mother said, turning around.

"Sorry. I just mean like. Wow. Um, hi!" Samantha's face turned bright red as her eyes darted back and forth between her mother and me.

"Hi," I laughed. "It's nice to meet you Samantha."

"You too." And then she stared at me silently, her eyes wide, and I wondered if she'd gone mute from excitement. She clearly wanted to keep talking but if I didn't say something, we were just going to stand there staring at each other for all eternity.

"So are you guys here on vacation? Or do you and your family live out here?" I asked after a moment, searching for something to say. I smiled at Samantha's mother, trying to include her in the conversation, but I didn't need to bother. Apparently, that had opened the floodgates.

"Vacation," Samantha said, "for one more week, and then I have to go to summer camp, which is the worst."

I asked her why she hated it so much and Samantha treated us to a five minute monologue about the general unfairness of not being allowed to stay home and watch tv all summer and having to go spend time *living in tents in the woods*, which was apparently a fate worse than death.

Adam was practically wheezing by the time Samantha and her mom got their ice cream and left, Samantha the proud owner of a new selfie with Ben Thomas who had—stupid asshole that he was—also promised to mail her a postcard at camp.

"Really bucking for Miss Congeniality there, aren't you," he smirked.

"Shut up." I rolled my eyes. "It'll make Shereen happy. It's a nice thing to do that requires like, no effort on my part. Well, except maybe finding a postcard. And stamps."

Thankfully, the older woman at the counter of the ice cream shop seemed to have no idea who I was.

"What can I get you?" she asked, sounding supremely bored. Music to my ears, really.

"Mint chocolate chip for me." I looked at Adam. "What are you having?"

"Oh, you don't have to—I can get my own," Adam said.

"Dude it's like, six bucks. Don't worry about it."

Adam sighed. "Fine. Salted caramel then. Show off."

We wandered over to a bench in a small park on the far side of the street and sat, looking at that the waves down on the beach.

"Don't even think about offering to pay me back for this," I said.

Adam frowned. "Anyone ever tell you you can be a real pill?"

"Yeah, but you like me anyway, right?"

"I don't have feelings, remember? I don't know where you got the impression that I did."

I smacked my hand to my forehead. "Silly me, assuming that someone whispering my name as they jerked me off meant something."

"Jesus, Ben." Adam's face turned bright red and he looked around the park in a panic.

"Oh, no one's close enough to hear." There were a few other groups of people scattered around but none of them seemed interested in our conversation. "Now tell me you like me."

"I thought I told you not to fish for compliments."

"Yeah, but I ignored you. Come on, say it. Say it say it say it."

I batted my eyelashes at him aggressively and leaned so far over to him on the bench that I was practically horizontal.

"Ugh, fine, I like you, jeez," Adam said, before looking down and yelping. "Hey! You're dripping on me!"

My eyes followed his and saw that my ice cream had, indeed, melted a bit and dripped down onto Adam's arm. I took a quick glance around us and, ascertaining that no one was paying attention, bent down and licked the ice cream off of Adam's skin.

"Fucking hell, Ben," Adam groaned.

"What?" I asked, sitting back up. "Don't tell me that grosses you out."

"The opposite," Adam grumbled as he straightened up as well. "But you're going to give me a boner if you do shit like that in public and that's gonna be awkward."

"I'll take that under advisement."

"Asshole," Adam muttered, his cheeks still pink.

"Ben? Holy shit, Adam? I haven't seen you in ages."

Both Adam and I turned around to see Luke walking towards us in a full suit and tie. I waved and Adam smiled but I noticed he moved further away from me on the bench.

"Hey Luke," I said as he got closer. "How's it going?"

"Eh, can't complain. Here on a client visit but at least I'm out of the city, right?"

"Fair enough."

Luke turned and looked at Adam. "Long time no see, dude. How long's it been?"

"Not sure. Since that awful rooftop party you dragged us to the summer after graduation?" Adam grinned. "You still selling your soul to the highest bidder down on Wall Street?"

"More or less," Luke said. "You still toiling away in noble but obscure poverty?"

Adam laughed. "Basically."

"Seriously, though, how are you?" Luke fixed Adam with one of his trademark *'you're the most fascinating person I've ever met, please tell me your life story'* stares. They could be a little disconcerting if you weren't used to them and I was pretty sure that's why he was so good at drumming up investments.

"Oh, you know," Adam said. "Had a mental breakdown, went to an inpatient psychiatric clinic for a month, discovered I was homeless when I got out. The usual."

"How boring," Luke laughed.

"I know, right?" Adam snorted. "Oh, and I'm gay now."

Luke grinned. "So passé. Isn't everybody?"

"I know. Just had to jump on the bandwagon." Adam shrugged.

"So what are you guys doing out here," Luke asked. He frowned at me. "Did you mention coming out here and I just forgot?"

"Nah." I shook my head. "I've just been under house arrest while my manager was taking care of some PR stuff."

"Ah, right." Luke nodded. "Yeah, I'd uh, heard something about that. How... are things?" He frowned. "I'm not sure what I'm really supposed to ask here. It seems weird to ask about your relationship when I could read about it in *US Weekly*."

"It's okay," I said. "It's a weird situation all around. We're just trying to take it a day at a time right now."

That seemed like a safe, non-committal answer. Dammit, I really did need to talk to Shereen. Luke was a friend but I knew Shereen would want me to keep the circle of people who knew the truth about me and Mia small. Which meant I really needed to figure out what my answer was. At least until I could be done with the whole fake relationship.

"Cool," Luke said. "Well, good luck. And you know, if you ever get tired of dating famous people, there are a couple of women in my office who would probably commit a felony to go on a date with you."

"Uh, thanks. That's... reassuring?"

"I gotta head back to the city," Luke said. "But we should all hang out sometime soon, yeah?"

"Sounds good," I said, looking over at Adam who nodded vaguely. He was being weirdly quiet and I wasn't sure why. "Oh, hey, while I'm thinking about it—can you move some more money over into my parents' account? Lacey just had some more tests done and I want to make sure they have enough to cover everything."

"Sure. Just email me the amount and I'll take care of it."

Luke waved goodbye and Adam and I finished our ice cream in silence. I kept waiting for him to say something but he didn't, so finally I just suggested heading back. I took his hand again once we were on the path home but Adam didn't seem to want to hold mine. His fingers were limp, loose, and eventually I just gave up.

"Okay, what's wrong?" I asked, unable to bear the silence any longer as we approached the final curve in the path back to Gray's place.

"What? Nothing," Adam said, looking up from where he'd been studying the sand underneath our feet. He looked surprised.

"You're doing it again. Your eyes are all far away. What are you thinking about?"

"Nothing," Adam insisted. "Really."

"I don't buy it."

Adam sighed. "It's really not important."

"Well it is to me, even if it's not to you. So come on. What's up?"

"I don't know," Adam began. He looked away from me before he spoke again. "I guess it's just that we're going back to the city tomorrow."

"So?"

"So this week is ending." Adam shrugged. "I guess I'm just feeling like, pre-nostalgic for it. Missing something while it's still happening. How messed up is that?"

"We can always come back, though," I said.

"Yeah. Sure."

"Seriously." I frowned. "Anytime. We could just rent a place or stay in a hotel or—"

"No, I know," Adam interrupted. "It's not that. It's just... ugh, I hate this."

"Hate what?"

"Hate liking you, okay?" Adam said, finally turning and looking at me again. His eyes burned angrily. "I hate that I like you and that this is going to end and I can't even just enjoy it for what it is, I have to go and ruin it by being sad before it's even over."

"Wait, is *that* what's bothering you?" I stared at him, comprehension washing over me.

"I said it was stupid. Look, I get it. I'm not trying to push for anything more. I just—ugh, this is why I didn't want to talk about it."

"Adam, no, stop," I said, reaching out and taking his hands in mine, then stepping closer to him. "I don't want this to be over. I don't want this to be just a—just a *here* thing. I want this to be an all the time thing."

"But you—but you said we should take it slow. I thought—"

"I said that because I didn't want you to freak out and over-think things."

"Well that plan failed," Adam said wryly. "I don't think you counted on my ability to freak out about any and every eventuality."

"Maybe not," I said, taking another step towards him. I

leaned in and pressed my forehead to his. "But I like you. I like this. I want... I want to keep doing this. No matter where we are."

"But what about—" Adam paused and took a deep breath. "What about Mia? And your whole image and everything? Like, have you even thought about what this would mean for your career? If you suddenly come out, if you're dating a guy—Ben, I don't want to fuck things up for you."

"Well maybe I don't come out immediately," I said. "I don't want to leave Mia in a lurch right now. And I need a little time to figure out how to do this. But that doesn't mean that I don't want to be with you. That I want this to stop."

"Okay." Adam frowned. "So what does that mean? I'm just your secret? Until you decide to come out?"

"It sounds really bad when you say it like that," I said, sighing. "Which probably means it *is* really bad."

"I mean, it's not great," Adam said, arching an eyebrow. "I get it, but I just... I don't know, after Ellis, I didn't want to hide who I was, or who I was with, again. I don't want to be ashamed of myself. Or with someone who's ashamed of me, you know?"

"I know. Fuck, I know." I stepped back and looked him in the eye. "Adam, I'm not ashamed of you. Or us. Or anything. And I want to come out. I want the world to know I'm with you. I just need a little time, you know? I mean, fuck, you could be a woman and the situation would be the same." Adam flinched and I grimaced. "Fuck, okay, that sounded bad too. I didn't mean—fuck, I don't even know what I mean. I'm sorry. I'm doing a really shitty job of this, aren't I?"

Adam smiled sadly. "Well I'm not really making it easy for you. I don't mean to be like, pushy and it's not really fair of me to—"

"It's completely fair of you," I interrupted. "To do and say whatever you need to. I never want to make you feel like I'm not proud to be with you, or to make you doubt my feelings for you."

"Yeah, but it's only been like, a week. You're allowed to not have it all figured out."

"And I don't," I said, "except for one part. I know what I feel for you. I know it's real. But I understand if you don't want to —if you don't feel like you can do this. Be with me when I'm not out. With all this Mia stuff going on. I—I get it."

Adam shook his head. "I think you're overestimating the strength of my principles. And it'd be pretty hypocritical for me to say you have to come out after what, a week of thinking you might like a guy, when it took me literally like, ten years to do the same thing. I—I'm not saying I love it. This being a secret. But I can do it."

"I hate asking you to," I said fiercely. "I promise, I'll figure this out."

"I know." Adam smiled. "I believe you, anyway. Same thing."

"Hmm. So maybe not the time for me to reveal that I tricked you this afternoon, then?"

"How so?" Adam frowned.

I grinned. "Do you realize what we just did?"

"Talked about our feelings like a bunch of weirdos?"

"Okay, that, yes. But also... we just went on a date."

"What? No we didn't."

"Uh, we 100% just did. We walked somewhere together. We held hands. We ate food, which I paid for, we sat on a park bench and were generally adorable, we talked about our future, and—" I broke off and leaned in, kissing Adam quickly on the lips— "and we kissed right before we got home. What is that if not a date?"

"It doesn't count as a date if I didn't know I was on it," Adam pouted. "Not fair."

"Complain all you want," I said with a grin. "Denying it doesn't change the fact that it happened. Now come on, tonight's our last night here. Let's enjoy it."

Later that night as we sat around the campfire, Adam leaned over and put his hand on my shoulder.

"I'm headed inside. Come follow me in five minutes. Meet me in the bedroom," he whispered, bringing his lips to my ear.

Well that send a bolt of electricity right down to my cock. I nodded vaguely and then tried my best to act interested in everyone's conversation for the next five minutes. It felt interminable and finally I stood up and stretched and announced I was going to bed.

"Smooth, dude," Gray said, snorting a laugh.

I flushed but let it go—I was too eager to get inside. I had no idea what Adam had planned but I couldn't imagine any scenario that I wouldn't be into. What I didn't expect, though, was for Adam to pull me into the bedroom roughly once I got inside, shutting the door behind me and pushing me up against it.

Adam's kiss was almost feral, and my cock was painfully hard by the time he pulled back.

"What was that for?" I asked, breathless, when Adam broke away.

"Didn't you say we should enjoy our last night here?" Adam said, a grin playing across his face.

"I—fuck," I murmured as Adam leaned in and kissed me again.

His lips were like silk, sliding over mine and then down onto my neck. I arched my back, pressing up against Adam, and he slid his hands to my waist and began to tug my shirt up. It was hot, seeing that Adam wanted me. I'd never felt more attractive than I did when Adam looked at me like this, like he could devour me or be devoured and be utterly happy either way.

I had the presence of mind to throw the lock on the bedroom door before we stumbled back towards the bed, shedding clothes as we went. Adam melted down onto the bed, pulling me on top of him. I loved the feeling of his hot skin against my own, the sight of his hard cock pointing up at me.

How had I gone so long, I wondered, seeing Adam's body as anything other than beautiful, all lithe lines and lean muscle? I wanted to taste every inch of him, possess him, in a way I'd never felt about anyone else I'd been with. The thought that someone like Adam—so talented, so sensitive, so smart—would want me had to make me the luckiest person in the world.

"Fuck," I breathed as I brought my body in line with Adam's. Our cocks touched and I reached down to stroke them together.

"Oh God," Adam moaned. "Ben, fuck, yes."

I leaned in and kissed his neck, tickling his skin with my tongue, and was rewarded with Adam hipping up into my grasp. I loved how pliant he was, how eager. He could be so prickly, almost spiky, most of the time but when it was just the two of us, sometimes he let his walls slip down and showed me a side of him no one else got to see.

I liked it, this softer, needier side of him. And I liked the idea that it was just for me. I ran my fingers slowly around the head of Adam's cock and he moaned again—but then he was pulling away.

"Hey, where are you going?" I asked.

"Shh." Adam slipped out of my grasp and then pushed me down so I was lying on my back. "Not going anywhere. Stay just like that."

He moved to straddle me and gave me a long, lingering kiss before bending down to lick at my left nipple, his fingers playing with the other. I gasped when he bit at it and my cock twitched, pressed between my body and Adam's.

Adam gave a low laugh and let his free hand trail down my stomach, circling the tip of my cock. I moaned into the silence of the room, the night air drawn close around us, and hipped up into his hand.

Adam kissed his way lower then and my breath caught. So far we really had been taking it slow. I hadn't wanted to press him into doing anything he wasn't comfortable with. But it was clear what his intentions were as he kissed down the light trail of hair on my stomach and my heart started pounding in my chest.

Pulling back, Adam pushed my legs apart and brought himself in between them. His green eyes glinted in the light as he looked up at me and when he licked his lips, my cock twitched again.

Christ, he was sexy. So often Adam was quiet, watching people from the sidelines. But tonight he was confident, completely in control, and I was in his thrall. I realized I'd do anything for him, just to see that smile spread across his lips like moonrise over the ocean.

But I only had a second to catch that look before Adam bent down again, kissing my stomach, my hips, the inside of my thighs—everywhere except my cock itself. I moaned louder this time, desperate to feel his mouth on my cock. Adam kept his grip tight around the base, at least giving me some-thing to thrust up against, but he seemed intent on torturing me, letting his tongue trace patterns on my skin as I writhed beneath him.

Finally, he pulled back again and caught my eyes. And then slowly, keeping my gaze locked on him, he bent down again, bringing his mouth just above the head of my cock before wrapping his lips around it.

A tremor ran through me at the feel of his soft, wet lips taking me in and I could see that glint in Adam's eyes again, knew that he knew just how much I liked it, just how much power he had over me.

I groaned, soft and broken, as Adam slowly took more of me into his mouth. It was hot, wet, and tight. Still locking eyes with me, Adam began to bob up and down on my cock, hollowing his cheeks out, and I could tell I wasn't going to last very long.

On each stroke, Adam took me a little deeper, then pulled up, swirling his tongue around the head of my cock, flicking the slit, and sliding it along the sensitive underside. And then, without warning, he plunged down and took all of me into his mouth, sinking down around my length. I could just feel the tip of my cock hit the back of his throat, heard the soft gagging noise Adam made, and trembled.

"Fuck, Adam," I whispered, my voice wrecked. "Adam, that's so good, you're so good."

Adam pulled back and smiled at me, then took one of my hands and moved it to the back of his head. My eyes widened but he nodded and as I laced my fingers through his hair, he took me in his mouth again.

Jesus, there was something obscene about this, my best friend's mouth closing around my cock. Something forbidden about the way my hand guided him down as my hips began to thrust up into his lips. And then Adam started to moan like he was the one getting pleasure out of this and that was enough to tip me over the edge.

"Fuck, Adam," I gasped. "I'm gonna—If you wanna—"

I moved my hand from his head but Adam didn't move. He just kept sucking me, his hot velvet mouth better than anything I'd ever felt, and I came, hard. Fuck, the sight of that, of filling my best friend's mouth as I released was the hottest thing I'd ever seen.

Adam's eyes locked onto mine again like they were wringing my orgasm out of me. My body was wracked with pleasure, convulsing as I came and I was pretty sure I would have left my goddamn body if his eyes hadn't anchored me down to earth.

Finally spent, I pulled Adam off and up. He started to wipe his mouth but I caught him in a kiss instead. I could taste myself on Adam's tongue and I realized at that moment how badly I wanted to know what he tasted like.

"Jesus, that was amazing," I whispered when we broke apart.

Adam gave me a lopsided grin. "Well, I'm not saying I've been thinking about that for a long time and wanted to make sure it was good. But I'm not *not* saying that either."

"Fuck, I should have gotten jealous of Nick earlier," I said, pulling him to my chest.

"What?"

"Nick sorta—" I laughed, "he sorta... helped me realize how I felt about you. I kept getting jealous of him and couldn't figure out why. Until Gray pointed out the obvious."

"You were jealous of Nick?" Adam asked, tilting his head up and looking at me. "That's adorable."

"You'd better not be making fun of me," I said, narrowing my eyes.

"I'm not, trust me." Adam laughed. "But you can also trust

me when I tell you there is no way in hell I could ever be into him."

"Why not?" I frowned. "Is it that unthinkable? He's nice, he's a good looking guy..."

"He's not you," Adam said simply.

"Yeah but—"

"He's not you," Adam repeated, his cheeks flushing. "And it's —I mean, I've always—it's just... Oh God, this is awful, why did I start talking?"

He turned and buried his face in a pillow.

"Hey, hey, it's fine," I said, turning onto my side and rubbing his back. "I like you too, in case you'd forgotten. What's wrong? There's nothing embarrassing about that."

Adam mumbled something incomprehensible into the pillow.

"What?" I squeezed his shoulder, then leaned over and kissed the back of his neck. "I didn't catch that."

"Nfs mrbsgh nwf flp wyvp hvmrrst," Adam said, louder this time.

"Adam, what's wrong? I'm beginning to think you're confessing to having murdered someone."

"It's embarrassing when you've felt that way for seven years," Adam said, finally turning around and pulling his face out of the pillow. "I was never going to like Nick, I was never going to like anyone else, because it's always been you. For forever."

"But you—I mean, Ellis—"

"Ellis was my misguided attempt to get over you," Adam said. "Only possible because you'd been gone for long enough for me to finally see how pathetic my crush on you truly was. But even so, I could never—"

"Hey," I said, interrupting him firmly. "It wasn't pathetic."

Adam raised his eyebrows. "You're trying to tell me that nursing unrequited feelings for your best friend for seven years and never telling him isn't pathetic?"

"But they weren't unrequited," I said, running my fingers up and down his back. "Just because I didn't realize how I felt about you doesn't mean that those feelings weren't there."

"It's not the same," Adam said, and his voice sounded pained.

"I know but—please. Adam, I don't think it's weird. I think it's..." I paused, trying to find the right words. "It makes me feel like I'm yours, you know?"

"Oh my God, why did I have to like the grossest, sappiest guy on the planet?" Adam groaned and covered his face with his hands, but at least he didn't turn away from me this time. "You're so sweet it's disgusting."

"You're just lucky, I guess."

I moved my hand to Adam's shoulder and drew him onto his side, then his back. Adam whimpered as I kissed him, drawing his bottom lip out and biting it gently before releasing it and kissing his neck, his collarbone, his chest. But when I moved lower, Adam's hands flew to my shoulders. I looked up in confusion.

"You don't have to," Adam said, knitting his brows together.

"I want to,"

"Yeah but..." Adam trailed off. I waited for him to finish but he left me hanging.

"Do you... not want me to?" I asked it with a smile, joking, but Adam flinched and I frowned. "Wait, do you seriously not want me to? Why?"

"It's not—it's not that I don't *want* you to. I just... I don't know, what if you don't like it? And then you change your mind about this whole thing? What if you think it's gross, or I'm gross, or—"

"I would never think that," I said, pressing a kiss to his sternum. "I love your body. I'm sorry, is my ever-present boner not enough evidence for you?"

"Yeah, but this is different." Adam frowned. "I mean, what, you go from wondering if you might like guys to giving your first blow job in one week? Are you sure you don't want to like, mull this over a little longer?"

"And what, return you to the store if I change my mind within 30 days?" I snorted. "'Cause it's too late. I already threw out the receipt."

"Ben, take this seriously," Adam said, sounding annoyed.

"I am taking it seriously," I countered. "I just don't see what the big deal is. I guess maybe it's a little fast but when you know, you know. You know?"

"But how can you know that when you don't even—I mean, do you even like other guys? Is it just me? Can't you see how it's a little weird for me to trust that you really want this when you've never been with anyone else?"

"Well what am I supposed to do, go blow five other guys while you watch just so that you'll believe me when I say I want you to be number six?"

"Okay, that's not exactly what I meant."

"I know, but—fuck, Adam, I don't know. I think I'm probably bisexual. Am I one hundred percent sure that that label is exactly what fits? No. And that's something I'm happy to keep exploring—with you. But I don't need to be with some other guy to know that I want to be with you. I don't want some other guy." I looked at him fiercely. "I want you. I like you. I would like to put your cock in my mouth."

"Jesus Christ," Adam said, a flush staining his cheeks. "You're shameless."

"When it comes to you, apparently yes." I smiled. "Look, I'll drop it if you really don't want me to. But just... don't say no because you think *I* don't want to. I might not have a lot of experience but I'm a quick learner. And I want to show you how I feel and I know this is just one way, but frankly, the thought of making you come, of tasting you when you do— fuck, I'm getting hard again just thinking about it. So don't say no because you think you're doing me some kind of favor, okay?"

"But what if you don't like me after?" Adam's voice was so small I could barely hear it. "Ben, you're my best friend and you're so fucking perfect and strong and caring and hot and you're nice to me and—"

"I'm *nice* to you? Adam, that shouldn't be a reason for you to like me, that should be a baseline expectation for normal human interaction."

"Well maybe it's not, okay? It's a big deal to me. You've never made me feel weird about who I am, you've never made fun of me or teased me even though you probably should because I'm a fucking headache and you're so fucking normal and I just—if I lose you, if you weren't my friend anymore, I'd fucking lose my mind, so maybe I'm a little nervous about all of this, okay?"

By the time Adam was done talking, there were tears in his eyes. He wiped at them angrily and I pulled him close. Adam buried his face in my neck and I felt his body shake.

"Fuck," he said quietly after a few minutes. "I never used to cry and now I do it all the time. I blame you."

"You can." I ran a hand through his hair. "And let's put the blow job issue aside for tonight. Just know that you're never going to lose me. No matter what."

"Okay," Adam said, his voice still a little sniffly.

I expected Adam to pull away then but when he didn't, I squeezed him tighter. Because I realized at that moment that as worried as Adam might be about losing me, I was 10 times as worried about losing him. It was all so fast, so sudden, but I'd never felt anything this real.

"Okay," I repeated softly. I took a deep breath, inhaling the cool, sweet scent of Adam's skin, and tried to calm down the frantic beating of my heart. Somehow, we were going to make this work. "Okay."

15

ADAM

"So, what's the problem?" Nick asked as we turned the corner onto Mercer Street. We'd met up for lunch and he was walking me back to Ben's apartment on his way up to Penn Station. "He wants to give you head and you're saying no because... why?"

"Because he says he likes me."

"And again, I say, what's the problem?"

I rolled my eyes. "Don't be cute. This whole situation is quite possibly the worst thing that's ever happened to me."

"Worse than being in love with Ben and convinced he couldn't possibly ever be interested?" Nick said drily. "Really?"

"Yes."

"Because..."

"Because now this is fucking happening, it's not just some

fucked up trash-fantasy that I carry around in my head like the garbage person I am. It's an actual thing. It had a beginning. And that means it's going to have an end."

Nick squinted at me. "I think you skipped a logical step there, or twenty. Why are we so convinced it's going to end?"

"Because it's *Ben*. The human embodiment of perfection. The platonic ideal of a person. Why would he want to be with a dumpster fire like me when he could be with anyone. Literally anyone, male or female. Though that's another thing—like, what the fuck? Since when does he like guys?"

"I don't know, dude," Nick said, shrugging. "Maybe he always has and just didn't realize. Maybe it's honestly new. People can change over time. Either way, human sexuality is complicated."

"So I'm just supposed to trust that in the space of a couple weeks he went from being straight to being all about dick?" I asked, crossing my arms as we walked.

"Dude, stranger things have happened. Don't look a gift blow job in the mouth, that's my advice."

"Can you admit that he's at least a much better person than I am?" I asked plaintively.

"And that would make you feel better *why*?"

"I just need someone else to acknowledge how deeply weird this all is," I said. "I can't really talk to anyone else about it since Ben doesn't want to come out yet and talking to him about it is no use because he doesn't see it as strange."

"I won't say he's a better person than you are but I will agree that he is a very good one." Nick shook his head and laughed ruefully. "Dude, you know how he's doing that benefit concert for the Family Futures Project? I mentioned to my boss that I knew him and he told me Ben donated a huge chunk of money to them this year too, but on the condition that it be anonymous."

"See, that's exactly what I mean," I said. "He's too good."

"Adam, it doesn't matter how good he is. If he likes you, he likes you. If he wants to suck you off, he wants to suck you off. Those things don't change just because he's the Mother Theresa of boyfriends."

"What if he hates it?" I asked, hating how needy my tone sounded. "What if he hates me after? And then he's disgusted by me and not only does he not want to hook up anymore—which, by the way, please don't jinx me and use the B word, we don't need to add that to this mess—but what if he doesn't even want to be friends anymore either?"

"A, I don't think that he's going to suddenly change his mind. And B, even if he did, you guys have been friends for seven years. Don't you think you could get past it and find a way to stay friends?"

"Not after having my dick in his mouth," I said, shaking my head. "That's like, the gay sex event horizon. You can't come back from that."

"Okay, well here's a radical thought: What if he doesn't hate it? What if you actually, you know, do him the favor of believing him when he tells you he wants this—and, shocker—it turns out he does. What if absolutely nothing bad happens as an outcome?"

"Unrealistic," I said flatly. "I think you've forgotten who you're talking to. *'Nothing bad happens'* isn't really an option in my relationship history.'"

"Adam, I say this with all the love and respect in the world," Nick said, arching an eyebrow, "but your relationship history is exactly one person long. That's hardly enough to form a pattern."

"Okay, my life history then. I'm not... the kid who things work out for. I don't get the popular guy, the homecoming king."

"Adam."

"Yeah?"

"You know you're not actually in high school anymore, right?"

"Harsh, dude." I glared at him. It stung, but I figured that probably meant he had a point.

"I'm just saying, yeah, you've gone through some shit. But that doesn't mean you're doomed to repeat it."

"I beg to fucking differ," I said, staring angrily at the stoplight as we waited at an intersection. "What the hell was Ellis if not just another example of me letting someone else hurt me? What the hell was me chasing a fistful of pills with lukewarm whiskey if not me continuing to make spectacularly bad decisions? If I'm not doomed to repeat that, then why the fuck does everything in my life keep going to shit?"

Nick gave me a considering look before speaking. "Do you want friend Nick or professional Nick to answer that?"

"Whichever one is going to agree with me that this is fucking scary as shit and I'm right to be suspicious."

"Okay, well, neither one is going to say that. Friend Nick is going to yell at you and tell you that not everything in your life is going to shit, that you've actually got a lot of great things in your life and maybe you need to start realizing that. You have people who love you and care about you, a job doing what you love, and a guy who as far as I can tell is head over heels for you and you're keeping him at arm's length because you're scared. Professional Nick says your feelings are valid and that it must be really hard and scary to be where you are right now. But that maybe, Ellis and that night at The Grasshopper weren't examples of you fucking up, but you starting to make changes for the better—realizing what you wanted and deciding you deserved to have something good. And yes, Ben wanting to be with you is terrifying, because it's something you've wanted for so long. And your fear is just doing the best it can, trying to keep you safe. But maybe it's outlived its usefulness here. Maybe you need to pick whether you want to let that fear rule you, or if you want to keep deciding that you deserve something good, if you want to give your hope and your strength and your courage a chance to direct you instead."

"God, Professional Nick sounds like a smug bastard."

"He might be," Nick agreed. "But I also think he might be right. What you and Ben are starting—this could be really amazing."

"Or it could be the opposite."

We'd reached the apartment building and I stared at the steps leading up to the entrance with misgiving.

"That's life, man," Nick said apologetically. "But if you run away from this, it's guaranteed to not be amazing. So…"

"Fuck you and your reasonableness."

"Oh, I didn't realize you wanted Unreasonable Nick. He's a third person entirely. He'd definitely tell you to run away, but he'd probably also get you drunk on absinthe and steal all your money first. So maybe not the best source of advice."

"This sucks." I sighed. "Why does being a responsible, emotionally-grounded adult have to involve so much, you know, being responsible and emotionally-grounded?"

"I don't make the rules, dude," Nick said with a laugh.

"Well if you ever find out who does, let me know," I said, putting my foot on the bottom step. "I'm going to leave them a scathing *Yelp* review."

"I'm out!" Lacey said, throwing the last card from her hand down onto the Uno pile on the table. "I win again!"

I grinned as I watched Ben grumble that Lacey must be cheating and pretend to check for cards stuck up her sleeves. They were at the end of the kitchen table; I was standing at the sink drying dishes. I'd been here enough times that I knew where to put them away and since Ben's parents had cooked, I'd insisted on cleaning up.

"Are you sure you haven't been training as a secret Uno ninja behind my back?" Ben asked, fixing Lacey with a suspicious glare.

"No." Lacey smiled brightly. "I was born th—" she cut off, coughing, and Ben was at her side immediately, rubbing her back and then holding her glass of water up when the cough subsided. His face was full of concern.

Mrs. Kowalski came into the kitchen from the living room where she'd been watching PBS with Ben's dad.

"Everyone okay in here?" she asked. "Lacey, are you alright?"

"Mom, I'm fine. It's j—" Another cough interrupted her speech and Mrs. Kowalski was next to Lacey in a flash.

"I think it's time for bed," she said, helping a protesting Lacey stand up. She glanced over at me and frowned. "Adam, honey, really, just leave those. I'll put them away in the morning."

"I don't mind," I said cheerfully. "Honestly, it's the least I can do after you were kind enough to have me over again."

Mrs. Kowalski fixed me with a stern look. "Sweetheart, you're family. None of my other ungrateful spawn help clean up, there's no reason you should either."

"Hey, I resent that," Ben protested as he swept the deck of cards up. "I got drafted into a vitally important Uno game. Like, critical to national security, Ma. I didn't really have a choice."

His mom smiled at him sweetly. "I'm sure your country thanks you for your sacrifice. But I'd better see you cleaning up after breakfast and not Adam."

I was sleeping on the pull-out couch again that night, but since Ben's sister Jessica hadn't come out for dinner this week, Ben was back up in the extra bedroom upstairs. As I lay in bed later that night, drowsily trying to read, I realized it had been a long time since I'd felt this happy. I knew Mrs. Kowalski was just joking about me being part of the family, but it was nice to pretend it was real.

Though if we were family, my desire to sneak into Ben's bedroom upstairs would probably be a little weirder. I stayed where I was, though. Mrs. Kowalski might like me now, but I wasn't sure I wanted to test her affections by getting caught trying to slip into Ben's bed.

I was just about to put my book down when I heard a creak on the stairs. I looked up to see Ben standing at the top of them, wearing just his boxer briefs.

"Hey," he said softly. "You awake?"

"Yeah." I tilted my head to the side. "What's up?"

"Couldn't sleep. Can I come down and hang out?"

"Of course, dude, it's your house." I laughed as Ben came down the stairs and then crawled under the covers with me. "I was just thinking about coming upstairs to find you, but I wasn't sure I wanted to risk having to explain to your mom why I was sneaking into your room in my boxers in the middle of the night."

"Eh, she'd probably be thrilled," Ben said, turning onto his side with a grin. "She always worries that Mia being my fake-girlfriend is going to result in me being for-real single forever. I think she'd start planning our wedding immediately if she found out."

"And you don't think that the fact that her son had a for-real *boy*friend would be a hiccup at all?"

"Hey, give her some credit," Ben protested. "Besides, you're not just some guy. I think she actually loves you more than she loves me, so—wait a second."

"What?"

Ben's smile lit up his whole face. "Did you just call yourself my boyfriend?"

I flushed. "You tricked me. My guard is always down here."

"Well I'll take my victories where I can fine them," Ben said.

He slid closer to me and put his head down on my chest and I wrapped an arm around him. We were quiet for a few minutes as Ben traced abstract patterns on my arm with his index finger. I could tell something was bothering him and I wasn't sure he wanted to talk about it. Eventually, though, I cracked.

"Worried about Lacey?" I ventured.

Ben nodded—I could feel his stubble scratch against my chest. "Yeah."

"I'm sorry." I squeezed him tight. "I wish there were something I could do."

"Just you being here is doing something." He sighed. "Mom says Lacey's been feeling weaker in the past couple of days —it's been this on and off pattern for a while now. They did some tests that came back negative but I just worry, you know. I try not to, but it feels like waiting for the other shoe to drop. Which is such an asshole thing to say. I shouldn't view Lacey as a problem."

"Hey, you're not an asshole. You just care. That's your thing."

I laughed. "Like this benefit thing—you didn't tell me you were also donating money to them."

Ben tilted his chin and looked up at me. "Who told you that?"

"Nick." I winced. "Sorry, I know you didn't want people to know. He just found out and mentioned it to me."

"It's not that I don't want *you* to know," Ben said. "I just didn't want to make a whole thing about it. Talking about that kind of stuff just seems like showing off."

"It's fucking adorable. You're perfect."

"I'm not," Ben said, his voice heated. "But if I'm going to have all this money, I might as well put it to good use, you know? What else am I doing with my life if I'm not helping people? Especially people who can't help themselves?"

"So, like I was saying, you're perfect."

"I don't know," Ben said. "I mean, if Lacey relapses... It's pretty selfish to be thinking about going independent when renewing with Greenleaf would be way more stable. I could do a lot more good if I were making the kind of money they're talking about."

That felt like a stab to the gut. Ben had been so positive about splitting with Greenleaf just a couple weeks ago. I couldn't blame him for having second thoughts. But what were the chances of him wanting to come out if he stayed with the label?

But I didn't want to say anything. Not tonight, not when Ben was already upset about Lacey. I'd pushed him enough back in Montauk.

"You have to do what feels right," I said instead. "I'm not saying it's bad to want the security that would come with Greenleaf. But if none of the other stuff that you disliked about working with them has changed..."

"Which it hasn't. Of course." He smiled. "God, when'd you get so wise."

I snorted. "I've just seen two very different people—my mom and my dad—live lives that revolve around money. And neither one of them is happy. Or a particularly good person, for that matter."

"You sound like my mom," Ben sighed. "Always telling me money isn't everything."

I rolled my eyes. "I guess that makes sense, seeing as how I'm her favorite."

"It really means a lot to me that you came tonight," Ben said, pressing a kiss down onto my chest. "Having you here, it's just... well, thanks."

"Of course," I said softly. "Anything you want."

Ben didn't say anything, he just leaned in and kissed me. I kissed him back hungrily, channeling all the worry inside me into want, my hands reaching up to cling to his body like a drowning man clinging to driftwood.

There wasn't much clothing between us to start with so it didn't take long to peel it off. I slid a hand down Ben's chest, across his stomach, and onto his cock as he lay back in bed. It was hot—and hard, a fact that never ceased to amaze me. When I stroked it, the smooth, golden skin sliding underneath my fingers, Ben shuddered.

I kissed his jaw, then his neck and collarbones, slowly crawling on top of Ben and reveling at the sight of his body stretched out beneath me. Ben was perfect, strong muscles and long lines, and when he smiled up at me, I shivered.

I couldn't figure out how to put everything I was feeling into words—the love, the fear, the hope and the confusion—but I figured maybe that was okay. Maybe I could show him how I felt. I slid down, kissing his stomach, and felt my spine tingle when Ben tangled his hand in my hair.

I liked how possessive Ben was of me. I wasn't sure I should, but I did. I liked knowing that he wanted me.

I'd been so nervous the first time I'd given Ben head and I still got a little thrill every time I sucked him off. Ben's cock was long and firm, the skin silky smooth, and I licked my lips, getting them wet before wrapping them around the tip and massaging him with my tongue.

"Oh, Adam, fuck," Ben moaned lightly, rubbing the back of my neck. The way he said my name, that reverent whisper, sent shivers across my body—and sent all the blood in my body straight to my cock.

I bobbed my head up and down, sucking more of Ben in with each stroke. I loved the way he tasted, salty and sweet, the tang of precum beading at his tip. I savored every minute of it. It still didn't seem real that Ben wanted this and I loved how eager he was, how appreciative.

Soon Ben was bucking up underneath me, his hips working in concert with his hand. I smiled around his cock. It was insanely hot to know that I could make him feel this good.

"You're so good, Adam," Ben whispered as I moved my hand in time with my mouth, knowing he was close.

It had only been a week since we'd gotten back from Montauk but I'd already learned to read Ben like a map, the topography of his body and the weather of his arousal. I moved my hand and took Ben all the way down, feeling the head of his cock hitting the back of my throat.

It always made me gag, just a little, but I liked that too, the strange feeling of helplessness. It didn't make any sense. Anywhere else in life, that feeling would make me cringe. But with Ben, somehow it felt safe. And hot, giving him that control. And it seemed to work for Ben, too.

"Adam, fuck, I'm gonna—" he whispered, and then he was coming down my throat. I kept my lips tight around him and swallowed, closing my eyes and listening to the way he whispered my name. "Adam, Adam, Adam."

When I pulled off, Ben drew me up to him and kissed me deeply.

"I love tasting myself on your tongue," Ben said, and I felt my cock twitch. Ben felt it too, and he laughed.

"Yeah, well that totally doesn't do anything for me at all." I rolled my eyes.

"Right," Ben said, rolling me onto my side and then running a hand up and down my chest. "You're clearly not into this."

"Nope." I shrugged my shoulders. "Could take it or leave it, really."

"And if I do this," he continued, dropping his hand to palm my cock, "you're probably just bored."

"Fuck," I moaned, then bit my lip. "Yeah. Might as well be reading the encyclopedia."

I could feel precum leaking from the tip of my cock and Ben ran his finger across it, then used it to slick his hand and stroke me.

"And this? You probably couldn't care less, huh?"

"Fuck, no," I said, breathing heavily. I tried and failed to stifle another moan. "Totally didn't—fuck—didn't even notice you were doing it. Til you—oh God—said something."

"I could probably blow you and you wouldn't even care," Ben said, flashing me a smile.

I tensed immediately. I didn't want to, but I did and Ben noticed.

"Sorry," he said quickly. "Sorry, I'm not pushing. Or, well, I am. But I'll stop. Just... consider this a gentle reminder of how badly I want you, okay?"

I'd been thinking about this ever since my conversation with Nick. Every cell in my body was on high alert, screaming in panic that this was a bad idea, Ben wasn't going to want me anymore, this was the beginning of the end.

But was I going to let that fear make my decision for me? Or was I going to try to be brave?

"Okay," I said, my voice tight. "You can—you can do it. If you want."

"Really?" Ben stared at me in confusion. "That... worked? Are you... sure you didn't mean to say, hell no, definitely not, never?"

"Hey, don't make me change my mind," I snapped.

"Adam, you don't have to," Ben said softly. "Really. You know that, right?"

"I do." I squeezed my eyes shut for a second. "I do know that. And I'm still nervous and like, convinced you're going to change *your* mind about me, but... I dunno, what's a relationship without trust and all that bullshit?"

"Relationship, huh?"

"Yeah, don't let it go to your head," I said, rolling my eyes.

Ben snorted. "Did I ever tell you why Rachel broke up with me, back in college?"

I frowned, confused at the non-sequitur. "No. Why?"

"She basically accused me of being in love with you. Said that I couldn't make time for her but I always had time for you. Her exact words were, *'I'm sick of being the third wheel in your relationship with Adam.'* So if you go by her definition, we've been in a relationship for a very long while. Plenty of time to build up trust and all that bullshit."

"I'm sure she'd be thrilled to know she was right," I said, forcing myself to stop turning the phrase, 'accused me of being in love with you,' over in my mind. It was just a figure of speech, it didn't mean anything.

Ben smiled, then picked up my right hand and kissed it. It was only afterwards that he seemed to notice it was shaking.

"Nerves," I said, shrugging in response to his silent question.

Ben smiled. "You ever think maybe I'm nervous too? What if I'm not any good at this? What if you don't like it?"

"It's a physical impossibility that I won't like it, trust me."

"Trust, huh?" Ben kissed my palm before setting my hand down on the mattress. "I'm going to hold you to that."

He pushed himself up onto all fours and then swung a leg over me as I lay on my back. I forced myself to take a deep breath. It wasn't that I hadn't been naked in front of him before, not after the past two weeks. But suddenly I felt shy, on display. I'd always sort of hated people looking at me, and then Ben had to go and look at me like I was something special.

"You're beautiful, you know that?"

I snorted. "That might be stretching it a bit."

"No." Ben shook his head emphatically. "You are." He bent down and ghosted his lips across mine. "Completely fucking gorgeous. And mine."

My cock twitched again at those words and Ben bit down on my lower lip, pulling it out with his teeth before releasing it. I whimpered in pleasure.

"I'm going to make you feel so good," he whispered. "I promise. Just relax."

Relaxed was the last thing I felt. Not just because I was nervous but because I was fucking hard as hell and my cock was desperate for attention. But I took another deep breath and tried to will my heart to beat a little slower, at least.

Ben slid down and nipped at my neck, licking and sucking at a spot that always made me weak. His body covered mine and he rocked it up and down as he moved lower, rubbing against my cock.

I tried to contain a whimper, not wanting to be too loud, but now Ben was kissing my stomach and then licking along the lines of my hips.

"Fuck, Ben," I moaned, unable to stop myself.

Ben looked up at me and his pupils were blown wide, almost obliterating the blue of his irises. Shit, he really did want to do this. The realization knocked the wind out of me so I was a little breathless when Ben nudged my legs apart, bringing himself in between them.

There was something extremely vulnerable about that position and I sucked in a hard breath of air, trying to remind myself to relax as I made space for him. This was Ben. I could trust him. He wasn't going to run away and change his mind, right?

I was still running around in circles in my head when Ben brought his hand to the base of my cock, then bent down and licked a long stripe up the underside of it. I shivered as he reached the tip and swirled his tongue around the head. And then he did it again, slowly, half an inch to the left. He kept it up until he'd covered every inch of my skin and I was twitching, desperate to feel his mouth on me.

"Jesus Christ, Ben," I whispered.

Ben's eyes flicked up to me and I blinked at the hint of fear I saw. "Was that—is that... not good?"

"No, it's *very* good," I said. "Just like, not what I expected from your first blowjob ever."

Ben flushed. "I might have watched a lot of porn. For research."

"Well it worked."

Ben grinned. "Good." And then he brought his lips down to the tip of my cock and slid my entire length into his mouth in one go.

"Fuck, Ben," I moaned, feeling the tight heat of his mouth around my shaft. "Fucking hell."

Ben looked up at me, his eyes intense, and holy shit that was hot, his face buried between my legs, his mouth around my cock. None of my fantasies could compare to the reality of actually seeing Ben sucking me off.

I could feel my body un-tensing, relaxing under Ben's touch. It was hard to stay nervous that Ben wasn't going to enjoy this when he was smiling up at me with my cock in his mouth. And then Ben started to move and I couldn't think coherently anymore. I wasn't relaxing, I was relaxed, full stop, and coming undone.

For all of Ben's research, it was still clear that he didn't have a ton of experience doing this, but that just made it hotter. It was sloppy, Ben's breath ragged, but what he lacked in finesse, he made up for in enthusiasm, his mouth so hot and wet. I could feel my orgasm building and when Ben pulled off my cock to suck my balls into his mouth, I knew it wasn't going to be long.

Not quite believing what I was doing, I opened my legs wider, giving Ben better access. Ben rolled my balls in his hand, tugging on them gently and I groaned in pleasure. When he moved his mouth back to my cock, I looked down and Ben caught my eye. And then I felt one of his fingers brush lightly across my hole and my body jumped.

That... wasn't what I'd expected. When the hell had Ben even gotten that finger wet? Well, he had, somehow, and it wasn't like I could deny what I'd fantasized about for years. Ben watched me, waiting to see how I reacted, and I gave him the tiniest of nods. Ben sucked down on my cock, stroking his finger across my hole again and I moaned.

It wasn't long before I was gripping the sheets, thrusting up into Ben's mouth as his finger circled around my hole.

"Fuck," I gasped, trying to focus, trying to warn him. "Fuck, Ben, I'm gonna come."

Ben didn't move, just kept sucking my cock, and suddenly I was coming. Fuck, this was the hottest thing I'd ever experienced. What would it feel like if Ben were actually fucking me, instead of just teasing me with a finger? I wasn't sure I could handle that much pleasure.

When I finally came back down to earth, I pulled Ben back up towards me and faced him on my side.

"Good?" Ben asked.

"Nah, terrible. I hated every second of it."

"That's what I thought," Ben said, making a face. "You faked an orgasm on me, didn't you?"

"Yep," I nodded. "That might have been a gallon of cum, but it was just pity cum, I swear."

"Well," Ben grinned. "Pity cum still tastes delicious."

"Suspicious. I might need to check that out myself. For research," I added, leaning in and bringing my lips to his. And yeah, okay, it did taste pretty amazing, in an obscene kind of way, like it shouldn't be allowed, and somehow, that made it even better.

When I pulled back, Ben was smiling at me goofily. "Verdict?"

"Not bad," I said, running my finger along his jaw. "We might have to do some more experimentation though. Just to be sure."

"Hey Adam?" Ben said, smiling at me.

"What?"

"I still like you. Just in case you were wondering."

"Eww, gross, get out of here." I shoved his chest with one hand. "We were having a perfectly nice moment talking about cum and you had to go and ruin it with your filth."

"Well to be really filthy, I should probably clarify that I like you a lot."

"Disgusting."

"In fact, I might even like you more than before," Ben said, taking hold of my hand on his chest and squeezing it. "I think you're just the smartest, funniest, sweetest, sexiest little creampuff to ever grace the earth and I'm thinking that maybe I should write a song specifically about how much I like you and be sure to include your middle name just to make certain that everyone knows it's really about you, and then everyone can listen to it all the time when it becomes the number one single in the country and—"

"Oh my God, someone kill me." I turned and buried my face in the pillow behind me. "Get out of here. Get out of this bed right now with that talk."

"Make me," Ben said, tugging on my hand that he was still holding and refusing to let go until he'd pulled me back and crushed me to his chest.

I rolled my eyes, but I had to admit, it felt nice lying there. We just had to make sure not to fall asleep like this. I snuggled up against him further, mortified at what I was doing and doing it anyway.

"So you did a lot of research?" I said after a minute. "Watched all the gay porn?"

"All of it," Ben said, laughing lightly. "I'm armed and dangerous now. I've got way too many ideas of things I want to do with you."

"Oh yeah?" I said, feeling a simultaneous thrill and clench in my stomach.

"Yeah." Ben paused and then pulled back a little, looking down at me. "I mean, only if you want to, that is. No pressure or like, rush or anything."

"I, uh, want to," I said slowly. "It's just..." I stopped and sighed. "Fuck, ok well I wanted to be drunk when I told you this but... I've never actually done it. Had sex, I mean."

"Wait, really?" Ben blinked. "But what about Ellis?"

"Yeah, that, um, was apparently his justification for cheating on me? So I'm just a big old virgin, basically. Emphasis on old. Embarrassingly old. I like, don't even know how to *gay* right."

"It's not embarrassing, it's fine," Ben said, his brow knit in confusion. "I'm surprised but it doesn't bother me."

"It's not that I never wanted to," I said, forcing myself to continue. I'd started explaining, I might as well finish. "It's just that I—God, this sounds so stupid but I wanted to wait until it was someone I was comfortable with and well, joke's on me because now I'm 25 and a virgin so good job, self."

"Hey, come here," Ben said, pulling me back to his chest. "It's seriously nothing to be embarrassed about. I mean, I've never done it either."

"Yeah but you've at least had sex. I know it was with women but it still counts."

"Right, but not actually with all that many people. And I totally get wanting to wait until you're with someone you feel safe with. Someone you trust."

"Ugh, but it sounds so gross and sad," I protested.

"It sounds sweet. I like it."

"Yeah, but we've already established that you have questionable taste. You like me, after all."

Ben laughed. "Good point. Okay, you're probably right, you're pathetic and I'm judging you really hard right now." He pressed a kiss to my forehead. "There, does that make you feel better?"

"Like 1% better. Could you work more disdain into your delivery next time?"

"You know," Ben said slowly. "We've never actually talked about this, so I don't know what you had in mind. I just kind of assumed that you'd be—well, what I'm trying to say is that I could, um, be on bottom. If that would make it better."

I frowned. "Wait, really?"

"Yeah, sure. Why not?"

I looked at him in confusion. "Because, I don't know. Like, do you *want* to? Ugh, I can't believe I'm asking this—"

"God forbid we talk about sex like adults—"

"—but when you've thought about it, is that what you've wanted? To bottom? Or are you just saying that for me?"

"Honestly?" Ben said. "No. I don't think bottoming would be like, my preference. Probably. But I don't know, I've never done it before. So maybe I'd like it more than I think."

"God, what planet are you from? How are you this perfect?"

"I just want you to feel comfortable. It's not going to be good for me if you're not into it, so I just—like, whatever would make you—I mean, we can—"

"I want you to fuck me," I said in a rush. Ben's eyes opened wide and I almost laughed at how shocked he looked. "I do. I mean it. That's... what I want. I just might need to take it slow. If that's okay."

"We can take it as slow as you want." He brought his lips to mine, his tongue diving into my mouth and taking my breath away before he pulled back. "Actually, that's probably a good idea anyway, because I think the box of condoms I have in the apartment is from like, three years ago."

I bit my lip.

"What?" Ben asked.

Oh God, this was excruciating. Goddamn Nick and his

goddamn advice. It was so much easier to just never tell people what you wanted. More effective? No. But easier? Hell fucking yes.

"So, I um—" I paused, then forced myself to continue. "I got tested. When I was at Peachtree. I mean, after I found out about Ellis. Even though we hadn't actually had sex, we'd done other stuff and it just seemed like a good idea. And I don't have anything. So if you were—"

Ben's eyes widened. "I got tested at my last physical, three months ago. We scheduled it in, mid-tour. Negative on everything. And the only person I've been with since then is you."

"I mean, we can still use condoms," I said. "If it like, grosses you out or something. But if you don't mind, it might—it might be fun to—"

"Adam Hart, are you telling me you want me to come in your ass?"

"Jesus," I whispered, feeling my stomach turn a somersault. I knew I was blushing which, honestly? I was almost surprised I still had the capacity to feel shame. But... "Uh, yeah," I said. "Yeah, I guess I am. If you want."

"Oh, I want." Ben brought his lips to my ear as his hand slid down to cup my ass gently. "I want to come inside you. But only after I've eaten you out. And finger fucked you. And then made you come so hard with my cock that you fucking scream. *Then* I'll come in your ass."

"Fuck."

"Too much?" Ben asked.

"No fucking way. Perfect. Just surprising. But no. Perfect."

It was, I realized, as Ben wrapped his arms around me tighter. Laying there, my head on his chest, I felt flayed bare —and safer than I ever had before.

I started to drift off to sleep, sure there was something I was supposed to remember, but not caring enough to figure out what it was. This was perfect.

So of course, I woke up the next morning in a panic. A noise at the top of the stairs had woken me up and I realized that Ben was still in bed with me. More than that, Ben was sprawled on top of me and we were both naked, a light blue sheet the only thing covering us.

"Ben," I hissed. "Ben, wake up."

I shoved him and Ben blinked his eyes open groggily.

"What?" he asked—but he didn't move.

"We fell asleep," I said frantically. "You never went back to your room and now someone's awake upstairs and you need to—"

But it was too late. The noises at the top of the stairs got louder and my eyes went wide as I watched Ben's mom descend from the second floor carrying a basket of laundry.

She stopped dead at the foot of the stairs, taking in the scene before her—her son in bed with his best friend, draped across his chest, both of us clearly naked. Ben's whole body was tangled up with mine and there was no hiding what had taken place the night before.

"Uh. Hi, Ma," Ben said, his voice bright. He made an apologetic face. "Sorry, uh, sorry for the surprise."

Mrs. Kowalski was quiet for a moment. She blinked once, then twice. And then she shook her head and smiled.

"I'll go get the coffee started," she said. And as soon as she was around the corner and in the kitchen, I heard a noise that sounded suspiciously like a giggle.

"Oh. My. God," I mouthed at Ben. I wanted the sofabed to fold up and swallow us. "Fuck."

"I guess we don't have to worry about how to break the news to her," Ben said with a grin.

"I want to die."

"Oh come on," Ben said, poking me in the chest. "You have to admit it's kind of funny."

"Funny isn't the word I'd use. Flesh-curdlingly mortifying is more like it."

"Please," Ben said, sitting up and stretching. "I told you she wouldn't care."

"I didn't plan on testing that theory quite so soon," I grumbled, feeling around in the sheets for my boxers. Ben flashed back upstairs as I got dressed and I waited for him to come back down, fully clothed, before I was willing to venture into the kitchen.

Ben's mom was sitting at the kitchen table, sipping her coffee and working on a crossword. She waited for us each to fill our mugs before turning and fixing us both with a stare.

"So. How long has this been going on?" she asked.

"Uh. It's uh, kind of new," Ben said.

"And is this one of those hook-ups people you millennials are supposed to be all about these days? Or is it something more serious?"

"It's serious," Ben said without hesitation. He took my hand in his own. "Adam and I are dating. He's my—he's my boyfriend."

When his mom didn't say anything, I started to panic again.

"Mrs. Kowalski, I'm so sorry," I said, tripping over my words in my haste to get them out. "I shouldn't have—that is, I know I'm a guest in your home and it was wrong of me to, well, I didn't mean for anything to—we just, we fell asleep by accident, we didn't mean to—not that it would have been better to lie to you, I don't mean that, it's just that—"

I cut off when Mrs. Kowalski set her coffee down and stood up, wondering if we were about to get a lecture, if I was about to get kicked out of the house.

And then she hugged me. It took me a full 10 seconds to realize what was happening, to remember that I was supposed to hug her back. I had to let go of Ben's hand to do so but his mom didn't seem to mind and just squeezed me tighter when I brought my arms around her. She pulled Ben into a hug next and was beaming when she finally stepped back.

"I couldn't be happier for you two," she said. "I'm glad you have the good sense to realize what you have in each other. Probably no need to mention the particulars of our meeting this morning to anyone else—your father might pass out from embarrassment—but I hope you weren't planning on keeping this a secret from everyone for too much longer. It's just wonderful."

And you know what?

It was.

16

BEN

"*B*en, fuck, I'm so—I'm almost—" Adam gasped as I moved my mouth up and down on his cock.

We were in the kitchen—Adam pressed up against the refrigerator door, me on my knees in front of him. Note to self: Don't come up behind Adam while he's putting away the milk and kiss him on the back of his neck—it only leads to compromising situations, ones in which neither of us wants to stop long enough to walk the 20 feet to the bedroom, ones in which I end up blowing him on the kitchen floor.

Except, who was I kidding. Note to self: Definitely kiss Adam while he's putting the milk away. Do it every goddamn day.

We'd slept in this morning and had only been awake for a few hours. Neither of us had bothered to get very dressed, which, I'll admit, had made the kitchen floor blow job even easier. There was no way for Adam to cover up how hard he'd gotten when I'd pressed him up against the refrigerator. No reason for him to.

I kept one hand on the base of his cock, used the other to massage his balls and extend just one finger back between his legs. Adam quivered as I stroked past his hole and looked down at me with lust-shot eyes. I knew I looked messy, spit and precum all over my lips, but Adam seemed to like it.

I liked it too.

I liked the taste of his cock, the feel of it sliding between my lips, over my tongue, down into my mouth. I liked the way his whole body trembled as I brought him closer to the edge, the way his thighs shook and threatened to give way. I liked the way he moaned, the way his hips thrust forward, stuttering, desperate for me to take more of him in my mouth. I liked seeing him there above me, knowing I could untie him like a ribbon, see him come rippling out of control.

I stroked past his hole again and then started teasing it with my finger, tickling, making his knees shake as I moved my hand from the base of his cock and sucked him all the way down. Adam moaned above me, a high, broken sound. His cock twitched in my mouth and then he came. I could feel him releasing, hitting the back of my throat and I swallowed hungrily until I finally felt him stop.

"You," Adam said, pulling me up for a kiss, "are a dangerous person to have breakfast with."

I smiled as his tongue slid across my lips, then pushed into my mouth. He tasted like coffee, like lazy Saturdays, like sex.

"Just wait til you see what I have planned for dinner," I said, wiggling my eyebrows.

Adam swatted at my chest. "You're going to make me take two showers today, huh?"

"Who said anything about showering?" I gave him my best leering smile, then leaned in to nip at his lower lip. "I like the way you smell after I'm done with you."

"That's a little—" Adam cut off, his eyes going from my face to some spot behind me. "Holy shit, is someone coming into your—"

"Fuck," I said, bending down quickly to toss Adam's boxers at him as I heard the lock in the front door start to turn. "Shit, it must be Shereen. She has another key—Go, bedroom, hide. I'll get rid of her."

Adam just barely had time to throw me a horrified look before I shoved him towards the bedroom and bent to find my boxer-briefs. I didn't even remember them coming off. I pulled them on, Adam closed the bedroom door, and Shereen opened the front door in quick succession. I ran a hand through my hair, breathing hard.

"Ben!" Shereen exclaimed as she stepped into the apartment and saw me. She was carrying a massive bouquet of what looked like roses, calla lilies and ranunculus. "I didn't think you'd be here. Didn't you say something about going up to the Cloisters today?"

"Yeah," I said, trying my best not to sound like I'd been naked up until five seconds ago. "We—I—I got a late start today. Decided to stay in and work on some music instead.

Didn't you promise to start knocking before you just walked in here?"

Adam and I *had* talked about heading up to the Cloisters today—it was one of my favorite spots in the city, a park and museum at the very tip of Manhattan and I'd only just learned that Adam had never been there. But when the alarm had gone off this morning, neither of us had felt like getting up and, well, here we were.

Shereen gave me a suspicious look but then shrugged. "I didn't think you were around. What's the point of knocking if you're not supposed to be here."

"The point of knocking is that you don't actually *know* if someone's here til you do it. That's like, common sense."

"You say common sense, I say pointless waste of time. I'm a busy woman, Benjamin. Anyway, it's actually good that you *are* here—I was going to call you but now we can just talk in person. Here, take these first."

Shereen walked forward and foisted the bouquet off on me, then fished in her giant bag and pulled out a bottle of *Moet & Chandon*.

"Are you trying to bribe me into forgetting your terrible manners?" I asked as I set the flowers and the champagne on the island in the kitchen.

"I'm shocked and hurt that you would suggest such a thing," Shereen said, her eyes widening innocently. "I never apologize for my behavior."

She flashed me a grin and I rolled my eyes.

"The flowers and champers are from Greenleaf," she said.

"They haven't forgotten that your contract's coming up in a couple weeks, nor have they failed to notice that you still haven't renewed it."

"Shereen, I told you, I—"

She held up a hand to stop me. "I know. Trust me, I've told them your concerns, told them what you're thinking. You have to make your own decision. But you can't expect them to let you go without a fight, Ben. Get ready for the full court press. You're going to be drowning in flowers by the end of the week."

"I'd rather be drowning in champagne," I muttered. "If I have to choose."

"I'll be sure to pass that along," Shereen said with a smirk. "Listen, you're going to be getting a lot of phone calls from them and while I don't know the particular details of what they're prepared to offer you, I've got a guess. And it's not the kind of offer you should turn down lightly."

"Oh?"

"You know the money you made this past year?"

"Yeah?"

"Double it. And then multiply by five. Because I'm pretty sure that's what they're going to offer if you're willing to sign a five-year contract with them."

"Jesus." I blinked. "That's…"

"A lot," Shereen said, nodding. "I know."

"Fuck."

"Listen, I'm not saying take it, I'm not saying don't take it,"

Shereen said, holding her hands up. "When it comes down to it, I'd rather work with happy artists than ones who hate their jobs and are just doing it to get paid. Just... think carefully, you know? You've still got some time to decide."

"I—I will," I stammered. "That's, uh, well—I will."

"Good."

"So was there anything else or..." I let the sentence hang unfinished, conscious of the fact that Adam was probably standing on the other side of the bedroom door, tapping his foot in annoyance.

"You've got somewhere to be?" Shereen said, giving me a doubtful look.

"Maybe I just wanna take a shower and don't want to keep standing here talking to my manager in my underwear."

"Prude." Shereen snorted. "But as a matter of fact, yes, there is something else. Quick update on Mia—she's checking out of Peachtree in a few days and is coming back to her apartment. I want to keep the media fuss to a minimum until she feels ready to deal with it. But then, I was thinking, we'll probably want to book you two to do press together. People will eat it up—pop music's power couple coming through a crisis stronger, more in love than ever."

"That's... okay. I guess, sure," I said, "if that's what Mia wants."

"That's what she's going to want," Shereen said, "once her publicist and I talk to her about it. Her image has taken a bit of a beating and we're going to have to do some serious rehabilitation work. We're probably going to delay the album for a few more months, too."

"I—are you sure that's all necessary?" I frowned. "I mean, maybe it would be better to just ask Mia what she wants to do, and just do that"?

"Oh, Ben. Sweet, innocent Ben." Shereen shook her head. "Sometimes I wonder how you go through life without getting robbed blind. You realize most people are assholes, right? Right now, when they look at Mia, they see an evil, crazy bitch who cheated, lied, and pretty much lost her mind. You don't just bounce back from that with a quick, *'Sorry, my bad.'* You have to make people want to forgive you, remind them why they fell in love with you in the first place."

I sighed. I knew Shereen was probably right. "I just wish it didn't all feel so fake. So calculated."

"That's why you have me to do the calculations for you. Of course, we'll have to figure out what to do if you don't renew with Greenleaf," Shereen said, cocking her head to the side in thought. "That could get messy."

"I don't want to fuck things up for Mia," I said. "But I'm just... I'm not sure I can keep doing this, you know?"

Shereen nodded. "I know. But if you want this kind of money, this kind of fame, you have to play the game."

I knew it was true. But the thought twisted my stomach. I didn't want the fame. That part, I could take or leave. But the money... that was the rub.

"Just think it over," Shereen said. "I'll get out of your hair now and you can tell whatever lady friend you have on the other side of the bedroom door that they can come out."

I nearly choked. "There's no—I don't have—I'm not—"

Shereen just gave me a withering glance. "I'll give you props for being discreet, at least, while Mia's been at Peachtree. There've been more pictures of you with your friend Adam in the past few weeks than there have been of you with anyone else."

"Uh. Yeah," I said, completely unsure of what to say to that.

"Just make sure you keep it under wraps," Shereen said with a hard look. "We don't need to add another angle to this PR nightmare."

And with that, she air-kissed me goodbye and left me standing in the kitchen, my head spinning so much I felt like I'd just chugged the bottle of champagne on the counter. I walked over to the bedroom, shaking my head, and opened the door.

"Coast is clear," I called. "You can—"

I stopped. Adam was sitting in the overstuffed leather chair in the corner of the room, staring at nothing. Well, technically at the wall, but I didn't think he was seeing it. He was hugging his knees to his chest and didn't even seem to have heard me.

"Adam? Are you—" I stopped again as he looked up, tears glittering in the corners of his eyes. "What's wrong?" I walked over to him, knelt on the floor, put my hands on his shins. "What happened, what can I do?"

"It's stupid," Adam said, shaking his head like he was coming out of a trance. "It's stupid, ignore me."

"Okay, well that's not going to happen, so why don't you tell me what's wrong instead?"

"I just—" Adam stopped, swallowed hard, and squeezed his eyes shut. "I feel like such an idiot. I know why you can't come out. I get it. And I feel so shitty about getting upset about it because it's not fair to you. I just... fuck, I just wish it were different. I wish I didn't have to sprint into the bedroom to hide from people. I wish—fuck, it doesn't matter. Forget it."

My heart clenched. If *I* didn't like lying about who I was, who I was with, how had I not realized how much worse that must make Adam feel? I hated seeing him in pain—even worse, pain that I had caused. Fuck, what a mess.

I had to find some way to fix it.

"Can you come with me?" I asked quietly, standing up.

I held my hand out to Adam and after staring at it with some misgiving, he took it and let me pull him up. Still holding his hand, I walked us into the bathroom and turned the taps on in the massive tub.

"If I promise not to try any funny business," I said, "will you get in here with me?"

Adam frowned. I couldn't blame him. I bent down to feel the water filling up in the tub, adjusted the taps to make it hotter, and began to strip. I stepped into the tub once I was undressed, the hot water prickling against my skin, and then sat down.

I looked up at Adam. "Can you come in here with me? Just to talk? I'm gonna fix things, I promise."

I wasn't sure if he believed me or if he just felt awkward standing there watching me while I sloshed around naked in a bathtub, but eventually he shucked off his boxers and stepped in. I pulled him back to lie on my chest once he was settled and made a mental note that maybe having a bathtub the size of an SUV wasn't actually the dumbest thing in the world.

Our bodies just fit together, it seemed. There weren't any good, romantic metaphors for it. There's nothing sexy about saying we fit together like *Legos*, or those twirly little wrenches and sockets you use when you're putting together *IKEA* furniture. But we did.

I wrapped my arms around Adam's chest and kissed the side of his neck.

"I hate that I made you feel this way," I said softly. "But I promise, it won't happen again."

Adam snorted lightly. "It's not that I don't appreciate it, Ben, but don't make promises you can't keep."

"Adam, I—"

"I'm not trying to be a dick," he cut in. "But as long as we're keeping this a secret, shit like this is bound to happen. And it's not even a problem. Not your fault, anyway. I know there are good reasons for you not to come out. I just... I just have to learn to get used to it. Hell, it shouldn't even be that hard. Five years? I liked you for seven and managed to keep my mouth shut about it."

"Five years?" I asked.

"I heard Shereen," Adam said, his voice heavy. "And I get it. That kind of money—it's not nothing. And it makes sense that you'd need to keep this Mia thing going. Keep up the straight Ben Thomas act, even if you guys did 'break up.' I'm not trying to ask you to do things you're not ready for. It just might take me a little while to get used to it, I guess."

I turned, closed my eyes, and pressed my face to his cheek. "What if I am ready?"

"What?"

I could feel Adam's whole body tense.

"What if I am ready," I repeated. "What if I want to—what if I want to do it now. To tell everyone I'm with you. To be honest. To be who I am. To be with you."

"You can't," Adam said, his voice sounding frantic. "You can't do that. You're still under contract, you're still supposed to be with Mia. You said it yourself, you don't want to leave her without any support."

"I'm only under contract for two more weeks. And Mia... well, I can talk to Mia. We have our eject button, you know? I think she'll understand."

"But you'd damage your marketability, or whatever. Ruin your image."

"Fuck my image," I said fiercely. "Maybe people are more ready for a bisexual popstar than we give them credit for."

"But the money—"

"There is no way in hell that money is more important to me than you are," I growled. "I can't believe I even thought, for a second, that I should say yes to that. Not when it would hurt you. I never want to hurt you."

"What if I ruin everything?" Adam said after a moment. "What if you come out, tell everyone we're dating, and then no one wants anything to do with you. You can't book shows, you can't sell records, everything just falls apart. I don't want to fuck up your life."

"You couldn't fuck up my life if you tried. So what if no one wants to see me perform anymore? I'll get another job. It's not the worst thing in the world. I'd rather be myself, be honest, than be trapped."

Adam turned around sloshily and stared at me. "You can't. You love performing."

"But I love y-"

But I couldn't finish the sentence before Adam slapped a hand over my mouth, sending droplets of water flying from his arm.

He shook his head frantically. "Don't say that."

I looked a silent question at him—silent because he wouldn't move his hand from my mouth—and Adam's eyebrows drew down.

"Please," he said, his voice tight. "Just please, don't."

He stared at me for a long moment before finally moving his hand.

"Why?" I asked, confused. "I know it's fast, but honestly, Adam, it's not actually fast at all when you think about it. Not when we've known each other for as long as we have. This is real. I know it is. So... why?"

Adam squeezed his eyes shut for a moment and when he opened them, they burned like green flames.

"If you say it," he said slowly, "that makes it real. This. Us. If you say it, you can't take it back. And then everything feels different and then if something goes wrong, it's going to make it so much worse."

"Why are you so sure something's going to go wrong? Don't you trust me?"

"I'm trying," Adam said. "Please believe me, I'm trying. I know this isn't any fun, I know it sucks to be with someone who's so messed up—"

"You're not, though."

"Ben, I am. It's sweet of you to say I'm not, but trust me, no one's like, *'Gee, I'd really like to date someone with an anxiety disorder, that sounds like a real picnic.'* I'm trying to be better. I don't like being like this, feeling broken. But I just... I need time, okay?"

Adam's eyes darted back and forth across my face, searching for signs of... something. That I understood, maybe. I thought I did. Even if I didn't quite agree. I reached up and brushed the pad of my thumb across his cheekbone.

"Okay," I said. "Okay, I won't say it. But you can't make me unfeel it. And I still want to come out. I still want to be with you. Publicly." I stroked his cheekbone again. "So there."

Adam laughed lightly and leaned into my touch. "I guess I can live with that."

"Good."

Adam turned around and lay back against me. I ran my fingertips up and down his chest, just enjoying the feeling of his weight on top of me.

"So how were you thinking of doing this?" Adam asked after

a minute. "Hiring a plane to write 'I like dick, specifically Adam's' in the sky over Midtown?"

"Oh, I was just going to take out a full-page ad in the New York Times."

"Too elitist," Adam said. "A man who hires a skywriter is a man of the people."

"Good point." I paused. "Just to clarify, it's really okay if I do this, right?"

Adam put his hand on top of mine. "Yeah. It's really okay."

"Good." I nodded. "As for how... I hadn't actually gotten that far. Maybe I could get away without saying anything specifically. Just like, making it clear that Mia and I were done and then, I don't know, trying to convince you to hold hands with me in public. That would probably take care of it. It'll probably be a big thing for a few days but I can give a couple of statements and then things should settle down."

"That's optimistic," Adam said. "I bet you're going to get offers to turn your story into a TV movie. Write a memoir. Go on *Dancing with the Stars*."

"Oh God, let's hope not."

"Either way, though, you might want to talk to Mia first," Adam said. "And make sure you wait til you're off Green-leaf's payroll."

"Yeah." I nodded. "Yeah, for sure. Anyone you want to tell before we take it public?"

Adam paused. "Esther, I guess. She'd probably be pissed if I didn't. But other than that, not really."

"What if we invite her and Mia over for dinner?" I said, the idea popping into my brain. "Mia's coming home from Peachtree in a couple days. We can ply them with booze and then tell them together."

"And hope that neither of them decides they hate us?"

I snorted. "Something like that. I really think it's going to be fine, though."

"I hope so," Adam said. "I just can't shake this feeling that this is a terrible mistake and I'm ruining your life somehow."

"That's like a physical impossibility. Even if I end up as a dental hygienist when all of this is done. It'll be worth it."

It would be. Realizing what I felt for Adam, discovering what we could have together—I wouldn't trade that for the world. I felt, somehow, like I'd become more myself now that I was with him. It was exhilarating. And terrifying.

I was in love with Adam. I hadn't even realized it until I said it—well, tried to say it. But now that I had, I knew it for a fact. I was in love with my best friend, and it made me feel, as he would say, all gross and warm and squishy inside.

All I could do was hope Adam felt the same way. Or at least would, one day. Because part of me wondered if his reluctance for me to say I loved him was a different kind of fear—he didn't want me to say it because he didn't love me back.

It was okay if he didn't now. I could live with that. But the thought that he might never get there... it hurt too much to think about.

I tried to tell myself not to worry. This was Adam. Adam

who'd move heaven and earth to do you a favor if he considered you a friend, all while denying that he'd done anything special at all. He was allergic to expressing his feelings, but that didn't mean he didn't have them. Right?

"Dental hygienist?" Adam said after a moment, turning his head and glanced back at me.

I shrugged and made myself smile, pushing down my fears. There wasn't anything I could do about them anyway. "I always liked teeth."

"You're full of surprises, Ben Kowalski."

"I am." I grinned. "In fact, bring that mouth of yours a little closer. Might be time for an oral examination."

"For my health, of course."

"Definitely," I said, flashing him a wicked smile. "For your health."

17

ADAM

"Hey, my check came!" I said as I walked back into the apartment. I shuffled through the rest of the mail in my hand to check for anything else interesting. "Drinks are on me tonight!"

Ben looked over at me from where he was stirring sauce in front of the stove. "Dude, we already bought wine."

"Well, you know. Metaphorically." I snorted as I walked over to him. "Probably better that way, I don't know shit about wine."

"Still, though." Ben set the wooden spoon down carefully and pulled me in for a hug. "That's awesome."

I frowned as I opened the envelope and saw the amount on the check. "Huh. This is only for two songs from back in May. Maybe the other ones haven't been processed yet?"

"I'm sure they'll come soon. And then you can buy me all the wine you want."

"Five cases of Two Buck Chuck," I said with a grin. "Shit, I might actually be able to start paying Esther back now, though."

Ben sighed and kissed the top of my head, a gesture I found equal parts sweet and annoying. "I'm sure Esther doesn't think you need to pay her back."

"Yeah, well. I want to anyway. It just feels weird, knowing she spent so much money on something that could have been avoided if I had my life for together."

"I'm not going to be able to talk you out of this, am I?" Ben asked, peering down at me.

"Nope." I smiled and poked him in the chest. "So don't even try. I should also probably start seriously looking for a new place, too. Now that I actually have income coming in. Wanna read Craigslist ads with me after dinner and compose drunk replies?"

"Oh." Ben frowned, drawing his eyebrows down in thought. "Uh, sure. I guess. Okay."

"What?"

"I just... I thought—I didn't realize you wanted to move out, I guess?"

"I... didn't realize I'd actually moved in?" I tilted my head up. "Did you want—I mean, it's fine if—"

"I just thought it sorta made sense, since we're like, you know—"

"God, we're both terrible at this." I rolled my eyes and forced myself to take a deep breath. "Do you want me to stay?"

"Only if you want to," Ben said in a rush. "If you don't, that's fine. I just, I don't know, I like having you here?"

"Doesn't it seem kind of weird? Me not paying rent?"

"Well, to be fair, I'm not paying rent either. Actually, Green-leaf is probably going to kick me out of this apartment once I go independent. But I thought we could maybe look for a new place together?"

I bit my lip. "That'd be... I'd—I'd like that. But only if you let me pay half the rent. I don't want to be a charity case."

"You won't be, I promise. But I might request that you pay your share in wine, rather than dollars."

I smiled. "Deal."

"Shit, Ben, this is really good," Esther said, twirling the last spaghetti noodle around her fork and popping it into her mouth.

We were sitting around the island in Ben's *haute couture* space station kitchen, drinking a barolo (not that I knew what that was, but Ben swore it was good) and finishing dinner. It had gone surprisingly well.

Not that I'd expected Esther and Mia not to get along, but I definitely hadn't expected them to both turn out to adore the same middle grades mystery book series. I'd never heard of the *Fern and Ivy Mysteries* and had completely missed Esther's childhood obsession with them, but apparently one of the books was set close to Ben's apartment.

Esther had referenced it when she was describing getting lost finding Ben's place and it turned out Mia had read and loved the series too. They'd spent the next half hour debating the finer points of... well, I hadn't quite been able to follow it. Something about secret subway stations, water towers, and attic crawl spaces that might or might not lead back in time. Apparently the New York Public Library was hosting an exhibit on the series and Mia and Esther had made plans to see it together the following week.

"Yeah," Mia said, bringing my mind back to the conversation. She swiped a finger through the puddle of bolognese sauce on her plate and licked it. "Since when can you cook?"

"Since always," Ben said, indignant. "There just aren't a lot of chances to do it when we're on tour, you know? I can't exactly make bolognese sauce in a hotel microwave."

"Fair," Mia said. "But I still think that as my devoted boyfriend, you need to start cooking for me once a week. For my mental health and all."

Ben laughed. "What do I get in return?"

"My undying love and encouragement?" Mia offered.

"I'd rather have you bring me wine."

"Hey, I thought that was my job," I objected.

"Speaking of which," Esther said, reaching out to pick up the second bottle of wine we'd opened. "Anyone want more?"

Ben glanced at me while Esther filled up our glasses, quirking an eyebrow. I knew he was asking if he should bring it up now. It was probably as good a time as any. I was in that perfect warm, slightly fuzzy place where I'd had just enough wine to relax and not enough to be sleepy. If Esther or Mia reacted badly, at least we'd had a good night up until now. I nodded at Ben.

"So," he said, turning back to Mia and Esther on the other side of the island. "We actually had an ulterior motive for inviting you guys here tonight."

Mia frowned. "If it was to get us to do the dishes, you're shit out of luck. I just got my nails done."

"No, it's... hopefully better than that. Um, so basically, the idea was to get you guys drunk and poised at the edge of a food coma so that you're in a good mood when I tell you I need to pull the ripcord." Ben took a deep breath. "Sesquipedalian."

"Oh." Mia paused. "Ok. Shit. What's up?"

Esther frowned and looked at me. "What am I missing? What's sesquipedalian?"

"It's their uh—it's about their... relationship?" I felt completely tongue-tied and like everyone was looking at me, even if there were just three other people there. "It's hard to—I mean, it's not—"

"Ben and I aren't really dating," Mia said, jumping in to save me. I flashed her a grateful smile. "It's just a thing our label wanted us to do for publicity."

"Oh." Esther's eyes widened. "I didn't know that was an actual thing people did."

"Yeah." Mia made a face. "It's pretty weird, I guess, but when you do this for long enough, you sort of stop realizing how weird all these things are that have just become a part of your normal life. Anyway, sesquipedalian is our get-out-of-jail-free card—if someone says it, that means they want out of the relationship. We break up, no matter what the label wants. So," she turned back to Ben, "Ben wants out. Which, I can't really say I blame you for. I wouldn't want to date me right now either. Even fake-date me."

"No, Mia, it's not that, trust me."

"Dude, I just had to go spend two weeks at Peachtree for exhaustion-aka-I-picked-the-wrong-week-to-stop-taking-my-mood-disorder-medication—God forbid we ever say those words out loud, though." Mia rolled her eyes and then glanced at Esther and me. "Peachtree's a fancy-pants psychiatric facility in Connecticut that tries to pretend like it's a holistic healing center."

"I, uh, I know," I said, smiling. "I actually just spent a month there."

"No shit? You're crazy too?" Mia grinned.

"Certifiable," I said with a laugh.

It was weirdly nice not to be the only person with issues in the room. Ben could say I was perfect all he wanted—I'd never get tired of hearing it, but I'd never believe him either. Maybe Mia had the right attitude though—just owning it, not worrying about how other people reacted.

"Okay, neither of you are crazy," Ben said—because of course he did, "but seriously, Mia, that's not why I need to break things off. I know the timing's not great and I'm happy to like, figure out how to manage the PR and all of that, but the thing is, I need to break it off because there's someone I actually *do* want to be with. For real. Well, *am* with, already. But we want to be able to go public."

"Aww, Ben. That's so sweet," Mia said.

"Yeah, yeah, sweet, whatever," Esther said. "What I want to know is who it is. Please tell me it's another famous person. I live for celebrity gossip. No offense," she said, turning to Mia.

"None taken." Mia grinned. "Me too, actually."

"So," Esther said, "who is it?"

The two of them stared at Ben, who looked at me. I knew I was being chicken, making Ben do all the talking so far. So I took another deep breath—and dammit, I was going to have to tell Nick that his stupid mindfulness techniques were actually helping—and looked at Esther and Mia.

"It's me."

"Wait, what?" Esther said, her eyes wide.

"Oh my God, really?" Mia squealed. "That's So. Fucking. Cute."

Ben smiled at me and put his hand on top of the island. I reached over and covered it with mine, feeling a million things all at once. Pride. Fear. Hope. And love. That was the strongest feeling of all, welling up inside me.

I made myself look at Esther and Mia. Mia had her hands clapped to her mouth, her eyes dancing above them. And Esther... Esther looked like she was going to cry.

"Es, are you—are you okay?" I asked.

Had I totally misjudged how she'd react? Did she think this was a bad idea? I thought she was okay with me being gay— she'd offered to murder Ellis for me when I told her and still vowed to accidentally sew up a surgical sponge inside of him if he ever landed on her table—but maybe it was one of those things that was easier to handle in theory than in practice?

But then she stood up, walked around to my side of the island, and threw her arms around me.

"I'm so fucking happy for you," she said, squeezing me tight. "So happy. You deserve this."

"Oh. Um. Okay." I wasn't quite prepared for that reaction either, and I wondered if Ben and Mia were staring at us.

But Esther wouldn't let go and eventually I hugged her back, burying my face in her long brown hair, getting a whiff of that same spicy, herbal shampoo she'd used for as long as I could remember. It reminded me of my childhood, of the few happy memories I had from back then.

Esther building forts with me in the attic, running through the woods with me outside, reading stories to me at night long after I should have been too old for bedtime stories. She was the one person who'd cared about me, who'd wanted me around. I owed her so much.

I could feel myself getting teary-eyed and I forced myself to blink that back. Finally, Esther stepped back, still teary-eyed herself, and smiled.

"I'm really happy for you two," she said.

"We're happy for us two, too," Ben grinned.

He took my hand again. And just like that morning in his parents' kitchen, I felt that flash of recognition—this was what family was. People who loved you. People you could be vulnerable with. It was simultaneously unsettling in its strangeness and stunning in its warmth.

"So how'd you two get together?" Mia asked.

"It's kind of complicated," Ben said.

I snorted. "No it's not. Basically, I had a crush on Ben since forever, I came out a month ago, and then I Jedi-mind-tricked him into liking me."

"Or maybe I just needed you to come out for me to realize how I felt about you all along," Ben said, rolling his eyes. "It's not like it took me that long to figure out I was crazy about you."

"Gross. Barf. Stop," I said, holding my hands up in protest. "It's bad enough to say shit like that when we're alone. In front of friends and family? Evil."

"I know, I'm terrible," Ben said with a grin. "What if I just exposure-therapy you until you're so desensitized that I can give you compliments without you protesting."

"You would, wouldn't you?"

"Honestly?" Ben took my hand again. "I would."

"Honestly," Mia broke in, "you two are so cute that *I'm* going to vomit. But before I do that, tell me what the plan is. How are you guys gonna come out?"

"Well, we wanted to talk to you first," Ben said. "I've decided I'm not going to renew my contract with Greenleaf. But I don't want to screw you over or anything."

"Pssh, that's fine," Mia said. "I'm the one who's been causing all the problems lately with my crazy. You don't have to worry about me."

"Good luck with that argument," I told her. "Ben here doesn't seem to see crazy. I keep trying to tell him I'm a mess but he won't admit it."

Ben rolled his eyes. "Honestly, Mia, your 'crazy' or whatever you want to call it is part of the reason we're even together. Shereen told me to lie low that week you were out in Vegas and LA, so Adam and I went out to Montauk for a while and—"

"Ooh, Montauk," Esther broke in. She looked at me. "Didn't you swear you'd never go back there after you drove Dad's car into the ocean?"

"Wait, what?" Ben stared at me. "How did I miss that story?"

"It's not really that good a story," I said, my cheeks heating up. "I was 16 and Dad was being a dick as usual. He'd decided I was going to a new school that fall, even though I'd finally gotten the assholes at my old school to leave me in peace, so I decided to teach him a lesson by taking his Benz for a swim."

"Jesus," Ben said.

I shrugged. "Yeah, it didn't go over too well with him. But it was worth it."

"I think you're my hero," Mia said, "My parents were assholes too, but I was always too scared of them to do anything like that. Anyway," she turned to Ben, "I'm happy to do whatever you want. Quiet, professional breakup statements released to the press or a loud screaming match in Times Square. Whatever you fancy."

"I was kind of thinking something more like the former," Ben laughed.

"Pity." Mia made a face. "I've gotten pretty good at hysterical public breakdowns recently."

"Ooh, we should compare notes," I said. "You might be able to give me some pointers."

"You have anything planned I should know about?" Ben asked, giving me a questioning smile.

"Nah," I shrugged. "Just never hurts to stay on top of your game."

The rest of dinner was relaxed after that and it was after midnight when Esther and Mia finally left. As Ben was walking Mia to the door, I pulled Esther aside.

"Hey, I wanna talk to you about something if you've got a sec," I told her.

"Sure. What's up?"

"I wanted—okay, backing up, I should start by thanking you. For everything you've done for me. I know I joke about it but it was really shitty, what I put you through. And I know I can't make it up to you, but I was thinking maybe I could like, pay you back for Peachtree?" The last sentence came out in a rush.

Esther's eyes went wide. "Oh, Adam, no, you don't—"

"No, listen. I couldn't do it all at once. But like, in installments. It'll take a while but I—I want to. I really do."

Esther's eyes darted across the room to where Ben was shutting the door behind Mia. I wondered if she was buying time to think of an excuse.

"Please, Es. It would mean a lot to me."

"What would mean a lot to you?" Ben asked, coming over to join us. He slipped an arm around my shoulders.

"Me paying Esther back," I said, trying to resist the urge to fall back against him, to let him hold me. "Which she doesn't want me to do, as you predicted."

"Oh." Ben frowned for a second before his face cleared. "Well, I do like being right. I guess now you'll have to use that money for something else. How about you pay for us to install a moonbounce in the new apartment?"

"Ugh, how about you support me here," I groaned. "I'm trying to be a real adult and you're ganging up on me."

"Not ganging up," Esther objected. "Just saying that you're family. And money doesn't matter. You know we'll always take care of you."

I could feel myself getting annoyed but tried to keep my voice even. "Okay, I appreciate that, but since I'm not actually a child, it'd be awesome if you stopped treating me like one. I don't need to be *taken care of*."

"Bad choice of words," Ben said, his voice soothing. "I'm just saying that I—that *we* love you." He corrected himself and I felt a stab of guilt about our conversation earlier that week.

God, maybe I was making too big a deal out of all of this. Did I have to be such a difficult asshole about everything?

"Fine," I sighed. "Fine, I'll stop complaining. But only because I'm so full of pasta that I can't think straight."

"You're welcome," Ben said, flashing Esther a smile.

"See," Ben said as we finally said goodbye to Esther and closed the apartment door. "That wasn't so bad, was it?"

I wrapped my arms around him and buried my face in his neck. It *had* been a good night, but exhausting, in a way. It was nice to be back to just the two of us.

"No, I guess it wasn't," I said. "Aside from all the gross feelings parts."

"Yeah, aside from those," Ben laughed.

And even the feelings parts weren't so bad, I reflected as we cleaned up the remains of dinner. If I had to have feelings, anyway, at least I got to have them for Ben. Who was, quite possibly, the goofiest person in the world, singing a song to himself about doing dishes and trying to get me to harmonize with him. The goofiest, but also the best.

"Joke's on you if I turn this into a real song," I said as Ben handed me a dish to dry.

"You'd better. It's going on my next album."

"Well then you can't blame me if I stay up half the night on my guitar, working out the—"

"What?" Ben asked.

I sighed. "I just remembered that I still haven't gotten my stuff from my dad's place."

"No rush," Ben said.

"I know." I frowned. "Part of me just wants to say fuck it and leave it all there. But I'm attached to that guitar."

"Which one?" Ben frowned. "I thought you had two."

"I did. But I sold one of them a few months ago, while you were still on tour." I laughed ruefully. "I kept the Fender Strat. The one you put a dent in sophomore year."

"In my defense," Ben said, "That dent makes it way more rock 'n' roll."

"In my defense, you're a giant nerd," I retorted. "But I'm a sentimental asshole who kept that guitar because of the dent. So I guess we're even."

"Want me to come with you?" Ben asked. "When you go up to get your stuff?"

I paused, thinking it over. "Actually, I think maybe not. I think it's probably something I need to do on my own. I'm just sick of having it—having him—hanging over my head, you know? I need to close the door on it all."

"Okay." Ben took the dishcloth from my hands as I put away the last plate and hung it over the towel bar, then took my hand and started walking us towards the bedroom. "But if you change your mind, I'm happy to. If you want some moral support. Or someone to punch your dad in the throat."

"Thanks," I laughed as he pulled me onto the bed. We collapsed in a heap on top of the covers and I rolled over to look Ben in the eye. "I know I don't really say it much, but, well—all that feelings crap? You know I feel all that stuff. For you."

Ben pushed himself up on his elbows. "Really?"

"Yes, really." I looked at him in confusion. "Wait, are you seriously asking me that?"

"I don't know, Adam." Ben's shoulders gave a little shrug and looked down, his hair golden in the low lamp light. "I mean, no, not really. But at the same time, sometimes it's like trying to guess with you. I want to believe you like me. I do believe it. But it would be nice to hear it sometimes. Without having to pry it out of you. Sometimes I wonder if I'm just an idiot, pouring my heart out to you and you're just like, *'Eh, he's alright.'*"

"Are you fucking kidding me? Ben, I... I like you so much there aren't actually words for it. I know I'm not good at talking about it, but that doesn't mean the feelings aren't there. Trust me, if you knew how I felt about you, how much time I spend thinking about you, how *long* I've felt this way... you'd be justified in taking out a restraining order against me."

"But you never say it. Not on your own, anyway. I always feel like I have to prompt you, ask for it. It feels... I don't know, I don't like it. It makes me feel needy."

"God." I ran a hand through my hair. "Fuck, I never thought. Ben, *I* feel needy when I say things, too. You're just so much better at this stuff than I am. Talking about how you feel. Emoting normally. I didn't realize..."

"That I need to hear it too, sometimes?" Ben smiled sadly. "Just because I'm 'better at feelings' doesn't mean I don't get insecure. And I just—Adam, I'm falling—no, I've fallen, past tense, so hard and I just—I don't want to be the only one. It's scary not knowing if you feel the same way."

Tell him. Just say it. Tell him you love him. He'll say it back. You know he will. Just say it.

"I do," I said slowly. "I do feel the same way. It's just, it freaks me the fuck out to say it. Because it means that if this doesn't work out, it's going to be that much harder to take. I don't—I don't know how I'd handle it... if things between us. I just... fuck, Ben, you're my best friend. If things go wrong between us, I'm not going to have anyone left."

"Things aren't going to go wrong. I promise. Adam, I—"

I leaned in and kissed him. There was nothing else to do. Nothing else I could bring myself to say, because I was a fucking coward. But maybe I could show him how I felt instead.

Ben kissed me back, hungrily, needily, and rolled me onto my back. My heart began to race as he climbed on top of me. Not nerves, exactly, just... awareness. Of how charged everything felt between us. How full the air was with everything unspoken.

Ben's weight on top of me, all taut muscles and hard warmth, was comforting and exhilarating. I ran my hands through his hair, wanting to pull him closer.

Ben's lips slid off of mine and onto my neck, his rough stubble scratching my skin. He bit down, just where my neck disappeared into my shirt, and I decided that *that* wasn't going to be enough. It took a minute to get undressed —two-bottles-of-barolo fingers aren't the most nimble at unzipping jeans—but then Ben was back on top of me, his hard cock brushing mine. I hipped up against him, our breathing hot, quick, and eager.

I love you. I love you. I love you. It ran like a soundtrack through my mind.

"I want you," is what I said, my lips sliding along his neck. "Fuck, Ben, I *need* you."

It wasn't enough, it wasn't what I wanted to say, but it was as close as I could get.

Ben seemed to understand—my urgency, at least—and tongued at my earlobe as he brought his hand between us. I struggled to hold on, not to get swept away on the tide of sensations rolling through me, as he stroked our cocks together. We were both leaking precum and Ben's hand was slick as he stroked us.

"Fuck, yes," I moaned, my hands clawing into his back. "Oh fuck, yes, Ben."

"What do you want me to do?" Ben asked, breathless. "Just tell me what you want and I'll do it."

"Fuck me," I gasped, my eyes closing in pleasure. "Please, I want you to fuck me."

A sharp intake of breath from Ben made me open my eyes. He was staring down at me, the piercing blue of his gaze the color of waves sparkling in sunlight. His mouth was parted in desire and surprise. I bit my lip, suddenly shy.

"Are you sure?" Ben asked. His voice was raw with want. "We don't have to. I want to do whatever you want."

"What I want," I said, sucking in a breath, "is to feel your cock inside me." I couldn't believe I'd said that, but fuck, it was true. "It's all I've wanted for years."

"Jesus, Adam," Ben said, shaking his head. "Do you have any idea what you do to me?"

I laughed. "I'm gonna guess it's something like what you do to me. Except I can't imagine anyone wanting anything more than I want you."

"Guess I'll have to prove you wrong, then," Ben said. He leaned down and licked across my Adam's apple, his hand teasing the tip of my cock.

"Fucking hell," I moaned.

"Hey Adam?" Ben asked, pulling back from my neck and looking me in the eyes. His gaze was nervous, excited.

"Yeah?" I said, surfacing through the haze of sensation surrounding me.

"Can I—can I rim you?"

My eyes widened. "You really want to?"

"Fuck yes," Ben said. "I wasn't kidding when I told you that before. I want—I want to taste you. Every inch of you. I want to make you feel good."

I stared up at him, his pupils dilated with desire. God, he really did want this. There was no way I could say no. I'd never let someone do that before, but then, I'd never had sex before either. And it was supposed to feel good, right?

And if there were anyone in the world I could trust, it was Ben.

"Yeah," I said, my voice breathy. "Yeah, you can do it."

"You sure?"

"Yeah," I said, a little louder this time. "I'm, uh, a little nervous. But I want you to."

"Thank you." Ben bent down to kiss me. It was soft, delicate. Our tongues swirled together for a moment before Ben pulled back. "I'm going to make you feel amazing."

"Fuck," I groaned as he brought his mouth down to my nipple. "Fuck, you already are."

"Even more amazing," Ben said with a little smile, pressing a kiss to my stomach. "I'm going to make you scream."

As he licked down across my belly and along my hips, he brought his right hand up to my mouth, brushing a finger across my lips. I opened my mouth to ask what he wanted and he slid a finger inside—Oh. I got it.

I sucked his finger in, rolling my tongue around it as if it were his cock and getting it as wet as I could before I moved on to the next finger. Only when Ben's hand was practically dripping did he move it back down to grasp my cock again and fuck, his warm, wet grasp felt amazing.

Ben slid further down the bed and I widened my legs to make more room. His lips went to the head of my cock, which was straining for attention, and sucked the tip in gently. I moaned as he slid his tongue around the crown and then sucked me in further, his hand moving in time with his mouth. I felt like I was floating.

Ben kept up the long and steady strokes with his hands, building tension inside me steadily, licking and sucking my cock in languid, sloppy motions. Just when I was starting to worry that I might come if he kept it up, he pulled off and licked a long stripe down the back of my cock to my balls, rolling them in his mouth and making me groan in pleasure.

"Adam," Ben said, his voice breathy. "Can you—can you sort of..."

"What?" I asked, trying to focus. God, coherent thought was hard right now. "What do you need me to—"

"Can you move your legs sort of back, and like, up? Just a little..." Ben trailed off as I bent my knees and he put his hands on my legs, guiding them into the position he wanted. It wasn't the most comfortable position I'd ever been in—in fact, I couldn't think of anything that had made me feel more vulnerable, lying on my back, knees pulled up to my chest, my ass completely exposed.

"Suddenly I'm feeling kind of grateful for all those yoga classes at Peachtree," I said, trying to crack a joke.

"I mean, there are other positions," Ben said. He smiled shyly. "But I—I like being able to see your face."

I sucked in a breath and nodded silently. Ben turned and kissed my inner thigh and I gasped. His touch was so delicate, feather light, as his tongue traced the soft skin there. I realized I was holding my breath, my mind only able to focus on the sensation of Ben's tongue as it traveled across my balls to the other thigh, where he pressed his lips down and sucked on my skin.

God, that was hot. I closed my eyes and let myself float back on the spirals of pleasure rolling off of my body. Ben's hands moved to my ass, spread it wide, and before I had a chance to panic, he licked one long stripe across my hole from bottom to top.

"Fuck," I breathed.

And then there was another lick, from the other direction this time, and then a third, slow and steady with the flat part of Ben's tongue. He pressed against my hole and lingered. My breath fluttered, wing-like, as I tried to keep a hold of myself. It was like nothing I'd ever felt before. Soft, wet, and sweet.

My eyes flashed open as Ben's tongue pushed down into my hole just a bit before pulling away. Ben's eyes flickered up to mine and I wondered what he saw, if I looked as wild and raw as I felt, flayed open with exquisite tenderness. And then his lips closed around my hole as he flicked his tongue back and forth in quick strokes like he was lapping me up. Fuck, the suction, the friction, the hot, slick feeling of his tongue was incredible.

"Fuck, Ben," I whispered.

"Good?" he asked and I could hear the smile in his voice even before I looked down to see Ben looking satisfied, his eyes heavy-lidded with desire.

"God, yes."

"Told you," Ben smiled lazily. "You taste amazing, by the way."

And then he brought his head back down, using his tongue and lips to tease me open, to lay me bare. I surrendered to it, to that sweetness, to letting Ben take care of me. Ben wanted me—all of me. I could just let go.

Ben's tongue grew more insistent. In between kissing my thighs and biting my ass lightly, he kept returning to my hole, pushing his tongue further inside each time. All the while, he stroked my cock and I realized I was going to come soon if he didn't stop. And while my body wanted nothing more than to give in to that, I didn't want to come until Ben was inside me.

"Jesus, Ben," I moaned, trying to pull myself down out of the clouds. "Fuck, I need—I need—"

"What? Tell me what you need."

"You," I groaned. "I need you. Inside me."

Ben smiled and licked across my hole once more. "Get the lube from the nightstand."

His voice was thick with desire, huskier than usual, and it ran through me like a current. I let my legs fall down onto the bed as I twisted, grabbing the bottle of lube from the drawer. Ben climbed up to meet me and I pressed the bottle into his hands.

He turned me onto my side so I was facing him, then hitched my top leg over his thigh and squirted a dollop of lube onto his hand. I tried to keep my breath even as he brought his hand behind me and a moment later, I felt the cool wet slide of one of Ben's fingers at my entrance, still relaxed and wet from his tongue.

Ben looked at me, his blue eyes dark with want, and I nodded, and then he pressed his finger inside. I gasped, clutching at his shoulder in reflex as it penetrated me.

"Fuuuuck," I moaned as it slid inside. "Fuck, fuck, fuck."

Finally Ben stopped moving and we breathed together in silence for a moment as I got used to the feeling. I'd fingered myself before, but something about Ben doing it, putting myself quite literally in his hands, made it so much more intense.

"Tell me when," Ben said and I inhaled once more, then exhaled, feeling my body relax around him.

"Okay," I said, and I leaned forward, pressing my lips to his as he began to slide his finger in and out of my hole. Fuck, that felt good. I found myself moving my body in rhythm with him.

"More," I demanded as soon as I knew I could take it, and I groaned as Ben pushed another finger in.

The second one was a stretch but it would be nothing compared to his cock, which I was determined to take tonight. Ben moved slower this time, kissing my neck as I adjusted.

"God, you're so perfect," he whispered. "So beautiful."

"You don't need to keep complimenting me, dummy," I said with a shaky laugh. "You've already got me in bed with you."

"Can't help it," Ben said, his teeth grazing my skin as he kissed my neck.

I exhaled softly as Ben started to move his fingers again, my eyelids fluttering shut.

"Fuck," I breathed. "You're so—it's so—fuck."

"Good?" Ben asked, bringing his lips to my ear.

"Fuck, yes."

"How about this?" Ben asked, and he did *something* with his fingers that I couldn't quite describe but it didn't matter because suddenly I was seeing stars and I couldn't think straight anymore anyway.

"Ben, God, fuck, yes, please, fuck," I said, incoherent words falling from my lips.

Ben was pressing against something inside me and it was taking my breath away. My hand dropped from Ben's shoulder to my cock and I stroked myself with stuttering movements.

"Your prostate," Ben said with a grin.

"Jesus. I knew—fuck, I knew that was supposed to feel good. I just never could like, reach it on my own."

"See. You knew there had to be a reason you were keeping me around. Even with all the feelings and compliments."

"Fuck, you can say whatever you want to me," I whined, "as long as you keep dooo—"

Ben slid his fingers out, then thrust them back in again, rubbing my prostate at the end of the plunge and I couldn't talk anymore. All I could do was moan, and that's all I did do. I tried, briefly, to move my hand to Ben's cock, pressing hard against my stomach. I felt bad for ignoring him, but Ben shook his head.

"No. I like watching you touch yourself."

Any shame that I might have felt at one point was gone, forgotten, and I had no problem doing what Ben asked. I felt wanton, lush with pleasure as Ben's fingers fucked into me and I rolled my hips back to meet him.

"Please," I begged when I remembered how to talk. My hand fell to Ben's arm, stilling him. "I'm gonna come if you keep doing that. I want your cock."

I felt Ben's cock twitch against me at those words and smiled.

"You sure?" Ben asked.

I nodded. "I'm ready. In fact, I think I might actually die if you don't fuck me in the next 30 seconds."

"Definitely don't want that to happen."

"I know." I grinned. "Imagine what you'd have to tell the medical examiner."

"Gross." Ben laughed. "I didn't think anything could turn me off right now, but you might have just found it. Please stop talking about dead bodies."

"Then hurry up and get your dick in me," I said, rolling my eyes.

Ben leaned in and bit my lower lip, pulling it out with a growl. He slipped his fingers out and I whined a little, feeling suddenly empty and not liking it.

"How do you," I asked, looking up at Ben. "How do you want me? On my stomach?"

"No." Ben shook his head. "No, I want to see you."

My breath hitched. God, how could he still do that to me, take my breath away, even now?

I let Ben roll me onto my back and handed him the bottle of lube as I spread my legs, bending my knees and putting my feet on the mattress. So much for vulnerability. I watched hungrily as Ben squeezed lube into his hand again and then brought it to his cock, sliding up and down his length in long, smooth strokes.

God, it was beautiful. And fucking pornographic. Ben's cock deserved a centrefold spread. It was huge. And about to go inside me.

Ben moved in between my legs, bending down to kiss me, his hands tangling in my hair. I could feel his cock, hard and slick, lying next to mine and I shifted my hips so that it fell and pressed against my ass.

"Fuck me," I whispered, and Ben's gorgeous blue eyes locked onto mine. "Fuck me, Ben."

Ben pressed his lips to mine once more, soft and sweet, before pulling back. He lined his cock up at my entrance. He wasn't even pushing and I could already feel myself starting to give way for him.

This was actually happening. My heart was pounding. This dream I'd had for literal years was finally coming true. I vowed right then to start being a better person, to become the sort of person who deserved something this good happening to me, who deserved someone like Ben.

And then Ben pushed into me and it was... everything.

Big was the first word that came to mind, as I felt my entrance stretching to take the head of his cock. I sucked in a sharp breath of air as I felt the tip piercing into me. So much bigger than his fingers. Once he was past the tight outer ring, Ben began to slide forward, but I had to reach up and put a hand on his chest.

"Wait," I said, breathing hard. "Just—wait a second."

"Of course," Ben said. He bent down to kiss my forehead but even that tiny move changed the angle of his cock inside me and made my breath catch again. Ben stopped and straightened out.

"Sorry," he said with a sheepish grin. He settled for running a finger across my forehead, pushing back a stray hair, and then stroking down my jawline.

"It's okay," I said. "I just need—just need to go slow."

It should have been awkward, the two of us freeze-framed like that, our bodies slick with sweat, Ben's cock just barely inside me. And yet, as Ben smiled down at me, it wasn't.

His eyes were filled with something tender—love, I realized. Ben loved me. And even if I couldn't say it, I loved him back. And somehow, that made this moment perfect.

"You can move again," I said once my breathing had returned to normal.

Ben nodded and I felt the slow movement of his cock in my ass, pressing further into me. It was so fucking big and for a second, I wondered if I'd actually be able to take it all. I bit my lip and Ben caught my eyes.

"You need me to stop again?" he asked. "Or pull out? It's not —if you want to stop, I don't mind. It's not something we have to do."

"Fuck you," I growled. "Fuck you and your giant fucking cock. We are not stopping."

"I'm not sure if I should apologize or not?" Ben said with a laugh, but he kept pressing in.

"Don't even think about it," I gasped. I was clutching at his shoulders now. It was such a stretch, I felt so full, but I was determined to take it. "I like it."

"Good." Ben smiled. "Then I won't tell you to apologize for how fucking tight you are and how incredible your ass feels."

"Fuck," I breathed.

"What?"

"Just... Jesus, you wait seven years to hear someone say something and it's just... fuck. You feel so good."

Finally, Ben stopped moving. I could feel his body pressed up against me and knew he was all the way in. I exhaled, trying to catch my breath and adjust to the sensation of being stretched and filled. I glanced up and saw Ben looking down at me with a completely ridiculous smile on his face.

"What's that goofy look for," I asked. "You're supposed to be thinking about having your cock buried in my ass."

"Oh, I am. I'm just also thinking about other things."

"Like what?"

"Like things I'm not allowed to say out loud. Per your orders." Ben flashed me a grin.

"Oh," I said quietly.

"Yeah. Oh."

I blushed, but somehow that was exactly what I needed. I

felt warm all over. Loved. Protected. And I could feel my body relaxing, accommodating Ben. It required giving up some control, trusting him not to hurt me. But I did. Looking into his eyes, I knew I did. So I let go.

Ben must have seen it in my eyes, because without me having to say anything, he rolled his hips once. Didn't even pull out at all, just pressed against me and released. I gasped. He did it again and I moaned, gripping his shoulders tight, feeling a wave of sensation rush through me as Ben drove into me.

He wasn't even moving his cock yet, just experimenting with pressure, and it felt so good. His cock was so thick, so hard inside me and I hadn't been prepared for this at all, not how helpless I'd feel. Or how amazing.

The next time he moved, Ben slid his cock out just a bit before pushing back in and I groaned.

"Fuck, Ben," I cried. "Yes, fuck."

Ben did it again, and again, his breath growing heavy as he thrust his hips forward. I wrapped my legs around him, offering more of myself up. God, I needed more of him, all of him.

"Oh my God, Adam," Ben breathed, his cock sliding in and out of me. "Adam, you're so good. So good."

"Please," I begged, desperate to feel more of this.

More heat, more force, more need, more pleasure. Ben moved with me, leaning in and kissing me as he thrust. Our lips crashed together, our bodies a wave of heat and longing. Our tongues tangled, hands in hair, and when we broke apart, I could feel Ben's breath on my neck.

"Please," I said again. "Please, I need—fuck."

I didn't even know what I was asking for but somehow, Ben did. He slid his hand in between us, found my cock. Wrapping his hand around it, he stroked me in time with his thrusts and I started moaning again, aware of how completely needy, how wrecked I sounded and unable to stop, unable to even care.

"Yes," I whined. "Fuck yes, just like that, fuck, fuck."

Ben pulled his lips away from my neck and looked down at me, his eyes bluer than blue, and somehow that one look was enough to send me to the edge.

"Fuck, Ben, I'm gonna come if you don't—"

"I want you to come," Ben said, his voice raspy with pleasure, his eyes locked onto mine. How the hell did he do that —how could he hold me so completely, make me fall so completely apart?

"But I want—I don't want to—not until you—"

"I'm right there with you, Adam," Ben said. "Trust me. Right behind you."

"Fuck, Ben," I breathed as he thrust into me harder.

"Come for me, baby," he said, and I came undone. My orgasm hit me like a tidal wave, smashing my senses to bits. It exploded through my body as I came into Ben's hand, long ropes of cum landing on my stomach. I felt his movements stuttering, his cock twitching, and he released, spilling deep inside me. The whole time, Ben's eyes were locked on mine.

Finally, he collapsed down on top of me. I clung to him, tired, sweaty, sated.

"Holy shit," Ben said, his chest heaving.

"Yeah," I agreed, breathless. "Holy shit."

"Stay right here," Ben said, kissing my forehead lightly before pulling out and hopping off the bed.

I felt a slight pang of loss but he was back quickly with two glasses of water and a washcloth that he used to clean us up. He held the glass of water to my lips and I drank thirstily, feeling a little silly letting him hold it for me, but letting him do it anyway. It was nice, okay?

Ben finished off his glass of water, set them both down on the nightstand, and then pulled the covers down, crawling into bed and pulling me against him.

"Good?" he mumbled into the back of my neck.

"Fuck yes." I settled back against him. "Good. I don't even have words, really."

"Same," Ben said, and I could hear his smile.

"It was..." I laughed. "Like, I've imagined that a lot. Years of building it up in my head, really. And somehow, it was still better."

"Shit. I'm glad you told me that after the fact. I might have gotten stage fright if I knew I was competing against imaginary Ben."

"Always looking out for you. Baby," I added with a light laugh.

Ben snorted. "I wondered if you were going to mention that. Is it—does it bother you? Me calling you that?"

I rolled my eyes at myself. "It probably should."

"But?"

"But... maybe it's not the worst thing in the world."

Ben hummed against the back of my neck in response and slid one of his legs over mine so that his calf was covering my shins. I laughed quietly, remembering all the nights in all the years before this when Ben would drape himself over me and drive me crazy. And now he was mine. How the fuck had that happened?

"Hey Ben," I said softly.

"Yeah?"

"I love you."

Ben laughed and kissed my neck again. "I know."

"Dick," I whispered, tracing my fingers up and down Ben's arm lightly.

"Yeah," Ben agreed. "Pretty much."

I could feel my body trying to drift off to sleep. It was tempting, so tempting. Ben's arms around me, the softness of the pillows, the safety of this space made for just the two of us. But I fought it for as long as I could, waiting for Ben to speak again.

He didn't. All I heard were his even breaths, growing deeper and slower as he was tugged towards sleep as well. Finally, unable to take it anymore, I shoved my elbow back, poking Ben in the chest.

"That's it?" I said, trying to hide the panic I felt from creeping into my voice. "I know? That's all you have to say?"

"Oh, I'm sorry," Ben said lightly. "Was there something else you expected?"

"Don't be cute. You know what I'm talking about."

"I can't imagine what you mean." Ben's voice was entirely too innocent.

"You have—you have to say it back," I said, hating how needy I sounded. "Otherwise it's not fair."

"Not fair, huh?" Ben said playfully. "That reminds me of something, what was it... It's almost like I wanted to tell you something earlier, and you wouldn't let me. Not only that, but you wouldn't acknowledge you felt the same way. God, this situation just feels so familiar..."

"Fuck you," I said, annoyed. I began to slide away but Ben's arms were strong and wouldn't let me go.

"Hey, Adam, no." Ben pulled me closer to him. "I'm sorry, I shouldn't have joked about it. Of course I love you. I love you so much and if I made you doubt that for even a second, I'm so sorry. Will you turn around so I can tell you to your face?"

I stopped struggling but I didn't turn around either.

"Please, baby?" Ben said, his voice soft and sweet.

Who was I kidding? I sighed and turned around. Ben brought his hand up, pushed a strand of hair off my forehead, then traced my jawline with his thumb. His eyes locked onto mine.

"I love you so fucking much and I'm going to make you sick with how much I tell you that," Ben said. He smiled ruefully. "So I guess remember how the last 30 seconds felt because that's the last time you're ever going to wonder about it."

"You're such an asshole," I said, but I couldn't keep myself from breaking into a smile. I buried my face in his neck and Ben's arms squeezed me tighter.

"I know," Ben said, his voice warm like honey against my ear. "I know."

18

BEN

"You'll call as soon as you're done, right?" I asked for the millionth time as Adam brushed his teeth that morning.

He rolled his eyes. "Yes, *Mom*."

"Hey, forgive me for caring about you," I said, frowning at his reflection in the bathroom mirror.

"Nope." Adam grinned through the foam on his teeth. "Unforgivable."

I laughed. How could I not? Things felt so different now than they had a week ago. I was just days away from the benefit, from being free of Greenleaf. From coming out and getting to be who I was.

And since that night after Mia and Esther had come over for dinner, something had shifted between Adam and me. He seemed more relaxed, more affectionate. And I knew, I finally knew, that he loved me.

I'd been a little scared that night about whether or not

Adam really meant it. But he hadn't pulled away the next morning like I'd feared. Instead, we'd woken up and spent half the morning in bed just watching YouTube videos and arguing over which delivery option to get.

At the risk of sounding like a complete idiot, things were pretty goddamn perfect. But if I were going to be goofy, stupid in love with Adam, at least the feeling was mutual.

I could tell Adam was nervous this morning though, even if he wouldn't say it. So even though I knew I was being annoying, I couldn't help following him around the apartment and swooping in, hummingbird-style, to kiss him as he swatted me away. As he poured coffee into a travel mug, I came up behind him, wrapped my arms around him, and nipped at his earlobe.

Adam laughed and set the coffee down, then turned around and twined his arms around my neck and kissed me firmly. When he pulled away I grumbled in protest.

"Don't stop," I complained, keeping my arms around him and taking a step backwards towards the bedroom.

"You've already delayed me an hour by not letting me get out of bed—"

"If you think I'm apologizing for that, you're very wrong—"

"—And I'm never gonna get there if you won't let me leave. Which means I'm never going to come back and you'll never get to ask me how it went and I won't get to be evasive and standoffish and then collapse into a puddle of hurt feelings and let you fuck me back together again. You're only hurting yourself here, really."

I burst out laughing. "I didn't realize you had the whole day planned out."

"Oh yeah," Adam said seriously. "I'm bribing myself with sex. It's the only way I can make myself do this."

"But consider this—what if you don't go see your dad and you just stay here and we go back to bed and have sex anyway?"

"But then I never get my stuff. I need my stuff."

"Dude, I'm rich now, remember. I'll buy you new stuff."

"You're only rich for like, one more week," Adam protested. "Then you're going back to being a starving artist. Besides, I need to do this. Grow as a person or something."

"Sounds suspicious."

"Suspect all you want," Adam said. "I'm still going. I like that guitar."

"Ugh, fine. Abandon me. See if I care. I'll just sit here all day and sulk," I said as I walked to the door with Adam and grabbed some boxes to take down to the car. He was borrowing the convertible to drive up to Connecticut.

"Oh please," Adam said, tossing an amused glance over his shoulder as he put the boxes in the trunk. "Don't you have a meeting with Shereen today?"

"Yeah, but I'll still be sulking on the inside."

Adam laughed and closed the trunk. But when he walked to the driver's side door, he stopped and bit his lip, just staring at the car.

"I can do this, right?" he said finally, looking up at me, his eyes hesitant.

"Absolutely." I resisted the urge to pull him into my arms again but I did take one of his hands in mine. "And even if I'm not there with you physically, I'll be there like, metaphyisically, yelling things like, *'You're a terrible father,'* or, *'What's wrong with you, you monster,'* silently. Anything to stick it to him."

Adam laughed. "Honestly, *'Hey guess what, I'm fucking your son,'* might be more effective at pissing him off."

"Then that's what I'll yell."

Adam looked down at the ground and I couldn't help it, I crossed the foot of space between us and pressed my body up against his, pushing him back onto the car. I slid one thigh in between his legs and rubbed just until I could feel us both starting to get hard. I ran my lips up from his neck to his ear and bit down on his lobe gently.

"The no visit, just sex and buying you things offer still stands," I whispered. "Just in case you've changed your mind."

"Tempting," Adam said, closing his eyes briefly before opening them, nodding, and pushing me away. "Very tempting. But no, I need to do this. I'll call you once I'm back in the car."

Because I'd somehow become the world's biggest sap, I waited until he'd pulled out of the garage and turned the corner at the end of the block before going back upstairs to the apartment. I grabbed the mail on my way up and flipped through it to check for anything actually important. Most of it was crap—despite the fact that my address wasn't supposed to be listed, I still got junk mail—but I'd gotten a hand-written thank you note from Samantha at camp and what looked like the last bill from Peachtree.

I sliced the Peachtree envelope open, feeling a little unsettled about the fact that I still hadn't told Adam about paying for it. I kept meaning to... and then kept finding ways to put it off. I didn't want to mention it when he was in a bad mood, but then whenever things were going well, like they had been recently, I didn't want to ruin it with that news.

It was a bill, as suspected, though it had a hand-written note at the bottom from Peachtree's executive director thanking me for my generous donation to their non-profit arm that ran mobile clinics in low income communities across the city. Had I done that? I had a fuzzy memory of maybe asking Luke to do that for me. God, he was right. I really did need to pay more attention to that kind of thing.

I pulled my phone out to call him and saw I'd gotten a text —well, a series of increasingly irate texts—from Shereen, starting at 10:10 this morning.

SHEREEN>> We're still on for 10 right?

And then at 10:15:

SHEREEN>> If this is a last ditch negotiating tactic and you're trying to play hard to get, don't bother. The label will bend over backwards for you if you say you've changed your mind

And at 10:20, just a few minutes ago:

SHEREEN>> Benjamin, I'm very busy and important, in case you hadn't realized. Do you need to reschedule?

Shit. Adam wasn't kidding, I really had made us late. I hadn't realized I'd gotten the morning quite so off-track. I texted back apologetically.

BEN>> So sorry, on my way now! Got held up

BEN>> Is it too late or have you already abandoned me forever?

SHEREEN>> I could have gone to a spin class, Ben. Caught up on my true crime podcasts. Done a sheet mask, at the very least.

SHEREEN>> But no, it's not too late. Get your ass over here

I put my phone back in my pocket and grabbed my keys. I'd deal with the bill when I came back—the meeting with Shereen wasn't going to take long. Slipping my hat and sunglasses on, I headed out the door.

"Benjamin, my one, my only," Shereen trilled as I poked my head into her office. "How are you my dearest?"

"I'm... highly suspicious of this." I arched an eyebrow. "Weren't you mad at me like, twenty minutes ago?"

"Ancient history," Shereen said. "Entirely forgotten."

"Really?" I asked, stepping into her office.

Shereen sighed. "Well, no. My pores will never forgive you. They could have been soaking in Aztec mud and snail mucin this whole time. But I was hoping some last minute obsequious fawning might get you to change your mind about leaving the label."

"Sadly, no," I said with an apologetic smile. "But still, it's nice to hear. I certainly don't object to being told how awesome I am."

"Nuh-uh," Shereen said, standing up from her desk and walking over to sit in one of the two arm chairs in front of her window. I joined her and sat in the other one. "No compliments for free, buddy."

"Is this really where we've ended up, Shereen?" I said with a grin. "If you want to compliment me, don't hold yourself back. Do what's in your heart."

"My heart says to lock this door and not let you leave til you've renewed your contract with Greenleaf," Shereen said drily. "I don't actually think you want to advise me to follow it."

"That depends. What do you have by way of snacks in here? How long could I last?"

"Diet soda and corn chips, I'm afraid. You'd definitely get scurvy." Shereen frowned at me. "Ben, are you sure you want to do this? I mean, I get it. Greenleaf's a machine. Music industrial complex and all that. It's not what you expected, I'm sure. But if you stick it out another few years, you'll be in a position to call your own shots. And in the meantime, you'd be making the kind of money you'd only dream of if you go independent."

"It's about more than just the money, though. More than the music, even. It's about being who I am. I never wanted to be this perfect, polished pop star. That's not me. And I can't wait around hoping it gets better over time. By the time I'm able to call my own shots, I'm afraid I'll have lost the parts of me that are real."

"Ugh, why can't everyone be as banal and shallow as I am?" Shereen groaned and I laughed. "Don't answer that," she said, flashing me a warning look. "And fine. I guess if you need to stand in your own truth or whatever, I get it. As your friend, I'm proud of you. As your manager, I'm pissed, because the label's gonna be maaaad. But as your friend..."

"Listen, there's something else I wanted to tell you," I said. "As a friend. Well, I guess kind of as a manager, too, but it's not really going to be your problem after next week, so more as a friend—"

"Okay, now I'm the suspicious one," Shereen said, cocking an eyebrow.

"It's not bad. I promise. Well, I don't think it's bad anyway and I don't think you will either. But the label—uh, they're probably not going to be thrilled. Which is why I'm going to wait until after the benefit, after I'm off their payroll to go public with this, but I wanted to tell you now, because it just seemed like the right thing and—"

"Oh for Christ's sake, Ben, spit it out. I could have gotten a pedicure in the time it took you to say all that."

"I'm bi."

"Really?" Shereen's face lit up. "That's awesome!"

"And I'm dating a guy."

"What?" If possible, Shereen's smile got even bigger. "Oh my God, seriously? Who? Since when? Do I know them? What's his name? What's his deal? Tell me everything."

"That's..." I laughed. "Okay, you're taking this way better than I thought you were going to."

"Well, like you said." Shereen mimed putting a hat on with her right hand. "Manager hat says that we need to talk to Mia and figure out a story for you guys breaking up. But friend hat," she mimed putting on a hat with her left hand, "says this is really great news. Frankly, I'm mostly just surprised because I haven't seen you date anyone in the entire year I've known you."

"Yeah," I laughed. "I know. It kind of took me by surprise, too? I've already told Mia, by the way. So that's taken care of. And... yeah. I don't know, the last month has just been kind of amazing."

"You know, I thought there was something different about you recently," Shereen said. "You've had this little glow— you're doing it right now!—on your cheeks that's just been way too adorable, even for normal adorable Ben. And it's— holy shit, he was there, wasn't he? That time I came over to your apartment last week?"

I blushed. "Yeah. To be fair, I did tell you to start knocking."

"How was I supposed to know this was the month you decided to start having sex in your living room?"

"Kitchen, technically," I said, feeling my cheeks grow even hotter.

"Wait." Shereen paused. "Isn't your friend Adam staying with you though?"

I smiled. "Yeah. He is."

"But then why wasn't he—" Shereen stopped and her eyes grew round. "Holy shit, it's Adam? Adam's the guy?"

"Yeah, Adam's the guy." My smile spread to take over my whole face. "He's the one."

"You are too fucking much. Haven't you guys been friends for like, ever?"

I laughed. "Yeah. It kind of came out of nowhere, I guess. But then again, it also kind of didn't? I don't know. It's just... It's good."

"God, people are going to freak—in a good way—when you guys come out." Shereen's eyes danced. "He's got that whole emo thing, you've got the all-American vibe. You're like a Taylor Swift song come to life."

"I guess that's one way to put it."

"So you talked to Mia," Shereen said, narrowing her eyes. "Have you guys given any thought to how you want to do the break up?"

"We were kind of thinking like, she does some cryptic Instagram posts with sad quotes and sunset pictures, and then maybe a joint statement like, we realized we were better as friends thing?"

"Ooh, I like it." Shereen nodded. "Would you guys be willing to do an interview together, maybe? Mia as the supportive ex-girlfriend would be so good for her right now. And then we could—" she stopped short and rolled her eyes. "Sorry, I need to remember that I'm not going to be your manager anymore after next week."

"Yeah, but if you think that gets you out of having to see me, you're crazy," I said. "It just means that now you'll let me actually drink when we hang—"

I stopped short when my phone started buzzing in my pocket. I frowned when I pulled it out. "That's weird. It's my mom. But we just talked yesterday. Usually she doesn't call unless—" I looked up at Shereen, a stab of worry pulsing through my gut. "Do you mind if I take this?"

"No, no, of course not."

"Thanks." I stood up and answered. "Hey Ma, what's up?"

"Ben?" My mother's voice was tight with worry. "Can you come down to Mt. Sinai? We had to take Lacey into the ER."

Two hours and 14 minutes. That's how long we'd been at the hospital, sitting in the plastic chairs by the nursing station, waiting for news. The surgery was supposed to be quick, they'd said when they'd taken Lacey back. But what did quick mean?

Was two hours quick, or did it mean something had gone wrong, something unexpected had happened? With each minute that passed, my stomach tied itself into more complicated knots. If something terrible had happened, wouldn't they have come out and told us? More time had to mean they were still working, that she was still okay. Unless she wasn't. I desperately wanted someone to come out and just tell us something. Unless the news was bad.

Fuck, I was a mess.

Compounding matters, Adam wasn't answering his phone. I'd called and texted multiple times since I got here but the calls went straight to voicemail and the texts went unanswered. And the longer I sat here without hearing from Adam, without Adam next to me, the more anxious I got.

Finally, the swinging double doors that led back into the operating rooms opened and the doctor who'd talked to us before they'd taken Lacey in for surgery came out. Her face was unreadable, but we all sat up, our eyes locked on her as she approached.

"She's in stable condition," the doctor said when she reached us. I felt myself sigh with relief, saw the same wave pass through my parents. "She's sleeping now, but you can go in and see her in a bit. One of the nurses will come and get you."

"Thank you," my mom said. She smiled at the doctor and squeezed my dad's hand.

My dad didn't say anything, just exhaled and nodded. He'd been practically mute since I'd gotten to the hospital. He doted on Lacey—we all did, but she and my dad had always been close.

"We will need to talk about long-term options," the doctor continued, her kind smile taking all of us in. "She'll need time to recover—her heart is still weak—but we're going to be looking at more surgery sooner or later."

"Thank you," my mom said again. "Thank you. We were hoping... well, we knew this would happen some day."

The doctor smiled sympathetically. "If you plan for it ahead of time and operate when it's not a crisis situation, procedures are usually a lot smoother and recovery time can be shorter as well. There's every reason to expect Lacey will have long, happy years in front of her. But we want to try to stay on top of this as much as possible."

My mom turned to my dad and pulled him in for a hug after the doctor walked away. I sank my head into my hands and sighed again, feeling suddenly worn out. Lacey was going to be okay. She was going to be okay.

She had been admitted with breathing problems, slipping in and out of consciousness, but it had turned out to be something with her heart. I didn't understand the medical terms. The bright side of going to an emergency room with breathing or heart trouble is that they admit you before everyone else. The down side is that if you're having either one of those issues, it usually really is an emergency.

I smiled sadly at my parents. I was glad they had each other. I just wished Adam were here with me. Or that he would at least look at his fucking phone.

I'd gotten to Mt. Sinai right about the time Adam should have gotten to his dad's, I thought. I'd called, left a message explaining what had happened, and then texted to update him on Lacey's status and to tell him which hospital we were at, in case he wanted to come.

In case. Who the hell was I kidding, I *wanted* him to come. And he'd promised he'd call me once he was leaving his dad's. So where the hell was he? And why wasn't he answering?

Of course, my mind had started spiraling, concocting insane scenarios, ping-ponging back and forth between annoyance at Adam and fear that something had happened to him. Logically, I knew that probably nothing drastic had occurred. But I was on edge, and right now, the unthinkable seemed, well, more thinkable than it usually did.

I pulled my phone out to give Adam an update.

BEN>> Lacey's out of the woods. Stable and resting. We should know more soon.

BEN>> Call me???

I hated how needy I felt. How off-balance.

"I should go call Jess," my dad said, standing up slowly. "She'll be done with her classes now and want an update."

"Tell her she doesn't have to come out yet," my mom said. "Traffic's going to be a nightmare for another few hours and everything's fine here."

"I'll tell her," my dad says, "but I doubt that'll make any difference. You know she'd rather sit in traffic for two hours instead of on her couch worrying."

He walked down the hallway towards the main lobby and my mom turned and took my hand.

"How're you doing, sweetie?" she asked.

"I don't know," I said, shrugging helplessly. "Fine? I guess? I mean, as much as you can be, right? God, I should be asking you that. Are you okay? Is there anything I can get you?"

"Thanks, honey." My mom patted my hand. "But I'm okay. Now that we know Lacey'll be alright, that's all I need."

I nodded and tried to give her an agreeing smile but my mom just cocked her head and squinted at me.

"Alright, out with it," she said after a minute.

"What?"

"Something's bothering you. Come on, no point in letting it fester."

"No, it's nothing," I said, sighing. "Really."

"Ben. Child of mine. I can read you like a book. Something's wrong."

"It seems stupid, considering..." I trailed off and waved a hand towards the doors the doctor had disappeared back through.

"Honey, just because we went through a scare today doesn't mean that your life doesn't count. What's wrong. Is it work stuff?"

I paused for a moment, then shook my head. "No. It's —it's Adam."

"Oh no, sweetheart. What's wrong? Is everything okay between you two?" My mom's voice was full of concern.

"Yeah, no it's not—it's not that. It's just. I dunno, I texted him hours ago and like, a million more times since then, called him twice and he... he hasn't picked up or responded or anything. And I just... I'm sure it's nothing and his phone just died or something but like, where is he?"

"Oh Ben," my mom said. "I'm sure he'd be here if he knew. He probably just hasn't seen any of that yet."

"Yeah, but he was supposed to call me when he was headed back today and he hasn't done that either."

"Where was he going?" my mom asked. "Somewhere where there's no service?"

"Fairfield County, Ma. Not really the boondocks."

"Well, maybe you're right and his phone just died."

"Yeah but what kind of person walks around with a dead phone for hours and never once thinks, hmm, maybe I should plug this thing in and see if someone's trying to get in touch with me? Maybe I should plug it in and actually *call my boyfriend back*." I couldn't keep the bitter taste of panic and frustration out of my voice.

"I know, honey, I know," my mom clucked. "It sucks."

I turned to her, my voice cracking. "I just... I hate feeling mad at him and I know it's not fair but if I don't get mad, I know I'm just going to start freaking out and wondering if something happened to him."

"Oh Ben, I'm sure he's alright."

"But—I can't—I just—he was going up to his dad's today and they don't get along and his dad's a real asshole and I just. I don't know, it's hard to explain but Adam's been... through a lot recently. And I'm just afraid that if his dad said something, or did something, maybe Adam's... maybe he's... fuck, Ma, I don't know what I'd do if something happened to him."

"Sweetie, come here," my mom said, pulling me in for a hug. She rubbed my back, just like she had when I was a kid, and I felt like an idiot, a grown man needing to be comforted by his mom. In public. When my problems paled in comparison to the reason we were even here. But I was so frayed, so worried, and coming apart at the seams.

When I finally let go, I felt a little better, if also a little silly.

"Everything's going to be fine, sweetie," my mom said. "I'm sure of it."

My mind flashed back to Adam on the beach out in Montauk, asking me how I could be so sure everything would be okay. Back then, I just was. But suddenly, nothing seemed sure anymore. Nothing, except that I needed him.

My dad was still out in the lobby when a nurse came back to tell us we could go in and visit Lacey, though he warned us she was still asleep. My mom squeezed my hand again.

"You go on in, honey," she said. "I'll go get your father."

I nodded and headed through the double doors with the nurse, following him down a hall and around a series of corners and passages until I was thoroughly lost. Finally, he pointed me to a room at the end of a hall.

I thanked him as he left, then walked over to the doorway and came to a stop, peering into Lacey's room. She'd had so many health problems that I was used to seeing her with tubes and IVs and all that. But still, it hurt to see her like this.

She'd always been small, but here, she looked positively minute. She did look peaceful, though. So there was that.

I walked over to her bed and sat down in a chair next to it, covering her hand with my own. Her eyes flickered back and forth beneath her lids but stayed shut.

"Hey Lace," I said, giving her hand a squeeze. "Looking good." I leaned over and brushed her hair off her forehead. "Your gown's pink, so they got your favorite color right, at least. Ma's gonna go back and get a bag of your stuff tonight.

I'll make sure she gets your sparkly lip gloss. Gotta stay fresh, even in here."

I brought her hand to my lips and kissed it. "God, you gave us a scare. What were you trying to do, kill me? If you wanted me to come over more, you could have just called. Dramatic much?"

I tried to laugh, but it felt hollow. "Lace, I swear I'm going to be around more. No more crazy tours. This year... it hasn't been worth it. I'm gonna be a better brother, okay. And I'm gonna bring Adam around more too. I don't know if mom told you but he... well, he's great. Which you know, obviously." I was rambling now, but somehow the talking was helping. "But he's also... Lace, he's my boyfriend. And I'm pretty much obsessed. So yeah, you're going to see more of both of us. Don't worry, though, I still think he might love you more than me. You guys can gang up on me playing Go Fish from now on, okay? It's gonna be great."

"You just gotta be strong," I went on. "The sooner you get better, the sooner you can go home and we can get that tournament started. Got that? So no malingering in here just because you think the doctors and nurses are cute." I barked a laugh. "Actually, the guy that brought me back here is pretty good looking. You're gonna flip when you wake up. I'll make sure Ma brings your lip gloss though."

"What's this about lip gloss?" my mom asked. I turned to see her walking in with my dad.

"Just saying you need to remember to bring it when you come back with Lacey's stuff." I grinned. "One of her nurses is really cute. She's gonna want it."

My mom rolled her eyes. "Honestly, between the pair of you. You leave that young man alone."

I laughed. "Don't worry, I'm just gonna wingman for Lace. I'm off the market."

"Honey, why don't you go home," my mom said, her eyes growing soft. "Go find him."

"No, it's not—" I shook my head. "I can stay. It's fine."

"Sweetheart, we're fine here. Lacey's fine. In fact, I'm pretty sure she'd yell at you to go find Adam yourself if she knew he wasn't here. Consider yourself under orders."

"I don't want to abandon you guys—"

"Son," my dad said. "If there's one thing I've learned over the years, it's don't disagree with your mother. She knows what she's talking about."

I flushed, but I was overcome at that moment with much I loved my family. God, it'd only been a few weeks and they'd completely adjusted to me dating a guy—dating Adam, in particular. My mom had had the usual mom questions, but they were the exact same ones she'd asked any time I'd started dating a woman. It was... really, really nice. Normal.

"Okay," I said finally. "But call me the second anything changes. Lacey wakes up, the nurse comes back in and declares his love, anything. I want to know."

"Of course, sweetheart," my mom said. "Now get out of here."

I gave Lacey a kiss on the forehead and hugged my parents goodbye, then walked out of the hospital, only getting lost once on my way back to the front entrance. I pulled my phone out for one last text.

BEN>> Dude, where are you? I'm coming home. Please text me back

But by the time I got off the subway—and amazingly, had only gotten stopped once by a fan while I was changing trains—I still hadn't heard back.

I shoved my phone back in my pocket and walked the short blocks from the subway stop to my building, trying to punch down my panic. But that didn't really help much, because as soon as the panic was out of the way, the annoyance came back stronger than ever. I knew it wasn't fair to blame Adam for not being with me at the hospital when he didn't even know I'd been there... but honestly, why the fuck hadn't he checked his phone by now? Or if it was dead, realized that and plugged it in?

I stepped out of the elevator and walked toward my door, vowing to remain calm no matter what had happened. But I didn't even have a chance to get inside before that was put to the test. I turned the key in the lock, pushed the door open, and stopped dead.

Adam was standing in the doorway, clearly on his way out of the building.

"Adam?" I was shocked, not quite able to make sense of what I was seeing. "What the hell are you doing here?"

19

ADAM

J told myself I was fine when I got in Ben's car and headed north out of the city. And I told myself again when I got on the highway, and again when I got off it. I was fine.

Sure, my hands were getting clammier by the minute and I was pretty sure I'd be sitting in a lake of my own sweat by the time I got there, but I was fine. I was just going to get there, get my stuff, and get out. Wouldn't take more than 15 minutes. Ben was waiting for me back home. I was fine.

I just wished I could do something about that sensation of dread, like there was an axe hanging over me, inching closer to my neck with each mile. I couldn't shake the memory of the last time I was here, my dad yelling at me and me just... crumpling, any self-esteem and self-respect just gone.

Maybe I should have let Ben come with me. It was a lot easier to be brave, to say stupid shit like, *'I need to do this on my own,'* when I was back in Manhattan, a river and a state line away from my dad. Why the fuck had I thought this was a good idea?

If I was honest, it was just because I hadn't wanted to risk Ben seeing my dad cut me down like that again. But it was the middle of the day in the middle of the work week. There was no reason for my dad to be home. Get in, get my stuff, get out. Simple as that.

So why the hell couldn't my stomach get on board with that? Why did it feel like I was going to hurl up everything I'd eaten in the past week?

I was supposed to be fine. But I wasn't.

But my only other option was giving up. Turning around, saying goodbye to my stuff. Honestly, if it hadn't been for my guitar, I probably would have. But I wanted that thing back.

I sighed as I turned onto Damson Lane and drove to the end of the street. Fine or not, I was going to do this

I pulled the car to a stop in front of the gates, rolled down the window, and punched the call button on the intercom without giving myself the chance to chicken out. I used to know the key code to punch in and open the gates on my own but when my dad had changed it a couple years ago, he didn't bother to tell me the new one and I didn't care enough to ask.

Lydia's voice came in over the intercom.

"Hello? Hart residence."

"Hey Lydia, it's Adam again," I said, forcing a smile. "I came to pick up my stuff?"

"Oh, Adam, sweetheart." Lydia paused and I wondered if

she was trying to decide whether to reference my last visit here. She must have decided against it, because all she said was, "It's so good to hear your voice. Come on back."

"Uh, wait, um." I took a deep breath. "Is my dad home?"

Lydia took a moment to answer and when she spoke, her voice was hushed—well, as much as it could be over an intercom. "He is, but he's in his study. If you come around to the back, you should be able to avoid him."

"Thanks."

Get in, get my stuff, get out. I barely saw the grounds as I drove through them and I pulled around to the service entrance in a bit of a daze. Lydia was outside waiting for me.

"Come here, you," she said, pulling me into a hug as soon as I stepped out of the car. And okay, despite my general principle that hugs should be used sparingly and never outside where other people might see you, I did feel a *little* better when she drew me in. "Two visits in one month. What did I do to get so lucky?"

I laughed when she pulled away. "I don't know that we should really count the last one as something lucky. I'm sorry that turned into such a, well, shitshow. I hope Dad wasn't too much of an ass about it."

Lydia glanced over her shoulder before giving me a conspiratorial smile. "He was pissed, but we were so busy getting ready for the party that he didn't have time to stand around and yell at us. Besides, Esther stayed a little longer after you and your friend left, and it was lovely to see her."

"Glad it wasn't a total disaster, then." I looked back at the house. "You said he's in his study? Would you hate me completely if I just kind of run in and get my stuff and then leave?"

"Not so long as you promise to call me later and set up a time for us to really talk," Lydia said with an admonishing look. "I miss you, young man."

"I promise," I said. "Scouts honor."

Lydia snorted. "You quit the Boy Scouts after you turned 8. I'm not sure how seriously I should take that."

"Very seriously," I grinned. "That just means I never had time to become disenchanted with it. It's an oath I hold in the highest regard."

With another hug, Lydia went back inside and ducked into the laundry room, leaving me to my own devices—which was just as well, since I wasn't sure I would have been able to keep up much conversation once I walked inside. I hadn't actually been inside my dad's house in years but that familiar feeling of low-key, near constant alarm settled back over my shoulders like a jacket as I walked through the kitchen and into the back hall.

There were three staircases in the house—the sweeping, ostentatious set in the main foyer right off the front entrance, the private set leading down from the master suite in the west wing of the house, and the ones right around the corner from the kitchen—actual servants' stairs, dating back to when the house was first built, over a hundred years ago.

Sometimes I thought my dad believed he actually lived in that time period. Frankly, his general air of assholery made a lot more sense from that perspective.

I walked up the stairs as quietly as I could. Even if my dad was on the far side of the house, there was no reason to go around announcing my presence. It might have been years, but my feet still picked their path up the steps with muscle memory, avoiding creaking boards and squeaky spots. The stairs went up to the attic, but I slipped out the slender doorway that led onto the second floor.

Memories rushed over me as soon as my feet hit that thick, butter yellow carpet that ran down the middle of that hallway. This had been the nursery wing when Esther and I were little and, later, after we moved up to the third floor, it was where my mom ate, slept, and did practically everything after she and my dad stopped keeping up any pretense of being together but before they'd gotten a divorce.

When I'd come back from California, I'd discovered that my bedroom up on the third floor had been converted into a gun room—always classy, my dad—and so I'd been assigned a small room at the end of the hall here. I padded along the hallway to it and stopped short in the doorway.

It was untouched, exactly the way I'd left it when I was 18—and since I hadn't spent more than ten nights here combined since then, it really was like looking at a time capsule. But it wasn't the Nirvana posters or books with bent spines scattered around the room that got me. It was the visceral punch in the gut of remembering who I'd been the last time I'd slept here.

I used to treat coming home like a nightmare. Trying to avoid, and then survive, my dad's tirades. When he'd been drinking, anything could set him off and there wasn't much I could do but try to go somewhere else mentally until he was done telling me what a useless, pathetic excuse for a son I was—usually loud enough for the entire household staff to hear. No matter how shitty my boarding school *du jour* was, it was always better than being at home.

Even after I left for college, the occasional nights I had to spend in Connecticut would throw me into a low-grade panic for weeks leading up to them and then have me counting the minutes until I could leave again. Coming home always made me feel small. Scared. Worthless.

But I wasn't that person anymore. Or he wasn't me. As I looked around the room, everything the same as I'd left it except for the stack of boxes and guitar in the middle, that much was clear. That version of me, scared to be myself, hoping to go unseen—I think I'd left him on the floor at The Grasshopper. Or maybe back in that tiny twin bed at Gray's beach house. Somewhere along the way, unbeknownst to me, I'd lost him.

I picked up the boxes and brought them down to the car in three loads, that feeling of distance, of remove, growing with each trip back up the stairs. What the hell had I been so worried about? I didn't feel any need to spend more time here—but I didn't need to be afraid of it either.

Which is why, I suppose, when I ran into my dad—literally ran into him—as I carried my last box of things down the stairs and into the kitchen, all I could think to say was, "Oh."

"Oh?" My dad's voice was cold, and between the smell of scotch on his breath and the empty tumbler in his hand, I got the feeling he'd come to the kitchen for more ice. "That's all you have to say?"

"Uh—I mean, it's not—" I stopped. What the hell was I doing? He was the one who was drunk before it was even noon on a work day. And why the fuck wasn't he at work, come to think of it? I didn't have anything to apologize for. "Yeah. Oh."

"What are you doing here?" he asked, his eyes narrowing. He took a step towards me, lurching slightly, and I stepped around to the far side of the long counter where Lydia usually did her cooking. Just because I didn't want to let him to intimidate me wasn't any reason to be stupid. He didn't look like staying upright was something he had the firmest grasp on right then.

I took a deep breath. I could do this. "I just came to get some things." I hefted the box in my hands. "That's all. I'll be gone soon."

"I'm sure." My dad's voice was full of scorn. "I'm sure it's pure chance that you're here right before I have clients coming. Just like it was chance you showed up before the board dinner, looking to cause trouble."

"Uh, yeah. It really is. Much as I'm sure it flatters you to think so, I don't actually spy on your schedule and show up just to torment you."

"Don't take that tone with me, boy."

"What tone?" I spit back. God, how had I been so scared of him all these years? Seeing him today, weaving slightly as he clutched his empty drink, his cheeks red with anger—and, let's be honest, alcohol—I felt pity, not fear. "This tone? This is just the way I talk to people who are assholes to me for no reason."

My dad's eyes widened in shock. "How dare you. After all I've done for you, that's how you talk to me?"

"All you've done for me?" I laughed. "Dad, all you've done

for me is make me feel like a piece of shit since I was four years old. All you've done for me is make it clear how much you wish you could trade me in for a better model, how much you wished they'd given you a better son."

"Can you blame me?" My dad was on the verge of shouting. "Who wouldn't want to trade you in. I wanted a son and what I got was... you. You've never been anything more than a skinny, pathetic, useless little wretch. *Sensitive*, they called you. Well I call it queer, and after everything I did to try to get you to change, you refused. Out of spite. I wanted a son, yes, but you're no son of mine."

I felt like I'd been slapped. It wasn't the first time he'd said it. It wasn't even the twentieth. But it hurt just as much now as it had the first time. The sick sinking realization that no matter what I did, I'd never be good enough for him. Never be what he wanted.

So yeah, it hurt. Words like that probably always would. But you know what? Fuck it. They were just words. Words that, honestly, had begun to lose their lustre. I mean, if he was going to continue to insult me, he could at least be a little more creative about it.

And while the words hurt, I wasn't going to give them any extra power. If someone yelled *'queer'* out their window when they drove by me, I'd be shaken, sure. But I wouldn't take it to heart.

My dad was an asshole. Honestly, I'd lend more credence to what random window-yelling guy said than anything that came out of my dad's mouth. So why the hell should I listen to anything he said?

"You know what?" I cocked my head to the side and looked

at my dad. "I'm done with this. And with you. I'm gonna go back to the city now. See you—you know, honestly, I don't particularly want to see you again. Ever. So... bye."

And with that, I turned around and walked through the kitchen, into the back hall, and out the door. My dad followed, spluttering something behind me, but I decided I didn't want to listen to it, so I just repeated, *'I'm leaving I'm leaving I'm leaving,'* to myself as I threw the last box in the passenger seat of the car, got in, and closed the door.

I made it as far as the gates before my hands started to shake and by the time I was two streets away, I had to pull over because I had tremors running through my whole body. I didn't even know how to describe what I was feeling. It wasn't sadness or anger, but it wasn't happiness either. Just... emptiness. A strange, confusing emptiness.

I'd stood up to my dad. Told him I didn't want to see him again. And it was entirely within my power to make that come true.

So why didn't I feel better?

I was supposed to call Ben when I was leaving. I'd just call him and tell him what happened. He'd be at home waiting for me when I got back. Everything would be fine. I'd start feeling better once I was back in the city, right?

I picked my phone up from where I'd left it on the dash. Fuck. It was dead.

Dammit, of all the nights to forget to charge your phone, I'd had to go and do it right before the day I was almost guaranteed to have a breakdown. Genius move on my part.

Fuck fuck fuck. I knew I should just drive home as fast as I could. Get back to the city and back to Ben. But as I started driving again, heading south, I realized I wasn't ready. I felt too raw, the confrontation too fresh. I needed time.

So I drove. And drove. I was somewhere in New Jersey when I realized the empty light was on. And as I sat there, waiting for the attendant to pump my gas, I sighed.

What the fuck was I doing? I didn't feel any better. And I probably wouldn't, not as long as I stayed away. Typical me, trying to feel better by avoiding dealing with my emotions, when actually confronting them was probably the only thing that would work.

I sighed and headed back to the city.

It was late afternoon by the time I pulled the car back into its parking space in the garage under Ben's building. Which was, for the record, still absurd. Who had a private garage in lower Manhattan? I was going to have to make the most of my opportunities to tease Ben about it until we had to move out.

But Ben wasn't home when I got up to the apartment. Fuck, he'd probably had to go out and had texted me and I, in typical messy fashion, hadn't gotten it. Now that I was back, all I wanted was to talk to him.

I rooted around the apartment for my charger for a few minutes before finally finding it in the kitchen next to a stack of mail. I flipped through the envelopes quickly on the off chance that another check had come for me. Nothing.

I sighed and turned to plug my phone in when another piece of paper on the counter caught my eye. That was Peachtree's logo. I'd seen it all over when I'd stayed there.

What the hell was it doing on what looked like a bill in Ben's name? I picked the paper up out of curiosity.

And for the second time that day, I thought I might throw up.

Dear Mr. Kowalski:

This includes the final statement for Mr. Hart's stay at Peachtree Wellness Center from June 24, 2017 to July 23, 2017. Below you will an account of your previous payments.

My eyes skittered down to the table below. Jesus Christ. My heart began to race. Jesus fucking Christ. Eighteen thousand dollars. That's what my month at Peachtree had cost.

We appreciate your prompt payment and please do not hesitate to contact us with any questions.

And then, below, a handwritten note.

Dear Mr. Kowalski,

Thank you so much for your generous donation to our Health on Wheels program. As you know, funding for this program supports Peachtree's mobile clinics located in various low-income neighborhoods in New York City. Your contribution is helping keep others healthy.

Yours gratefully,

Gretchen Borthwick

Executive Director, Peachtree Wellness Center

Fuck. It wasn't enough for Ben to pay for my fucking mental health care, he had to go and make a giant fucking charitable donation on top of it?

I felt sick. Eighteen thousand dollars. I'd known Peachtree was expensive—I'd done a little googling after I came home. Unsurprisingly, Peachtree didn't advertise their rates. But I'd found enough information to get a general idea of how much Esther had shelled out for me.

Except it hadn't been Esther. It had been Ben. And they'd both been lying to me about it. For the past two months.

I was mortified. How the hell could Ben do this? Spending that kind of money on someone who wasn't even family. And then not telling me about it? Letting me think it was Esther? I felt like an idiot.

Somehow, it made everything feel so much worse. Not only was I messed up enough to have to go to the clinic in the first place, but Ben didn't even trust me enough to tell me he'd paid for it? To offer, and give me the chance to say yes or no.

It made me feel like a child. Like a burden. Like the broken mess I'd always known deep down that I was.

I'd thought Ben and I had something special. And this whole time, he'd been looking down on me. How could I ever look into is eyes now, and not think of how much I owed him? How indebted to him I was?

My skin was crawling. Sweat broke out across my brow and I really did think I might throw up. And I still had no idea where Ben was. I grabbed my phone and charger, shoving them into my pocket. He could be coming home any minute.

I couldn't handle the thought of seeing him right then. I was too mortified. God, and to think I wouldn't have ever found out if I hadn't needed to plug my phone in. How the hell could he have lied to me like this?

I'd just put my hand on the door when I heard a key slide into the lock from the other side. Shit. I barely had time to panic before the door opened.

Ben stared at me in shock from the hallway.

"Adam? What the hell are you doing here?"

"What the hell are you doing here?"

Adam's face contorted. "I have to go."

"Wait, what?" I moved to the right as Adam tried to step past me. "Where? Why? Adam, I've been trying to get a hold of you all day."

"Please, I just need to—" Adam took another step forward but I blocked his path. He looked down and sighed.

"What's wrong?" I asked, peering at him. "Adam, what happened? Please, tell me."

Adam's eyes flashed up to mine and they were filled with anger. And hurt. What the hell had happened?

"I can't—" he said, shaking his head slowly. "I can't talk to you right now."

"What do you mean you can't talk to me right now?" I put a hand on his arm but he flinched away like I'd burned him. "Adam, what the hell, what's wrong?"

Suddenly there were tears in his eyes. "How could you—why would you lie to me like that?"

"Like what?" I stared at him.

"Don't pretend you don't know."

"Adam, honestly, I have no fucking clue what you're talking about." I was starting to get annoyed. I knew I shouldn't, knew I was just frayed from worrying about Lacey, but I couldn't keep the edge out of my voice. "I've had a shitty fucking day and I don't have the energy to figure this out on my own, clearly, so will you just tell me what's wrong?"

"Peachtree," Adam said, his voice shaking. "You paid for it."

"That's what you're so upset about?" I said, my eyes widening. "Seriously?"

I'd known he wasn't going to be happy about it, but suddenly, something as small as who paid for what seemed so trivial.

"Yes I'm fucking *upset*," Adam spit. "You've been lying to me for months."

"Okay, lying to you is a stretch," I said, feeling a little defensive. Well, a lot defensive.

"Right, because I've only mentioned thousands of times how I wanted to pay Esther back and you never once thought to say, 'Hey Adam, actually, that was me.'"

"Jesus, Adam." I scrubbed a hand through my hair. I didn't have the stamina for this fight right now. "Look, I know it wasn't a great thing to do. Not telling you. But please. Can't we just—does it have to be that big a deal?"

"Of course not," he said, his voice thick with scorn. "It's only eighteen thousand dollars. That kind of money doesn't mean anything to you. Why would it be a big deal?"

"That's not what I—"

"It's bad enough that I had to go and have a mental fucking breakdown in public and then needed to go to Peachtree in the first place. Worse that I couldn't even pay for it myself, that I needed family to do it. But it wasn't even family, it was you. How the hell is that not supposed to make me feel pathetic?"

"That's not how I see you and you know it." I shot back. "Look, I knew you weren't going to like it, but you needed the help and I had the money and it felt good to be able to do something for my friend. Some things are more important than money."

"Then why the hell did you lie about it?"

"Because I didn't want you freaking out, which clearly was a pretty reasonable thing to worry about."

"Well great job, Ben. Good plan. It went splendidly." Adam shook his head, his eyes narrowing. "Were you seriously never going to tell me?"

"I don't know," I said, throwing my hands up. "Honestly. I don't. Because whenever I thought about doing it, I didn't want to because I knew something like this would happen. You'd overreact and have a meltdown about something that, in the grand scheme of things, really doesn't fucking matter. Money doesn't matter. You being alive? That does."

"A meltdown?" Adam stared at me. "Jesus, that's really how you see me, isn't it?"

"Adam, no. Please." I reached out to him again, put my hand on his shoulder, but he shrugged me off. "That's not what I meant. I didn't mean—I just—fuck. Look, I just spent hours in the hospital with Lacey. It's been a rough day. I didn't mean that. What I said."

Adam frowned. "What happened with Lacey?"

I couldn't help arching an eyebrow. "Oh, now you want to stop and talk?"

"Oh fuck you, just because I'm mad at you doesn't mean I don't care about her. What happened?"

"She had to have emergency surgery. Something was wrong with one of the valves in her heart. I mean—more wrong than we already knew about. She's—she's fine now. But she's going to need more surgery and it was long and scary and I didn't know where the hell you were." I could feel my voice breaking. "It was just a really shitty day, okay?"

"I'm sorry," Adam said. "I didn't know."

"It's okay," I said. God, I was exhausted. Words were swimming around in my brain and it was an effort to take a deep breath and focus. "Can we—can we please just stop fighting? If today showed me anything, it's how important the people you love are. I'd do anything I could to keep Lacey alive and healthy. Safe. I'd do the same thing for you. And I don't think that's something I should have to apologize for. I love you."

"But you don't respect me," Adam said, his voice frustrated, angry. "That's the problem. Not when you treat me like I have to be handled with kid gloves. Just one more person you have to take care of."

"Well sometimes you fucking do need to be taken care of, or did you forget how you wound up in Peachtree in the first place? God, you're the one who's always reminding me how fucked up you are."

Fuck. Adam blanched and stepped back like I'd punched him and I hated myself. Why had I said that? I shouldn't have said it. I hadn't *meant* to say it. I was tired, and pissed, and hurting, but that was cruel.

"Yeah," Adam said sadly, shaking his head. "I do say that a lot. But you're the one who's supposed to tell me that's not true. I guess that's not really how you see me, though."

"Adam, I'm so sorry. I shouldn't have said that, that wasn't right. There's no excuse for me to—"

"Don't you get it, Ben?" Adam said. "I don't like being broken. I don't want to be. But what you did—lying to me, not trusting me—you took away my chance to be anything else."

"Adam, I'm sorry." I squeezed my eyes shut to blink back the tears suddenly pressing against them. "I'm so sorry. I didn't mean to take that away from you. I didn't mean to lie. And I didn't mean to fight like this. I don't think you're broken. Fuck, I just—this has been such a shitty day and I'm sorry I'm not handling this very well. Please, can we just talk this through? Let me apologize? Let me make this right?"

"I have to go," Adam said, pushing past me. "I'm sorry."

"Adam, wait—" I grabbed his arm and he turned back to look at me over his shoulder.

"I can't do this anymore, Ben."

"Do what? This conversation? Or us?"

"Either. Both." Adam shrugged his shoulders helplessly. "I just can't."

He pulled away and walked out into the hall, turning left quickly and walking to the end where the stairs led down to the lobby. And I just stood there and watched him leave.

21

ADAM

I didn't know what the fuck to do after I left Ben's apartment. I wandered around aimlessly, feeling physically and emotionally exhausted. Just drained. All I wanted to do was go to sleep. But where was I supposed to do that?

I couldn't stomach the thought of going back to Ben's. And being some sort of child he had to take care of. God, those words coming out of his mouth had cut deep. He thought I was helpless. Broken. I didn't think I could look him in the eyes anymore.

So I did the only thing I could think of—made someone else deal with my problems.

In this case, Nick. I found a coffee shop, plugged my phone in just long enough to turn it on, and called him to ask if I could come over. I had three texts from Ben, but I didn't read them. I didn't think I could face them right now.

"Jesus, you weren't kidding," he said as he opened the door to his apartment for me. "You look terrible."

"Yeah," I said absently as I walked in. "I know."

Nick's apartment turned out to be a tiny one bedroom at the top of a six floor walkup. The living room, such as it was, spilled into the kitchen, the sofa, coffee table and single armchair less than 6 feet from the kitchen counter with two cramped bar stools shoved underneath it. There was a bedroom barely visible behind a cracked-open door and, I assumed, a bathroom somewhere.

And the whole place was covered in books. Books in shelves that lined the walls, books in piles on the coffee table, books in stacks on the floor. Between the books, the low lighting from a fringed lamp in the corner, and the casement windows, it looked like the kind of place a rogue librarian might live in the 1890s.

"Dude, do you live in La Boheme?" I asked, looking around. "This is the kind of place you live when you have tuberculosis and you're scribbling away at a manuscript in the corner."

"The electricity probably dates to back then, at least, and the air conditioner's broken," Nick said. "But it's worth it for the balcony."

I nodded wearily. "Do you mind if I—" I gestured towards the couch and Nick waved me towards it. "I just... need to lie down for a while."

"You wanna talk about it?" Nick asked, moving a stack of books from the armchair to the floor so he could sit down across from me. "You didn't exactly say what was wrong on the phone but..."

"No," I said, shaking my head emphatically and then regretting it. Fuck, when had I gotten that headache? I felt hungover somehow—emotionally hungover. "No, I really don't."

The thought of having to explain was excruciating. Having to put what Ben had done into words somehow made it even more embarrassing. I just wanted to crawl into a hole and forget that it—and maybe the past two months—had ever happened.

"You sure you're okay, man?" Nick asked. "I have to head out for the night shift at Peachtree pretty soon, but I could call in sick if you want me to stay with you tonight."

I shuddered at the thought of Peachtree. Fuck, I wished I could forget I'd ever been there.

"No, it's fine. Really." I pulled my phone out of my pocket—two more texts from Ben—and turned it off. "I honestly just want to pass out for a while, if that's okay."

Nick gave me a long look but finally nodded. "Okay. I'll be back tomorrow, then."

"Got it."

I lay down on the couch, turning my face towards the back of it. I could feel sleep pulling me under and I didn't even hear Nick leave.

I wasn't sure quite when I woke up next, but it must have been after Nick got back the next morning because there was a glass of water and a granola bar waiting for me on the coffee table. I swallowed some water, heard Nick moving around in his bedroom, and immediately put my head back down and closed my eyes.

I didn't want to talk to Nick, or anyone, yet, and I knew he'd probably insist on me processing or some dumb shit like that if he knew I was awake. And eventually, I'd kept my eyes closed for long enough that I fell asleep again.

When I woke up a second time, there was a note on the coffee table from Nick, along with a pile of delivery menus.

At work. Please eat something. I'd rather not have to explain why you died in my apartment. Also Ben's texted me like 20 times in the past 24 hours. Assuming that has something to do with why you're on my couch. I turned your phone on and plugged it in. Wanna maybe get in touch with him? Home by 7. —N

The thought of eating anything right then turned my stomach. I knew I was supposed to be hungry—it had been 24 hours since I'd eaten anything, but I couldn't seem to summon up an appetite.

I pushed myself up from the couch. Fuck, I still had a brutal headache, though at this point that probably had more to do with dehydration and lack of food than anything else. I looked around Nick's place, disgruntled. My phone was on the floor in the corner next to an outlet and I could see it flashing at me, telling me I had a new text message. Probably more than one.

Fuck.

Ignoring my phone, I forced myself off the couch and grabbed my water glass. I shuffled to Nick's bathroom and searched the medicine cabinet for painkillers, tossing two Advil back with a glass of lukewarm tap water. When I closed the cabinet, I regarded myself in the mirror.

I looked terrible. Frankly, I looked like someone who hadn't slept in a week, when in fact, I'd basically done nothing but sleep for the last day. Dark circles under my eyes, pallid skin with two feverish spots of color in my cheeks. You could see the veins running down from the corners of my mouth to my chin, stark and blue under the harsh bathroom light.

What the fuck does it matter what you look like. It's not like you have anybody to impress. Or like you ever impressed anybody in the first place, for that matter.

My lips twisted bitterly. I'd thought Ben might actually feel something for me. But it turned out it was nothing but pity. I was pathetic.

I glanced at the clock on the wall. 6 p.m. Nick would be home soon. And he'd probably yell at me if I hadn't at least attempted to eat something. Since I didn't have anywhere else to crash right then, I figured I'd better not press my luck, so with misgiving, I went to grab my phone from the charger and call in some delivery.

My stomach sank when I looked at my messages. Ten from Ben since yesterday. I didn't really want to read them, but I found myself opening up the messaging app anyway with a feeling of sick fascination in my stomach.

The first ones he'd sent started out the way you'd expect.

BEN>> Adam, please, come home. Can we talk?

BEN>> This isn't fair Adam, you can't just leave and not tell me where you're going

BEN>> Where the hell even are you right now?

It almost made me feel better to see those. Ben being mad at me was something I could handle. It made me mad right back. But after I didn't respond to those, the tone shifted.

BEN>> God, Adam, I'm sorry. I really am. I didn't mean to upset you. I just really want to talk to you right now

My stomach turned. *'I didn't want to upset you'* made it sound like I was some fragile piece of porcelain. And yeah, I got it. I was a little fucked up. But I didn't need it rubbed in my face.

BEN>> Can we at least do that? Please

BEN>> Fuck, Adam, you can't just ignore me

But of course, I had.

BEN>> Please. I'm sorry. Will you at least let me know where you are? That you're safe?

BEN>> I'm worried about you, dammit, and I know that's probably going to make you mad to hear but I just need to know you're okay at least. Will you please text me back and let me know you're alive?

Mad? It didn't make me mad, it made me want to vomit, I was so disgusted with myself. One more way I'd managed to get Ben to think I was broken instead of someone he could actually be with as a partner.

BEN>> Fucking hell, Adam. What the fuck? Are you honestly just going to never talk to me again?

And then, the last one, from this morning:

BEN>> Okay. It's clear you have no intention of responding. I... don't know what to do about that, because this all feels incredibly sudden and I just... Adam, I'm so sorry. I fucked up. I should have told you. I never should have kept it from you, I should have told you from the beginning. But I was so worried you'd say no and that you'd hurt yourself somehow while I was gone and I know you don't want to hear that but you were telling me not to come home and I didn't know what else to do. I love you. I have loved you for so fucking long and I'm sorry it took me so long to see it but I do now and all I want is to be with you and make this up to you somehow. Please let me try and fix this. Please. I love you. And the thought of never talking to you again is killing me. Please, if you change your mind. Please call me. I love you

And now I fucking wanted to cry. Goddammit. Why couldn't I just be mad at him?

Instead he had to remind me of just how fucked up I was. How fucked up I'd always been. I was a complete fool to think he'd ever see me as anything but broken. Someone to be taken care of. Someone weak.

I jumped when suddenly my phone started ringing. It was Esther. Another person I didn't want to talk to, considering she'd been lying to me too. I let it ring. But of course, she couldn't let it rest and ten seconds later I had a text from her as well.

ES>> Pick up asshole. It actually rang this time, which means your phone's on again, which means you're alive.

Yeah, like that was going to happen.

ES>> Seriously, call me back or I'm coming down there. I know you're at Nick's and if you think I haven't Google stalked him and found his address, you're a damn idiot

Fuck. She might actually do that.

ES>> Adam I swear to God

I sighed and tapped out a reply

ADAM>> *Jesus give it a rest. I'm fine*

She didn't even bother to reply, just called me again, immediately. I rolled my eyes and answered.

"Hey."

"Hey yourself, dumbass", Esther said. "God, would it kill you to pick up your phone and let me know you're okay?"

"Es, what do you want?"

"What do I want?" Her voice went up an octave. "I want to make sure my baby brother didn't jump off the deep end. I want to make sure you're okay. I want to—Adam, God, I'm sorry. Ben told me what happened. I didn't mean to lie to you. I just... I was so worried about you and I wanted to make sure you were okay and—"

"Right," I said flatly. "Right. Well, sorry for making your life so much harder. I'll try not to *worry* you ever again."

"Adam, that's not what I meant. There's nothing wrong with caring about someone."

"Yeah but there's a big fucking difference between caring about someone and treating them like they're a child who can't take care of themselves."

"Adam, I—" Esther sighed. "You're right. You're right. I really don't have any excuse for it at all. I wasn't thinking straight and I should have told you."

And somehow, all the wind left my sails.

"Well, thanks," I said bitterly.

"Adam, I am so sorry."

"I just... Es, do you have any fucking idea how embarrassing this is? It's bad enough that I'm such a fuck up that I needed to go to Peachtree in the first place. It's bad enough that I couldn't afford it, that I needed—"

"Hey." Esther interrupted me sharply. "Listen—I will cop to having fucked up about lying to you. But I am not going to listen to you fucking put yourself down like this. There is nothing *bad* about needing help. Nothing bad about needing people, needing to lean on family or friends."

"That's easy to say when you're not the screw up."

You think I'm not screwed up?" Esther exploded. "Adam, I've been diagnosed with depression since I was 19. I've never managed to date anyone for longer than three months. I have this supposedly adult job and there are some week-ends I can't even get off the couch to go to the fucking corner store for string cheese and I have to have it delivered."

"Oh." I paused. "You never told me any of that before."

"You never asked." Esther sighed. "And I guess I didn't want to burden you. Which I realize now sounds incredibly hypo-critical but seriously, I wouldn't be here today if I didn't have people I could turn to for help."

"You've never asked me for help," I said, frowning.

"I know," Esther said. "I know. And I should have. I don't think mom and dad really raised us to be good at this shit. Or talk about things."

"Or really raised us at all, when you think about it."

"True," Esther snorted. "Look, I know I fucked up. But... I love you, okay?"

It was almost exactly the same thing Ben had said in his last text. But somehow, coming from Es, it was easier to handle. I guess if one person's allowed to see you as needy, it's your older sibling, right?

"Yeah," I said after a moment. "Yeah. I know."

"Ben's really worried about you."

"Not a great choice of words, Es," I said flatly.

"Okay, trying again. Ben feels awful about what happened and he wants to talk to you again. Adam, he called me five times last night and when I didn't pick up—because I was on shift, incidentally—he waited outside my apartment til I got home."

"Goddammit, Ben," I sighed.

"He's the one who called Nick," Esther said. "I think he's been haranguing him too."

"Yeah. I know."

"Consider talking to him, then. Maybe? Just think about it."

I felt awful. I knew I was supposed to say yes. But I just felt so embarrassed and gross inside. So I said nothing.

Esther sighed. "Fine. But know that I love you and I'm probably not going to stop bugging you about it."

"Why am I not surprised."

We hung up and I felt... unsettled. Esther's words bounced around in my head as I ordered delivery, getting enough for

Nick, too, but I still hadn't figured anything out by the time he got home.

"You're up!" Nick said, smiling delightedly when he walked in. "I half expected you to still be lying down."

I snorted. "Believe me, I gave it serious thought. But it's easier to eat chow mein when you have full use of your arms."

"Fair point," Nick said. "You get me any?"

"Yeah." I gestured to the extra containers on the coffee table. "I wasn't sure what you liked so I went with the classics."

Nick bent over and inspected the tupperware on the table. "General Tso's and Chicken with Broccoli. Sweet."

"So," Nick continued after taking a few bites of General Tso's and sprawling out in the armchair. "I take it you're feeling a little bit better."

"Define better."

"Upright."

"Well, if that's all it takes, sure."

"You talk to Ben?" Nick asked.

I frowned.

"Look, I obviously don't know what happened," Nick said. "But Ben has been calling and texting me somewhat obsessively since last night and he obviously wants to talk to you. He also—and I'm just going to say this and then get out of the middle of whatever's going on between you two—he also said to say he was sorry. And he seems pretty fucked up about this—whatever this is."

I slumped further down in the couch, even though that position made the noodles harder to eat.

"I wouldn't bring it up," Nick said after more of my silence. "But you seem more... sad than mad, I guess. So if you wanna talk about it..."

I sighed. "It's so fucking embarrassing."

"Welcome to the world dude. Fifty percent of your life is just making an ass out of yourself for other people."

"Yeah, I get that part," I grumbled. "I'm used to feeling embarrassed about shit I do to myself, but this wasn't that."

Nick just looked at me sympathetically until I broke down.

"Apparently back when I agreed to go to Peachtree, Esther told Ben about it. And he said he'd pay for it. Except he also asked her not to tell me."

Nick frowned. "I can see how that would feel... not great."

"Yeah. Do you have any idea how fucking expensive that place is?"

"Actually, no." Nick barked a laugh. "My position is a volunteer one so I've literally never talked to anyone in their billing office."

"Eighteen thousand dollars. For 30 days. And he just dropped it like it was nothing."

"That's... wow."

"And he just didn't tell me. It's so fucking—I don't even have the words for it."

"That sucks."

"That's it?" I stared at Nick. "Come on. Out with the helpful friend bullshit."

"I honestly don't know what to say," Nick said apologetically. "You seem really upset by it."

"Well wouldn't you be? If you found out your boyfriend had been lying to you?"

Nick cocked his head to the side. "It's hard to say. But it doesn't matter how I'd feel. It's how you feel that counts."

"I feel like a fucking idiot," I said. "I was so fucking proud of myself for getting someone as amazing as Ben to fall for me and the whole time, he's treating me like a fucking child who can't take care of himself and can't be trusted with the truth."

"I doubt that's how he saw it," Nick said slowly. "I'm not defending what he did, exactly, but I very much doubt that's how he saw it, from what I know of Ben. That guy was head over heels for you since before you started dating. That doesn't change how you feel, of course. But I'm just saying. Dude would do anything for you."

"Then why wasn't he honest with me?"

"I don't know. Why do you think?"

"Fuck." I sighed. "Because he knew I'd do this. He said it himself—I'd go off the deep end and freak out about it and now I'm fucking proving him right."

"Have you actually talked to him? Since you found out?"

"No. I'm two trillion times too embarrassed for that."

Nick nodded. "Alright."

"Alright? What kind of help are you? You're supposed to tell me what to do, not just sit there eating chicken."

"Sorry, man. I can't. That's honestly something only you can decide."

"Well I don't fucking know," I said.

"Why don't you know? What are you conflicted about?"

"I just—I feel like a fucking dumbass because I'm so mad at him and fucking hurt but I just—I just want to see him." I could hear myself getting worked up and, of course, I couldn't do anything to stop that. Story of my life. "Like at the same time as all of that shit, I just miss him and want to be with him and I hate that. I fucking hate that. I hate how much I need him and how fucking weak I feel and I can't control any of this shit. All I've ever wanted is to fucking control things and I just can't. Not my own brain. Not how people treat me. I just—I hate it."

"Adam, loving people, needing people—that doesn't make you weak. It makes you human."

"Well being human sucks."

"Sometimes," Nick agreed. "But sometimes it's the most amazing gift. Yeah, you can't control shit. That's one of the sucky parts. But honestly, Adam, would you want to control other people?"

"If it meant I didn't get hurt, maybe," I said mutinously.

"But it would also mean you'd never feel love. Or be loved. For that to happen, you need people to be able to give themselves freely. And not having love... that's kind of the whole point of this whole being alive thing."

I stared at the floor, letting his words wash over me.

"You can't control other people," Nick continued. "You can't even control your feelings, not really. But in every situation you're faced with, you've always got a choice of how to act. That's the only thing you can control. And it's kind of an amazing power. What you choose to do."

"I love him," I said, my voice broken. "God after all of this, I still love him. So much."

"Of course you do. One mistake, one action doesn't make love go away. And this doesn't have to be the end."

"But how do I trust him again?" I asked, looking up. "How do I know he doesn't see me—see me the way I see myself?"

"I don't know," Nick said. "But I don't think it's fair to look at trust as just a feeling. I think trust is a choice. It's an action, something you do in thousands of small moments every day. And maybe it's hard at first and maybe it feels scary. But eventually, it starts to feel right. If you decide it's worth it."

"How do you know, though? If it's worth it?"

"I don't know," Nick said. "Maybe you just try it and see. But if you don't want to spend your life cut off from everyone, you've got to trust someone. Only you can decide who that someone is."

22

BEN

*G*ray took one look at me as I walked into Maggie's and winced.

"Alcohol or caffeine? You look awful."

"Caffeine," I said, sliding onto a stool at the bar. "I have a show tonight."

"Jeez, try to contain your enthusiasm, Ben, you're scaring people with your joy."

I sighed. "It's just—it's been a really shitty week."

Gray frowned as he walked over to the espresso machine. "Wanna talk about it or wanna just get really amped and pretend nothing happened?"

"Won't work," I said. "I've tried. After a day of panicking and two straight days of wallowing, I tried obsessive working out and positive thinking and telling myself it would magically get better. It didn't."

"So you're back to wallowing?" Gray asked, sliding my coffee over to me.

"Pretty much." I stared at my coffee, not even remotely in the mood to drink it.

Gray folded his arms across his chest and nodded. "Alright. Well, what's Adam say about it?"

"Yeah, that's... the shitty thing." I looked up at him. "It's Adam. I... fucked up."

"Ohhh."

"Yeah." I swallowed. "I mean technically, it's more that I did something fucked up a while ago. But he found out about it now. And, completely understandably, did not take it well."

Gray puffed air out of his cheeks. "That's rough."

"I don't know what to do. I know it's my fault, I just—he left. And he won't answer my calls or return my texts. I fucking went up to Harlem to go to his sister's apartment because I thought he'd be there. He wasn't, but that's how much of a fucking stalker I've become. I know he's at Nick's now, but I can't make him talk to me. Like, that's not going to make it better, right?"

"I don't know," Gray said slowly. "How did you guys leave things?"

"Not good."

"Well, presumably he's still got stuff at your place, right? Isn't he going to have to come back and collect that?"

"Fuck, Gray, we were supposed to move in together." I shook my head. "And I have to move out of that apartment in like, days. What the hell am I supposed to do? Just sit there and refuse to leave until he comes back?"

"I'm sure he'll talk to you again," Gray said. "You're just having a fight. Give it time. The way he looks at you? He's not gonna stay away forever."

"I think you're underestimating how much Adam hates... everything. Do you have any idea how hard it was to get him to ever admit he felt anything in the first place?" I snorted. "Nevermind that he says he felt it first. It was like dragging it out of him. Adam fucking hates being vulnerable. And I—I did just about the worst thing I could have."

Gray arched an eyebrow. "What, did you murder someone? Several someones? Puppies?"

"Okay, well, worst thing in Adam's eyes. When it comes to us. When it comes to him. I made him feel..." I trailed off and stared into my coffee for a moment. "Have you ever watched a butterfly come out of its chrysalis?"

"Uh, no. I definitely have not."

"I have. Our kindergarten class had a pet caterpillar. We brought it in and kept it in a birdcage all year. Watched it make its cocoon. And then one day, it finally came out. They're all wet, you know. When they break free. And they can't fly yet. They just kind of like, shudder. You've never seen something so delicate, so defenseless." I paused. "I basically just crushed that fucking butterfly."

Gray made a face. "I think the beauty of that metaphor is a little lost on me. I hate butterflies."

I stared at him, uncomprehending. "How can you hate butterflies?"

"Uh, are you talking about the same satanic hellspawn that I'm talking about?" Gray shivered. "Anyway, agree to disagree."

"I just—this whole time, I kept rushing things, kept pushing Adam and all he was ever trying to tell me was to slow down, to give him some time to adjust. I never even stopped to listen to him, to think about what he wanted. To wonder if I was treating him like—like an equal."

"Sounds like you need to tell him that," Gray said.

"Well how the hell do you recommend I do that when he's not answering my calls?"

"Didn't you say you had some big concert tonight?"

"Yeah, but I can't like, do anything. Not in public. It's a benefit, for one thing. Plus Adam would murder me. Being the center of attention is *not* his thing."

"Then say it a different way," Gray said. "But I'd bet you serious money he's gonna be watching tonight."

Gray's words stayed with me for the rest of the day. Was it completely self-centered, delusional to think that Adam would be watching tonight?

He'd never missed one of my shows before, as long as we'd been in the same city—he'd even tagged along to a stupid sweet sixteen party I'd performed at right out of college. But then again, I'd never broken his heart before either.

There were tickets with his name on them if he came and

Shereen had promised to keep an eye out for him but for all I knew, he wasn't even in the city anymore.

The concert itself snuck up on me. I spent hours in rehearsals, then meetings about logistics, then hair and makeup—insomnia, I explained, had produced those dark circles under my eyes. Inexplicable insomnia, definitely not the kind caused by losing the love of your life and your best friend in one week.

And the whole time I kept wondering if I should call Adam once more. Just in case. I didn't want to push him even further away, though, so I just stared at my phone the whole day and agonized.

I still hadn't brought myself to do it when it was time to go up on stage, but I couldn't make myself leave my phone behind. I turned it on silent and stuck it in the back pocket of my jeans, even though I knew my stylist would be pissed at me for ruining the lines of my outfit.

Taking the stage—the lights, the noise, that hum in the air that you can kind of feel in your chest, that collective energy of the crowd—it was honestly a relief. Something kicked on inside me as soon as I felt the heat of the lights on my face.

Honestly, it didn't matter if it was a hushed group of five people or a stadium full of thousands. There was a connection you got when you performed. You became greater than yourself, somehow. You and everyone in the room. You built something together, greater than the sum of all your parts. And it was different every night, every room.

"Hey guys," I said, grabbing the mic. It felt odd to smile out at them, with everything so unsettled with Adam. But this was also the first time I hadn't felt completely shitty the whole week. "How's everyone doing tonight?"

Cheers and screams echoed back at me, filling the air. It was electrifying—it didn't shock me, anymore, how excited people got, but it never quite felt normal and it was impossible to take for granted. Even if it wasn't me, the real me, that they loved. Me singing brought them something that made them happy. And that was something to be thankful for.

"Thank you guys so much for coming out tonight," I continued. "All of your ticket sales are going to support the Family Futures Project which does such great work here in New York. Intimate partner violence affects thousands of women, men, and children, and the Family Futures Project makes sure that survivors don't have to go it alone, that they have a safe place, a helping hand.

"I was lucky enough to grow up surrounded by a loving family, with my parents and sisters who I knew I was safe with. But not everyone is that lucky. And it's up to us to do everything we can to—"

I stopped, mid-sentence, suddenly hearing the phrase that was about to roll off my tongue.

To help those less fortunate than ourselves.

What a shitty way to say that. How condescending. I'd hate it if someone said that about me. Made me nothing more than a statistic, just a passive recipient of care.

A burden. It hit me like a lead weight smashed into my chest. That's what I'd been doing to Adam.

Fuck.

I blinked, suddenly realizing that I was still standing on stage, my mouth hanging open, mid-sentence.

"To do everything we can to work together," I finished. "To make the world a place that's safe for everyone."

I cursed myself silently for how lame an ending that was. But no one seemed to mind. People were cheering like I'd just told them I'd cured cancer.

I wanted to rush off the stage right then. Call Adam, *find* Adam. Apologize again, tell him what I'd figured out. But of course, I couldn't. So I launched into the first song, still shaken from that realization, and it reverberated through the night, coloring every note I sang.

I wished Adam were there. Found myself squinting out into the crowd, as though there were any chance of seeing him even if he had shown up. I counted my way down through the setlist, eager for the night to be over.

And then I thought about what Gray had said. I didn't want to make the night about me. That wasn't the point. But my last song, by happenstance, in a setlist I'd planned ages ago, was called *Bow and Arrow*. One of the few songs from my demo that I'd fought tooth and nail to get onto my debut album with Greenleaf. Adam had written it, of course.

Maybe I could say something.

I turned to the crowd, and smiled.

"Guys, you've been so amazing tonight. Thank you all so much for coming out. This one's gonna be my last song for the night and if you'll let me get sappy here for a minute—" the crowd quieted down—as quiet as a crowd that size could get, anyway, "if you'll let me get sappy here, this song reminds me of someone I love. Someone really important to me. Someone I couldn't live without. And, well..." I stopped and laughed as I heard muttering in my earpiece. "Someone backstage is really pissed at me right now because I'm rambling and taking more time than I'm supposed to." The crowd laughed. "I started talking without really knowing where I was going. Don't go off-script, guys, it makes your manager freak out." More laughter. "Anyway, I guess I just wanted to say that sometimes we take the people we love for granted. We hurt them in ways we never mean to." I stopped, swallowing hard. "So I want everyone to go home tonight and reach out to someone you love—whoever that is, your mom, your friend, your dog, your mailman—and tell them how much they mean to you. Got it? Can you do that for me?"

The crowd roared and I smiled.

"Okay, I guess I'm gonna sing this song now before they drag me off-stage."

It occurred to me that maybe there actually was a silver lining to mostly singing the perfectly calibrated, slick pop songs Greenleaf had decided would be my bread and butter. Since I hadn't had a hand in writing those, I wasn't emotionally attached to them at all.

But *Bow and Arrow* was different. Adam had written it over the course of one afternoon, the two of us sitting around in Washington Square Park watching the sun slip lower and lower in the sky. It had a steady, propulsive baseline and this really thrummy, sort of juicy hook and a chorus that got your blood flowing. Even when you played a stripped down version of it on an acoustic guitar, it was electric.

But this time, that driving force that ran through the song only wound me up more, made me realize how badly I needed Adam. I got through it, somehow, thanked everyone again, and walked off-stage as quickly as I could without actually running.

I could see Shereen already giving me a raised eyebrow from across the room but I got pulled into the press room for interviews and photos before she could say anything. I checked my phone—nothing from Adam—and I tried to tell myself it was going to be okay. I was going to find him. I was going to fix this. If I could ever get out of this interminable round of photo-ops.

And then I saw Nick walking up to me and I swear to God my heart almost stopped.

"Adam," I said, grabbing Nick by the arm and ducking clumsily out of a conversation with the president of the board for the Family Futures Project. "Is he here? Is he with you?"

"He's not here," Nick said, shaking his head. "I asked if he wanted to come, since I had to be here for work anyway, and he said he wasn't up to it. But—I think you need to see this."

He pulled his phone out and I squinted at the screen, then felt my eyes widen as I realized what I was looking at. Or more importantly, who.

"Holy shit."

*I*t was the first show of Ben's that I'd missed.

It felt weird.

It would have been weird enough if it were as simple as that, me missing his show because I had a dentist appointment or something. I know no one goes to the dentist at 9 p.m. on a Thursday but you know what I mean. With everything else that was going on though?

I loved watching Ben perform. The way he connected with a crowd, no matter how big or small, was breathtaking. It was the kind of thing that electrified you if you were just in the audience and gave you chills if you knew enough about music to know just how good Ben truly was.

The first time I'd seen Ben sing, fronting a random band during college, was only a month after he'd finally broken through my self-righteous, self-imposed social exile and forced me to start hanging out with him. We'd dicked around a little bit in our dorm room a few times, me making up riffs and Ben inventing lyrics on the spot. Or, more often,

Ben insisting I play Heart's *Alone* so he could work on his upper registers and I told myself to stop being emo and taking the lyrics to heart.

But that night on the patio of the L Village Apartments, something had rushed through me during Ben's first song. Like being shocked by a current—I'd literally felt my body kind of twitch in response (and no, not just my cock, though... that too). It was like standing at the top of a skyscraper and leaning over, losing your balance and getting a taste of the freefall before being pulled back at the last second. It was intoxicating.

But when Nick had said he was going to the benefit tonight and asked if I just wanted to come and stand in the back, I hadn't been able to say yes. I'd wanted to. God, part of me wanted to so badly. But there was something around me like an anchor, pulling me back stubbornly, reminding me how weak it would be to go.

I'd spent my whole life fighting that. Fighting that desperate, dark, clammy part of me that was just so fucking thirsty for love. So terrified of asking for it and not getting it. If I went to Ben's show, it meant I was asking for it. And it meant putting myself at risk again of getting hurt. It meant admitting how broken I really was.

But after about 30 minutes of being cooped up in Nick's apartment after he'd left, I started to get twitchy. I needed to go somewhere, anywhere, just to move. So I went for a walk and before I knew it, I found myself standing in front of Ben's apartment, contemplating the building's smooth, impassive surface.

I could just go up and get my stuff now, knowing Ben

wouldn't be there. Or, I could just go up and wait for him. Surrender. Curl up in bed and wait for him to come home.

God, I wanted to do that.

But Ben hadn't called or texted since that first day at Nick's. What if he'd changed his mind? What if he'd decided I really was too much to put up with?

I hated that I might have ruined things with Ben just because of my stubborn pride and then I hated myself for thinking that. I wasn't supposed to still want Ben. But I did.

Eventually, I realized I'd been staring at the building for so long that someone might think I was going to rob the place, so I started walking again and somehow, my feet took me to Maggie's. I went in, for lack of anything better to do.

Whatever buzz Mia's party had generated earlier that summer, it apparently didn't translate to Thursday nights. There were about six other people in the place so it wasn't difficult for Gray to look up from the bar and see me as I walked in.

"Hey," he said, his easy-going bartender's smile only slightly marred by a note of confusion. "How's it going?"

"It's... okay," I said, walking over and squinting at him. "Have you, uh, talked to Ben recently?"

Gray nodded. "Yeah. He was just in here earlier today, actually."

"He tell you?"

"The outline of things," Gray said with a sad smile.

I felt my lips twist. "Yeah. I figured."

But what had I expected? Gray was Ben's friend. And I was the dumbass who'd walked in here.

"You want a drink?" Gray asked.

I did. I wanted about five drinks. But I was trying to be less of a mess, not more of one, so I shook my head. "Seltzer water?"

"No problem." Gray filled up a glass with some ice and added seltzer, then garnished it with a lime and grinned. "Lime's on the house. Plus it makes it look like you're actually drinking."

I snorted. "If I were the kind of person who drank gin and tonics, I guess."

"Or vodka tonics. Or, worse, vodka sodas." Gray shuddered.

"Eww. Who the hell would drink that? That's just watery vodka. With bubbles."

"People who care enough about being 'healthy' to not want the calories of tonic but not enough to actually stop drinking alcohol," Gray said, rolling his eyes.

I snorted. "I don't even care enough to pretend," I stirred the seltzer with the tiny black straw he'd given me. "If it were me, honestly, this would probably be Everclear and 7-Up."

"Frat party drink of choice. Classy," Gray said. He walked down to the other end of the bar to get two more beers for a pair of girls standing down there before coming back my way. He narrowed his eyes. "I can't believe I'm asking this, but, have you talked to Ben?"

I shrug-sighed, the kind of move you make when you're too

exhausted and embarrassed to fully commit to either. "No," I said simply.

"You gonna?"

I sighed again—a real one this time, and answered Gray honestly. "I don't know."

"You know he has some show tonight, right?" Gray cocked an eyebrow. "You're not going?"

"It's complicated."

Gray folded his arms across his chest and gave me a long look.

"What?" I asked, fully aware of how petulant I sounded. "You have an opinion you'd like to share?"

Gray snorted. "Not an opinion. I don't know the details of what happened and I don't want to. I left middle school a long time ago, thank you very much." He shook his head. "But whatever happened, Ben feels awful. And he looks atrocious. Worse than you, which is saying something."

"Hey."

Gray held his hand up peaceably. "I'm just saying, would it really be so bad to talk to him? Just to talk and hear him out?"

"Yes," I said, annoyed. "Yes, actually, it probably would, because the second I did, I'd just end up forgiving him and saying it's okay just because I don't want to be alone. Because I'm weak. Because I'd rather be broken with someone than try to be whole on my own."

Gray whistled. "That's... quite a statement."

"Yeah, well if you didn't want to listen to other people's self-indulgent melodrama, you picked the wrong line of work. Besides, you asked."

"I did," Gray said with a little laugh. "That's true. I just... Adam, look, I'll drop it after this but, you know that needing people doesn't make you weak. And good luck trying to heal anything on your own. We're all broken, man. We're all walking wounded. Other people... other people are how we heal. If the process stings sometimes, that just means it's working."

"Gross."

"Hey, you get to be melodramatic, so do I." Gray shrugged. "Just think about it. Because honestly, Adam, I know this feels really big and terrifying but I've been around long enough to recognize a good relationship when I see one. Ben is stupid in love with you. And it's pretty clear you're a wreck without him. Don't throw this away because you're scared."

Another customer called for Gray's attention and he pulled away, leaving me chewing on the lime from my seltzer and his words. I wondered if he was right. I hated, hated, hated needing people. But hating it didn't make it go away. And if Gray had the right end of the stick—was I just fighting a losing battle?

There was one thing I was sure he was right about, at least. I *was* a wreck without Ben.

Gray seemed content to let me be as he worked. Every so often Micah or he would swing by to check on me, refilling my seltzer as I sat there and tried to sort things through. I was content to be left alone. There was a perfect amount of people in the bar now, just enough so that it didn't feel empty but not so much that it got loud or uncomfortable.

It wasn't until Micah came out to fix the string of lights running along the top of the shelves behind the bar that I started paying attention to what was going on around me, and that was only because he called my name.

"Adam, can you hold this for a sec?"

I looked up and saw that he'd taken down the guitar that hung on the wall so that he could reach the lights better. I reached out and took it from him, then stared at it in surprise.

I'd never actually looked at it closely before—it was usually shadowed up there and I'd always assumed it was just some chintzy decoration. But it was actually a decently made acoustic guitar. Classical, not my normal style, but good craftsmanship. I strummed my fingers across the strings and winced. Desperately out of tune.

"How'd you end up with this?" I asked Gray when he came over and watched me tune it.

"It was my aunt's," Gray said. "She left it to me, along with the bar. I don't know shit about guitars but it didn't feel quite right just getting rid of it.

"It's a nice instrument," I said, twisting the tuning key for the D string and plucking it. Still sounded a little flat. It twisted the peghead some more and then strummed a few chords, nodding to myself. Better. It was actually—

"Oh, shit, sorry," I said, slapping my hand down over the strings to quiet them when I realized what I was doing. "Bad habit. I see an instrument, I play it, unless someone takes it out of my hands."

I made a face and offered the guitar back to Gray but he shook his head.

"Don't apologize at all. Honestly, do you want the thing? It's not doing me any good up there."

I laughed. "No, dude, definitely don't just give it away. You could get a couple hundred dollars for this at least."

I looked down and ran my hand over the wood. It was obvious Gray's aunt had taken good care of it and from the little bit I'd played, it had a nice sound. I strummed again and nodded. Warm and resonant. Like morning sun shining through a cedar forest, all golden and rich.

I couldn't resist giving it a little flourish, running through the opening riff to *Sweet Child of Mine*, which sounded absolutely ridiculous on an acoustic guitar but was pretty fun to play. And it had the added benefit of looking more impressive than it actually was.

A woman sitting two stools down from me at the bar turned away from her conversation with her friend and looked at me, her eyes wide.

"Oh my God, do you play the guitar?"

Crap. Should have known that would happen.

"Uh, yeah. Not usually in public though," I said, laughing a little bit and hoping I came off sounding relaxed. I could feel myself blushing.

"Dude, there are like, 10 people in this bar right now," Gray said. "I don't really think it counts as public."

"Oh my God," the woman went on, pushing her hair behind her ears and smiling. "I always wanted to play the guitar. Will you play something for me?"

"Yeah," her friend put in. "Please?"

"Um." The problem wasn't that I didn't really want to. It was that I couldn't think of a good reason to say no. It would be far less awkward to just say yes. "Sure, I guess."

I frowned down at the guitar and suddenly, a snatch of *Bow and Arrow*, one of the first songs I'd ever written with Ben, popped into my head. Stupid subconscious. But it was an easy song to play and dammit, I liked it.

It was nice to lose myself in it, too, to forget for a second why I was here alone. Of course, it always sounded better when Ben sang it but somehow, singing it made it feel a bit like Ben *was* there. Which was mortifying and sentimental but who the hell was I even kidding anymore, mortifying and sentimental was basically homeostasis for me.

"That's a Ben Thomas song, isn't it?" the woman asked when I finished.

I smiled. "Yeah. Yeah, it is. I know, he sings it better."

"No! You were really good," the woman said. She leaned over the empty stool between us and smiled. "I'm Rosa, by the way. This is Beth."

Beth smiled and I nodded to both of them. "Nice to meet you guys. I'm Adam."

"Can you play *Torn*?" Beth asked, her eyes lighting up.

Double crap. That was the problem with agreeing to play one song—too often it turned into a string of songs and suddenly you were that asshole who brought an acoustic guitar to every party in an attempt to look like a sensitive, tender bro and get laid. I hated that guy and even if that wasn't what was happening, I still felt grossed out by myself.

Luckily...

"Sorry, I don't think I know that one," I said. It was true, too. I had no idea what she was talking about.

"No, you do," Beth insisted. "Here, it's the one that goes like—"

She started humming. Fuck. I did know it, and she must have seen that moment of recognition in my eyes because she cut off and smiled.

"See, told you."

There was nothing to do but play it. Thank God Rosa and Beth seemed to know the lyrics by heart because I was patchy in some places and needed them to fill in for me. It wasn't until I finished that I realized Rosa had pulled her phone out and recorded the whole thing.

"You're like, *so good*," she said, giving me the intense stare of the very earnest or the very drunk. Or, possibly in this case, both. She turned back to Beth. "What should we ask him to play next?"

I felt my face heating up as they started arguing about 90s pop songs and turned to see Gray smirking at me from behind the bar.

"You want a beer or something?" he asked.

"Nah, I'm good." And strangely, I was. It was weird, playing sober. But not bad, exactly. Probably because I was only playing for a crowd of three right now. "I don't know why they're making such a big thing of it," I added under my breath.

Gray laughed and leaned across the bar. "I mean, you are good," he said, his voice low and amused. "So there's that. But they'd do it anyway."

"What? Why?"

"They're flirting with you."

"They're not—" I stopped, my mouth dropping open and my cheeks flushing. "Oh my God."

"Foreign concept?" Gray asked, his eyes dancing.

"I just never—" I glanced over my shoulder to see Rosa and Beth talking to some guy with glasses who'd just approached them. "Do you think I should tell them I'm not—"

"Hell no," Gray said. "Flirt back and tell them to bring their friends in. Maybe I'll actually make some money tonight."

Rosa leaned over then and asked if I could play *Hallelujah*. I was still trying to figure out a graceful way to get out of playing at all, but she and Beth and whoever that guy was were so enthusiastic it was just easier to say yes. And I didn't actually mind, I realized. I didn't feel uncomfortable so much as I *expected* to feel uncomfortable and was trying to back out by habit. Well, that and the fact that I knew I'd inevitably disappoint them because whatever version of the song I picked, the original or one of the covers, they'd somehow be expecting something different.

I looked up when I was finished playing. Rosa and Beth had

both been recording me but the guy with glasses standing next to them was just staring.

"You're Adam Hart, aren't you?" Glasses said, his tone sounding 50% excited and 50% accusatory.

"Uh, yeah." I felt sort of like I was copping to a murder charge.

"Shit, you're amazing."

Rosa looked at me in confusion. "Wait, who are you?"

"No one, really," I said, wincing. "It's not a big deal."

"Fuck no," Glasses said. It seemed like he might be drunk too or, at the very least, felt very strongly about defending my honor. "He's famous." He turned back to me. "Didn't you like, write all the songs on Ben Thomas's last album?"

"Only a couple, actually." But that was mostly because of all the one's I'd written on his demo, only a few had carried over onto the album he'd put out with Greenleaf.

"He has his own band, too," Glasses continued, evangelizing me to Beth and Rosa. "They're really good, though they haven't played since... oh."

Glasses stopped and looked sheepish.

"It's okay," I said, laughing a little. "It's not like I'd forgotten."

It felt oddly good to laugh about it. Just like it felt strangely okay to be playing in front of people. I just...

I wished Ben were there.

There was no point in denying it. I just did. I was playing in public and I didn't hate it and the only other times I hadn't hated playing had all been with Ben. And maybe it was weak and maybe it was pathetic and maybe I was drunk on seltzer water but fuck, I just wanted him back. And I might have ruined everything.

And before I knew what I was doing, I'd launched into *Underwater*, another song from Ben's demo, and then Glasses, who turned out to be named Jonas, asked if I could play *Cardiology* and it turned out that if I just pretended I'd written the song about Ben, I didn't actually hate having to play it, even if it did still make me sad.

And at some point, I looked up again to realize that the bar that had been empty earlier that night was now packed with people and I was playing to a rapt audience, still sitting on that same bar stool. Gray looked overworked and overjoyed and mouthed a silent *'thank you'* over everyone's heads from the far side of the bar.

"Can you play *Everlong*?" someone shouted out from the back of the crowd.

"I, uh—" I stopped.

"Play whatever you want," Rosa said, frowning, as though she hadn't been issuing demands for songs up until 10 minutes ago. "Don't listen to him."

"No, it's—it's fine." I laughed and raised my voice a little. The bar wasn't huge, but it wasn't like I was on stage with a mic or anything. "I used to make fun of this song so much and people who wanted to hear it. But the fact of the matter is, I'm a giant fucking sap and the song makes me feel all kinds of gross feelings inside and *that's* why I didn't want to play it. But fuck it, I've lost that battle, clearly. Yeah, I can play it."

I started strumming the first few chords and then surprised myself by stopping.

"Um—" I said, wincing at my goddamn earnestness before I'd even spoken. "I'm uh, gay."

"Wanna go out with me?" called a voice from somewhere in the middle of the crowd, and everyone laughed.

"Uh, right. So yeah, I'm gonna change the pronouns in this song. Hope that's cool. If it's not, uh, I guess drink some more until your hearing gets slurry? And tip your bartenders."

Everyone laughed like I'd said something funny and I shook my head. I'd just come out myself to a room full of people— some of whom were still recording me—and nothing... bad... had happened? That was fucking weird. Or maybe it wasn't, and I was the weird one for thinking anyone would care.

I felt drunk at the thought. Why did I get caught in my head so goddamn much when really, no one gave a shit? And if they did, why did I think it mattered? I shook myself, realizing I was keeping people waiting so I started playing. It wasn't until the middle of the song that I finally let myself hear the words. Which was a mistake.

And now, I know you've always been

Out of your head, out of my head I sang

Definitely a mistake. I was starting to fucking tear up. And by the time I got to the second round of the chorus, I could hear my goddamn voice crack and I had to look down at the guitar, not because I needed to pay attention to my fingers —for as much as I'd refused to play this song, I also knew it by heart—but because I was afraid I was going to start to cry.

If everything could ever feel this real forever

If anything could ever be this good again

The only thing I'll ever ask of you

You've gotta promise not to stop when I say when

Fuck, this was embarrassing. This was why I didn't play in front of people. Not sober, anyway. Because everyone looked at you like you were the key to something in their lives, like you could solve something for them with this song you were playing and you couldn't even solve your own fucking life. It felt like they were trying to pry inside you and for years, everything in me had screamed 'No'—don't let them look, don't let them see you're not good enough.

But I was tired of feeling not good enough. I was tired of just being so afraid all the time. And hell, I'd just told a room full of strangers I was gay and no one had batted an eye. Why couldn't I just let go?

So I made myself look up again, completely aware of the tears leaking out of the corner of my right eye. When I finished the song, people clapped and someone whistled.

I wiped the cuff of my hoodie across my eye and laughed. "See, told you guys it made me sappy."

"Me too," said a woman's voice from somewhere near the front

The crowd laughed and I joined in. I strummed across the strings absent-mindedly, wondering the last time I'd felt this... free. This unencumbered.

It came to me in a flash—in bed with Ben the first night we'd fucked. The first time I'd felt truly seen. The first night I'd really trusted.

Trust is something you do, Nick had said. I was so afraid of being broken. But if Gray was right, if we were all broken?

"You guys mind if I play one more sentimental song for a minute?" I got encouraging shouts from the crowd. "I'll, uh, take that as a yes. Fair warning, it's an original song, so you might not like it. But I promise I'll go back to covers after. I just..." I shrugged. "I feel like moping a bit for tonight. So this is gonna be a love song. For someone I pushed away."

I took a deep breath and began playing the song I'd been working on all summer, the one Ben had first played for me that night at the piano after Mia's party. God, that felt like ages ago. I could barely remember being that Adam. So scared, so brittle. So convinced that nothing good could come into my life.

And then it had. I'd let Ben in. And I'd become something more than myself.

Love was a bit like music in that way. It made you bigger than you were, took you out of your own body, made you something greater—together.

I'd called this our song by mistake. But I'd ended up thinking of it as exactly that. And the lyrics—I'd been riffing on the ones Ben had sang to me that night on the couch, just playing around with them, and somehow I'd landed on something so sappy, I hadn't even been able to show Ben. But tonight, as I sang them, I realized how true they were.

You take up space inside my heart

Pushing, pulling, making room

And as I lie here in the dark

And tell our story to the moon

There's nothing I want more, my dear

No feeling I would rather chase

I need your touch, I need you here

Inside my heart, you take up space

I didn't want to go back to being brittle old Adam. I didn't want to go back to being alone. Scared to let anyone in. And so I played, and sang, and I knew I was getting emotional but I didn't even care. It was the most amazing thing, to be so sad about what I'd fucked up with Ben and yet to feel okay in myself for once.

When I came to a stop, the room was silent for a long moment, then broke out into applause. I flushed.

"Thanks guys. For listening to me mope. Honestly, anyone else wanna take a turn at this? I'm mostly just playing because Gray's been putting up with my sorry ass all night and I'm trying to make it up to him by getting you to spend all your money on drinks." Everyone laughed as I held up the guitar but no one rose to take the bait.

"Okay then," I said, rolling my eyes. "Uh, I promised fun stuff. Who's up for some Backstreet Boys?"

An hour later, I was exhausted. The crowd had only gotten bigger, people were still recording me, and even though I'd made other people come up and sing with me, I could feel my voice going. It was time to leave. Time to find Ben—past time—and ask him to forgive me.

So I smiled at the crowd and waited for them to quiet down before telling them this would be my last song. I heard people murmuring in the back—even more people joining the crowd probably—and I gave everyone an apologetic look.

"Really, it's been awesome, but I'm beat and if I keep it up my voice is going to sound like nails on a chalkboard and that's no fun for anyone. So this is gonna be the last one. Any requests?"

"Can you play any power ballads?" shouted a voice from the back of the room. "*Total Eclipse of the Heart*?"

My head snapped up in shock.

That was Ben's voice.

I scanned the crowd, trying to figure out where it had come from, and saw a ripple in the back. And then the swarm of people in front of me parted and I could see Ben, standing next to Nick, of all people, at the back of the room. I swear to God I heard an actual gasp go through the bar—echoed, obviously, by me.

"Ben." The room was so quiet that everyone heard me, even though I'd said it softly.

"Hey." Ben said, taking a step forward. He stopped. Took another step, then stopped again. "I wanted—fuck. I didn't think this through." He glanced around and seemed to notice for the first time that everyone was watching him. He laughed nervously. "Do you wanna maybe, um, I mean, you don't have to like, but if you wanted maybe we could—"

"Just get the fuck over here and kiss me already."

And he did. He crossed the space between us in an instant and I had just enough time to realize what was happening, to shove the guitar at someone, before Ben pulled me into his arms, my hands went to his face, and he kissed me.

Everyone cheered.

Ben's lips were warm, soft, and God had I missed them. It felt like months since I'd kissed him, not the five days it had actually been. I opened my mouth, deepening the kiss while I pushed so hard against Ben's body that he actually stumbled back, pulling me off the bar stool before we caught our balance. When we finally broke apart, I was breathless, and everyone was still fucking clapping.

"I'm sorry," I whispered into Ben's ear.

"I'm sorrier."

"Debatable," I said with a smile. "How did you—how did you know I was here? Aren't you supposed to be—"

"You're trending on Twitter right now." Ben said. "Someone's been putting video of you up online—'Adam Hart plays surprise show at Maggie's in SoHo'—and Nick saw it somehow. Showed it to me at the benefit. You were playing—you played Everlong. And I thought maybe, somehow that meant that you might—"

"Well, obviously." I could feel my cheeks flushing.

"I wouldn't—I was so sure you'd written me off. But when you said—when I heard you—"

"Oh God, it's bad enough that I said it in public. Hearing it out of your mouth is too much." I looked up at him and smiled. "But it's all true. I love you."

"I love you too."

The night was hot and humid as we walked back to Ben's apartment, the darkness drawing close around us like curtains. I didn't say much. At first I was waiting for Ben to speak, overwhelmed with the need to say too many things, to say everything, and then I was quiet because I realized that right now, I didn't want to say anything at all. Right now, walking home, Ben's hand holding mine, was enough.

"Gray's gonna be happy," Ben said absently as we turned onto our block. *Our* block. *Ours.* "I've never seen his place that crowded."

"Yeah." I nodded. "I should probably demand free seltzer for life from him."

It was light, inconsequential talk. But it was almost like we had to build up to the rest of it. The rush, the heady feeling of Ben crashing into me, wrapping me up, had knocked us flat in a wave and then ebbed, leaving us lying on the beach, trying to pick ourselves up.

And now it felt like we were standing next to this ocean, vast and deep, knowing we had to swim across it. We would— together. But for now, it was enough to hold hands on that beach, breathing in time to the waves lapping at the shore, and dip our toes in.

"How was the benefit?" I asked after a moment.

Ben smiled. "Good. Raised a bunch of money. Only lost my shit thinking about you once."

"Nice. How'd it feel? The concert, I mean. Your last one for a while."

"A little sad, maybe," Ben said, shrugging. "End of an era and all that."

"You could still change your mind," I said. "Doesn't your contract technically end tomorrow? I'm sure Shereen would be thrilled."

Ben laughed. "She would be. But no. Not for a second. This is the right thing."

"Good." I squeezed Ben's hand and he squeezed back.

"Missed you, though," Ben said. "At the show."

I smiled sadly. "I wanted to go."

"You had reasons."

"I know. But... next one. I'll be there. I don't want to miss anymore."

"Next one," Ben said, pulling me up the steps of the building to the front door, "next one I want to do together."

I blinked. Play a show together? We'd worked together, sure, written together. But we hadn't played a show together more than two or three times. I'd never been that comfortable up on a stage. But now?

"I mean, only if you want to," Ben added, opening the door. He smiled at me nervously. "But what's the point of going independent if I can't be with you, you know?"

"I do," I said after a moment. "And yeah. That sounds... that sounds amazing."

Things felt softer, safer, as soon as the door to the street closed, and even quieter, almost reverent, when we got into the apartment. I stared around the shadowy space, the wall of windows in the living room letting in the moon, and streetlights, and the headlights of cars arcing across the walls.

"Is it weird to say I've missed this place?" I asked.

Ben came up behind me, slid his arms around my waist, and pulled me back against his chest. "No. Because God did I miss having you here."

I turned around and kissed him, feather light, on the lips, and then took Ben's hand and walked back towards the bedroom. What I'd missed most was the feel of Ben's skin on my own. Not even sex, specifically—though, fine, that too—but the sense of having nothing between us. Our bodies touching, breath and heartbeats mingled. That was when I felt safe, and whole.

I needed to feel that again.

So we walked into the bedroom, that quiet spell as yet unbroken, humming in the air around us. I stripped, frankly and unselfconsciously for once, then looked over my shoulder and arched an eyebrow at Ben, who was staring with a dumbstruck smile on his face.

"You just gonna stand there all night?" I asked with a grin.

Ben shook himself a little and started pulling off his shirt. I crawled into bed, pulling the comforter up to my waist, and watched as Ben undressed, his pants falling into a heap on the ground. He picked them up immediately and pressed them flat, laying them gently along the back of the armchair in the corner of the room.

I smiled. My own clothes remained in a puddle on the floor but I wasn't going to pick them up now. I had more important things to do, like watching the muscles ripple in Ben's back as he hung up his shirt and tucked it in the closet, then bent down to strip off his socks. Fuck, his ass was perfect.

I blushed out of habit, remembering all the times over the years I'd tried to stop myself from staring at Ben, tried to keep my eyes from doing what they longed to do, roaming over his unclothed body, memorizing every inch of his skin.

Then Ben turned and in one swift movement, shucked his navy boxer briefs. My stomach turned over in excitement as his cock sprang free. Fuck, he was already hard.

Ben was gorgeous. And improbably, unbelievably, he wanted to be with me.

Ben caught me looking. He arched an eyebrow and shimmied his hips for a second. "I would have put on more of a show if I knew you were watching."

"Have you really not gotten used to the fact that I'm totally fucking creepy? Ben, I'm always watching." I rolled my eyes. "But I'm out of cash at the moment."

"I can think of other forms of payment," Ben said. "There's plenty you could do."

"Not with you standing all the way over there, there's not."

Just looking at Ben had my cock hardening and God, I needed to feel him pressed against me. I lifted up the corner of the comforter and Ben dove in. He slid to the middle of the bed and hadn't even stopped moving before I launched myself at him, wrapping both arms and one leg around him like a koala—which, yeah, might have been a little needy but why bother even pretending not to be at this point? Besides, koalas are cute.

I buried my face in Ben's neck as he hugged me back and breathed deeply. Citrus shampoo and fucking liquid sunshine. I'd missed the way he smelled. Finally, I was home.

Ben's fingers traced little spirals up and down my back. "You wanna talk about it?" he asked after a minute.

I cracked an eyelid open. "I mean, no. But we probably should, I guess."

Ben laughed and pulled back to look me in the eye. "Well then let me start. Because I have some major groveling to do."

I pushed back, raising myself up on my elbows and preparing to disagree but Ben shushed me. "No. I do. And I need to say it and then you can argue, okay?"

I rolled my eyes and flushed, then made a big show of plumping up a pillow and leaning back on it. "Fine. I consent."

"You're too kind." Ben glanced down at the covers for a moment, then took my hand before looking back up at me. "I was so, so scared when I found out about the accident. You were my best friend, Adam. But that was the first time I'd ever thought about how it would feel to lose you. And it ripped me apart."

He ran the backs of his fingers up and down my arm as he talked and gave me a small smile. "I didn't realize it at the time, but I was in love with you, even back then. I just needed a push to see it. When Esther told me she was worried, when she mentioned Peachtree, I didn't think twice about offering to pay for it. And I would do that again. But I never should have asked her not to tell you. I should have talked to you, from the beginning. And I should have listened. I should have trusted you."

"Thanks," I said softly. "That—thanks." I swallowed. "I probably shouldn't have reacted the way I did. I was just— it's just that my whole life, I've been told I'm not good enough, that something was wrong with me. And even if I'm supposed to know that's not true, it kind of fucked with my head, thinking that was how you saw me too."

"Oh, Adam." Ben squeezed my hand. "I'm so sorry."

"It's just—you've always been, like, my person, you know? The one person who didn't judge me, who saw past all my bullshit and decided you liked me anyway. The thought that you didn't anymore—that scared me more than anything. But I don't *want* to be scared anymore. I don't want to like, keep pulling back because I'm afraid of letting someone—of letting *you* in. I just—I don't want to be alone, you know?" I started to cry and wiped the tears from my eyes angrily. "Jesus, I'm a fucking waterworks over here. I can't talk about buying groceries without tearing up anymore."

"You're perfect," Ben said. He brought his hands to either side of my face and pulled me in, kissing my cheeks, kissing the tears away. When he pulled back, there were tears in his eyes too. "I know—I know I can be a little overbearing sometimes. And pushy. I need you to tell me when I'm doing that, when I need to let up, okay? It's a bad habit, I know. I was just trying to help, but I didn't realize—I didn't realize how much trying to take care of people can feel shitty from the other end."

"Okay." I bit my lip. "But I... would it be okay if sometimes I want you to do that? If sometimes I like, need you to take care of me?"

"Yeah." Ben was really crying now. "Yeah, it would."

Our lips crushed together, both of us messes, but for once, I wasn't self conscious about it. If I couldn't let go in front of Ben, who could I let go in front of? Who could I be myself with, if not him?

Ben smiled as he pulled back. "You're the best person in my life, Adam. I could never—you're not even *real* sometimes, you know that? It kills me how smart and talented you are, I'm honestly in awe of you. And you're so sweet and you cut through my bullshit and you make me laugh and when I see you, something in here—" he brought my hand to his chest, placed my fingers right on his sternum, "lights up. You make me a better person. So please don't think that I see you as anything less than the amazing person you are."

"Well now I'm thoroughly embarrassed," I said, feeling my face flush.

"Yeah, I know," Ben laughed. "I'm expecting to be kicked out of bed shortly."

I pulled him closer. "Fuck no. I might not understand why you want me, but as long as you do, I'm going to make the most of that."

"I will always want you," Ben whispered. "I think I always have."

My eyes widened in surprise and Ben looked at me. "What? What's wrong?"

"Nothing." I shook my head in disbelief. "Absolutely nothing's wrong. I just... eww. I just realized that this only works, we only happened because we each like, opened up to each other. And were vulnerable. Ugh, this is disgusting. Nick's gonna be so fucking smug when he finds out we're back together."

"Better make it worth it then," Ben said, leaning forward and kissing me.

His lips were soft and sweet, his tongue darting out to flick inside my mouth and taste me. I moaned, pressing hard against Ben's body, his cock grinding next to mine, and then pushed Ben over onto his back. I crawled on top of him, then trailed my lips from his mouth across his jaw to his ear.

"It's been way too long since you fucked me," I whispered. Ben's eyes widened and I smiled. I loved that I could still startle him.

I traced my way down Ben's neck, nipping and sucking as I went. I wanted to leave marks, wanted everyone to know that Ben was mine, just as much as I was his. Ben arched his back up, his cock, already leaking precum, leaving a trail on my stomach. I reached down in between us and began stroking him as I kissed his chest. Ben's hands tangled in my hair.

Of all the magical, specific little details that I'd learned about Ben's body over the past month—things I never could have imagined when I was just daydreaming about us being together—his nipples were probably my favorite. I loved how sensitive they were, twitching any time I touched them. It made it damn hard to resist.

I flicked my tongue across his left nipple, swirling it around, then sucking it into my mouth before kissing across his chest to do the same to the right one. I bit down on it hard and Ben gasped, his hands pulling on my hair.

I took that as a sign to move lower but as I started to shift, Ben grabbed my shoulders.

"What?" I asked, looking up.

"Can we—" Ben blushed, which looked incredibly sexy. "Was was thinking... can we sixty-nine?"

Like I was going to say no to that.

It was a little awkward, getting into position, me on my hands and knees above him, but then I felt Ben's hand on my cock, guiding it towards his lips, and I decided I didn't care. I leaned in, my hand circling the bottom of Ben's shaft, and brought the tip to my mouth. I let my lips slide over it as my tongue swirled around the head.

Fuck, Ben tasted good—like apple pie and Friday nights and a happy childhood. I slurped along his length hungrily, loving the salty tang of prcum leaking from his tip. I took more of Ben into my mouth but suddenly it was hard to concentrate as Ben's mouth closed around my cock. He kept his lips tight, his tongue moving, knowing just the pace that drove me crazy.

Just when I thought I was going to have to ask Ben to stop, to slow down or I'd come, he did. He even let go of my cock.

But then I felt his hands move to my ass, massaging me as he pressed his lips to one cheek, kissing it and then biting down gently. Fuck, that was hot.

My stomach fluttered as Ben's hands gripped me strongly, spreading my ass and exposing me. It used to make me nervous—and okay, it still kind of did, but that was part of the thrill of it—but Ben seemed to love rimming me. I shuddered as he slid his tongue across my entrance, wet and velvety. When he started to flick his tongue back and forth, then pressed it into me, I felt my knees go weak.

"Fuck," I gasped, pulling off of Ben's cock so I could steady myself. "Oh fuck, Ben."

"You're so fucking perfect," Ben said, swirling his tongue around my hole for emphasis. "God, someday I'm going to make you come just from this."

My eyes widened. "Keep it up," I groaned, "and that day might come a lot sooner than you planned."

"Hold that thought," Ben said. I heard movement behind me and when I looked over my shoulder, he was reaching into the nightstand to grab the lube.

Jesus, he was going to prep me like this? God, that felt almost slutty, my ass up in the air like I was on display. But fuck, it was also hot.

When I felt Ben place a cool, wet finger against my hole, I shivered, expecting him to work it in. But instead he just held it there, rubbing his other hand over my ass.

"Push back, baby," he said.

My stomach fluttered. This felt so much more erotic, me

seeking it out rather than letting Ben set the pace. Slowly, I pushed my hips back and felt his finger enter me.

"Oh fuck," I moaned as it went in.

"You're so fucking sexy," Ben whispered as it slid all the way in.

It took me a minute to get used to the feeling but once I'd relaxed around him, I started experimenting, pulling forward and away from Ben before sliding back onto his finger. Fuck, it felt good, firm and hard, filling me up. But it wasn't enough and soon I was begging for more.

"Please," I panted, looking over my shoulder. Ben's eyes looked drunk with desire and he licked his lips as he lubed up a second finger and held it next to the first. I pushed back slowly, feeling them pierce me.

"Fuck, fuck, fuck," I whined as they thrust inside me.

"Take your time," Ben breathed.

"Fuck taking my time," I growled, settling all the way back onto his fingers. "We've got the rest of our lives to take our time. Tonight, I want you *now*.

My eyes flew open wide as I registered what I'd just said. I whipped my head around in a panic, ready to qualify it, explain that I hadn't really meant '*the rest of our lives*,' but Ben just smiled.

"I'm holding you to that," he said, and he flexed his fingers inside me, making me see sparks as he pressed against my prostate. I groaned, arching my back and pulling forward before rocking my hips back onto his hand again. It was so good, too good, almost. Ben knew what I liked and for once,

I could let go of that worry, that layer of self-consciousness that held me back. For once, I could just let Ben take care of me.

"Jesus Christ, you're so hot," Ben purred as I rutted back onto his hand, his fingers sliding into me with slick, wet sounds. "You look so gorgeous, fucking yourself on my fingers."

All I could do was moan in response. I was beginning to sweat and my arms and legs were starting to shake. I drew a trembling breath.

"I need you," I whispered. "I need your cock."

I heard Ben's breath hitch and looked over my shoulder to catch his eyes looking wild, lust-shot. I whimpered as he slid his fingers out but I crawled off of him and began to lie down. Ben put his hand on my thigh and stopped me.

"I was thinking—I want you to be on top. I want to watch you."

His words sent a current through me but I nodded, shifting my left leg over Ben so I was straddling him. I sat down on his thighs just below his cock and looked into his eyes, grabbing the bottle of lube. I squeezed some into my right hand and brought it to his cock, stroking his shaft up and down. Ben watched, hypnotized.

I might not always have been comfortable performing for a room full of people, but for Ben? I could put on a bit of a show. I parted my mouth, running my tongue along my lower lip before sucking it in and biting it gently. Ben's eyes widened and I smiled, brought my left hand up to my mouth, and sucked my fingers in one at a time. Once they were wet, I closed my eyes and trailed my hand down my chest until I found my cock and began stroking myself, both of my hands pumping in unison now.

"Fuck, Adam," Ben said, his voice raw.

His hands rubbed my thighs, his fingers digging into my muscles. I liked his grip, liked feeling like he had me. But as fun as it was to put on a show, I didn't have the patience to keep this part up much longer. I needed to feel him inside me. Opening my eyes, I lifted up and shifted forwards, guiding his cock to my entrance.

"Ready?" I asked, trying for saucily confident and mostly just ending up sounding fucking wrecked.

"God, yes," Ben whispered.

I sank down onto him slowly. Fuck, he was huge. It didn't matter how often we'd fucked in the past few weeks, I still wasn't quite used to taking his cock up my ass. And it had been five days since the last time—120 long, dry hours. Entirely too long, in my opinion.

I loved the feeling of Ben filling me up. But I still needed to go slow. Once his cock was all the way inside me, I had to stop and breathe while I adjusted, feeling myself mold around him.

"You feel so good," I moaned, bringing one hand down to my cock, resting the other on Ben's stomach. "So fucking huge."

"You're so tight," Ben breathed. "God, Adam, it's ridiculous. Do you have any idea how hot you are?"

"No," I said with a grin. "But I have a very good idea how hot *you* are."

Ben groaned in pleasure as I squeezed my ass tight around him, then raised my hips just an inch and let them fall back down on to his cock. This position was definitely one of his better ideas. I loved seeing him beneath me, getting to watch his reactions play across his gorgeous face. And fine, maybe I couldn't resist keeping the performance going a little longer.

"God, you're amazing," I whispered, moaning as I lifted my hips up again and slid back down on his shaft. "So fucking hard, so hot, sliding into me. I could fucking ride you forever."

Ben's eyes widened and his breath caught. Perfect. It was intoxicating, seeing what I could do to him. And not bad for the self-esteem department, either. There was no way to deny that Ben was as turned on as I was.

His hands moved to my ass and he gripped it tightly, moving me up and down on his cock. I let him set the pace, arching my back and rolling my hips in rhythm with the motion. It felt incredible and I knew it wasn't going to be much longer before I came.

"Ben," I whined as he thrust into me. "Fuck, Ben, yes."

I wasn't trying to flaunt anything anymore, didn't have the presence of mind to keep up the performance. It felt too good, his cock driving into me, and I lost myself to the sensations. Every word from my lips now was wrung out of me in pure pleasure.

This was all I needed, just this moment, forever. Not

worrying about what anyone else thought of me, not caring what anyone else wanted. Just me and Ben together. Letting Ben take care of me, and giving him what he needed right back. This was enough.

Ben shifted on the bed, bending his knees and using the new position to thrust up into me harder from below. I groaned at the additional force, his cock slamming into me as I rode him. The cool cotton of the bedsheets was the only thing anchoring me to the earth now—the rest was hot, wet heat from our bodies, the sound of skin on skin, the rush of pleasure coming off of us in waves.

"Come here," Ben gasped, pulling me down. I collapsed onto his chest, let him catch my mouth in a kiss. His lips tasted salty. "Fuck, I need you."

He drove into me harder, filling me utterly. I could feel myself letting go, getting pulled under as my orgasm built. My cock slid between our bodies, the friction growing and I wasn't going to be able to hold it off any longer.

"God, yes," I groaned. "Fuck, Ben, I'm gonna come. I can't—Ben—"

"That's it, baby," he whispered. His words fell on my skin like silk, stealing my breath. "Just let go. Come for me, Adam."

I cried out, feeling myself release. Cum spilled from my cock, splashing onto his chest. I came harder than I ever had before, feeling flooding me and knocking me senseless. I couldn't think, couldn't speak, couldn't do anything except float somewhere up in the stars.

My whole body tensed with my orgasm, clenching and

releasing, and I felt the moment that Ben's thrusts began to stutter, losing their smooth momentum as he came. He exploded into me, filling me up, and it felt incredible, the two of us connected in a way no one else could share. Ben pumped into me until he was done, his last strokes forceful, his arms crushing me to him.

We lay pressed together like that in the still night air for long moments, the beat of our hearts mixing, our chests rising and falling in time. I didn't want to move yet, didn't want to break the spell of what the two of us had shared. It was enough to just lie here, with him.

Finally, I slid off of Ben and made him lie still while I went to the bathroom to get a wet washcloth. He smiled deviously after I dabbed him clean and then used the washcloth on myself.

"What?" I asked, not sure I trusted that impish smirk.

"Careful," Ben smiled. "The way you look when you do that. You're gonna make me hard again if you keep that up."

I laughed and tossed the washcloth aside, then slid back under the covers next to him. He rolled onto his side and pulled me to him, crushing his chest against mine.

"Impressive," I said. "I'm pretty sure I just came hard enough to fucking power a jet engine. I'm gonna need a minute."

"I'm not going anywhere," he said. He rubbed my back with his free hand, then pressed a kiss to my cheek. "That was pretty impressive, huh?"

"Mmhmm." I murmured my agreement into his neck.

"Maybe we should break up more often," he laughed, "if that's the kind of sex it leads to."

"Don't even think about it," I snorted. "Hell, on second thought, I'd like to see you try. You're not getting rid of me that easy."

"That," Ben said with a smile, "sounds just about perfect."

BEN

"*H*ey, it's the men of the hour," Gray said as we walked into Maggie's.

I held Adam's hand as we walked into the bar and smiled at the crowd of people waiting there for us. Adam gave it a little squeeze and grinned at me.

It was the night of our first show together, a month after I'd broken away from Greenleaf. We'd been playing around, still writing songs together but not really playing seriously yet, when The Grasshopper had called and asked if we wanted to do a last-minute show. We'd said yes.

"We have enough material," Adam had reasoned. "Besides, I'd like to have a memory of playing there that doesn't end in an ambulance. Or even just a memory I can actually remember. I'd settle for that."

We'd gotten dinner with my family at Peking Palace before the show and stayed to talk to them a little bit after, promising Lacey we'd come by to see her in a couple days. She claimed she was the expert on teen girl tastes and therefore should be the arbiter of what went on the new album. Then we'd followed the rest of the band across town and joined everyone here.

"Here you go," Micah said, coming up to the two of us with glasses in hand. Some kind of fruity, sour cocktail for me and seltzer for Adam, who'd decided he didn't want to drink when he went out anymore.

"Thanks, man," Adam said to Micah. "You make a mean club soda."

"I aim to please," Micah grinned. "Ben, how's the cocktail? That's actually a new invention of mine."

"It's, um," I paused and took another sip. "Very grapefruity?"

"Excellent," Micah said. "Exactly what I was going for."

"What's the new recipe for?" I asked. "Angling for a raise with Gray?"

"Nah, he doesn't bother doing anything special for that," Gray said, coming up to us and joining the conversation. "He just asks me every day."

"Hey, I gotta eat, right?" Micah laughed. "You might be a man of leisure but some of us are still out there hustling on a daily basis. Though, I guess your ass is about to get a little less leisurely, actually."

"New business venture?" Adam asked Gray.

"New business *opportunity*," Gray corrected him. "Potentially. I'm probably not going to take it."

"He's totally taking it," Micah said with a smirk.

"Maybe," Gray countered.

"Definitely," Micah replied. "And he's going to need someone to watch the bar while he's, shall we say, otherwise engaged. So I'm preparing for when I become the man in charge around here."

"Another reason for me to say no," Gray said. "If I turn my back for half a second, you'll probably turn this place into a tiki bar or something equally as cheesy."

"Just because you don't understand that tiki bars are cool again," Micah said, "is no reason to hate on people who are hip and cultured enough to know these things."

He looked at me and Adam who were staring at him doubtfully and added, "that's me, dummies, in case that wasn't clear."

"Sorry, I guess we weren't hip and cultured enough to understand that," Adam said with a grin.

"So what's the business opportunity?" I asked, turning to Gray.

"It's..." Gray trailed off and I was pretty sure he was actually blushing. It was strange seeing someone as put together and confident as him looking even the slightest bit embarrassed.

"It's amazing, is what it is," Micah said. "Gray's gonna be a movie star."

"What?" I blinked. "Seriously?"

"No." Gray shook his head. "Not seriously."

"Yes, seriously," Micah argued. "He's just saying that because he's being modest." He leaned in conspiratorially. "There's this gay romance novel that's getting made into a movie. They asked Gray to be in it."

"That's awesome," Adam said. "Congrats."

"Don't congratulate me yet," Gray said. "I haven't even officially been offered the part. Or said that I'd do it if they did offer it to me." He snorted. "I'm pretty sure they just asked me because they know I'm not gonna be too prudish about sex scenes."

"That's one way of putting it," Micah said with a smile.

"Anyway, it's still very much in the development stages," Gray said. "So I'm trying not to talk about it until we know more either way. This one only knows," Gray said, jerking his thumb at Micah, "because he walked in on the meeting I was having about it in my office."

"Which is another way of saying I'm super nosy." Micah grinned shamelessly.

"Well, come help me be nosy behind the bar, if you really wanna show me you can run it," Gray said. "We've got people to serve."

"My life of drudgery never ends," Micah said with a sigh. He smiled at us as he walked away though. "Congrats again on your big night!"

It was one of those busy nights where you only just manage to stop talking to one person before another one takes their place and all you're trying to do is get to the side table where the baby carrots are and you can't.

It was actually a pretty awesome crowd. Mostly people we knew, even Shereen showed up to congratulate us—and offer to sign us as a group act, of course—but still, by the time we got to the food, there was only celery and raw broccoli left and I think I speak for everyone ever when I say: fuck raw broccoli.

"Honestly," Adam said, holding up a sprig and inspecting it. "Just off the top of my head, I can think of 10 better uses for this than putting it in my mouth."

"Pumice stone," I suggested. "For exfoliating your feet."

"Mistletoe substitute," Adam returned. "For hanging from the ceiling and making awkward kisses happen."

"Feather duster."

"Insulation in your walls."

"Beanbag chair stuffing."

"Block your nostrils with it," Adam said, taking a second sprig from the tray and holding them up to his nose, "for when you have to sneeze but you don't have a handkerchief handy."

"And who does, these days?" I agreed. "Much easier to just keep some broccoli in your pockets, honestly."

"Ooh! Pocket square," Adam said excitedly. "Keep it in the breast pocket of your blazer. Practical *and* fashionable."

"This is why I love you," I said with a laugh. "Like, the sex and companionship and emotional support is nice and all, but if I'm being honest, it's because of your genius brain."

"And my keen fashion sense," Adam said. "Don't forget that."

"Who's got a keen fashion sense?" Nick asked, coming up to join us on the side of the room.

"I do," Adam said, gesturing to the Clash t-shirt and jeans he was wearing—jeans I was pretty sure hadn't been washed in at least two weeks. "Obviously."

"Obviously," Nick agreed. "Congratulations on the show. You guys were amazing."

"Thanks," Adam grinned. He proffered Nick the vegetables in his hands. "Want some broccoli?"

"I swear I just saw you put that up your nose, so I think I have to decline," Nick said.

"Wise choice," I laughed. "It tastes terrible enough even when it hasn't been used as a tissue."

"So where've you been, dude?" Adam asked. "I feel like we haven't seen you in weeks."

Nick winced. "I know. I'm sorry. Things have just been crazy, gearing up for the next semester. I've been finishing out a couple of my internships and trying to get ready for a new part-time job and things have been a little nuts with family stuff. I don't know, none of it's really interesting but suffice it to say, I've been busy."

"Fine," Adam said, looking at him doubtfully. "But you'd better start hanging out with us again or I'm just going to call and have trays of raw broccoli delivered to your house every day until you do." He grinned evilly. "I'll do it, too. Ben's way richer than I thought, even if he is off of Green-leaf's payroll."

"Yeah, I'm rich because I don't spend all my money airmailing crudite to people," I snorted. I frowned at Nick. "Everything going okay? Sounds like things are a little intense."

"Yeah," Nick said with a shrug. "It'll pass. Just a busy time." He smiled after a second. "And it's not all bad."

"What's his name?" Adam pounced.

"What?" Nick asked, looking confused. "Who?"

"The guy you're so clearly talking about. *It's not all bad*," he mimicked, batting his eyelashes dreamily.

"I'm not—"

"No, you definitely are," Adam said. "Ben back me up on this."

I gave Nick an apologetic smile. "I gotta go with Adam on this one. You've got that goofy grin people get when they've got a crush. Trust me, I was wearing that look myself not too long ago."

"And it looked very cute on you, too," Adam said, tapping me on the nose.

I scrunched my nose up and threw a stick of celery at him, then turned back to Nick. "So, spill."

"It's not—" Nick paused, looking flustered. "It's stupid. It's not even a crush, not really. I like, barely know the guy."

"Whose name is...?" Adam said expectantly. "You still haven't answered that part."

"Eli," Nick said, and that smile crept back onto his face. I didn't think he even realized it. "His name's Eli."

"Cute name," I said. "So what's the deal?"

Nick shook his head. "We—it's hard to even explain. We met in Penn Station, of all places. It was after my overnight shift at Peachtree. We were both taking the first train out in the morning and we just started talking. And then I just kept running into him on Sunday mornings and..." He stopped and blushed. "Well, yesterday, we were talking down on his platform and right before the train pulled out, he wrote his number down on a Dunkin Donuts receipt and kissed me."

"What?" Adam's face lit up. "That. Is. Fucking. Adorable. God, you're disgusting."

"Not a lie," I agreed. "That's pretty damn gross."

"I know!" Nick exclaimed. "It's like, too perfect right now. I'm afraid to call him and ruin it."

"Nick." I gave him a level look. "Don't even. You're calling him."

"Nick and Eli, sitting in a tree," Adam began as Nick groaned. "When are you coming down out of your tree so that we can meet him?"

"Oh my God, maybe give me a chance to actually call him before you plan the wedding?" Nick begged.

"Fine," Adam agreed. "But that means you have to actually follow through on this."

"And I can't wait to tell this story *at* your wedding," I put in. "Everyone will just eat up how shy and nervous poor Nick was before he made that first call. It's gonna be the most precious thing ever."

Nick rolled his eyes. "You guys are ones to talk. You realize you're actually at the top of the disgustingly saccharine scale, right? You've achieved peak cute-vomit levels."

"Trust me," Adam said, looking pained, "I know. It's hazardous to our health."

"I've actually developed diabetes," I said, putting my arm around Adam's shoulders and smiling at him. "We're way too sweet to each other."

Nick laughed and went off to go get a drink, promising to come back and tell us the full details of the Eli story. Adam looked up at me and frowned.

"You know, I think Nick's right," he said. "This is a state of emergency. I don't think my body knows what to do with this much unironic joy and happiness. We need to be meaner to each other, starting now."

I leaned in and kissed him on the cheek, then gave him the meanest look I could muster which was, admittedly, pretty weak. "You got it, asshole."

"Right back at you, dipshit," Adam said solemnly.

It was a struggle to keep a straight face as I tucked a piece of broccoli into the pocket of his jeans. "Fucker. I love you."

Adam snorted and grinned up at me.

"I know."

∼

THANKS FOR READING!

Check out some of my other books no the next page! But before you do... want to know what's next for Adam and Ben?

ALL I NEED

Free Bonus Chapter

You can read *All I Need*, a free, explicit bonus epilogue for *Adam's Song*, just by joining my mailing list. *All I Need* is an explicit follow-up, taking place after the end of *Adam's Song*. Sweet and sexy, it's the perfect happy ending for Adam and Ben (at least until I cave and write even more for them...)! You know you want that, right?

Oh, and also, you'll be notified of my new releases and when I have more free stuff, you'll be the first to know.

Sign up at: http://eepurl.com/deH7Z1
www.spencerspears.com

ALSO BY SPENCER SPEARS

Check out the next *8 Million Hearts* book in the series!

Gray For You

You might also like my *Maple Springs* series!

Billion Dollar Bet

Beneath Orion

Sugar Season

Strawberry Moon

Gray For You
Who auditions for gay porn without realizing it? Me,
apparently...

Gray: I'm not the kind of guy you take home to meet your
mother. I'm an ex-adult film star with a GED and a giant
co...llection of movie credits I can't talk about in polite
company. I might be good at helping other guys get their
happy endings, but I've more or less given up on finding one
of my own.

Until Tyler Lang walks into my life.

That's right, my co-star for my final film is Tyler Lang--
America's heartthrob, until he disappeared from the radar
last year. Tyler's got a reputation for being a bad boy, a
partier, and apparently straight, but the sweet, vulnerable-
looking kid who shows up at auditions is completely
different. And now that I'm getting to know him, I can't help
wondering what it is that's made his eyes so sad--and
wishing there were some way I could make it better.

I'm not supposed to get a happy ending. So why the hell won't my heart listen?

Tyler: I know what you've heard about me. Another spoiled child-actor, all grown up and out of control. I wish I could tell you you're wrong, but the truth is, I'm a little bit of a mess. Okay, so maybe I'm a *giant* mess. And now, after getting arrested with an ez-bake oven's worth of drugs I don't even remember buying, I'm washed-up at the grand old age of 21.

After a year of rehab and community service, all I want is to work again. So when my agent sends me a new script, maybe I don't read the fine print as carefully as I should. Which is how I end up auditioning for an adult film. A high-brow, literary adult film. But still. There's no way I can go through with this. After all, I'm so deep in the closet I'm not sure I'll ever find my way out. And I *wouldn't* do this movie-- except for one thing: Gray Evans.

Strong, kind, and honest, Gray makes me feel seen in a way I've never been before--and makes me want to be better. And somehow, around Gray, everything seems possible. Like maybe there's a world where I'm not a total screw-up. Maybe there's a world where I can come out, and not tank my career. And maybe, just maybe, there's a world where Gray, who's smart and brave and so together, could want someone like me.

Gray For You is Book 2 in the 8 Million Hearts series. While each book can be read on its own, they're even more fun to read together. Gray For You is a 150,000 word m/m romance full of snark, sweetness, and a healthy serving of steam. Movie star romance and hurt/comfort themes. No cheating, no cliffhangers, and a guaranteed HEA.

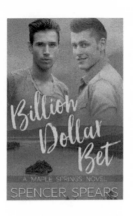

Billion Dollar Bet
What would you bet for a chance at true love?

Hopeless romantic Kian Bellevue can't help falling for the
wrong guys. Maybe it's because he lost his parents so young,
maybe it's just his caring nature, but he can't stop diving in
when he should be heading for the hills. And just when he
decides to swear off guys for the summer, he meets drop-
dead gorgeous Jack Thorsen, who might just be the man of
his dreams.

It's not fair, because Kian doesn't even have time for guys
right now. His hometown of Maple Springs, Minnesota is
considering selling miles of pristine wilderness to a Wall
Street billionaire who wants to open a resort and play at
being a hotelier. But Kian's spent his whole life fighting
against big businesses and he's ready to go toe-to-toe with
the mystery mogul - until he realizes that the billionaire is
Jack himself.

Billionaire Jack Thorsen is married to his work and likes it that way. Growing up in foster care taught him to look out for himself and since the day he left for college, he's never stopped striving. Despite his best friend's urging, he's not looking for a guy. Even after he meets sweet and sexy Kian Bellevue, he's still determined to keep his guard up. People can't hurt you if you never let them close.

But it's not like Jack doesn't have a heart. When he finds out that Maple Springs, the home he left behind, is on the brink of bankruptcy, he proposes to buy their unused public lands and create an eco-resort. It's an obvious win-win - who could oppose it? That is, who, other than Kian, the guy he can't get out of his head.

Jack needs Kian on his side if he wants the town to vote in favor of his resort and he's not afraid to play dirty. His proposition: Kian spends the summer with him. If Jack convinces Kian to support him, Kian will get the town on Jack's side. But if he fails, Jack will withdraw the proposal completely. It's a crazy bet, but Kian would be crazy to turn it down - right?

There's only one problem. Jack - tall, handsome, and emotionally unavailable - is exactly Kian's type. And Kian is surprisingly good at breaking down the barriers Jack spent years putting up. With their hearts on the line as well as a hotel, will both men risk it all for a chance at love?

Billion Dollar Bet is Book 1 in the Maple Springs series. While each book focuses on different characters and can be read on its own, they're even more fun to read together.

Billion Dollar Bet is a 55,000 word m/m romance novel with sizzling summer heat. No cheating, no cliffhangers, and a guaranteed HEA.

Beneath Orion

What happens when two stars collide?

The first lesson Colin Gardner ever learned was not to trust. The second was that love hurts. Growing up in an abusive family, he turned to the night sky for comfort and buried himself in science. It wasn't easy being the only gay guy in school and Colin made peace with the fact that he'd never fall in love. He won't risk that pain. Especially not for a guy who's never dated men before. No matter how much he's tempted.

Charlie Keller doesn't date. How could he risk his kid growing attached to someone when it might not last? The divorced dad's life revolves around his daughter, his dog, and his job as Maple Springs' resident handy-man. But when Charlie helps Colin out in a pinch, his world changes forever. Charlie can't ignore his attraction to Colin, but he can't act on it either - can he?

As winter deepens, Charlie and Colin are drawn into each other's orbit. But when Charlie's ex-wife threatens to move his daughter across the country, he realizes his worst fears might come true. And when Colin's past comes calling, it raises demons he's not sure he's strong enough to fight. Will Colin and Charlie's love flame out, or can they find a way to make a new constellation - just for the two them?

Beneath Orion is Book 2 in the Maple Springs series. While each book focuses on different characters and can be read on its own, they're even more fun to read together.

Beneath Orion is a 55,000 word steamy, contemporary, gay-for-you M/M romance. No cliffhangers, no cheating, and a guaranteed HEA.

A MAPLE SPRINGS NOVEL
SPENCER SPEARS

<u>Sugar Season</u>
They say it's better to have loved and lost. They have no idea what they're talking about...

Police officer Graham Andersen already had his happy ending. A whirlwind romance, a young marriage, more happiness than he knew what to do with. And then it was over, almost as soon as it began.

After his husband Joey died, Graham knew he'd never find that kind of love again. But what he'd had with Joey was more than some people ever got in life. He'd had his chance at happiness. He couldn't ask for more.

When chef Ryan Gallagher is swindled out of his savings right before he can open his restaurant, it almost seems right. One more failure for his long list, one more way he'll never measure up to his older brother. Joey might be gone, but he still finds a way to overshadow Ryan.

With no money and no prospects, Ryan has no choice but to move home to the family that rejected him and his sexuality.

But when he goes out to the local bar one winter night, he never dreams the hot guy he's hitting on used to be his brother's husband.

Both men insist that they're not interested. And yet neither can resist the desire they feel. But relationships require love. Love requires risk. And both Graham and Ryan know this life offers no guarantees. After a long winter in both their hearts, are they finally ready for spring?

Sugar Season is Book 3 in the Maple Springs series. While each book focuses on different characters and can be read on its own, they've even more fun to read together.

Sugar Season is a 75,000 word steamy, contemporary, second chance m/m romance. No cheating, no cliffhangers, and a guaranteed HEA.

<u>Strawberry Moon</u>
Trevor: It was supposed to be a one-night stand.

Josh isn't even my type. I mean, physically, sure, with those hopeful green eyes and hips that fit perfectly in my hands, he's insanely sexy. But the guy talks too much, tries too hard, flirts way too shamelessly. From the moment I met Josh, I knew he'd drive me crazy.

I didn't think it mattered for one night. I suck at relationships, so I stopped trying long ago. I didn't expect to ever see Josh again. And I definitely didn't expect him to turn out to be sweeter, kinder, and genuinely a better person than a guy like me deserves. I should know better than to want someone like him.

It was supposed to be a one-night stand. So why the hell can't I let him go?

Josh: It freaking figures.

The night I finally have some meaningless fun--and,

incidentally, the hottest hook-up of my life--I manage to pick the one guy in the bar who I'm gonna have to see for the rest of the summer. How was I supposed to know that Trevor had a competing claim on my grandma's cabin? Or that he's the only person who can help me get it ready to sell by the end of the season?

It would be so much easier if I could hate him. Trevor's got that whole tall, dark, and mysterious thing down - emphasis on mysterious. He's aloof to the point of arrogance and deals with emotions about as well as a tree-trunk. He swears he's no good for me, but the more time I spend with him, the more I know he's wrong.

It freaking figures. So what the hell am I supposed to do now?

Strawberry Moon is Book 4 in the Maple Springs series. While each book focuses on different characters and can be read on its own, they've even more fun to read together.

Strawberry Moon is an 85,000 word m/m romance with enemies-to-lovers, out-for-you, and hurt/comfort themes. No cheating, no cliffhangers, and a guaranteed HEA.

Check out the rest of my catalog at:
www.spencerspears.com